# Dragon Stone

## BOOK ONE

## by
## D. A. McIntyre

*For Greg on his 46th Birthday! Enjoy!*

**Dragon Stone**

**BOOK ONE**

**by D. A. McIntyre**

*Webby McIntyre*

**dedicated to Shane**

**In real life,
we cannot always protect our heroes,
no matter how much they are loved,
no matter how brave they are.**

# INTRODUCTION

It was winter 2002 and I had just finished reading Tolkien's works again. I first read the Hobbit and Tolkien's Lord of the Rings trilogy during my college years, soon after Tolkien's death. I will admit to sulking for a time. I usually do when I finish a good book. There would be no more Tolkien works, after all. Dead men don't write. (sigh)

I missed his gentle, elegant style. I have many favorite authors, but Tolkien was the one who sparked my addiction to fantasy. Could I write a book like Tolkien's work? Well, not really. I am not Tolkien by any stretch of anyone's imagination. In addition, should any writer wish to write like another? No, probably not. However, this gives you an idea of my frame of mind during the long, cold winter of 2002 when I began to write this book.

In Dragon Stone, the first book in a series of three, we meet our first young hero, Althus, and send him on a quest to find the Wizard who raised him. Along the way, he gathers valuable allies and terrifying enemies and finds himself the subject of chilling prophecy. Suddenly, he finds himself responsible for the lives of the people he left behind.

I wrote Dragon Stone for young adults as well as adults who are young at heart. I apologize for the few big words my editor couldn't persuade me to eliminate. I attribute my overblown vocabulary to the many books I read as a child and I would like to make my own contribution to yours. The writing style is a bit formal. You may find the hidden logic in it as the story moves through books two and three.

There is a list of characters at the end of the book to help you keep them straight.

May you find as much pleasure reading Dragon Stone as I did in writing it. Sulk just a little when you are done. Book two will be available in February 2005.

## PROLOGUE

Jonah ran through the village, calling his son's name. The blowing smoke hindered him. He could not see far beyond the ruins of the nearest buildings. There were shouts all about him as the other Riders searched for survivors. He found his wife lying dead in the street before her mother's house. He should never have let her leave the safety of the Hall. He was too late. At the sight of her lifeless body, he felt his heart shatter within him.

Their friends, Kate and Abraham Peregrine, lay dead nearby. There was no sign of his son, no sign of Kate and Abraham's son, Joseph. He fought the terror that gripped him when he thought of his small son and young Joseph at the mercy of the huge Orcs that had invaded this remote mountain village. They were only two small boys. What chance would they have against such creatures?

Jonah had only recently given Solomon his first weapon, a knife that almost served as a sword in Solomon's small hands. Joseph's father, a cabinetmaker, a quiet, thoughtful man, was unlikely ever to arm his son at all, even though Joseph promised to grow to be one of the tallest of the mountain Elves with the strength and agility to become a fine Rider.

Jonah prayed they were together. He prayed that somehow they had escaped. He searched through streets that ran red with the blood of his people and shouted for Solomon until the smoke took his voice from him.

He stopped to catch his breath, standing in the middle of what once served as the town square, turning to look helplessly at the devastation about him. They had come too late. This town, the town where his wife was born and where she had died was not likely to survive this attack. He had lost her and now it seemed he had lost his son as well. He shouted his son's name once more in desperation and thought he heard an answer. He headed toward the sound, hoping the desire to hear his son's voice once again was not deceiving him. Another shout brought a response that seemed closer. Jonah broke into a run, the direction clearer now.

He found his son in the ruins of the council house, desperately trying to shift the corpse of a huge Orc, his soot stained face streaked with tears. Jonah swept his son into his arms, dragging him away from the grisly corpse.

Solomon began to sob as his father wrapped his arms about him. "Help me, father," he gasped. "Please, help me."

"Shhhh, I am here now. I will take you away from here. We will go home soon. We have to find Joseph first."

"It is my fault. I was not thinking clearly. The Orc came after us. I was not thinking. When I killed him, he fell so quickly. I am sorry. Please help me."

"You killed this beast, Solomon?"

"I did not mean for it to happen, father. I killed him, and he fell so quickly."

Jonah could not help but smile at his courageous little boy. "We will retrieve your knife, son. Do not worry about it now."

Solomon looked up at his father. His eyes were dazed, confused. It was not until then Jonah noticed the bloody gash across his son's chest and the blood that trickled from beneath his curly hair.

Jonah watched anxiously as Solomon struggled to catch his breath. "Joseph is beneath the monster, father. I cannot free him."

With an oath for his own stupidity, Jonah called to his fellow Riders. He soon held Joseph in his arms while he watched Augustine tend to Solomon, relieved to find them both still alive.

He had lost his wife and Solomon his mother, but Joseph had lost both his parents and grandparents and two older brothers that day. Jonah worried that grief would kill him. He held Joseph close, his hand pressing Joseph's head against his chest, reaching to touch the emotions Joseph was too stunned to express. Joseph rested in Jonah's arms, silent, staring, his dark eyes empty.

Solomon sat with his hand on Joseph's shoulder, the golden eyes that marked him as his father's son never leaving Joseph's face as Augustine dressed his wounds.

Solomon's wounds would heal. Joseph was not injured. Jonah was grateful for that. Solomon, knocked senseless, was spared the sight of his mother's death. Joseph had most likely witnessed it all and still carried Solomon to safety.

Jonah took Joseph and Solomon back to the Hall of the Riders. He mourned his dead wife, thankful the Creator had spared his son and the son of his friends. They needed him. Together they found the strength to live on. Slowly, Joseph recovered and came to think of Jonah as his father and Solomon as his brother. Jonah raised Joseph with as much love and care as his own son, grateful to have two fine children to call his own.

Solomon and Joseph were inseparable although opposites in many ways. Solomon was quicksilver, nearly as tall as Joseph, but slight of build, agile and lively, and Joseph was iron, one of the tallest of the mountain Elves, solid and strong. Both became Riders, following in Jonah's footsteps, taking the oath to protect their people, as the Brotherhood of Riders had for thousands of years.

Φ                    Φ                    Φ

The dark Wizard took the bundle from the nurse's arms, opening it to reveal the newborn infant.

"He is dead, then?" he said, his deep voice devoid of emotion, examining the small body closely with his dark eyes while the nurse shivered on his doorstep. Fear made her shiver. The night was warm. Fear of the Wizard, fear for what he intended to do with the body of this newborn child.

"Yes, stillborn," she answered, struggling to keep her voice from quivering.

The Wizard regarded her closely. "And the queen?" he asked.

Elinor stared at him. What would he have her say? The queen had lost her firstborn son. She suspected the king and his court Wizard, Borgas of having a hand in the child's death. How did he expect the queen to survive such a thing?

The Wizard sighed as if her silence was all the answer he needed or expected.

This Wizard, Euwyn, was a different sort. At least, he seemed a just and honorable man. Still, he was a Wizard. He may have had a hand in it as well. Why else would he have an interest in the dead child's body?

"I will care for the child's remains, Elinor. You may go now."

"Yes, sir."

"You will tell no one of this, Elinor. No one." He looked deep into her eyes and whispered a few words to her she could not quite hear or perhaps they were in a language she did not understand.

"Thank you for delivering this package of books, Elinor. Tell the queen I will take care of them as if they were my own."

Elinor felt a moment of confusion. "Oh, yes, thank you Euwyn. I will tell her." It seemed rather strange to Elinor that the queen had asked her to deliver books to Euwyn in the middle of the night. Still, powerful people often did unexplainable things.

Euwyn turned to the child as soon as the door closed behind her. He knew the woman well enough. Perhaps he could have trusted her. He shook his head at the thought. From this day forward, where this child was concerned, he would trust no one.

The child was so tiny. He had held very few infants this small. The superstitious farmers of Anduin seldom called upon him to serve as a midwife unless the woman or the child was in dire trouble. Even when he was called upon, he was usually a last resort and often too late to save them. He cradled the infant in his arms and spoke the words that would set him free from the death spell triggered by his birth. There was no response. Euwyn took a deep breath, trying to shake the panic that ate at the edges of his mind. He tried once more with no better result. Had he thwarted the Wizard Borgas only to unwittingly serve as the king's executioner in his stead? He had set a spell of his own before that of the Wizard, Borgas. His intention was to save the child, but to set one spell atop another was a dangerous ploy, especially for one so small. He sent a prayer to the Creator for help and spoke the counter spell once more.

He was wiping his eyes and reaching for the blanket to wrap the child's body when the infant gave a slight twitch followed by small squeaky cry. Euwyn held the child close and smiled down at him as he opened his eyes for the first time. They were a startling shade of sapphire. Euwyn had seen such eyes before. They were curious, inquiring, clearly focusing on his face, even at this young age. The blood of the queen's ancestors ran strong in her child. Still, he was his father's child as well.

Euwyn felt as if the child held his heart in his tiny fist. He would soon find loving parents to raise him, but, for now, he was too fragile to leave in another's hands.

Euwyn was a healing Wizard. He would make sure the boy was healthy before he left him to another's care. He held the child's tiny face against his and closed his eyes, trying to imagine what life held for this precious bit of humanity, gathering his wits for the task he was about to undertake. Nothing in his books had prepared him to care for such a small child. It would take every bit of resourcefulness he could muster.

If anyone had told him that day the tiny child would remain in his care until he grew to adulthood, Euwyn would have said they had taken leave of their senses. A child needed a mother. He adored children of any size, but he was not fit to raise one.

Somehow, the boy the queen named Althus never seemed ready for another's care. The right time, the right people to serve as his parents never came. The queen encouraged the arrangement. She trusted Euwyn to keep the child safe. It was four years before Euwyn allowed anyone to know the child existed, even then, allowing everyone to assume the child newly adopted.

## Chapter One

## DARK LORD

The Dark Lord, Adolphus, was smiling. He paced the perimeter of the flaming pit that lit the heart of his underground domain, his pets scurrying, slithering, hopping across the shadowed floor to stay out of his reach, their rustling almost lost in the roar and crackle of the flames. A smile on the Dark Lord's face was seldom a good omen for those who remained close to him.

He was home again, restless, full of himself. The fire played across the smooth planes of his face, a perfect face by the standards of any of the higher races. Perfect enough that most who faced him wondered why they could not look at it without experiencing a sharp stab of uneasiness.

His hair and skin were pale. His eyes captured the dancing flames of the fiery pit and held them when he turned away. The flawless perfection of his face was the very thing that wove itself into the nightmares of those unfortunate enough to draw his attention. It was a face of perfect symmetry, wreathed in madness.

A striking visage for a powerful being, it had served him well in the other world, a world where youth and beauty would bring him anything he desired, anything that existed in that world. It could not offer him the two things he truly desired, the power of magic and the pleasure of revenge. Only this world could offer him those.

The misery he had caused in that other world, the power he had drawn to himself there was hollow. There was no challenge there. He controlled them all with the mere wave of his hand.

All things considered, the world to which he had fled was not entirely unsuited to him. Life had been easy for him there, the Humans of the other world more corruptible, more easily bent to his evil ways than he dared hope, but he possessed no magic there. In that world, machines ruled and those with the knowledge that made and controlled the machines. He was native to this world where each of the higher races wielded their own magic. Some were born to it, as were the Wizards and Elves and, to a smaller extent, the Dwarves. As with the Giants and Humans, some possessed the ability to learn small bits of magic.

Only the lowly creatures that served him wielded no magic of any sort. The Orcs and Goblins had no desire for magic in any case. They desired only the destruction of those who possessed it. They fed on such creatures, killing and torture their only pleasures in life. That was why they served him well.

He had spent more than a thousand years in exile, his lust for revenge, the emptiness he experienced while denied the use of his magic, eating away at his sanity. He was rich and powerful in that world. His sins and excesses, his wild, unreasoning rages only earning him the reputation of an eccentric.

Only recently had he found a way to return. He had intended to return immediately, using his powers to leap back into his own world when he recovered his strength and the danger to him had passed, before the three Elven races grew strong once more and his forces were scattered to the four winds. He had not considered the possibility there would be no magic in the world to which he escaped. He waited over a thousand years before the Humans of the other world discovered the technology that allowed him to return to this one.

Even now, very few knew of the portals through which he traveled between worlds and those few were Human. He would kill them all eventually, when it pleased him to do so. His willingness to give them as much money as they wished to fund their research captivated them. They did not stop to consider what his true motives might be. The great minds of the computer age that swept the world of his exile did not want to see him as he truly was.

He used them to develop the portals and then slipped back into his own world, this world, right under their very noses. He laughed aloud as he considered what these learned scientists would think if they knew he was here to conquer the world they were so intent on studying.

They were fools, all of them. In honor of his support, they had let him choose those who traveled the portals, and he had chosen those he thought the least likely to interfere with his plans. They were the oldest, least fit, most gullible of those few invited to apply for the task, the least likely to have the strength or the courage to oppose him in the unlikely event they discovered his true purpose. He had nothing but contempt for Humans. They were easy prey, becoming old and defenseless, and often witless, so quickly.

The closest to his lair was a woman, a photographer. The most intelligent of the lot, but still a Human, and a woman at that, and therefore no threat to him. Still, she was an enigma to him, a puzzle to solve. He would take her apart, piece by piece some day soon and see what she was made of. He kept her closest. She would be the last to die.

At first glance, he had not discerned anything remarkable in her. She seemed as easily duped as the rest, a small sparrow of a woman. As the time neared when the researchers he funded would transport the chosen to various outposts throughout this world, she began to stand out as someone who would bear watching. He began to distrust her, but by the time he had marked her as unusual, it was too late to replace her without arousing suspicion.

She refused him at first, when invited to travel the portals. She had a husband she adored and a comfortable home. She was a professor of photography, dedicated to her students and their work.

No one would deny him anything he desired. He had taken her husband from her and then, as an afterthought, her position at the university. That had been enough to make her accept his offer. She sought an escape from her world and its painful memories and he graciously provided it.

He set her in the outpost closest to his lair and watched her carefully. He found her amusing in a way. She was resourceful. He had installed her in the harshest environment imaginable and still, she adapted far more easily than the others.

He had set the ground rules for those chosen. They were to have nothing to do with any of the intelligent races of this land. They were to observe and take notes, but only observe. All had readily taken an oath to do just that. It would be wrong to interfere with the natural order of things in a world where they did not truly belong. They had all agreed, seeing the logic of such a precaution.

A thousand years was not so long for one who would live forever, but there were matters he would put to rest here. Revenge to seek. He returned to the world others had forced him to abandon to find his faithful wraiths had survived within the influence of the stone some called the Dragon's Egg, hidden in his underground lair. They waited for his return as faithful hounds, setting events in motion even before his return, enabling him to regain his lost power quickly.

Borgas was entrenched in Anduin, the once mighty king of that land a puppet to the evil Wizard, controlled by shards of the Dragon's Egg. Another shard melted from this powerful stone held the Dwarves of Stonehaven as slaves to his will.

In the two years since his return to this world, he had recovered all that was once lost to him. He gathered the remnants of his scattered army about him once more, breeding foulness of every sort in the hidden passages of his underground kingdom, arming his Orcs and Goblins with Dwarf-forged weapons.

He reveled in the feel of magical powers once more at his disposal. With the help of his powerful stone, he grew stronger each day. He controlled the kingdom of the Dwarves. Anduin, the land of Humans was all but his to do with as he wished. With the help of Borgas and the wraith that bound the Wizard to him, Anduin would soon lie totally under his control.

The thought of Borgas abruptly erased the smile from his face. That Wizard was certainly one of his trusted servants, but the entire race of Wizards would be difficult to conquer. He was born a Wizard himself. He knew their foolish dedication to good and justice well. Until he had found the Dragon's Egg and devoted his life to it, he had been an ordinary, everyday Wizard, just as foolish and dedicated. Powerful, but not unusually so. He no longer considered himself one of them.

The race of Wizards was, for the most part, solitary, roaming the lands with no permanent dwellings, and very hard to locate unless they wished to be found. He had found two of them, lesser members of the brotherhood. When he had taken all he could from them, he destroyed them. He held another of their kind to the stone in the Dwarven kingdom of Stonehaven. Adolphus could feel him weakening, his defenses failing and his works throughout the land that protected the goodly races failing with him. Certainly, if he could destroy this powerful young Wizard, Euwyn, he could find and destroy any that might remain. Euwyn was the most powerful Wizard of his time and growing even more powerful as years passed. This was knowledge granted to Adolphus by Euwyn's mentor, one of the Wizards he drained of all knowledge before killing them. Adolphus wondered what talisman Euwyn held that magnified his powers to such a degree. Even Euwyn's teacher had not possessed that information.

Another bit of information from the Wizards he held captive gave him the location of a promising young Wizard who was vulnerable, unaware of his own worth. That knowledge died with the Wizards Adolphus held, the same ones who exiled the young Wizard to the realm of the Sea Elves. Now, only Adolphus knew of his existence.

That Wizard was an itch beneath his skin, the itching of a lost limb he could not truly scratch. Someone had set him free. When Adolphus had sent his creatures to fetch him, he was no longer on the island where he had been imprisoned. Still, Adolphus would find him.

He growled to himself, his eyes reddening with anger, his long, delicate hands clenching into fists at his sides. He would find the rest of them as well. They would not hide from him forever. With the help of the stone, he would detect them through their use of magic and then he would destroy them as he would soon destroy Euwyn.

He turned his thoughts to the three Elven nations, his anger deepening as he considered them. His smooth, pale face showed distaste for them even he, a master of disguise, so practiced at hiding his thoughts behind a mask of serenity could not hide. They were powerful as well. He understood the magic of Wizards, magic used as a weapon more often than not. The magic of the Elves was a puzzle to him. Theirs was a magic of perception, of feeling. They were readers of souls, attuned to the world around them. He once thought their powers useless, laughable, but they had defeated him soundly a thousand years ago. He would not underestimate them again.

He instructed his massed forces to avoid the realm of the Mountain Elves for now, leaving only a small force of Orcs and Goblins to harry them and keep them distracted. He would need to fully conquer Anduin and the realm of the Wood Elves before he attempted to bring the Mountain Elves, an even more ancient and fierce race, to their knees.

He had corrupted one of the Riders who protected the Mountain Elves.

That feat astonished even him. That one desired power above all else. Adolphus would give him just enough to keep him at his side. When he was done with him, he would show him what became of traitors, even one who served the Dark Lord against his own kind. Still, this one would be useful for a time. He had already given Adolphus information that could give him control of a power beyond even his most ambitious dreams.

His thoughts turned to the Elf that had escaped him. He had entrusted too much to his foot soldiers and the wraiths that commanded them. At the time, his only aim was the capture of Augustine's Second-in-Command. That alone would have been a severe blow to his hated enemy. His forces had been too eager. They had killed Augustine's Second, or so he thought. His spy had informed him otherwise, but it no longer mattered. The Elf was beyond his reach, his mind destroyed by the acts of Adolphus' own wraiths. He wandered the mountains, drawn so deeply within himself even those he called his brothers could not reach him.

Too late, he had discovered the true value of this one small Elf. Adolphus' creatures watched him, even so. If, by some chance, he escaped the living torment Adolphus' wraiths had cursed him with, Adolphus would know it.

That mistake ate at him. He had come so close to possessing him. That man's father would have served him just as well, but that knowledge had come too late as well.

Jonah was dead, taken from Adolphus by his own wraiths when Jonah and his Riders strayed too close to his hidden lair. They had summoned a demon at great cost and had succeeded in killing only Jonah, the one Rider who could also have given Adolphus the great power he sought. Still, Jonah's son, Augustine's latest Second, still lived, wandering the mountains, his mind shattered. Adolphus would watch him and wait.

If all went well, he might only need to conquer Anduin fully before he turned his attentions to the Elves that dwelt in the mountains nearby. Patience. He would need patience! He had time to gather strength and hone his plans to a fine edge. The Elven nations would fall, one by one. He would bend few Elves to his will. He knew that. He would have to kill them all, but perhaps not all at once. They would serve as amusement for a time.

He remembered those that opposed him in the past. Augustine of the mountain Elves and Gilden of the Wood Elves had been young then, very young, and still, Gilden's people, their numbers strengthened by an alliance with the sea Elves, had driven Adolphus' forces from the Dark Forest and southward into the mountains.

Deep in the mountains where Adolphus sought to hide, Augustine's Riders took up the chase. Augustine and Jonah, his Second, had cornered Adolphus there. They would have put an end to him if he had not slipped from their world in search of another.

Adolphus had led his own forces then, anxious to share in the killing of Elves. He would not make the mistake of leaving his lair again. He would stay close to the stone he called the Dragon's Egg, the source of his power. Gilden and Augustine were leaders of their respective races still. His smile returned as he considered ways to make them suffer for their arrogance.

He mourned the fact few travelers chanced the mountains now. He killed the last of them in his grasp nearly a year ago. He remembered the pleasure of torturing the creature. One of the small Mountain Elves, he thought, traveling the mountains with goods to sell. By the time the creature had died, he could not have said for sure to what race it had once belonged. He missed the little man. His tortured cries were only a pleasant memory. Adolphus would amuse himself for a time, trying his methods out on a few of the Orcs close to hand or a goblin or two. They would not be missed.

He had other captives, of course, but they were too valuable for him to risk harming them. Some day they would be expendable, but for now, they were his honored guests. There would soon be the Humans of Anduin to feed his cravings. Perhaps he would soon possess one of the Brotherhood for his amusement, if his servant among the Mountain Elves proved his worth.

The thought of that possibility sent him off to see Daystar. He would taunt the captive beast for a time with that knowledge.

## Chapter Two

## ALTHUS

Tristan regarded his father across the table, a forkful of eggs halfway to his mouth.

"You expect me to play nursemaid to this Althus?" he asked. "Who is this youngster the queen has recently added to our ranks?"

"You have seen him. He is Euwyn's adopted son. He is not much younger than you are. The queen asks that we watch over him until he has settled in."

Tristan could see his father, captain of the Anduin guard, was not joking. Still, he could not understand why this Althus should receive special consideration.

He did remember him. The soldiers called him 'the Wizard's bastard,' the words often accompanied by a sign to ward off evil. Those words were never spoken where the Wizard could hear and not where Tristan's father, Captain Manton, could overhear either.

"I suppose I must teach him to use a sword as well, then."

"He knows the use of a sword better than you, Tristan. Better than I, and I taught him the skill. He has surpassed me. I have never seen his equal, except perhaps among Lord Gilden's Elves."

Tristan sat gaping at his father, his forkful of food forgotten. "That quiet boy who barely speaks unless spoken to? He cannot be as good as you say."

Captain Manton saw an opportunity to spark Tristan's interest.

"Try him, then, and tell me what you think of his skills. You will see."

"I will do that, father, but I cannot see how you expect this silent, bookish Wizard's son to fit in with our rough lot of soldiers."

"There is no shame in having a good education, Tristan. You are better educated than most of my men and still you should apply yourself more diligently to your studies if you expect to serve as Captain after me. As for his silence, Tristan, what would *you* say to those who called you bastard behind your back when they think you do not hear? I know you, Tristan. You would be picking fights in the streets. Believe me, he knows what people say of him and he does not like it, but he deals with such matters in a different way than you. He holds his temper as Euwyn has taught him and does not respond. Does that make him less of a man than you?"

Tristan's face turned as red as his hair. He did not have an answer and turned his attention to his breakfast without another word.

Φ        Φ        Φ

He found Althus later that morning atop the southwestern tower of Castle Anduin. Tristan took a moment to study him as he paced the battlements, standing watch. Althus carried himself like a soldier. He looked every bit the soldier in the black and silver of the Anduin guard, but the intelligence that shone from his eyes marked him as a different type of man from most of the ruffians populating the Anduin Guard. That was what set him apart from them. That was why they baited him. They would bring him down to their level if they could.

He thought of his father's last words to him that morning. As was usually so, Captain Manton was right. Althus would need a friend among the ranks if he were to remain in Castle Anduin.

When Tristan stepped into Althus' path, Althus saluted him, standing at attention. As a sergeant, Tristan outranked him. They stood face to face in silence, appraising each other. Tristan thought Althus might look away or show some sign of uneasiness if confronted by a superior officer. His sapphire eyes regarded Tristan calmly, steadily. Tristan was the first to look away, his green eyes sweeping the panorama of Anduin's farmlands beyond the city walls, showing the first signs of spring. Teams of horses and oxen dotted the landscape, moving slowly as they tilled the fertile soil bordering the river Anduin from which the kingdom took its name.

He was the one who felt uneasy, guilty. He did not know how to begin. Had Althus ever overheard the word 'bastard' from his lips? He did not think so. His mother, Elinor did not approve of the term. He seldom used it.

"A beautiful sight, is it not, Althus? All seems well in our kingdom. The bitter winds that blew in over the sea cliffs all winter have given way to warmer winds from the south. Spring has come to Anduin."

"Yes, sir, the smell of the sea has been replaced by that of freshly turned soil." Althus answered. His voice was clear, ringing. Tristan heard the Wizard's tones in it.

Tristan offered his hand. "I am Tristan. Captain Manton is my father. You may call me Tristan when we are alone. I suppose you should call me 'sir' when in the company of others, but it is difficult to begin a friendship if one of us must continually call the other 'sir.'"

Tristan noted with satisfaction that Althus' face showed a hint of surprise as he shook his hand. He drew Althus toward the wall where they stood side by side, looking toward the Hoary Mountains whose snow-capped peaks shone in the distance. "Tell me, Althus, how did you find yourself here as a soldier in the service of Anduin? Has it been a lifelong ambition of yours to become a warrior?"

Althus gave a short laugh. "I must be truthful, Tristan. This is the last thing I wanted. I will do as I must to the best of my ability, but I am no warrior. I have no heart for killing."

"And yet, my father tells me your swordsmanship is without equal."

Another look of surprise crossed Althus' face. "Did he truly say that?"

Tristan nodded. "He said you surpassed him."

"He has been my instructor since I was very young. I did not know he thought so much of my skill. It pleases me to know he feels I have become more skilled than he is, although I doubt it is true."

"You have worked very hard to become a swordsman, and yet you do not aspire to become a soldier," Tristan asked, "why?"

"I would protect my father, Euwyn. He has dedicated his life, his powers of healing, to the people of Anduin and he has no one else. It must seem strange to you. He is a powerful man, but I have watched him risk his own life to reach someone whose life is in danger. He seldom receives anything in return. He will not ask for anything in return, especially now that so many of our people find it difficult to keep food on their tables and clothing on their backs.

"I suspect he often went hungry when I was young, just so I had something to eat. As I grew older, I became more able to make sure there was food on the table for both of us, but now that I am fully-grown, I would protect him when he is in danger as well. He deserves someone to care for him as he has cared for me and for the people of Anduin. I can be that someone now."

"You speak of him as if he were old and feeble and not a man in the prime of his life as he appears," Tristan said.

"Yes, he is strong and hard and youthful for a Wizard, but his mind is not always on his own safety. When he sees someone in trouble he often does not stop to think, but plunges in blindly."

Althus turned his head so their eyes met. There was an angry look hidden in their depths.

"He has left me here to wait in safety like a small child while he travels to Stonehaven. He fears some evil or other has overcome the Dwarves and he has gone alone to see what he might do to help them. He would not take me with him. He is a powerful Wizard and I am not. I could not stop him, and I could not follow him. I do not understand why he cannot see me as an equal. Will he always consider me a child?"

Tristan smiled at him, shaking his head. "We will always be our fathers' children, Althus. They will always be older and wiser no matter how old we become. At least my father is only Human. He is difficult enough to deal with. Your father is a very powerful Wizard.

"I do not envy you, Althus. As he grows older, he will become even more powerful. You and I will remain Human for the rest of our days and there comes a time for us when we will become old and feeble and even less than we are now. This does not happen to Wizards.

"Perhaps you seem very vulnerable to him. You do not have his powers and he will outlive you by centuries unless some accident befalls him. He must live in fear of losing the few years you will have together."

Althus nodded sadly. "He has said as much to me, but I think there is something more to it than he is willing to admit." Althus looked to the west where the Forest Road disappeared into the distance and sighed. "I have a feeling, a premonition of trouble. He should have taken me with him."

Tristan wondered at how wrong he had been about Althus. A boy he had thought of as sullen and silent had just admitted his deepest thoughts to him for no more than an offer of friendship. He found he liked young Althus very much. Watching out for him would not be such a difficult thing after all. He was looking forward to it.

He laid a hand on Althus' shoulder. "Come," he said. "Your replacement arrives. Your watch is over. I would see some of this amazing swordsmanship you are said to possess."

Φ      Φ      Φ

Althus was an amazing swordsman. He defeated Tristan easily that day and just as easily on the days that followed. They became fast friends. Althus never forgot to call him 'sir' in the presence of others, but 'Tristan' when they were alone together.

Tristan chose a horse for Althus and taught him to ride. They spent many hours following the queen as she traveled about her kingdom, seeking out those in need. Althus was aware the number of Anduin's people who found themselves in need had increased greatly in the past two years. The king levied ever-higher taxes and still, the dikes, roads, and granaries of Anduin were falling into disrepair. Many were finding it difficult to feed and clothe their families.

Tristan did not ask Althus more of his private life until many days later when they sat in the shadow of the castle walls, stripped to the waist and sweating from an afternoon practice session with quarterstaffs.

"So," Tristan began, plunging into the subject without preamble. "It was a hard life with the Wizard, Euwyn."

"No," Althus said, laughing at Tristan's typically abrupt approach. "I was happy with Euwyn. He taught me many things and made it all a game. There was not a day went by I did not learn something from him and not a day went by we did not find something to laugh about. Euwyn's stone tower is full to the rafters with amazing things.

"There are hundreds of books on the shelves. Maps cover the walls. The stones are always warm when Euwyn is there as if the sun shines on them at all times when he is present. I know some fear him because of what he is, but to me he was and is a dear and gentle father. I have tried to be as good a son to him as he has been a father to me."

"It seems we are both fortunate in our fathers, then," said Tristan.

"Tell me, Althus," he continued, "when did my father find the time to teach you swordsmanship?"

The question seemed to take Althus off guard. He hesitated a moment before he answered. "Your father came with the queen when she visited Euwyn. She usually came at least three times a week when the roads were passable. Sometimes more and sometimes less."

Tristan gaped at him. "The queen visited you? My father never told me of this. Did she speak to you?"

"She always took time to speak with me. Sometimes she spent more time with me than Euwyn. She watched my sessions with the sword until I once took a minor cut. She always left us alone after that. She said the sight of blood made her feel faint."

"How long has this been going on, Althus?"

"For as long as I can remember."

Tristan was silent, digesting this bit of information. What was the queen's interest in this young man? He had seen the queen's eyes on him as they accompanied her on her rides through the countryside. They almost never left him. She requested he ride at her side at all times. Tristan was silent, puzzling over this mystery.

Euwyn may have left Althus at the Queen's side to protect her. He may have left Althus with the queen for his own safety, but that did not explain the queen's unusual fascination with him.

"Please, Tristan," he said. "Tell no one the queen has spent so much time with me. The other men seem to know I am a favorite of hers already, but I would not have them know how close we truly are. I do not know why she has singled me out in such a manner. She and Euwyn are very close. I suppose that would explain her interest in me, but I would not have the others know of it."

"Your secret is safe with me, Althus. We will not speak of it again," he said. Perhaps Althus was right. The queen was only showing her friendship for Euwyn by befriending his son.

Φ   Φ   Φ

The Elves arrived two weeks and a day after that. Althus and Tristan were in the courtyard surrounding the stable area, having just returned from an outing with the queen. They were caring for their mounts and the queen's black mare when they heard the sounding of horns from the direction of the main gates.

"Elves," Tristan said. "Elven royalty would be my guess."

"How do you know?" Althus asked.

"No one sounds a horn as clear and sweet as the Elves. I have not heard such horns in many years. It makes the hair on the back of my neck stand up to hear them."

Althus nodded. He could still hear the horns echoing in his head even though their sounding had been brief. It was a wild, untamed sound that made his heart beat faster. He thought of Euwyn's tales of his time with the Elves and wondered if they would look as he imagined them. He was soon to find the Elves of his imagination did not compare to reality. They appeared in the courtyard soon after Tristan and Althus had finished with the queen's horse and were tending to their own.

Tristan bent close and whispered in Althus' ear as they approached. "None other than Lord Gilden of the Wood Elves and his son, and heir, Rowan," he said.

Althus felt his mouth go dry, his tongue cleaving to the roof of it. Gilden and Euwyn were close friends and yet he and Althus had never met. He was about to find himself face to face with the ruler of all Wood Elves.

Gilden and Rowan caught sight of them and moved toward them. The Elves were tall. Euwyn towered over Althus' six-foot height by at least a head. Gilden and Rowan were every bit as tall, and as fair as Euwyn was dark. They seemed to draw the sunlight after them as they moved across the courtyard.

Their horses followed freely, stepping boldly after their masters. Althus was surprised at their size. They were not the fine-boned and hot-blooded horses he had imagined, but broad and heavily muscled, horses bred more for armed warfare than speed. They moved with deliberate grace, their eyes taking in their surroundings, pacing lightly as if they could walk without touching the ground if they wished.

Gilden held out his hand to Tristan.

"You are Captain Manton's son," he said. "How you have grown! You are changed, but I could not mistake your red hair."

"Welcome to Anduin, Lord Gilden and welcome to you also, Rowan," Tristan said easily as if he shook the hands of royalty every day. Althus envied him since his own tongue still seemed stuck irretrievably to the roof of his mouth. "It has been a long time since you honored us with a visit."

"It has been much too long," Gilden answered.

Before Althus could gather his scattered wits, Tristan was introducing him and Gilden was offering his hand. He prayed he was not gaping at them. He seemed to have gone numb from the neck up and hardly knew what he was doing. He wanted to make a good impression on these men who were part of Euwyn's past and the Wizard's closest friends.

Gilden's hand was warm. He did not let go of Althus' hand as he had

Tristan's after taking it, but stood looking down at him. Their eyes met. Gilden was smiling at him. Althus fought a wild urge to run.

"Althus?" Gilden said. "Euwyn's son? Are you *that* Althus?"

Now Rowan turned to stare at him as well. Gilden still held his hand in a firm grip or he might have run.

Althus managed to loosen his tongue enough to answer. "Yes, I am," he said. He did not know how to address Lord Gilden so he did not add 'your majesty' or 'my lord'. Gilden did not seem to notice.

"We were hoping to see Euwyn while we are in Anduin. We are fortunate to have found you here. You can tell us where to find him. Perhaps you can be spared from your duties here in Castle Anduin long enough to take us to him."

"He has left for Stonehaven, sir. He left almost a month ago and must have reached there by now," Althus said.

"Stonehaven," Gilden repeated. "It does not please me to hear he is there, and yet, it does not surprise me. Something is definitely amiss in Stonehaven. Neither am I pleased nor surprised he did not ask for my help. He is as stubborn and independent as a Sea Elf.

"I have not received more than a few brief messages from him in the years since he took you in, but I thought I detected an improvement in his behavior since then. He displayed more caution than in his younger years."

Gilden sighed, as if resigning himself to Euwyn's absence. He placed his free hand on Althus' shoulder. "It is reasonable for you to worry for him, Althus, but you should not feel guilt for not accompanying him. I have known him for well over two hundred years and I have never been able to make him listen to reason when it concerns his own safety."

Althus stood in silence, wondering how Gilden knew what he was feeling.

"May we tend to your horses, my lords?" Tristan asked.

"No. Thank you, sergeant," Rowan said, "but, you could show us where we might turn them out when we have cared for them."

Tristan led them off towards one of the unoccupied paddocks. Althus did not move from where he stood. He admired the horses as they walked past. Gilden rode a blue roan and Rowan an iron gray. They followed their masters without guidance as if they knew what was required of them. Rowan's gray rolled an eye at him and tossed his head as he passed. Althus could have sworn the horse was laughing at him. He should have said more to them. The brief encounter left him feeling confused and stupid. Gilden must think Euwyn had adopted a very slow-witted son.

## Chapter Three

## LORD GILDEN

Gilden and Rowan soon left the stables. Althus and Tristan made sure someone informed the King and Queen of their arrival and led them to suitable rooms in the southwest tower of Castle Anduin.

"So, that is Euwyn's son," Rowan mused as they dropped their saddlebags on the floor of their common sitting room. "I have always wanted to meet him, and yet, he barely spoke to us. What do you think of him?"

"I think we caught him by surprise. He wanted to make a good impression, but did not know how to begin.

"I am disappointed to find Euwyn has left Anduin. These people will be in dire need of him soon, but I am pleased to find his son here. There is much of Euwyn in him, not the power of a Wizard, but still, a sense of right and wrong. He will be true to the people of Anduin and to Euwyn. I had hoped for Euwyn's help, but Althus will help us if he can. I felt that much from him."

Rowan laughed softly, "He is a son worthy of our friend Euwyn, then?"

"I would wish Euwyn the happiness I find in my children and it seems he has reason to be proud of Althus."

"You read him so thoroughly in such a short time?" Rowan inquired.

"Yes, there is innocence and openness about him. He is not one who guards his feelings from others easily. I suppose he may have some Elven blood in him. Euwyn did not disclose his origins to me. Perhaps he does not know them."

"Come, Rowan," he said, as he headed for the door. "We cannot keep Queen Maris waiting any longer."

Althus was there to admit Gilden and his son to the queen's quarters. Gilden was tempted to ask him to stay, but allowed him to return to his post outside her door. He could not resist the temptation to connect with him once more, however, and briefly placed a hand on Althus' shoulder as he passed. The boy's feelings still came readily to Gilden through his touch and once again the emotions he drew from the boy impressed him. Althus would protect the queen at all costs. Gilden was startled to find himself assessed and then dismissed as an opponent. He and Rowan went unarmed within the castle walls.

Maris greeted them with an embrace for each. Gilden was not surprised to find her feelings guarded. The queen was half-Elven, a descendant of sea Elves. They were a wild and proud race and did not give their feelings readily. She seated them close to the fire and took a chair between them.

"I have spoken with two of your guards, Maris," Gilden said. "One of them, the one who guards your door, tells me he is Euwyn's son."

Maris' green eyes regarded him carefully. "What do you think of him, Gilden?"

"It seems Euwyn has raised a fine son. He must be very proud of the boy. Tell me, Maris. Why is he here, dancing attendance to you and not with his father as he wishes?" Gilden asked.

The question had the desired effect. Maris colored slightly, hesitating before answering. Gilden knew she did not want to tell him the truth, but she could not tell him a lie either.

"I requested he stay here with me."

"Why?" Gilden asked.

"To keep him from harm," she answered, still avoiding Gilden's eyes. "I am very fond of him."

"He is Euwyn's son and would have gone with Euwyn if he had been permitted."

"Yes, he would have. Euwyn would have led him into danger," Maris answered softly.

Gilden let the matter rest. There was more to it than Maris was telling. He wondered at it, but other matters seemed of more importance.

"What brings you to Anduin, Lord Gilden? You certainly did not come here to discuss my choice of guards?" The queen asked.

"We came to warn you of an army gathering in the wild lands south of our kingdoms and to offer an alliance. I fear evil is on the march and it has set its sights on Anduin."

Queen Maris rose from her chair. The rustle of silk followed her as she stepped to the window looking out over the farmlands south of Castle Anduin. "It has come, then. The thing I feared most has come to pass. Our enemies see us as easy prey. Somehow, they know we lie defenseless before them. I fear the king will not heed your warning, Gilden. He has become a useless puppet of that fiend he calls a court Wizard."

"It is true, then, Maris? I had heard as much, but hoped things were not as bad as that."

"It is much worse than you know," Maris said. "I fear by the time this army marches into Anduin, Borgas will control the king so completely he will open wide the gates of the city and invite them in."

Φ          Φ          Φ

Gilden and Rowan approached King Allen that very afternoon, hoping against hope he was not as far gone as the queen feared.

Gilden's warning drew a scornful laugh from the king and an answering snort from Borgas.

"You think to draw my forces into a skirmish with the bands of Goblins that beset your borders when your own patrols should be dealing with such small matters," King Allen said, waving his hand at Gilden as if to dismiss him. "Please do not take me for a fool."

"My scouts tell me this is more than a few bands of Goblins looking for trouble. There are Orcs and other foul creatures gathering to our south as well, thousands of creatures. We will deflect them from our borders, but they will head for your kingdom when that is accomplished. They will know our strength as well as we know theirs. They will know how matters stand here," Gilden said, casting a glance at Borgas. "Your kingdom is in peril, King Allen. I am here to warn you. You must prepare for war."

Borgas bent to whisper in the king's ear. King Allen laughed. "Perhaps you should return to your wood and hide, Lord Gilden. If what you say is true, why are you here? Why do you not look after your own people and leave the people of Anduin to me? I have a great Wizard at my side and an army to defend my kingdom. Why do you pester me with your fears like an old woman?"

"I will stay for a time, your majesty. There are those here I have not spoken with in years and some I have just met I would know better,"

"Stay, then, Lord Gilden, or go slinking back to your wood. I do not care either way," the king said.

The sour look on Borgas' face as they turned to leave the king's quarters told Gilden the Wizard did not want them to stay in Anduin. That made Gilden even more determined to see this matter to its conclusion. He would keep an eye on the Wizard.

Φ         Φ         Φ

Queen Maris stood before the fountain that graced the center of the castle gardens, idly watching the water that spilled over the lip of its basin trickle through her fingers. If King Allen would do nothing to defend the people of Anduin, she would prepare them without the king's consent. Captain Manton had not taken Gilden's warning lightly. She watched the Captain grow more desperate as the days passed and Gilden did not make any headway with the king.

She was so absorbed in turning the problem over in her mind she did not hear Borgas' approach. She was startled to find him at her side, leering at her with an insolence that made her ache to slap him.

"I have come to give you a piece of advice, Maris," he said.

"I have never been known to seek your advice, Wizard," she said, her voice as cool as the water that trickled from her hand, "nor do I ask for it now."

"You would do well to take it if you care for Gilden and his son. The king wishes them to leave Anduin. If they do not, I fear something unfortunate will happen to them."

His purring voice close to her ear made her shiver as much as the advice he offered.

"It is *your* wish they leave Anduin, Borgas. If the king wishes it, then it is only from the poison that continually pours into his ear from your mouth. Gilden has nothing to fear from you. He has been as a brother to King Allen in years past. If you push the king too far, he may remember it. Your plans for Anduin could fall to dust at your feet."

"Why, Maris, what could you mean?" he said, all innocence. "King Allen rules Anduin. I have no plans for Anduin that do not reflect his desires for his people."

"You will not have Anduin, Borgas. Gilden and I will stop you."

She turned to leave him, dismissing him, as if his words meant nothing to her, as if they did not frighten her.

Borgas' temper got the better of him. He did not like such an insolent tone from one who would some day be his. She would be part of the spoils of war when the Dark Lord's army took Anduin. He grabbed her roughly by the arms. She would learn to fear him.

A blade held firmly to his throat caused him to let go of her abruptly, raising his hands defensively. Where had this fierce guardsman sprung from so suddenly? He had thought no guard had the temerity to cross him.

"You will never touch the queen in such a manner again," a firm voice said as the owner of the blade moved to face him. A lowly guard, Borgas realized, relieved to know he was not facing Gilden. He would kill this youngster as easily as he would crush a beetle in his path.

"Althus, no!" the queen shouted as the young guardsman stepped between them. Borgas could see fear in her eyes as she looked on from behind the young man's shoulder. He could make her beg for this man's life before he killed him. He began to wonder why that was so.

Borgas' eyes shifted to meet the guard's eyes. Who was this Althus? He was not afraid, although he should have been. Borgas caught sight of Gilden and Rowan approaching. Too many present now to risk killing this upstart. He would bide his time and find another opportunity to put an end to him. He turned his back on them, fleeing before the Elf lord, his face dark with anger.

They would pay, but he would not risk killing them where others could see. Not yet. The young guard would die first. He would be easy enough to kill. A stray arrow from a crossbow as he kept watch, an unfortunate fall from the ramparts. Gilden and his son would be more difficult to catch unaware, but he would kill them as well, and with the king's blessing. The queen would be his to do with as he pleased as soon as he ruled Anduin openly.

The queen rounded on Althus as soon as Borgas was out of sight. The anger in her eyes drove him to step back. "You are foolish beyond belief, Althus! He could have killed you easily! You must not cross him again! In fact, you must stay out his way entirely!"

Althus regarded her with a look of astonishment. Where had this harpy come from? What had happened to the serene and majestic woman in whose wake he followed so faithfully?

"Ease up, Maris," Gilden said, amused and puzzled by her anger. "You have given him a job to do and now he has done it, you are angry with him. Did you expect him to stand by while the Wizard handled you so roughly?"

She rounded on Gilden as if she would give him a piece of her mind as well. His look, curious, calculating made her think better of it. Althus watched as she made a visible effort to bring her anger under control.

"I am sorry, Althus," she said, outwardly calm once again. "I am shaken by his threats and cannot be expected to behave rationally." She walked away from them, leaving Althus gaping at her.

Gilden put a comforting hand on his shoulder. "Do not let her anger keep you from your duty, Althus. You did very well. Not many would risk making an enemy of Borgas. I will watch over her until her anger cools. It will give me an opportunity to speak with her privately concerning a few matters that have recently come to my attention."

Althus was glad to escape the queen's presence while he puzzled over her strange behavior. He left her to Gilden.

He was pleased as well to have Rowan accompany him to the kitchens where he found a bite to eat in a quiet corner.

Rowan sat across from him. Althus watched his graceful hands as he tore a roll in half and buttered it, setting it beside the bowl of soup Althus downed hungrily. The young Elf seemed at ease sitting at the crude table in the corner of the bustling kitchen. Althus liked him for that, even though he suspected Rowan was there to protect him.

Tristan appeared with a group of soldiers, each bearing a saddlebag over their shoulder. His look of relief when he caught sight of Althus was almost comical.

"Althus," he said. "Thank the Creator you are safe! I have been searching everywhere for you. It is the talk of the barracks you faced down that snake, Borgas."

"Tristan, that happened little more than an hour ago!" Althus said, astounded by the speed at which gossip traveled within the castle.

"The men are talking of nothing else. I have come to drop a warning in your ear. You have the support of those still loyal to the queen, but you will not be safe from Borgas. There are men within these walls who answer only to him."

Althus nodded. "I hear you," he said. "Where are you bound, Tristan?"

"Father is sending us to guard the southern border," Tristan answered. "We are leaving as soon as our provisions are packed."

"I thought the king has refused such measures," Rowan said. "Has your father succeeded where mine has failed?"

Tristan looked at them both, a frown creasing his face. "We are to tell no one of our destination. I do not believe the king knows of it. I knew I could trust you two to keep our secret."

"Your father risks much in doing this," Althus said.

"He thinks of the welfare of the citizens of Anduin before his own. It has always been so," Tristan said.

Althus nodded. "I have seen as much, Tristan. I suppose the queen has forbidden me to go with you."

Tristan did not answer immediately. He and Althus stared at each other across the table.

"I wish you were at my side in this, Althus," Tristan said, finally. "There is no one I trust more than you. I fear I will be safer at the borders than you will be here in Anduin.

"I must go," Tristan said, abruptly taking up his saddlebags. "Watch your backs, both of you. Watch out for each other as best you can."

Φ                    Φ                    Φ

Lord Gilden and Queen Maris stood atop the battlements of Castle Anduin. The queen faced him, her back to the wind and her hands wound into her thick chestnut hair to keep it from her face. Her anger had cooled quickly, replaced by a worried frown.

"He is not safer here than he would be on the open road, Maris," Gilden repeated. "The Wizard sees him as only a guardsman. He will think him easy prey and someone who no one will miss if he disappears. You should think seriously about the danger facing him. I will not ask you why you care so much for him, but I know you do. I care for him as well. He is Euwyn's son. Euwyn saved the lives of Rowan and his sister, Bree, when they were young and I would return that favor.

"Euwyn has been gone far too long. He is in peril. You know that is true and Althus knows it as well. Let him go, Maris. Castle Anduin is no longer a safe place for him. He has drawn the attention of Borgas and Borgas will soon learn Althus is Euwyn's son. That will give him even more reason to want him dead."

Maris would not give in easily. She regarded Gilden, a stubborn look in her eyes. "He is only a boy. You would send him to his death."

"He is no longer a boy, Maris!  He is a grown man, and he would be long gone from here if you would release him from his duty to you!  If he must die, Maris, at least he will die for a cause that matters to him!"

"No!" Maris shouted.  "Anduin matters to him!  He cares deeply for the people of Anduin!"

"Let him go, then, Maris.  If Euwyn does not return to Anduin before this army reaches your gates, most within these walls will die and those who do not will wish they had," Gilden said softly.  "You know that is true as well, Maris.  I can try to protect him if you will send him after Euwyn.  I cannot promise he will survive such a quest, but I will do all I can for him."

Maris sighed and nodded.  Tears coursed down her cheeks, but she held her head high.  "We will petition the king tomorrow for men to accompany him."

Gilden wondered if it would not be wiser for Althus to leave Castle Anduin without informing the king and his Wizard of his departure, but did not say so to Maris.  He meant what he said.  Gilden did not have much hope of persuading Rowan to leave his side and accompany Althus on his journey, but he knew very well the powers his son possessed.  Rowan had already summoned help from the Dark Forest.  He did not doubt help would arrive in time for Althus' departure from Anduin.

Φ        Φ        Φ

The eldest citizens of Anduin said the king of that land had once been the fairest and most beloved king in all the lands and he and his queen once seemed to be of one mind in all things.  Now the queen appeared before her once beloved husband as no more than one of his many petitioners.

Althus did not remember him as anything but a man everyone feared.

He followed Queen Maris from the doors of the throne room to stand at her side before the king.  Borgas, standing in his usual place behind the king's left shoulder, favored him with a look of pure hatred.

Althus was relieved to find Gilden sitting at the king's right hand and Rowan standing at Gilden's side.  The king did not look at Althus.  He was a lowly guard, after all, as easily overlooked as the dust motes that hung in the sunlight streaming through the colored glass of the palace windows, but when Queen Maris approached, the king's gaze shifted to regard her absently.

Althus stood to the queen's left, watching King Allen as Borgas spoke in his ear.  He studied the sunlight, colored by the tall stained glass windows that lined the huge vaulted chamber, as it played across their faces, noting Borgas and King Allen wore identical pendants bearing milky white stones.  Althus thought they were rather ugly pieces of jewelry for two such men to wear. They began glow as he studied them and for a moment, he felt sick and dizzy, unable to tear his eyes away from them. His knees were failing him when he thought he heard his name, spoken softly. Suddenly, he found himself looking into Gilden's eyes, vaguely confused and wondering what had just occurred. Gilden was staring back at him intently. A smile flitted across Gilden's face before his attention turned to the queen.

Althus was tempted to step closer to her. She stood before the king, her hands clasped before her, colored sunlight creating a dazzling display against her gleaming, chestnut tresses. She looked vulnerable, standing alone before the king. Althus began to wonder if the king had forgotten her.

Althus' resemblance to King Allen struck Lord Gilden suddenly as he sat at the king's side. Why had he not noticed it before? The young man seemed different, as if he saw him clearly for the first time. Had Euwyn been protecting his adopted son somehow? If so, what had happened to weaken the enchantment preventing those Althus encountered within Castle Anduin from seeing his striking resemblance to their king? Gilden wondered if they were not too late to save Euwyn from whatever trouble had befallen him.

Gilden had been close to the king in his younger days. They had been great allies in the Goblin wars, but now the king had become like a stranger to him. Not a hint remained as far as Gilden could see of the charming and powerful young man he once knew and respected, a young man so much like the one who stood at attention before him. He was not sure what to think of the enigmatic Althus. Many kings kept bastard sons close to them, giving them positions in their court in deference to their lineage, but never actually acknowledging them as their offspring. However, King Allen was all but oblivious to the young man's existence while the queen held him in the greatest regard. Why, if he were the result of a king's indiscretion, did the queen care so much for his welfare? But, then he had known Maris for many years and the fact she was half Elven made her heart open to anyone who was worthy.

His attention turned to the king as the queen addressed him.

"Sire," she began, "I would ask permission to send young Althus with a few men to seek out the Wizard Euwyn who has been absent from our kingdom far too long."

Althus watched the king's eyes harden as Borgas spoke into his ear.

"What need have we for your Wizard friend, Maris?" King Allen said, smiling condescendingly at the queen. "We have a court jester if you desire some diversion. What can he do our true court Wizard cannot surpass tenfold? Why do you cling to this charlatan even though he has been replaced by someone more suited to the job?"

"Your majesty, perhaps you have forgotten the many lives he saved, including your own during the Goblin wars less than thirty years ago. We should at least make some attempt to find him and rescue him," she answered, her pale cheeks coloring slightly.

"What do you suggest, my queen?" the king responded angrily. "Do we send our troops on a wild goose chase to find a man who may not wish to be found? Perhaps he has found a place with Gilden's people in the Dark Forest. He is probably hiding from the imaginary foes Gilden himself warns us of."

Gilden turned his attention from the king to Althus. He had already spent much time arguing with King Allen, and the king's slight did not anger him. The king's refusal to see what lay ahead only saddened him. Althus was barely holding his anger in check from the look in his eyes and the clenching of his jaws. King Allen still did not seem to see him.

The king sighed as if in resignation. "Very well, Maris send one of your guards if you must waste a man on some meaningless errand, but I will not waste my soldiers on it."

"Please, your majesty, I would send young Althus here, but I cannot send him into the wilds alone!" the queen pleaded.

Borgas whispered once more into the king's ear.

"Very well," the king said, his smile matching the oily grimace of his counselor. "Borgas has suggested he can spare two of his personal guards to accompany young Althus. You are fortunate he is willing to accommodate you in this matter."

Althus thought he would much rather face the dangers of the wilds alone than have two of Borgas' assassins riding at his back. Still, he was pleased they had settled the matter so easily, and his anger cooled at the thought of escaping the confines of the castle. He had no fear of Borgas' men.

Gilden, on the other hand, found the ease with which the king acceded to the queen's request and Borgas' supposed assistance troubling. Althus and Borgas' men were set to depart at daybreak the next day. He and Rowan had much to do before then, if he were to protect the queen's favorite guardsman.

He and Rowan went straight from the king's presence to their rooms where Rowan went to a window and opened it. There, his imitation of a hawk's cry rang out over the castle walls. Soon, a small sparrow hawk spiraled down from the cloudless sky to perch on his shoulder. Gilden quickly penned a message and Rowan read it aloud before inserting it into a tiny container bound to the hawk's leg. The little bird was released to soar over the battlements with his message.

"I hope Kestrel has a safe journey, father," Rowan said as the little hawk soared off.

"He has never failed us, Rowan. Let us hope he succeeds this time as well. I fear the fate of the people of Anduin and eventually the fate of our people go with him."

From the castle walls, a pair of dark, furtive eyes marked the path of the bird's coming and going. With a few words and gestures, the bird fell from the sky to lie helpless in Borgas' hands. Borgas altered the message and re-inserted it, and set the bird free once again, shrieking with indignation, to deliver his message. Borgas gave a dry laugh as he rubbed his hands together. The Dark Lord's wraith sharing his form had almost caused him to crush the life from the small hawk as he held it in his hands, ending its journey. Borgas persuaded the creature the hawk's message would prove invaluable if it he could alter it and send the bird on his way. "How foolish are these Elves," he chuckled. "One way or another, this young fool the queen holds in such high regard will die soon after he enters Gilden's wood. When the queen hears of it, the Elven Lord's influence upon her will end. She will send him packing and I will see he and his son do not leave Anduin alive." The wraith shifted, pleased with the cruelty of Borgas' plan.

Borgas barely noticed the feeling any longer, the feeling of something slithering about just beneath his skin. At first, he thought the wraith he had accepted from the Dark Lord in order to communicate directly with his evil master would drive him mad, but with his power growing and the conquest of Anduin at hand, the wraith's presence had become tolerable. He would soon rule Anduin openly as he now did in secret and the Dark Lord promised the Dark Forest would be his as well.

The one he hated most, the Elf lord, Gilden, would die screaming for mercy, as would Euwyn, soon enough. Euwyn was close to death even now. The Dark Lord's powerful stone would break him before long. It was only a matter of time before Euwyn would no longer be a threat.

The wraith's slithering dance subsided to become a mere tickle beneath his skin as he summoned the men he would send with Althus. They would need careful instruction. He would leave nothing to chance. Althus would not survive long after he crossed into the Dark Forest. Borgas would make doubly sure of that.

He did not like the look of the young guardsman, a look of determination he had seen somewhere before. Borgas could not put his finger upon where, but he would kill this Althus who had dared to put a sword to his throat. Althus would not live long enough to reach Stonehaven. Borgas would see to it.

Φ                    Φ                    Φ

At first light the next morning Althus and his two traveling companions were prepared for their journey and ready to mount their horses. Althus was pleased to see Gilden approaching them.

"I have come to wish you good luck on your journey, Althus, and to give you something to speed you on your way," he said.

"Thank you, Lord Gilden, and thank you for persuading the queen to send me. I wish now we had become better acquainted. Our ways seem to be parting now and I fear I may never get another opportunity to know you better," Althus said.

Gilden smiled at him. "I know more of you than you might think and I am sure our paths will soon cross again. Here is Rowan with a gift for you."

Rowan appeared leading a horse obviously meant for an Elf lord. He was jet black over most of his body with a proud white face and sturdy legs, white to the knees. Althus could only stare dumbly. This could not be a gift for him. Everyone said such horses would never carry anyone not of Elven blood and even if they would, they never passed from Elven hands for any price.

He continued to stare, dumbfounded, as Rowan proceeded to move his gear to the black horse's saddle. Gilden's voice strong and clear at his side brought him to his senses. "Althus!" he shouted, putting his hand on the young man's shoulder and shaking him gently. "You will never get very far just staring. You must mount him. You will find his gaits smooth and he is unsurpassed in speed and endurance."

Still speechless, Althus mounted and sat while Rowan murmured softly to the horse in the Elvish tongue, their foreheads touching.

"His name is Gust, and if you are kind to him he will carry you anywhere you wish You will need no bit or spur, but only your mind to direct him," Rowan said when he had finished.

"Farewell, Althus. Watch your back!" said Gilden, earning himself a malevolent look from Althus' companions.

"Take care of him!" said Rowan as they rode off.

Althus stopped and turned Gust about to face him. "I will!" he answered, breathless with surprise.

Rowan stepped forward and offered Althus his hand. "I was speaking to Gust," he laughed. "I suspect from the look on your face you will be looking out for each other."

They parted at the gates of the castle. Althus and his unsavory-looking companions were soon on the road beyond the walls ringing the surrounding city. Had he looked back, he would have seen Queen Maris watching him depart from the battlements, weeping as though her heart would break.

Althus could not help feeling happy despite the company he kept and the daunting task he faced. With a powerful horse beneath him, his broadsword at his side, Castle Anduin behind him and the road before him, he truly felt free for the first time since he had parted from Euwyn weeks before.

## Chapter Four

## BREE, CHESS, AND THORNY

Chess shaded his eyes with one hand as he watched the small hawk spiral downward through the opening in the trees above the tiny stone cottage.

"Thorny!" he shouted, "I think it is Kestrel! Maybe father has finally sent us a message!"

"Let us hope so," said his twin, emerging from inside. "It has been a long time since we last heard from him."

The hawk circled once, just out of reach over Chess' head as if to tease him, and then landed on his shoulder with a shrill cry.

"What has your feathers in a ruffle little bird?" he asked. "Did you meet a bigger bird on the way?"

The bird struggled and cried shrilly while Chess removed his message.

"What's biting him?" Thorny asked, frowning.

"I have no idea. Must have had a rough trip. Let us see what the note says."

Chess read the letter and then read it over again. It was a short message. He sat staring until Thorny said impatiently "Well, what does it say?"

"It says, 'Find the man named Althus. He is traveling in your direction with two companions. He is dressed in the uniform of the Anduin guard. You must kill him.'"

"What?"

"You heard me, Thorny. I read it word for word"

"That does not sound like father, asking us to kill a man without reason. Something is not right, Chess. Father has never killed a man as far as I know and I find it hard to believe he would ask us to kill for him."

"I wish Bree were here. Where is she, Thorny?"

"Up on the hill, watching for Eagle," he replied.

"Perhaps she saw Kestrel arrive and will be back soon. Let us hope so."

Bree arrived at the outpost within the hour. Her brothers watched her ride toward them across the clearing, her passing stirring up a cloud of small insects that shimmered in the setting sun behind her. She slid off before the horse had come to a complete stop and stood expectantly before her twin brothers. The looks on their faces caused her smile to fade.

"What's wrong?" she asked, "Was that Kestrel I saw? Did father send us a message?"

"Yes, but it is a very strange one. We are hoping you can unravel the mystery for us," answered Thorny.

Sitting at the table inside, Bree read the message carefully and then looked up at her brothers, puzzled. She went to the porch of the cottage and called the little hawk to her as Rowan had done. When he flew down to her, she carried him inside and set him on the table. He shrieked when he saw the message lying there, snatching at it with his sharp beak.

She murmured softly to the bird and stroked his head to calm him.

"Our only hope is that Rowan thought to read the letter aloud within Kestrel's hearing before he sent it," she said. She folded her hands about the bird and bent to touch her forehead gently to his. Moments passed while her brothers sat across the table from her in silence, waiting.

She finally released the bird and he fluttered to the mantle and sat quietly preening himself. Bree picked up the scrap of paper once more and looked at it carefully.

"I heard Rowan's voice speaking through Kestrel. He clearly said to help Althus, not kill him. I also heard Rowan say he is Euwyn's adopted son. See, here where the message has been altered somehow and it looks as if the bottom of the message has been cut," she said pointing to the bottom of the slip of paper where the edge was not quite straight. "I suspect it is father's hand except for this word. Someone has changed the word 'help' to the word 'kill.' There is treachery afoot in Anduin even father does not see. Someone who can read and write in Elvish wants this man's death and has the power to accomplish it if he can knock a bird from the sky and send him on his way again. It is fortunate Kestrel came to us and not to one of the other Elven patrols. Wherever this Althus is, he needs our help. I hope we are not too late.

The Elves packed their gear and saddled their horses with the speed of those accustomed to travel at a moment's notice, riding off into the fading twilight. The hoof beats of their horses echoed about them as they sped through the groves of huge and ancient trees and darkness closed about them.

Gilden's twin sons and only daughter had left their mother in Borias, the fair capital city of the Elves, and taken up their duties with the border patrol when word of unrest in the lands to the south reached them. Gilden and Rowan had left days before on their long journey to Anduin. It was a dangerous time for Elves and Humans alike.

## Chapter Five

## CULLY AND GARTH

Althus enjoyed his newfound freedom and the awakening spring as it burgeoned about him. His distrust of his fellow travelers abated a bit in the days that followed their departure from Anduin. After crossing the great stone bridge beyond the city walls, the road swung southwest, following the course of the broad Anduin River toward the shallow ford that marked their entry into Gilden's realm.

Althus knew from his maps this was the only way to reach Craglith Pass that bisected the northern arm of the Hoary Mountains. He hoped Euwyn's maps, tucked safely in his saddlebags, would enable him to find Stonehaven, the kingdom of the Dwarves. Unless some misfortune had befallen him soon after leaving Anduin, Euwyn should have passed this way before him.

His companions were Cully and Garth. They spoke to him very little, following behind at a short distance, talking between them.

Gust seemed greatly annoyed by their mere presence and showed his displeasure by baring his teeth and flattening his ears at them if they approached too close. They kept their distance from him after a day or so and Gust seemed content with that. At night, they sometimes found an inn where they spent the night, asking the regulars if they had seen the errant Wizard. Sometimes they spoke to one or two who remembered a tall stranger, a young Wizard, with dark hair and dark eyes. They seemed to be on the right path for the moment and Althus pushed his companions as quickly as he dared, fearing he would find the Wizard too late.

More and more frequently, as they approached the borders of Anduin, they slept under the stars just off the road. The first night sleeping under the stars after leaving Castle Anduin, he tethered Gust to a tree near the other horses. He awoke with a start that night to find Gust standing over him while he slept. Cully, standing first watch, informed him the horse had coolly and skillfully untied himself and come directly to Althus. Cully seemed disturbed by the animal's behavior, but Althus found it a comfort in such doubtful company and did not attempt to confine Gust from then on. When he awoke to stand watch or when morning came, Gust was always watching over him.

They soon re-crossed the river at the broad, shallow ford that separated the kingdom of Anduin from Gilden's realm. The trees grew larger and more ancient in the Dark Forest, their dense canopies shutting out much of the light, the road becoming narrower and less traveled in their shade. Althus' maps showed the road continuing on to follow the border between the Dark Forest and the wild lands for many leagues.

They would leave the road to travel south, entering the wild lands through the Craglith Pass at a point halfway between the borders of Anduin and the great sea that formed the western border of Gilden's realm.

Whose lands they would cross before they reached the lands inhabited by the Dwarves and the Dark Giants was unclear. Althus suspected no one race laid claim to them. They were a no-man's-land, a wilderness of hills and scrubland between Gilden's forest and the southern arm of the Hoary Mountains. Dwarves lived in those mountains, digging great kingdoms beneath the earth. The hidden lands of the elusive Dark Giants lay in the foothills and the lower slopes of the mountains.

Giants and Dwarves were allies. He had never seen individuals of either race and wondered what an army consisting of a mixture of Giants and Dwarves could possibly be like. It would seem the Giants would have the upper hand, but Euwyn had taught him Dwarves were the fiercest of warriors and Giants were a timid, peaceful race, despite their size.

His companions were uneasy since the border crossing. They cast their eyes here and there as if expecting an attack at any moment. He overheard them muttering something to each other about Elves and Orcs, but when they noticed him watching them, they fell silent. He supposed they considered him a friend of the Elves and did not want him to hear them speak ill of them. Althus supposed he *could* call himself a friend of the Elves as Gilden and Rowan certainly seemed to wish for his friendship. The thought of their kindness made him smile as he patted Gust's neck.

He was certain the Elves detected their passage into the Dark Forest as soon as they crossed the border into Gilden's realm. The Elves were ever vigilant. He expected they would encounter their patrols soon enough. Perhaps Gust was his guarantee of safe passage through their lands.

The first night in the Dark Forest they camped not far from the road among some boulders, sheltered from a stiff breeze springing up out of the west, sighing mournfully through the ancient trees. Cully and Garth were unusually quiet as they sat close to the fire. Watching Althus start a fire with only his hands and a few words, without the use of flint or tinder, still moved them to silent wonder. They seldom spoke to Althus in any case, but passed the time regaling each other with tales of their prowess with women or of brawls they had taken part in. Althus doubted they had ever seen a battlefield or traveled so far from the castle in their lives. They played the hero in most of their tales and Althus suspected most were figments of their fertile imaginations. They seemed to have run out of stories to tell this night. They started at every sound in the forest about them. They were more uneasy by far than Althus, who had spent many nights sleeping in the forests of Anduin with Euwyn, learning the sounds and habits of the creatures that lived there. He laughed at his companions when the eerie cry of a fox searching for a mate had them reaching for their swords. Althus felt as if the ancient trees watched them as they settled down beneath their branches, but this was Gilden's wood and the feeling comforted him.

The night passed uneventfully and the next morning they prepared to set out once again. Cully and Garth were unusually slow about stowing their gear and Althus wondered if lack of sleep was plaguing them. He waited impatiently, fingering the reins while Gust stamped and snorted with impatience, eager to be off.

They had ridden through the morning mists, Cully and Garth lagging far behind, for less than a league when Althus noted an unusual rock formation he recognized from his maps. They were close to the borders where the Dark Forest and the wild lands ran together. At this point, the giant trees had receded and the surrounding forest was denser with smaller trees and patches of brush. He turned to point the landmark out to his companions and found them gone. He turned Gust about and stared back down the road straining to hear the sound of their horses. The forest was silent, unusually silent. No rustlings in the forest floor. No birds chattering in the trees. Gust shook his head, the bridle making a slight jingling sound in the deep stillness. A prickling assailed his spine. Gust snorted and turned about staring into the surrounding forest straining his ears forward, showing the whites of his eyes. They stood on the silent path for what seemed an eternity, waiting.

Φ                 Φ                 Φ

Cully and Garth headed back toward Anduin as fast as their mounts would carry them.

"Kinda sad to leave the youngster to the Orcs, ain't it Garth?" said Cully.

"We done our part, Cully. Borgas said we was to see he got this far and didn't turn off the road. I feel worse about leavin' his gear for the Orcs," growled Garth. "That Althus gave me the creeps. Startin' fires with his hands. Ridin' that Elf horse. How does he know the stuff he told us about the lay of the land? It ain't natcheral, I tell ye."

"Maybe the Orcs won't get him" said Cully.

"Yer gettin soft, Cully. Besides, Borgas said if the Orcs didn't finish him off, the Elves would."

"How so, Garth? Seems to me he and the Elves are friendly like."

"Don't rightly know how, Cully, but one thing I will say about Borgas, when It comes to creepy ..."

Φ                 Φ                 Φ

Suddenly the wood about Althus erupted with terrible shrieks and howls. Orcs! Gust did not hesitate long enough for Althus to count, but there seemed to be hundreds of them. Gust leapt into the forest at an all-out gallop with Althus forced to bend close to his neck to avoid the lower branches of trees. Luckily, they soon found themselves back among the giant trees where their way was clearer, but the Orcs were ahead of them there. Orcs armed with bows stood atop huge boulders ahead. Althus had little doubt he had fallen into a carefully laid trap. Gust swung about quickly, fleeing to his right, turning again to avoid more Orc bowmen. They were surrounded. Gust flung a screaming challenge to the sky and swung about once more, heading directly away from the road now, deeper into the Dark Forest, his ears flattened against his head as he flew over the rough ground. Althus clung to him, praying he could stay with him as he leapt deadfalls and boulders, twisting and turning amongst the trees. They approached the Orc archers again and the boulders that barred their path.

Gust skidded to a stop beyond the range of the Orcs' bows and stood turning his head from side to side, his ears pinned. He snorted once and danced in place as if to gather himself and then he was off again, shooting toward the clustered boulders at top speed. Althus felt Gust gather himself and watched in disbelief as the huge boulders loomed ahead. Surely, no horse could hope to clear them. He shut his eyes and knotted his hands in Gust's mane as the horse left the ground with a powerful thrust of his hindquarters. Gust would have left him behind if he had not. They landed atop the largest boulder, Gust skidding on his haunches, slewing sideways slightly and bowling over the Orc standing there. Althus' last view of the ugly face before Gust's heavy shoulder catapulted it from the top of the boulder was a mouth lined with sharp teeth and yellow eyes opened wide in astonishment. Gust took a shortened step atop the boulder and leapt down, stumbling as he hit soft ground on the opposite side. Althus was unseated and Gust slowed as Althus struggled to regain his balance. That momentary hesitation proved their downfall. Althus felt the sting of two arrows in his back as they sped away. Gust gave a grunt of pain as an arrow buried itself in his hindquarters.

The Orcs swarmed from the rocks and the surrounding forest in pursuit, many mounted on foul wolf-like creatures Althus could not bring himself to look at too closely. For a time their harsh cries receded as they fled through the forest, but Althus' wounds soon made him unsteady and Gust began to travel more carefully. He knew he would fall unconscious from Gust's back if he did not dismount first. There was no sense in Gust carrying him any longer. He was forcing the horse to travel too slowly. Perhaps he could hide somewhere and send Gust on. He brought the horse to a reluctant halt and slid from his back. There was no sense in letting the Orcs kill Gust, he thought as the world began turn gray about him. He carefully plucked an arrow from the horse's sturdy hindquarters and prayed the animal's size and strength would prove too great for the poison the Orcs used to make their arrows more deadly. He knew he was a dead man. The two arrows were already doing their venomous work. He turned Gust toward what he hoped was his home and slapped him on the rump. Gust took a few strides in that direction, but wheeled about when Althus sank to his knees, coming to stand over him, shaking his proud head and regarding him with an anxious look. Althus tried once more to drive him off, but his strength was failing and now he was too weak to pull himself back into the saddle.

"All right, beast," he said, dragging himself to his feet to lean against Gust's side, drawing his sword. "We will die fighting anyway, you and me. May Gilden and Rowan forgive me for being the cause of your death. I have failed Euwyn as well."

Gust screamed another challenge as the shrieking horde of Orcs drew nearer. Althus fancied he heard an answering call from a tiny hawk hovering over his head. "Perhaps it is death come looking for me," he thought, but the tiny hawk turned and sped off in the direction from which it had come, deeper into the forest darkening about him.

## Chapter Six

## MANTON AND ELINOR

Captain Manton retired to his rooms soon after he watched Althus ride out of sight from the castle walls. Elinor, his wife, was there to greet him. He sighed wearily as he sank into a chair at the small table where they took their meals.

It still amazed him each time he found her waiting in the humble rooms allotted to him within the walls of Castle Anduin. His hair was graying, his body beginning to show the ravages of the harsh life he led, and yet, she still loved him passionately after all these years and did not hesitate to tell him so. She was a beautiful woman. The few strands of gray in her red hair and the lines that appeared at the corners of her green eyes when she smiled at him only made her more beautiful.

Elinor came to stand behind him, her arms about his neck and her face against his. She felt frustration radiating from him like heat from a forge. He was not a large man, but solid with broad, muscular shoulders, still as trim and strong as the youngest of his men. She felt secure when she was with him. Lately, it was the only time she felt secure within the walls of Castle Anduin. His worried frown made her uneasy

"What is it, Manton? Is there more amiss than usual in Castle Anduin?" she asked.

"I have just watched young Althus ride away with two companions I would not send to tend a goat," he said.

"How has this come to pass, then? I thought Althus was a favorite of the queen. Where is he off to and with whom?"

"They have sent him off to the mountains to find Euwyn with two of Borgas' men to guard his back." Manton's dislike of Borgas and his men hung palpably in the air.

"I think Gilden felt Althus was in danger here at the castle, but I do not think it was his choice to send him off with two men who will probably knife him in his sleep," said the Captain. "Still, Gilden has given him an Elven horse and will no doubt send word ahead to his patrols. Perhaps Althus is safer on the open road than here where that sneaking excuse for a Wizard can get his hands on him."

"Do you know why this young lad is so important to Gilden and the queen and, to his misfortune, Borgas? It seems everyone has some interest in him," asked Elinor. "Is he not just another member of the Anduin guard?"

Deep in thought, Manton missed the tone of her voice that would usually have alerted him she was hiding something of importance, probing to see how much he knew.

"I do not know for sure," he answered. "I simply like the boy, and I suspect Gilden sees something special in him. At any rate, Euwyn raised him and that makes him precious to many, especially if Euwyn does not return. I am not sure why the queen has always been so taken with him, but I am beginning to suspect he is more than just our friend, Euwyn's adopted son.

"Borgas hates him for a more obvious reason. Althus caught him with his hands on Queen Maris and nearly slit his throat. It is a pity the boy does not have a taste for blood. He could have rid us of Borgas for good. Perhaps it is just as well. Althus would have paid with his life." Captain Manton allowed himself a small smile. "I would have given a month's pay to have been there to see it," he said.

Elinor laughed at the look of pure pleasure that lit his face. "That is not all, is it?" Elinor pressed him. "Something else is amiss."

"Oh persistent little woman," he growled, standing to take her in his arms. "You are a breath of sanity in an otherwise insane world. In our twenty and two years of marriage, I do not think I have ever been able to hide anything from you. Yes, there is more, although I would like to spare you some of the dark thoughts in my head."

She gave him a hard look and, as usual, he could not keep his worries from her.

"My best men are disappearing. Desertion, says Borgas. Corny and Bellweather are gone, Max and Dell to name a few. Most of my trusted men have just up and disappeared. What is worse, that slimy Wizard has selected all of their replacements. Some, I suspect, are not fully human."

Elinor looked up at him, concern for his safety and that of his men etched on her face.

"What about Ryder and Best?" she asked, concerned for Manton's highest ranked and most trusted men.

"Fortunately, I sent them off to our borders with a patrol when Gilden appeared with a warning of unrest to our south. I have sent Tristan with them, hoping he will be safer in their company than he would here in this accursed castle."

Elinor nodded in agreement, concerned for her grown son and their only child.

"The king said he would not send troops beyond the borders of Anduin, but he did not say I could not send them *to* the borders. Gilden and the queen are planning to evacuate the outlying farms and bring all the citizens of Anduin within the protection of the city walls when word comes of enemy forces crossing our borders. Given the instability of our beloved king and the fact he has expressly forbidden any act of preparation for war, I fear they are putting themselves in great danger. Without my most trusted men, it will be difficult to protect either of them. They may save the lives of the people of

Anduin, but it may cost them their own."

"Perhaps the king will not realize what is happening until the enemy is at our gates and then what can he do but be grateful to Gilden and his queen? He has paid little enough attention to the affairs of his kingdom in the past few years, leaving them to his Wizard," said Elinor.

"There is no hope of that, Elinor, with Borgas whispering in his ear. Borgas would like nothing better than to have the Elf lord and his son dead at his feet. I shudder to think what the failure of our alliance with the Elves would cost the people of Anduin."

Manton sighed and sat back down at the table, dragging his hands through his hair. "It would be better for Anduin if our king were dead. I never thought it would come to this. He was a great king once, before this Borgas showed his face. People say the loss of his only son made the king what he is today, but I saw a change in him before that. I saw it happen when he dismissed Euwyn and took on this Borgas as court Wizard."

"You cannot mean you are thinking of assassination," Elinor said in a hushed voice.

"No, Elinor, I am the king's man, captain of the guard. I cannot harm the king. I only hope he does not lose his kingdom to an enemy that will make the lives of all who survive the coming battle a living torment and I cannot defend Anduin with men who are in league with the foulness gathering in the mountains to our south."

## Chapter Seven

## GILDEN'S CHILDREN

The three Elves had ridden steadily southward for nearly two days. Bree and Thorny continued onward while Chess headed for a nearby outpost to see if the Elves stationed there had any news to share of strangers crossing their borders. Bree sent Kestrel to scout ahead once more for any signs of Althus and his companions. As the sun approached the western horizon, the tiny hawk returned, flying down to perch on Bree's shoulder, calling shrilly.

"What do you suppose he is on about now?" Thorny asked.

"I do not know, Thorny, but it seems we should investigate," answered Bree.

They continued southward, veering to follow the hawk's flight through the trees. Chess soon rejoined them, accompanied by four Elves from the nearby outpost.

"There are Orcs in the forest. They have crossed our borders and headed north. A force of a hundred or more according to our scouts," Captain Cedar informed them as he rode alongside. "My Elves and I were riding south to intercept them when Chess overtook us. We are fortunate you headed this way. They will be no match for Bree's bow and the combined might of our swords." There were grim smiles all around as they rode swiftly through the deep forest.

Φ                    Φ                    Φ

Althus held his sword before him, swaying on his feet, unsure if he still possessed the strength to swing it if he had the opportunity. The Orcs, armed with bows, did not need to approach within the reach of his sword to kill him. They would not even need to waste their arrows for that matter. They would merely have to wait for the poisoned arrows he already carried in his back to finish their work. The foremost of them caught sight of him. Their hideous faces and cries of triumph almost sent him to his knees again. Gust pressed close to his side, his ears pinned, pawing the ground threateningly. His challenging call rang through the forest once again. Althus listened to the horse's scream echo through the trees behind him. It was a brave sound. He would stand with Gust as long as he was able. It did not help that the ground seemed to tremble beneath his feet and a thundering sound roared in his ears, accompanied by the sound of Gust's challenge, echoing endlessly from somewhere behind him. He watched in confusion as the yellow eyes of his pursuers shifted from him to something beyond him that made their jaws drop. They began to gibber with terror and all but a few of them took to their heels, howling with fright. Gust turned to face an approaching sound and, with the last of his strength Althus turned also, hoping some new terror was not coming to assail him.

Elves! He could tell from the horses they rode and the uniforms they wore they were indeed Elves. They rode at full gallop directly toward him, their mounts exhaling great puffs of vapor with every stride. All wore coats of mail and hooded cloaks that billowed out behind them. The Elf in the lead, armed with a bow, loosed arrows with deadly accuracy, dropping an Orc with each arrow, as the rest of the troop, swords drawn, swept by him and after the retreating Orcs. He saw them hesitate, milling in a tight knot for a moment as if to confer and then all but the leading archer continued out of sight. The remaining Elf rode back toward him and dismounted. Althus' sight was dimming, his head swimming, but there was no mistake. The archer was a beautiful female Elf. She wore her golden hair cropped short, but there was no mistake. His legs failed him and he fell to his knees, but he could not take his eyes off her face.

"Easy, brave warrior," she said. Her voice was beautiful and clear even to his failing senses. "You are safe now."

"The horse," he managed to gasp, fighting for breath, "He has been wounded. He belongs to Lord Gilden and his son Rowan. Please. Take care of him. I cannot survive the poison in me, but he may have a chance."

She sank to her knees and cradled him in her arms like a child, removing her cloak and wrapping it carefully about him.

"Tell me your name, Human," She begged softly.

"Althus," he replied. With the last of his strength, he was able to swallow some of the liquid she offered him from a small vial. For the next few days as his mind wandered the border between life and death, his concern for Euwyn and various other fears and concerns giving him little peace, that clear, soft voice was often his only link to reality.

Chess and Thorny returned before long to find Bree still sitting on the ground, cradling Althus in her arms.

"Is this Althus? Is he alive?" Thorny asked.

"Barely," she replied. The concern in her blue-green eyes told them all they needed to know.

"Captain Cedar is going on to hunt down the stragglers. Hickory's band, tracking them from the south, joined with us. I think we killed most of them," said Chess. "Cedar said his troop would move on to the next outpost and we are welcome to occupy this one as long as we like."

"We will take the young Human there and care for him," said Thorny. Chess lifted Althus gently and handed him to Thorny who gathered him into his arms as he sat astride his horse. "If he survives the trip to the outpost, he may yet live. He must have a good amount of fight in him if he was willing to stand alone against a hundred Orcs."

Althus did survive the journey to the outpost, but there were moments when Bree and her brothers thought he was drawing his last breath. He would lie quietly for a few hours, ghostly pale and sweating and then awake in a state of delirium. Thorny and Chess held him down while he screamed in pain and terror and Bree attempted to calm him with her voice and persuade him to swallow the draughts that would help him fight the poison coursing through him. He sweated and shook for two days, at times delirious and, for fleeting moments, lucid. He asked about Gust in a lucid moment, and Bree assured him he was recovering quickly. Althus rested quietly then, until the wee hours of the third day. Bree's voice usually helped to calm him, but some unknown terror had seized him. It was all her brothers could do to hold him down while she attempted to drug him again. By the time he was quiet once more, lying pale and exhausted, Bree had shouted at her brothers for holding him too roughly and they all were uncharacteristically out of sorts.

Near dawn, Chess and Thorny retreated to the porch to watch the sunrise. The outpost was within the edge of the forest on a rise that allowed them a view of a small, crystal lake nestled in a clearing. The horses grazed peacefully below, between the cluster of small stone buildings and the lake.

"He is strong, for a Human," said Chess. "I hope he comes to his senses before he regains his full strength."

"I must agree with you there, brother," Thorny agreed. They were silent for a time, deep in their own thoughts, afraid Althus would not recover.

"Is Bree still hoping for word from Bull?" Thorny finally asked.

"Yes, but no Eagle so far. I hope we hear soon. Searching the wild mountains for Euwyn without his help will be nearly impossible," replied Chess. "Whether Althus lives or dies we will have to make an attempt to find and rescue the Wizard."

"I think father considers Althus very important to this quest," mused Thorny, staring out across the lake.

"Let us hope he recovers soon, then," said Chess "I do not think he will survive much longer unless we can get more food and water into him and I am not looking forward to another struggle like the last."

As the sun rose above the horizon, they left the porch and headed down to look after the horses.

Bree was feeling a bit foolish for shouting at her brothers when they were doing their best to be gentle under impossible circumstances. Althus was resting peacefully at last. She laid a hand upon his forehead and found it cooler to her touch. His breathing had become deep and regular as if he slept normally. She sat on the floor, resting her arms on his bed and watched him sleep for a time, pleased he had finally conquered the poison that nearly took his life. Exhaustion soon claimed her and she fell asleep by his side.

Althus woke to find her there, her head cradled in her arms, her glorious face so close to his he could feel her breath on his cheek. His mind was still confused. Was he awake or dreaming, alive or dead? He reached out tentatively and touched a shaking hand to her hair. She was instantly awake and her clear eyes stared into his, unbelieving for a moment.

"Althus," she cried. "You are awake!"

Her smile and her touch as she laid a cool hand to his brow, made him very aware he was alive. "My brothers and I have been very worried about you." She stood up, glancing toward the door. She looked back at him, smiling. "They will want to know your fever has broken and you are awake at last. I believe they are down by the lake. I will go and fetch them."

To his weary brain, she seemed a confusing whirlwind of sound and motion, but he returned her smile as she snatched a cloak and headed out the door. She had not even given him the opportunity to speak, but he felt sure she would soon return. He wondered how far away this lake was. It made him terribly thirsty just thinking of it. He managed to sit up, although the effort made his head spin. His vision cleared after a moment and he could see an earthenware jug on the table with a cup next to it. At first, he was prepared to await the Elves' return, but his thirst got the better of him. He made his way unsteadily from the bed to the table where a scrap of paper with a message written in Elvish lying next to the cup caught his attention. His name on the paper prompted him to pick it up and read it. The message contained two words that set his head spinning. He read the message over, but there was no mistake. Gilden had instructed his Elves to kill him. Those two words echoed relentlessly through his already muddled head. Panic seized him. She had seemed so happy to see him awake. Were they waiting to extract some information from him before killing him? Was he a prisoner here? He could not think of anything he could possibly tell them they did not already know if they were in communication with Gilden. He was not privy to any court secrets. If no one ever saw him again, would anyone but Euwyn miss him? Would Euwyn ever return from Stonehaven to know he was gone? The king would certainly pay no ransom to have him back and the queen, well, the queen had many guards.

He could see Rowan's laughing face. He had cherished his parting words the entire journey. He had treasured their gift of the horse. She had gone to get the others. He had to escape. Euwyn needed him. He would puzzle it all out later. He found his boots and breeches and managed to pull them on. He could not find the rest of his clothes. He wore only a loose linen shirt that was not his, but he could not bring himself to steal something warmer. He could not even take Gust if the opportunity presented itself. He belonged to Gilden and the Elves. He could only hope to get far enough away, to find somewhere to hide until his head cleared and his strength returned.

He stumbled out the door and into the forest, making his way southward. He did not know where else to go. He prayed there were no Orcs remaining in the area. He was truly alone now and not in the best of shape. As time passed, he began to realize how weak he was. He could not say how long he had been ill. His wounds pained him. He began to feel dizzy. He was soon crawling on his hands and knees, still terribly thirsty. Why had he left without taking a drink? Althus struggled to keep moving. He was already beginning to shiver and realized too late that he was not likely to survive alone in the forest for very long. A sudden shower drenched him, but did little to ease his thirst. He was sodden now, wet to the skin and shivering in earnest.

The sound of trickling water drew him toward a small stream issuing from a jumble of rocks into a small pool and running away again, toward where he believed the lake must lie. He knelt beside the pool and drank, then crawled away into the gathering of rocks.

There he sat, his head in his hands, trying to shut out the voices his fever ravaged mind heard from within. "Failure" one cried. "Bastard" cried another. He heard Euwyn's voice crying out in despair, begging Althus to help him, accusing him of forgetting him, but the greatest horror was a dark, faceless form that beckoned to him amid the turmoil that assailed his mind.

He feared that dark figure more than all the rest, but could not say who or what it was. A clear, insistent voice had warned him many times he must not respond to its call no matter what it promised. The darkness whispered to him of peace and the soft, clear voice told him this creature's peace meant death. The voice that had called him away from the darkness was absent now. Only the voices that mocked him remained.

He almost wished he had let the Elves kill him where he lay. Too late, he wondered why they had not. He had been too hasty to leave them and now he would die here, a pathetic failure, sitting in the mud with his head in his hands. He could not muster the strength to find fuel for a fire to warm himself, even if he dared draw attention to his whereabouts by lighting one. He shivered as his eyes closed and he watched the dark figure move toward him, laughing, ready to claim him as he grew weaker, unable to resist its call.

Bree found her brothers with the horses, halfway down the western shore of the lake where they had taken them in search of better pasture. Her excitement over Althus' recovery soon drew her brothers back to the outpost. Not soon enough, however, to prevent his departure. The look on Bree's face as she beheld the empty cabin was one of pained disbelief.

"Do not worry, Bree, we will find him," Thorny assured her. "He will not get far in his condition and Chess and I can easily track him."

"No, let me look for him, Thorny," she said. "Something has frightened him. Perhaps his fever has returned and he is not himself. You may only frighten him more."

"Bree you talk as if he were a child," Chess said gently. "You say he is not himself, but we do not really know who he is. We know only his name and that Euwyn raised him. If he has lost his mind, he may be dangerous. He may hurt you."

Bree was adamant, however. They reached a compromise. Bree agreed to take her short sword and her brothers would follow within the sound of her voice. They hurried off through the massive trees following Althus' obvious trail.

Althus felt his consciousness slipping away as he sat shivering against the stones. He had managed to shut out the voices in his head, but he knew they would return. He tried to hang on to consciousness and his last shred of sanity, realizing too late it was the female Elf's voice that had called him away from the brink of death.

Suddenly, without a sound to alert him, she stood before him. He looked at her warily, unsure if she were real.

"Althus?" she said, the same voice, sweet and clear as it had been in his dreams. "What are you doing out here? You should not be out of bed. You are not well enough yet. You will die out here in the cold."

She was so beautiful. With her voice filling his ears, the other voices fled further from him. He could not run from her. He could barely stand. His legs would no longer support him. He noticed she was armed. If she wished to kill him, she could easily do so. She carried a razor sharp Elven blade. Unexpectedly, he saw in his mind's eye the Elven archer leading the band that had saved his life. She was that deadly archer. He remembered her arms about him and wished she would hold him again.

He clenched his teeth in an attempt to keep them from chattering. He wanted to hide his face again, but her gaze held him. "Althus, what is wrong?" she said. She took her cloak off and gently wrapped it about his shoulders. It carried the warmth of her body to his.

"I s-saw the note," he said. "The note from G-Gilden... instructions to k-kill me" He wished his teeth weren't chattering so. He sounded like a child, accusing and distrustful.

A puzzled look flitted across her face, then a look of consternation. "Oh, Althus," she sighed sitting down so close to him he could feel the heat of her body against his side. "I am so sorry. We should not have left that note lying about, but who would have thought you could read it, written in the Elven tongue as it was. I guess we should not have underestimated you or your teacher, Euwyn. We kept it because we were trying to determine who could have altered it after Rowan sent it."

"Altered it? What makes you think it was altered?" Althus asked. He hoped the answer would put his doubts to rest, but even if he still had doubts, what were his options at this point? He could die where he sat, shivering in the mud or he could return to the outpost with this beautiful Elf.

He was startled to hear a male voice answer. Two more Elves had silently appeared crouching side by side before him. He thought of Rowan who was equally fair, but slight in comparison.

"Because Gilden would not ask us to kill someone we could easily detain. You are only a Human after all, traveling through the Dark Forest of the Elves alone. You are no threat to us. Moreover, he knows we could not kill someone without knowing why he considered it necessary. To help someone in peril without specific reasons is a simple thing, easily done, but killing a Human or any member of the goodly races is a very serious matter to Elves," said one.

"Your illness is keeping you from thinking clearly," the second Elf added.

Althus had to nod in agreement

"If we wanted you dead, we would have left you to the Orcs. It would have been much easier to let you die at their hands than to try and kill you after Bree spent three days and nights at your side using every means at her disposal to keep you alive. I would sooner tangle with a she-bear defending her cub. It would be much safer."

"Chess!" Bree lobbed a pinecone at his head. He deflected easily with an upraised hand. She lobbed one at Thorny who was laughing as well with as little effect.

"My brothers, Althus. Chestnut and Hawthorn. They fancy themselves court jesters," said Bree.

Bree. She had told him her name in one of his first lucid moments. "I am sorry, Bree," he said, offering her his hand.

She took his hand in both of hers and looked into his eyes intently, then turned to look at her brothers. A look passed between them Althus could not see.

"Go ahead and get his bed and some food ready for him, Bree," said Thorny. "Chess and I will help him back to the outpost." Bree hesitated and then nodded. Althus watched her departure, feeling as if the light had left with her.

"Listen, young warrior," Chess said in his clear voice, bringing his face close to Althus' "You are not our prisoner. We wish to help you. We hope you will eventually look upon us as friends. However, if you choose to leave us and die somewhere alone and cold, lying in the wood, you will break Bree's heart and for that we could never forgive you." Chess' tone was rather threatening and Althus, looking up into his azure eyes, felt the incredible power behind his words. Still, Chess followed them with a smile and strong hands that gently helped him to his feet and back to his bed.

A fire crackling on the hearth warmed the cabin, but Bree's smile of welcome warmed him more. They stripped him of his breeches and boots once again and put him to bed, but allowed him to sit propped up by pillows. Althus gazed about him at the room he had occupied for days but had never really seen. The outpost was small, the walls of its single room made of stone. A table and chairs dominated the center of the room with a few more chairs placed before a large fireplace. He occupied one of four beds set against the walls.

Bree gave him a clear liquid to drink that made his wounds feel less painful and helped to clear his head so he was able to enjoy the brothers' silly banter over who had gathered the most eggs and how they should cook them. Bree moved gracefully about, avoiding collision with her active brothers in the close quarters they shared and shaking her head at their antics.

Althus felt pleasantly relaxed now, a bit drowsy, but too interested in the Elves and his surroundings to sleep. He continued to look about the cozy stone cottage. His eyes eventually found the small hawk dozing in the rafters.

"That is Kestrel, our messenger," said Bree, noticing the direction of his gaze. She brought him a plate of food and sat on the floor beside his bed holding a cup of water for him. "He brings messages to the border patrols, but particularly to us, as he is the link between Rowan and I. Anyone can read the written messages he carries, but I am the only one who can hear anything Rowan says within the bird's hearing by touching him. That is one of the ways we knew the message was false. I could hear Rowan telling us to help you and that you were Euwyn's adopted son. It is fortunate Kestrel came to us and not another Elven patrol. Perhaps he knew something was wrong with the message."

"He was definitely out of sorts when he arrived," Chess said.

"That is amazing," Althus said, pleased to find Rowan was a friend to him after all.

"Kestrel is also the one who led us to you when the Orcs were about to overtake you," said Chess.

"Then I owe him and you my life," said Althus. He stared hard at his plate, silently searching for the appropriate words. "I owe you my life and I have behaved terribly. How could I have doubted you? I hardly deserve your friendship and yet for Euwyn's sake, if not for mine, I hope you can forgive me."

"Lie down now, Althus," said Bree, taking his empty plate, pulling extra pillows gently from behind him and settling him under warm blankets. She laid a gentle hand on his forehead, smoothing away the dark hair that fell over his brow. "You were forgiven long ago. I should not have left you here alone so soon after you awakened. Sleep now. Your wounds are healing, but it will be days before you can travel again and we have much planning to do. Do not trouble yourself over what is past and forgotten."

Althus dozed on and off for the remainder of that day, the terrors of his dreams kept at bay by the three Elves who watched over him. When night fell and the Elves sat talking to each other softly in the firelight, Althus lay half-awake studying each face for some time. Their faces shone in the darkened cottage with a faint inner light that enabled him to see their features clearly. Chess had a round, childlike face surrounded by a halo of golden curls. He had a disposition to match. His words seemed to spring straight from his heart, voicing his thoughts without much consideration of their impact. Fortunately, he had a generous heart.

Thorny had a thinner face and very short, straight golden hair and was more reserved than his brother. He considered his words more carefully, but his heart was no less generous.

He stole a longer look at Bree. She sat across the small room from him with her face turned only slightly away from him. She was much smaller than her brothers with a delicately featured face, but he could still see her in his mind's eye riding toward him, leading the Elven warriors with her deadly bow in her hands. He concluded she was probably not as fragile as she appeared. Her brothers treated her as an equal. He felt safe among them. His dreams were untroubled for the first time in many nights.

## Chapter Eight

## AT THE OUTPOST

Althus awoke to the smell of breakfast and the sound of Chess and Thorny singing as they cooked. It was a merry song and the brothers sang it with gusto as they worked together. He looked for Bree, but did not see her. A burst of laughter and the sound of hooves on the flagstones outside gave him a clue to her location. She must be just outside caring for the horses. The song ended and Chess noticed that Althus was awake.

"Good morning, young warrior, the day is warm and sunny. Would you take your breakfast on the porch this morning? You have a visitor waiting to join you there," he said helping Althus up to sit on the edge of the bed.

Thorny had buried his head in a cupboard, but soon emerged carrying a pile of clothes. "I am afraid your fine black and silver uniform was beyond repair, Althus. You will have to dress like the Elven patrol until you can return to Anduin. These should fit you well enough, I think."

Althus felt honored and thanked the brothers for their generosity. He doubted just any stranger was allowed to dress in the uniform of the Elven patrol. The patrol's insignia, a golden tree, emblazoned the shoulder of the dark green coat. He donned the clothes carefully with the Elves' help, wishing he had a mirror to see the effect. Did he really look like one of them? Probably not, he decided since they were all so fair and he was dark-haired. His eyes were as blue as theirs were, but by dark brows and lashes framed them. Still, he was happy to be dressed as one of them. He thought how pleased Euwyn would have been to see him in the company of Elves. The thought of Euwyn brought a look of pain to his face and the twins, thinking his wounds were troubling him, gently helped him onto the porch and settled him into a chair.

A visitor? He remembered some talk of a visitor. Had the other Elves returned? He knew who the visitor was when he heard the sound of horses thundering up from the lake. Bree had taken them all down for a drink and Althus watched her clinging without saddle or bridle to the back of her dapple-gray as the four horses surged up the steep hill. He was amazed to see how similar the horses were in size and build, but how different in color. One was the color of a newly minted copper coin, with one white sock in front. One was the color of ripened wheat with a black mane and tail and all four legs white to the knees, a white face and one bright blue eye and one brown. Bree's horse was a silvery gray with a darkly dappled coat. However, he spared only a passing glance at the other horses and gazed happily at Gust as he sped up the hill. He caught sight of Althus and threw in a few squeals and bucks before sliding to a halt at the stone steps leading to the porch. Althus was attempting to rise from the chair unaided when the horse calmly walked up the steps and came to him. Gust examined him thoroughly, his warm muzzle still damp from his trip to the lake. When Gust was finally satisfied with his inspection and leapt off the porch to join the other horses, Althus and the Elves sat down to breakfast. He smiled at Bree whose ride up from the lake had made her cheeks pink and her eyes sparkle. She smiled back as she piled enough on his plate for two men.

"If you smile at her again, she will feed you till you burst, Althus," laughed Chess.

He found he was extremely hungry and the Elves regarded him with amusement as he attempted to eat all he was given. Althus was eager to discuss the continuation of his quest, but held his peace until all had eaten. When they had finished, Althus regarded them all expectantly. He was still feeling a bit embarrassed by his actions of the day before and hoped someone else would speak first. He was not disappointed. Thorny pushed back his chair and Bree pulled hers closer to Althus as Chess began to speak.

"Well, we all know Althus is not yet able to travel," he said, raising a hand to still Althus' objections. "Be still, Althus, and do not be foolish you know it is true. That gives us a few days to prepare."

"Bree, do you think there is still a chance Eagle will come with word from Bull?" asked Thorny.

"I am still hopeful he will find us before we leave this place. It would save us a great deal of time once we reach the mountains to have our brother, Bull, to guide us."

"Who is Bull?" Althus ventured to ask, his head full of questions.

"Bull is our foster brother who lives at the base of the mountains. We grew up together until he was old enough to leave us and find his own people," Chess said. "He and his wife, Liddy, are raising a family at the very doorstep of Stonehaven. If anything is amiss there, he will know of it. We only hope he and his family are safe. Eagle carries messages to us from Bull on occasion, but it is a great distance and we have been on the move of late."

"Is Eagle a real eagle or is that just his name?" Althus asked. "Does he carry messages to Bree as Kestrel does?"

"Yes, Eagle is the largest of the tribe of eagles that inhabit the hoary Mountains and, no, I cannot hear Bull's words through him. He carries written messages as is usually done."

"How is it you can hear Rowan's words then, Bree?"

"Rowan is my twin brother. Chess and Thorny are twins and so are Rowan and I. This may have something to do with it, but it is hard to say. There are very few twins among our people and to have two sets of twins in one family is unheard of. Chess and Thorny do not communicate in this way, although sometimes it seems to me they read each other's thoughts," answered Bree. "Rowan and I are very close."

Althus digested this bit of information with surprise. "Then you are all Lord Gilden's children!" he said in amazement, somehow pleased to know Bree and Rowan were brother and sister. "You are Elven royalty, and yet you are out here in the wilds serving in the Elven patrol."

"Ah, yes," said Chess, "but we command the Elven patrol because we *are* Gilden's children. We are required to serve in this manner if we are able while our mother, Linden, rules our land in father's absence. Rowan is also part of the patrol. However, he often accompanies father to other lands as he is the one to succeed father and it is necessary he know the people who dwell in the lands near to ours."

Althus thought of Gilden and his generosity. He had thought Gust a great gift, but now he was sending three of his children to accompany him on a dangerous quest from which none might return. "Why are you so eager to help me?" asked Althus. "I greatly appreciate your kindness, but what have I done to deserve it?"

"Well, Althus, Elves are in some ways more perceptive than Humans. We can see what is in your heart with a touch. When you were ill, your mind was in great turmoil, but now, when our hands are upon you, although we do not read your thoughts, we can sense some of what you are feeling. Bree tries to hide her talent, but she can know if you feel pain by a mere touch," said Thorny. "That is why she stays close to your side and why you cannot hide your true nature from us. Until the time we could know you, Father's obvious regard for you guided us. No Human has ever been given one of our horses as his own."

Althus sat in silence for a while before he could answer. "I am not sure Gust is mine to keep," he said reluctantly. "I think he was given to me only for the duration of my journey, to keep me safe."

"No, Althus," said Bree, "that is not possible. Once an Elven-bred horse allows a rider upon his back, he will accept no other unless his chosen rider bids him to. Rowan called Gust from our lands to accept you as his master. You are bound to him and he is bound to you. He has accepted no other rider than you. Only death will take him from you. Our horses were bound to us when we were young. My horse is called Moon, Chess' mount is Sand, the dun colored one, and the chestnut is Ochre and he is bound to Thorny. Father's intent is clear. Gust is yours."

Althus could not speak. He looked to where Gust cropped the grass near the lake with the other horses and tried to make some order of the thousand questions that swirled through his head. It was a little disconcerting to think they knew what he was feeling with just a touch. That would take some getting used to. He remembered Euwyn telling him Elves were at a disadvantage when it came to lying. He could see why if they could read each other's feelings.

"There is another reason why we wish to aid you in your quest and it has very little to do with you, but more to do with Euwyn," said Chess. "Years ago, even before Thorny and I were born, when Bree and Rowan were tiny children, Euwyn risked his life to save theirs.

"I am told they were always getting into mischief, unlike Thorny and I, who were model children. However, that is neither here nor there," he continued quickly when Bree choked in protest. Even Althus could not believe the rambunctious brothers had been quiet children. "Mother and Father were near the western border of the Dark Forest hunting stag when Bree and Rowan wandered off from their camp. The Dark Forest is usually safe enough for Elven children, but a band of Goblins had crossed our borders undetected and happened on the Elven camp. They loitered about some distance from the camp for a time and, as luck would have it, Bree and Rowan decided to venture into the wood alone while the Goblins were at watch. The Goblins soon snatched them up and headed quickly for the border. The Elven hunting party searched until they happened on the Goblins' tracks and set off after them, fearing the worst.

Fortunately, Euwyn also happened to be in the area and caught sight of the Goblins before the Elves could overtake them. He could see they were carrying something alive in sacks over their backs and decided to find out what they had poached from the Elves' forest, never suspecting Gilden's own children were in those sacks and in grave danger of becoming dinner. When the Goblins shook open the sacks and two children fell out, Euwyn went howling into their midst like a madman. I think the element of surprise must have saved him, for he was a very young Wizard then and not nearly as powerful as he is today. He stood alone against an entire band of Goblins. The Elves counted ten dead, but we do not know how many may have escaped into the wood. They found Euwyn nearly dead of his wounds. He held Bree and Rowan in his arms, very frightened by the experience, but unharmed. The hunting party took Euwyn and the children back to Borias and healed him. When we were all very small, he would visit us in Borias, staying among us for a month or more at a time, telling us of his travels and adventures. He taught Bree some of the skills that healed you, although her skills involve less magic and more knowledge of the proper potions to use and how to make them. She has always had an interest in healing and spent much time learning what she could from Euwyn and the Elven healer, Taxus. When Euwyn told us he had adopted a son and would not see us for a time, we all begged to meet you, but Euwyn said we would have to wait until the time was right. You are somewhat of a puzzle to us, Althus, but we feel as if you are also part of us."

Althus smiled at the thought of Euwyn doing battle with the Goblins. He always had a soft spot in his heart for any child. No matter how grimy or ill behaved he would take the urchins of Anduin in and feed them when times were hard. Althus had felt very special indeed that Euwyn had chosen him as his son from all who would have gladly taken his place.

Later that same day, Bree brought him a bow and arrow and placed it in his hands. He looked at her curiously, as she sat down at his side.

"How are you with a bow and arrow, Althus?" she asked.

"Not nearly as good as I am with a sword," he admitted. "This is a beautiful bow, Bree. The carvings are unlike any I have seen before."

"It is an Elven bow and a very good one. Rowan made this bow. He is the best at this craft of all the Wood Elves. I would like to teach you how to use it while we wait for your strength to return."

"I would love to learn such a skill from you, Bree," said Althus. "I am told you are the best archer in the Dark Forest and if that is true, and I am sure your brothers would never say it if it were not true, I am sure you are better than any archer on this earth."

Bree was smiling at him as she showed him how to string the bow and fit an arrow to it. He was eager to draw it, but she gently took it from his hands. It was not until then he realized her hand was resting on his shoulder. She knew his wounds were causing him some pain. He blushed, embarrassed by his inability to hide his weakness, but she laughed softly and kissed him gently on the cheek, ruffling his dark hair.

"You cannot lie to me, Althus, but I cannot lie to you either. Do not be ashamed to feel pain. It is the Creator's way of telling you to rest, and I must admit I am weary also. We will start tomorrow and you will become an archer without equal in Anduin."

Soothed by Bree's willow bark tea, Althus lay in his bed listening to Gilden's children breathing softly around him and turned the things he had learned that day about in his mind. He had been so fortunate in the last few days. His purpose, once in doubt, now seemed possible once more and he had learned more about the Elves in one day than he had ever hoped to know in his lifetime. There were still puzzles to solve concerning his origins, but perhaps they were not so important. He was content simply to be one of the Elven patrol for now.

## Chapter Nine

## ATOP THE TOR

Bree, true to her word, set up a target the next morning consisting of concentric circles on a scrap of cloth tacked to the trunk of a dead tree. Althus felt his strength returning and strung the beautiful ash bow without help. He was good with a crossbow, but the true art of archery with the more traditional Elven bow was new to him. He found his concentration less than perfect, hampered by Bree's arms about him, her face close to his, as she showed him the proper way to sight his target. The challenge of the task soon took his full attention. His aim, at first, was less than accurate, but when the lesson was finished, Bree seemed pleased with his progress, promising another lesson the next day.

Althus and the Elves took lunch on the wide porch. He was happy to be with the Elves, but anxious to resume his search for Euwyn. He asked them when they might leave the outpost. Thorny put a hand on his shoulder looking deep into his eyes. "I think you should rest for two more days, Althus," he said after a few moments. "Even I can feel you are in pain. If Bree says you are well enough by then, Eagle or no, we will start for the Hoary Mountains." Althus tried to be content. Thorny was right. That morning, he had felt well enough to travel. Now, his hands shook when he took the cup of tea Bree brought to him. It served to put out the fire someone had lit in his shoulder, but made him feel sleepy and a bit dazed.

"We are as anxious for Euwyn's safety as you, Althus," said Chess. "We will teach you the secret ways of the Dark Forest in the next two days. Bree is already making you into an expert archer. By the time we leave here, you will be a proper member of the border patrol.

"You have a great store of knowledge, Althus. Much of it, such as your memory of Euwyn's maps, we would like to learn. Are you a Wizard as well as a warrior?"

Althus was embarrassed to have deceived Chess somehow into thinking he was either of those things. "I must tell you honestly I am neither a Wizard nor a warrior. I have never killed any creature not meant to be my dinner and most of the little meat Euwyn and I ate came already dead and dressed to our table in payment for his services. As for being a great Wizard, Euwyn was only able to teach me a few simple spells. I have no discernible talent for wizardry."

"Well," Chess reassured him, "One must be born to it, I suppose, and we know you are not Euwyn's son by birth, but by his choice. As for being a warrior, you will prove yourself soon enough. Besides, anyone who can face a hundred Orcs with two arrows in him and still think to swing a sword is enough of a warrior for us."

Althus smiled at Chess' uncharacteristically careful choice of words. He missed Euwyn's council more each day, but the Elves' kindness eased his loneliness. His mind worked constantly now at the puzzle of Euwyn's whereabouts. He hoped the Wizard's journey had not taken him in a different direction than originally planned. His original intent to visit the Dwarves' kingdom was all Althus had to use as a guide.

He was lost in thought when Bree came to lay a hand on his shoulder, testing the effectiveness of the herbs she had given him. With his physical condition still under observation, she gazed off into the distance toward the far end of the lake where a small, bare hill thrust up through the trees. Still, he thought he could feel the warmth of her touch spreading through his body, reaching out, testing him gently. He looked up at her, wondering what she was thinking of him. What did she feel when she touched him beyond his physical state?

She smiled reassuringly back at him before raising her eyes to sky.

"I must ride to the hill to look for Eagle," she said after a thoughtful pause. "Perhaps he will arrive today." Althus watched her walk away toward the horses that grazed between the cabin and the lake. When she reached them, she leapt on Moon without saddle or bridle and cantered off along the edge of the lake, soon lost from sight among the trees pressed close to the shore. Althus spent the next few hours resting in the sun while Chess and Thorny discussed the terrain they could expect to encounter during their upcoming journey and shared some of the wood lore and the history of their people. He could not help but worry about Bree who was across the lake, alone and undefended. He noticed Chess and Thorny often looked off in the direction she had traveled and seemed as relieved as he to see her returning safely. When asked if she had caught sight of eagle, she shook her head sadly and sat down with her back against a post, hugging her knees. She scanned the skies and sighed, "Perhaps tomorrow."

The next day passed much like the previous one. Althus' archery improved with Bree's careful instruction and another trip to the hill across the lake proved as fruitless as the day before. Despite his eagerness to be off, Althus enjoyed sharing his knowledge with the two brothers who listened attentively to everything he told them of Anduin and its surrounding lands.

Their last day at the outpost dawned gray and cloudy with a few passing rain showers that kept them indoors during the morning. By afternoon, the sun broke through the clouds once again. Bree left the cabin the moment the skies cleared. Althus followed her to find her saddling Gust and Moon, who stood patiently by the cabin while she carried gear from a nearby shed. Gust nickered at him and tossed his head in greeting.

"Althus," she called to him when she caught sight of him "will you come with me to the hill today? We can take our bows and practice our archery. Perhaps you will bring us luck and Eagle will appear." Althus eagerly agreed to accompany her. The thought of spending the day in Bree's company and testing his returning strength lifted his spirits. They were soon riding down the hill toward the blue waters of the lake.

They rode side by side at a leisurely pace. Gust and Moon traveled close enough that his knee and Bree's often touched. Bree watched him closely, testing him to see if he was ready to make the long journey they planned for the next day. Gust's smooth pace did not cause him much discomfort. A long ride would be difficult, but his confidence rose as they traveled toward their destination. The hill, little more than a jumble of huge boulders sunk deep into the ground, was too steep for the horses to climb. They dismounted, leaving the horses to enjoy the grass growing about the base of the rocky tor while they scaled the smooth boulders to reach the top.

They sat and rested for a time, enjoying the view and the warmth of the sun. The lake glittered like a jewel to their south, the warm gray stones of the outpost easily visible against the dark forest beyond. A sea of treetops spread in every direction as far as the eye could see. Bree pointed to where her home lay, just out of sight over the horizon. Althus was amazed at the size of Gilden's Realm, marked by the unbroken canopy of the forest.

It struck him again that Bree was Elven royalty. Rowan, her twin brother, would one day take Gilden's place and rule this land all the Wood Elves called home. He thought how fortunate the Elves were to have two such men to rule them. It was easy to see Gilden's quiet strength in his son. He admired Gilden and his children and treasured their growing friendship. He could not help but compare the idyllic realm of the Elves with the conditions in Anduin, wishing he had some power to change what was happening there. Maybe Gilden or Queen Maris could make King Allen see reason, but he had seen no signs to give him hope. Gilden could not stay in Anduin forever. Althus hoped he would escape before the army rumored to be building in the south took Anduin, as it surely would if that army caught them unprepared. If Anduin fell, the Dark Forest would need every Elf to defend it.

"You seem troubled, Althus," Bree said softly.

He told her of his concerns while they sat resting back to back, hugging their knees in the sunlight that bathed the ancient tor. They scanned the skies for a sign of the eagle. Occasionally Bree would send out an imitation of an eagle's cry so real it sent chills down Althus' spine.

"I too have been worried about father since he left for Anduin. Sometimes he does things even he cannot explain," said Bree. "He follows his intuition in such matters. It tells him Anduin needs him now and he will stay until it tells him it is time to depart. He is always right when all is said and done. Let us hope this time he is right as usual. His people miss him sorely here in the

Dark Wood. The Orcs grow bolder. I have never seen as many within the forest as the force sent to kill you, Althus. Someone with great power wants you dead. Someone with the power to command these foul creatures and send them into our forest when they know their lives will end the moment we discover them within our borders."

Althus could guess who sent the Orcs into Gilden's realm. The disappearance of Cully and Garth before the Orc attack did not seem a coincidence. Borgas was behind the attempt to kill him. He could not be certain Borgas did not have King Allen's blessing as well. It was probably assumed he was lying dead somewhere in the Dark Forest.

Althus sighed sadly and looked toward his homeland. What was in store for the people of Anduin? He had left them in the hands of a mad king and an evil Wizard. Still, he was as powerless to change that fact as any of its citizens. His only hope was to use the connection he had with Euwyn to find him alive and return with him to Anduin.

They set up a target of small rocks set upon a larger one and practiced with their bows for a time. Bree admired his progress, and then made him laugh at his newfound skill by showing him what she could do with her bow. She never missed, no matter how small the pebble or how far she stood from her target. He admired her strength and grace as she concentrated on her target and pulled the bow to its limits.

They sat down to rest and talk once more while the sun moved inexorably toward the western horizon. The air had begun to take on the chill of evening, when they heard a cry in answer to Bree's. They both leapt to their feet and scanned the skies in the direction from which it had come.

"There he is!" shouted Bree, pointing to the southern sky. Althus could not see as well as an Elf, but he soon caught sight of a large bird winging its way toward them. Eagle landed before Bree, the rush of wind from his wings briefly ruffling her short hair. The very size of Eagle made Althus apprehensive for Bree's safety. The bird stood nearly as tall as Bree, its fierce eyes meeting hers at the same level, its sharp beak only inches from her face. They bowed amicably to each other, Bree greeting the bird formally as if addressing royalty.

"Greetings, Lord Eagle, I hope your journey was not a difficult one," she said.

Eagle screeched in reply, ruffling his feathers and shaking his snowy white head. Bree lifted a small cylinder attached to a light chain from about the bird's neck. She opened the cylinder and unrolled the message it contained while the eagle stood watching.

"It is a short message," she said, "but it is the answer I was hoping for." She took out a quill and paper and penned a note she inserted into the cylinder she replaced about Eagle's neck. Eagle spared a glance for Althus, his golden eyes fierce and appraising. Althus bowed in response. As if satisfied, the giant bird lifted off to head southward, back the way he had come. Bree and Althus watched him disappear into the southern sky before riding back through the twilight to the outpost where Chess and Thorny readied their gear for the next day's journey.

There was much excitement over Bull's message. They all stood looking over Bree's shoulder as she unrolled it on the outpost table.

The message read:

*Dearest Little Bree, Thorny, and Chess,*
 *I pray my missive reaches you in time. Indeed, there are foul things infesting my beloved mountains. I have been watching the paths in and out of Stonehaven, the dwelling of the Dwarves, and have seen the coming of many creatures of the foulest nature. Most numerous among these are Orcs. I fear, as you do, that an army of evil gathers within the Hoary Mountains. Whether they are in league with the Dwarves or have enslaved them, I do not know. I returned to my home to find Eagle impatiently waiting to deliver your message into my hands and I am afraid my absence has delayed my reply. I am most anxiously awaiting your arrival. We will join forces to seek out Euwyn if he is, as I fear, held captive and defeat the evil that holds him.*

*Your brother,*
*Bullroar*

Althus read the message with great interest. He could see why the Elves were anxious to hear from their foster brother. His knowledge of the mountains would be invaluable. He was surprised Elves would live so far from the Dark Forest, but he supposed they were Mountain Elves and not Wood Elves. Something Bree had said about him finding his own people made him feel Bull was not a Wood Elf in any case. As they turned their attention to preparations for their departure the next morning, he wondered about Bull, trying to imagine what he might be like. He wrote in a precise hand, his words clear and to the point. Althus did not find an opportunity that night to ask about Bull, but hoped to learn more on their way to the mountains.

He expected sleep to be difficult to come by, but the excitement of the day had tired him more than he realized. He slept soundly until dawn.

## Chapter Ten

## CAPTAIN CEDAR'S COMPANY

On the morning of their departure, a thick fog swirled and eddied about the ancient trees like ghostly figures, dancing with a gentle breeze that had arisen with the sun. The Elves, having served in the Elven patrol for much of their lives and therefore more used to traveling constantly than they were to staying in one place were well prepared for travel.

When Althus expressed concern over the desertion of their post, they assured him part of Captain Cedar's troop had long ago taken over their tasks so they could care for Althus. Althus vaguely recalled seeing more than three Elves when they rescued him from the Orcs, but his memory of that event was insubstantial at best. He wished he could meet Captain Cedar and his troops before he left the Dark Forest, but their mission was urgent and there was no time to waste seeking Cedar's roving patrol. Bree assured him they were more than a day from the point where they would cross the border into the wild lands and they could yet meet with one of the patrols, perhaps even Cedar's Elven patrol, before that time.

The Elves presented him with more gifts. Thorny gave him a set of mail so silvery, light and supple he could not feel its weight when Thorny helped him put it on. Chess dug a gray cloak out of his gear for Althus to wear, identical to those worn by Bree and her brothers. Chess told him the cloak would not only keep him warm and dry, but would also conceal him if he wrapped himself in it and kept very still.

Althus gave a last look about him as they left the outpost. It seemed almost like home to him, a place where he was reborn. He hoped to return some day.

The four companions rode through the thinning mists silently for a time. Althus admired the huge and stately trees about him and wondered if he would ever see the cities of the Elves. He tried to imagine dwellings, roads, built in the branches of the trees, full of light, and music as Bree described them. As matters stood now, it was not certain he would see his own home again or, if he did return to Anduin, it would ever be the same.

The Elven horses traveled tirelessly, their swift paces so well matched they rode two by two easily the entire day. Bree and Althus rode first, followed by Chess and Thorny who never seemed to run out of tales to tell. Their easy laughter made Althus smile despite his uneasiness concerning the wilderness they would encounter in the days ahead. They were finally on their way. That eased his mind and enabled him to join in their laughter. The morning passed quickly. When the fog lifted at mid morning, Bree began to call his attention to the shy animals that marked their passing from the cover of the deep forest. He was not sure he would have noticed them if she had not pointed them out. They saw a solitary gray wolf, looking down on them from a boulder top and majestic stags that leapt off through the forest at their approach. The different birds and animals foraging about on the forest floor and pacing the branches above them were too numerous to count. Althus occasionally glimpsed a large creature just at the edge of his sight, traveling through the forest parallel to their path. When he mentioned it to Bree, she merely nodded. Althus continued to catch glimpses of the animal, but although he caught a flash of brown or black, he could not quite make out what type of creature it was.

By the time they stopped for lunch, Althus was glad to rest. The wounds in his shoulder ached. After resting a hand on his arm for only a moment, Bree set out the ingredients to make him some willow bark tea. They ate a meal of bread, cheese and fruit beneath the trees. When they were finished, making ready to depart, Althus stood staring off into the forest, wondering if the beast pacing them was gone. Thorny walked to Althus' side idly tossing an apple hand to hand.

"Would you like to see this wild beast?" he said.

"You have noticed it, too. What kind of beast is it, Thorny?" asked Althus, full of curiosity.

"Come," said Thorny with a mysterious look. "I will capture it for you to see."

They walked a few paces into the forest and Thorny gave a loud, clear whistle, echoing through the trees. Althus heard and saw the creature then as it approached. It was a horse. A bay horse, red brown with a black mane and tail and black legs. On its forehead, it bore a white star.

"He is called Mars," said Thorny. "I called him just before we left the outpost. He has been running wild in the forest since we last saw Euwyn years ago. He belongs to Euwyn, but the Wizard rode him only when he was with the Elves. He has been a little shy of us. If Euwyn were with us, he would have come to us at once. He is confused by the Wizard's absence, but when we have rescued Euwyn he will need his horse as we must then travel swiftly to Anduin."

The animal approached hesitantly, sniffed at the offered apple and then took it from Thorny's hand. He made a great mess of it, the juice dripping from his mouth as he ate. He inspected Althus closely as if wondering what this creature might offer him. Althus gave him a piece of the apple he had saved for Gust. He had seldom seen Euwyn riding a horse. The Wizard seemed to prefer his own feet. Perhaps he did not wish to ride any horse but Mars. Thorny was right, they would need an extra mount for Euwyn if they were to return to Anduin. The confidence Thorny showed in Euwyn's rescue was comforting in any case. The horse accompanied them back to the others and when they were once more on their way, he followed obediently as if he had always been a part of their band.

Althus now rode beside Thorny. He wanted to ask about the calling of the horse. He remembered Bree saying Rowan had called Gust from the Dark Forest to Anduin as a gift for him, and wished to know more of the Elven brothers' amazing talent.

"I am not as skilled as Rowan," said Thorny when asked, "but Mars was not so far from here. I cannot explain it to you very well. It is just our thoughts and our need for them that bring them to us, no more than that. Chess and Bree can also call horses to them if need be, although no one but Rowan can call from so great a distance as Anduin. It is a talent only the ruling Elf Lord and his children possess and it has been so for many thousands of years. Perhaps it was something the old lords needed to protect their heirs in times of peril, but I do not know how my people came by this talent. We are simply born with it."

Althus was greatly impressed. To communicate one's thoughts to an animal from as far as Anduin seemed impossible, but he could not deny he had not seen the Elves ride into Anduin with any horses but their own and yet Gust was there for him when he left Anduin.

"I hope to see Gilden and Rowan again some day so I may thank them for all their help. It seems they aided me in ways I did not know until now," said Althus

"I would like to think we will see them again soon," said Thorny, a frown of worry crossing his fair face as he gazed in the direction of Anduin. "I hope we return to Anduin in time."

Althus also worried about Gilden and Rowan. The king was becoming more unpredictable by the day and Borgas clearly wished to rid himself of the Elves. Much could happen to them alone in a castle full of soldiers sworn to obey their king no matter how insane he became.

They rode in silence for a while. Althus was beginning to tire and found Thorny's quiet presence comforting. Bree and Chess rode behind them speaking quietly to each other and faithful Mars trailed along behind. Althus thought to ask how old Mars was as he showed little signs of advanced age, but Euwyn could not have ridden him for more than twenty years.

"Our horses are blessed with immortality as we are. It is common for them to live as long as their riders," said Thorny. "Many of them die of sorrow if their riders are slain. That is one reason why we never allowed Humans to possess them. It might condemn them to an early death. It is a great thing to have them as eternal companions, but a sad thing indeed to think if one is killed in battle or by accident one's faithful friend will probably die also."

Althus thought of Gust pining away after his death. Somehow, it was hard to imagine Gust fading away to an untimely death for anyone. He decided Gust would probably be the exception to the rule. He leaned forward to look him in the eye. Gust rolled an eye back at him with a loud snort, causing Althus and Thorny much amusement. It felt good to laugh. Althus had found little to laugh at since Euwyn's disappearance. He was quiet by nature, but Euwyn could always make him laugh. He found it easier to laugh again in the company of the Elves and imagined this was what being part of a family with brothers and sisters must be like. The Elves had become like family to him in a few short days. Perhaps it was because they could know what was in his heart.

Soon after, Thorny called Althus' attention to the ground before him. "Look, Althus there are hoof prints on the trail before us and droppings that are fresh. We are nearing the border now. You may get your wish. I think we are following Captain Cedar and some of his patrol. We can share camp with them if we catch them before nightfall."

They increased their pace from a leisurely trot to a gallop. For a moment, Althus recalled his flight from the Orcs a few short days before. It made him feel a bit light-headed at first, but when a clearing appeared before them and their hand gallop evolved into an all-out race, he forgot the past in the joy of the moment. He loved the feel of Gust's compact, muscular body laboring beneath him and the muffled sound of the horses' hoof beats on the soft turf beneath their feet. He thought he had won until a streak of gray went flying past and Moon and Bree took the lead. They slowed when they reached the edge of the clearing and allowed the rest to catch up.

"Not fair," complained Chess. "You do not weigh as much as we do, Bree. It gives you the advantage."

"You are a sore loser, Chestnut," she laughed, crowding Moon up to him and trying unsuccessfully to push him off Sand's broad back.

"Here!" called a voice from the edge of the forest. "That is no way to treat the Lord's patrol! Show some respect!"

"Cedar!" laughed Bree. "We were hoping to catch you and share a last camp before we crossed the border."

"We thought we were being pursued by wild men from the sound of you. You are fortunate we recognized your voices before we ambushed you," answered Cedar.

Much to Althus' enjoyment, they soon sat about a warm fire sharing a meal and tales of the Elven patrol. Thorny introduced him to Cedar's three companions, a young woman named Willow, patrol officer Maple, and an Elf they called Sailor. These four Elves made up Cedar's small band of Patrolmen. Sailor fascinated Althus. His features were definitely Elven, but his hair was as dark as Althus' and he was no taller. Chess remarked on their resemblance as they greeted one another, standing face to face. Althus was struck by the fact Elves were not all light haired and tall. Of course, almost all of the Elves he knew until now were closely related to each other so it was not surprising they were similar in appearance. His curiosity aroused, he sat on the ground next to Sailor to eat his evening meal. Sailor smiled at him over his plate and when they had finished, he proved to be as curious about Althus as Althus was about him. Althus learned he was one of the race of Elves who sailed the seas to the west of the Dark Forest. He had left the sea to wed the lovely Elf, Willow, and join the Elven patrol.

"We do not call him by his true name. It is as long as your arm and so we call him Sailor. I thought we would never teach him to ride a horse," laughed Maple. "He was off more than on for the first month no matter how hard Quinn tried to stay beneath him. We were unsure whether to lash him on or leave him behind. He eventually got the hang of it. Willow will make a patrolman of him yet. He was a natural with the sword, at any rate. That is one thing they taught him while he was bobbing about on the wild ocean."

"Enough about me," growled Sailor in feigned annoyance, "I want to know more about you, Althus. Last time we set eyes on you we thought you would be dead by nightfall, and yet you have made a miraculous recovery and are off on an adventure into the wild lands beyond our borders."

Althus shared all he could about his purpose and his destination while Cedar and his crew listened intently. All were impressed by their daring mission and wished them good fortune in their travels. The Elves made a toast to their success and to Althus who cheated death to make this journey. The Elves were soon singing songs and telling tales around the fire while Althus sat quietly enjoying their high spirits and camaraderie. Cedar came to sit beside him and speak to him alone.

"I cannot help but think if you succeed in this quest of yours, it will help our people as well, Althus. I am sure that is why Lord Gilden was so eager for you to make this journey," said Captain Cedar. "If the evil force behind this army of Orcs gathering in the mountains succeeds in taking Anduin it is certain it will next set its sights on the Dark Forest. With the resources of Anduin behind them, we would be sore pressed to defeat such an army. Rumor has it Orcs are gathering in Stonehaven from every corner of the wild lands. Your journey will be perilous once you cross our borders."

Cedar laughed, then, shaking his head. "I am sorry, Althus. I guess your journey has already proved to be perilous. It is an embarrassment to the Elven patrol that you were nearly slain by Orcs within our borders."

Althus looked at his hands lying open on his knees for a long moment before he spoke. "As Bree has said, someone very powerful wishes to keep me from finding Euwyn. Euwyn was a good father to me when it was his nature to live a life of solitude and Anduin needs him. I have to do what I can to find him. I have seen his face before me in my dreams and somehow I know he is in danger. Captain Cedar, I have not proven myself as a soldier. I have never slain a man or even an Orc. I have never even seen battle. I am unsure of my path once we reach the mountains and I worry that I lead Bree and her brothers to their death. It is my greatest fear I will lead them from the safety of their own land and one or all of us will never return."

Cedar smiled sadly at him. "Now you feel the burden of leadership, Althus. It may ease a little when you are more experienced, but it will always be there as long as others follow you into danger."

"But I am *not* a leader. I have been a soldier for little more than two months. I have never been a leader in my life. I am but a quiet scholar, and soldiering, I fear, was merely Euwyn's idea to keep me safe within the castle walls until his return. I have trained as a soldier and can handle a sword tolerably well, but I have never tested my skills in battle."

"There are three things I would ask you to remember," replied Cedar, "Those who follow you do so of their own free will. Perhaps this is because they see something in you that you do not recognize in yourself. It is easier for Elves to know your heart than it is for you to know your own. Second, Gilden has put his faith in you and his intuition has always proven right. He felt you were the man for this mission and that is enough for me to know you are the right one. Finally, the Elves owe much to Euwyn. He traveled this forest for years with the blessing of the Elves and did much good here. He saved my life once as well as Bree and Rowan's lives as they probably have told you. There are many who would follow you on these facts alone and, with or without you, we would make an attempt to save Euwyn from whatever keeps him in the Hoary Mountains.

"Perhaps you alone must save him when all is said and done, but Thorny, Chess, and Bree will help you find him and you will be far safer traveling with them than with any others, Human or Elf. I know they have seemed kindly and gentle to you, but they *have* been tested in battle. They are the fiercest of warriors and yet, they have chosen to follow you."

"I am not sure they follow me so much as I follow them, but thank you for your kind words, Cedar. I will keep them in my heart and think of them when I need strength," said Althus.

Cedar smiled and laid a hand on his shoulder. "Do not worry, Althus. I, too, find no fault in you and I am never wrong either. Well, hardly ever. However, you are obviously still feeling the effects of your wounds and need your rest."

Althus looked at Bree and then at Cedar, but before he could ask, Cedar laughed, "No, I cannot sense pain with a touch as Bree can. That is a talent I do not have, but I do have eyes in my head and you look dead tired to me. Elves often do not sleep, especially under the open sky, and I fear we will talk the night away. You, on the other hand, need to sleep, so do not feel you will offend us if you wish to do so." Althus wondered wearily as he rolled himself into his blankets if all Elves worried as much for the welfare of foundlings who wandered into their lands. Their concern would have embarrassed him if he were not so tired.

## Chapter Eleven

## AT THE FORD

Althus awoke at daybreak to Chess' hand on his shoulder. He opened his eyes to the Elf's smiling face and a golden sun just peeking through the forest canopy.

"You seem to have slept well, Althus," he said. "I trust we did not keep you awake last night with our carousing."

"No, Chess, I did sleep well. Your voices around me made me feel very safe," Althus reassured him.

"And our dull stories and our singing would put any man to sleep," Chess laughed merrily. "I will get us some breakfast while you prepare for the day," he said heading for the cooking fire while Althus went to find soap and water.

He was sitting beside Chess, hungrily downing a hearty breakfast when he noticed Chess had stopped eating and was watching him.

"You are staring, Chess. What is it?" asked Althus.

"Oh, sorry, Althus," Chess apologized. "I was thinking how ill you were just a few days ago. At times, we were all certain you would die and now you seem nearly recovered. You amaze me, Althus. I do not want you to think I do not hold the race of Humans in the highest regard, but are you sure you do not have some Elven blood in you?"

"I would like that, Chess," said Althus, suddenly struck by the possibility. "The truth is, I have no clue who my parents were. I think Euwyn knows something, but what he knows he does not share with me. Perhaps he does not know or he cannot say. Perhaps it does not matter."

Chess digested this quietly for a time. He knew Euwyn had taken Althus in as an infant, but he was somewhat surprised to find Althus did not know who his parents were. He tried to imagine what that would be like, but Elves held to each other so closely, parent and child, he could not fathom it. Althus seemed to have made peace with the situation, but Chess could detect a remnant of longing running through him. He thought how strong this young man was to accept this and go on with his life as if it did not matter.

"You have a fine father in Euwyn, Althus, and when we find him perhaps he will tell you all he knows. Until then, you will think of us as your brothers," Chess said, throwing an arm about Althus' shoulders roughly and giving him one of his radiant smiles.

"What about Bree?" asked Althus, turning to look at Bree and Willow who were talking animatedly to each other beside the campfire, hoping to hide the emotions Chess had awakened in him, his desire to be part of them. He realized how foolish a hope that was when Chess kept an arm draped about his shoulders. Chess would know what he was feeling.

The two women stood facing. Each was holding the other's hands as if saying farewell to a dear friend.

"I think," said Chess, leaning over to speak close to his ear, "Bree would *not* like you to think of her as a sister." Chess left his side then, leaving him staring at Bree in surprise. She turned to smile at him before turning back to greet Sailor who had come to join them. His thoughts were racing. Suddenly, he knew why he needed to know where she was at all times. He had so little experience with women. What should he do? What would Gilden think if he knew Althus had fallen in love with his daughter? The thought of making Gilden angry with him in any way gave him pause. He remembered reading if an Elf loved a mortal, they were no longer immortal. He could not do that to Bree or her brothers. It was wrong even to think of Bree in that way. He tried to push the thoughts Chess had given rise to from his mind, knowing they were now there to stay. He sighed. He would have to let them stay for now. What else could he do?

He heard Kestrel's cry overhead and saw him land on Bree's shoulder. He went to her side to see what message the bird carried from Rowan.

"Things in Anduin remain the same," Bree sighed. "The king does not move to defend Anduin and father and Queen Maris fear for the people of the outlying farms. They will begin gathering the people within the walls of the city and risk the king's anger soon. Perhaps King Allan is so far out of touch he will not take notice. At least we were able to tell father you are well and we have heard from Bull. I sent the message soon after we met with Eagle, telling Rowan of our plans to head south the next morning. Their thoughts are with us and they pray for our safety. That is all Kestrel has to tell us, Althus. I am relieved he has found a way to enter and leave Castle Anduin safely. Perhaps he waits for nightfall. He is certainly not a stupid bird and will not be easily intercepted again."

"It is something to know matters have not yet become worse there," Althus said. "The king has lost touch with his people. That is certainly true, but I fear Borgas will not let anything that would further turn the king against your father go unnoticed."

"Well, I guess it is up to us to tend to the task we have been given and hope matters in Anduin turn out for the best," said Bree. Althus did not miss the worried look that briefly crossed her face.

They departed from Cedar's small band with many farewells and promises to meet again and share the tale of Euwyn's rescue. They headed south toward the border. By mid morning, they reached the road Althus had taken from Anduin. At this point, it had dwindled to a path only wide enough for them to ride two by two, as they had in the trackless forest. They joined it at a point some leagues west of the Orc ambush, very near the point where they would cross into the wild lands beyond.

As one, they stopped and stood looking back into the Dark Forest, reluctant to leave its familiar shelter. Too soon, they turned and left the forest behind. They left the trail behind as well in a very short while, setting off cross-country, using the mountains' jagged peaks ahead as their guide. Their course wound through a forest populated by small trees and saplings that deteriorated into a brushy marshland that sucked at the horses' feet. They allowed the horses to pick the best path through the tangle of brush and bog, as they seemed to have an unerring sense of the safest path. Despite the rough conditions, they made good progress. After an uneventful day of travel, they found a fairly dry hill on which to set up camp and spent an equally uneventful night.

Soon after starting out the next morning, the boggy fen became a dry wasteland of coarse rock and sand dotted with clumps of tough, wiry grass. A strong wind, harbinger of bad weather approaching, hissed through the grass, sending the sandy soil seething about the horses' feet as they passed.

They came across a rough track through the sparse vegetation, heading in the direction they wished to travel, marked by the tracks of Orcs and Goblins and creatures unfamiliar to Althus. After some discussion, they decided to follow it until they crossed the river Anduin whose upper reaches now lay between them and their destination.

As expected, the roar of the young river passing through its deep, rocky bed soon reached their ears. As they had hoped, the path they followed led to a ford where they could negotiate the river's banks in relative safety.

Althus surveyed the rushing water with some doubt. It was a deep, swift ford that would involve some swimming on the part of the horses. Thorny and Chess assured him it was only a matter of hanging on to Gust's mane and giving him his head. The horses would swim with little more than their heads out of the water so the force of the water would separate them if he did not hang on tightly. Althus assured them if he and Gust separated, he could swim very well, having grown up on the banks of the Anduin. They decided Thorny would go first, then Chess, Bree and finally Althus. Ochre splashed willingly into the swift stream and was soon swimming strongly with Thorny clinging doggedly to his mane. They reached the opposite shore with little trouble. Chess reached the far shore on Sand with the same success. Mars, lacking the direction of a rider, decided he would be the third horse to cross and soon stood patiently waiting for Bree and Althus alongside the other horses. Bree and Moon splashed into the stream as confidently as her brothers did. She was near midstream before Althus caught sight of the danger surging downstream. Urging Gust into the river, he shouted to warn her of the submerged tree headed toward her, turning and bobbing just below the surface. Even over the river's roar, her sharp hearing caught his warning shout, but it came too late.

The huge tree headed downriver toward them, hidden from Thorny and Chess by a steep bank. Althus' shout and his sudden entry into the rushing stream alerted them something was wrong. Bree and Moon could not avoid the tree bearing down on them. Althus' heart stopped as it struck Moon broadside, tangling her legs and rolling her under in the swiftly moving stream. Moon resurfaced quickly, snorting and blowing, kicking herself free, but Bree did not reappear. Gust had reached midstream by then and Althus deliberately parted company with him. He struggled for a moment, searching his mind for the spell Euwyn had taught him as a boy, a spell that would enable him to breathe underwater. He recited what he prayed were the right words and dove below the surface, headed after the tree where he feared Bree was entangled. Fortunately, the tree slowed briefly, caught in an eddy near the far riverbank, slowing its progress enough for Althus to reach it. He swam desperately among the branches for what seemed an eternity, praying the current would not dislodge the tree while he searched.

He caught sight of her, floating motionless in the current, caught by the strap that held her quiver of arrows. Using his short dagger, he hacked desperately at the branches between them. He freed her quickly, surfacing blessedly close to shore. He felt a moment of panic, uncertain if he could remember the spell that would allow him to breathe air once more. His first attempt was not quite right. He laid Bree's still form on the stony beach, struggling to breathe, cursing his imprecise memory of the words while he pressed water from Bree's lungs. A second try was more successful. He managed to take a few deep breaths before he placed his mouth over hers and attempted to refill her lungs with air as Euwyn had taught him. He was so intent on saving her, he did see or hear their horses leave the water to stand over them or the arrival of Thorny and Chess soon after, all watching hopefully as he tried to bring Bree back to life.

Minutes seemed like hours. How long since she had last drawn breath? Could he possibly revive her? She had been under water for a long time. He had almost given up hope when Bree took one breath on her own and then another. He helped her to her knees, kneeling beside her while she coughed up the rest of the water she had inhaled, gathering her into his arms and holding her close as they knelt by the rushing water. It was not until Thorny and Chess wrapped a dry cloak about each of them that he found the strength to move again. He was still shaking when he picked Bree up, cloak and all and carried her away from the Anduin to a small grove of trees. He was amazed at how light she was. She weighed almost nothing in his arms. At any other time, he might have wondered if her brothers were equally insubstantial, but now his heart still pounded with fear for her. Thorny and Chess started a fire to warm them and dry their clothes, but Althus was still shaking when Chess and Thorny brought them something to eat. He could not seem to stop.

Chess broke the silence first. "Well, we all got across the river safely."

At first, everyone looked at him in disbelief and then, Bree began to laugh. Soon they were all laughing.

"You are the very personification of serenity, Chess," said Thorny. "Althus is still shaking. I will not ever look at a river crossing with the same confidence, but you only see we all got across somehow without getting ourselves killed and that is good enough for you."

"Well, we *are* across and we *are* all alive so with your permission, Thorny, I will cease to worry myself about that which is over and done and has had a good outcome," Chess said as he turned to rummage about in his saddlebag. "In fact, I think this calls for a drink of Maple's famous border patrol brew. *I* think Bree and Althus could use a drink to warm them after nearly drowning in the cold waters of the Anduin."

"Chess!" cried Thorny. "You have been holding out on us. We could indeed use a mug of brew. Maybe it would help Althus to stop shaking and then we could ask him how he stayed under for so long without drowning. I was so sure we had lost them both."

Althus gratefully accepted Chess' proffered drink. It was not ale as he remembered it from his short time with the Anduin guard. It was clear and sweet, warming him to his very toes and it did help him to stop shaking even though he was not shaking from cold. Bree came to sit by his side and he could not help putting an arm about her shoulders, holding her close when she smiled at him over the brim of her mug. He was left without any resistance. He needed to be close to her.

Chess was not going to let the matter of Althus' swimming ability rest. "So, tell us, Althus, how did you hold your breath underwater for so long?" he began, "and how did you bring Bree back to life when she was obviously dead? I thought you said you were not a Wizard and yet if you can bring the dead back to life you are a most powerful Wizard, indeed."

"Please, Chess," begged Thorny, "stop saying dead and Bree in the same sentence. It makes my flesh crawl and yet you say it so casually."

Chess seemed suddenly struck by what he had said. "I apologize, Bree. I must say it disturbed me to see you look so dead. To see you lying dead with Althus struggling to make you live again was not an easy thing for me."

"Chess, stop!" Thorny begged.

"I think we understand what you are trying to say, Chess, although you are very bad at expressing it," Bree said. "You would miss me if I were dead, almost as much as you would miss Sand if anything should happen to him."

"Exactly," said Chess. Althus was laughing at him. Chess reran the discussion through his head. "No, Bree. I would miss you every bit as much as Sand."

Bree was glaring at him now.

"What?" he asked, perplexed.

"I should think I would mean more to you than your horse." Bree said.

Chess seemed to consider the matter. "Yes, I guess you do, Bree."

"You guess? You are not sure?" Bree said.

Thorny begged them both to let the matter drop and let Althus speak.

Althus was sorry Thorny had interrupted their lively exchange, but he was resigned to explaining his actions to them somehow.

He began, carefully choosing his words to make what he was about to tell them clear.

"First of all, I was not holding my breath under the water." He paused, expecting some comment, but the Elves sat silently, waiting for him to finish. "I was using a spell Euwyn taught me as a very young boy. It enables me to breathe as a fish does until I say the counter spell."

"I knew it!" Chess said. "He *is* a Wizard. Tell us about the spell that brings people back to life, Althus."

"I will admit there was some magic in my ability to breathe underwater, Chess, but the few minor spells I know do not make me a Wizard in any way. Please do not think of me as a Wizard. I will never be a Wizard like Euwyn. Believe me, I tried to learn the craft from him, but I could only master the most elementary spells. You could do better than I if you had Euwyn to teach you. I am happy with the abilities I have, but magic is not a discipline at which I excel." Althus continued hastily before Chess accused him again of bringing the dead back to life, "As for Bree, she was not dead, but had only stopped breathing or my efforts to revive her would have been useless." He had to take a drink to steady himself at the thought of Bree stretched lifeless on the bank of the river. He did not want Bree to feel him shaking again.

"I could easily teach anyone to do what I did. I have taught many of the people of Anduin. It is a good skill to know when you live on the banks of a river. It can be used on anyone who has stopped breathing for any reason. It often works, but as I said, it will not bring the dead back to life and there is no magic in it whatsoever, Chess."

Chess looked somewhat disappointed, but comforted himself with the thought Euwyn might teach him some magic if only he could be rescued.

The afternoon was only half spent and Bree was all for traveling further before nightfall. However, Althus and her brothers thought it best for her to rest until morning. Althus worried she might become ill from inhaling so much river water, but Thorny assured him it was not likely. The water ran clean through the unpopulated wild lands and Elves were not so delicate as to become ill from such things. In fact, illness was unknown amongst the Elves. Althus was about to say how great a thing that would be, until Thorny informed him they were as easily killed by injury as any mortal and may even die of grief if they lost a loved one to war or accident.

Althus himself did not remember ever being ill, but had witnessed illnesses that sometimes ran through the population of Anduin and killed many people. He could not imagine, however, going through life with a heart so vulnerable to grief one could die from it. He thought of how easily the Elves had opened their hearts to him and what risks they took every time they came to care for someone who was as mortal as he. He hoped that alive or dead, he would not be responsible for anyone's death.

"Well," said Chess, "you two have chosen a very gloomy subject to discuss. Come on, Thorny, let us practice some swordplay while we have some spare time. Perhaps Althus will join us."

"I will watch you two at play for a time," said Althus. "I have not swung my sword since I was wounded. I may be stiff at first."

The Elves faced off on a grassy hilltop against the sun lowering in the west. Althus was glad he had not joined them when their exercise began. They were amazing swordsmen. They wielded their beautiful glittering swords like dancers. Each movement was a wonder to him. They fought so fiercely if he did not know how much they loved one another he would have feared for their safety. There was no wasted effort on their part. Each stroke and parry was perfect and precise. Bree was enjoying the spectacle as well and when asked which one of the brothers would win the contest, she informed him they merely called it a draw at the end of each session.

"They are different in many ways, but in swordplay, they are equals. I have never seen one win over the other."

Althus thought how much alike they became in temperament when they wielded their swords. Chess became more serious and fiercely competitive. The usually more serious Thorny became almost playful with a sword in his hand. Althus was sorry to see the contest end and was a little embarrassed to even to hold his sword in their presence. He soon faced Chess across the grassy hill and tried to hold his own with the sword he carried from his days in Anduin. Chess contested with him for a while and then called a halt to their session.

"You are very good with your sword, Althus, perhaps your shoulder is somewhat stiff, though," Chess said. "Let Althus use your sword, Thorny. It is lighter than his. It will be easier for him to swing until his shoulder is better healed."

Thorny was smiling when he offered his sword, hilt first, to Althus with a flourish.

"Come on, Althus, show young Chestnut here he can be bested with a sword," he laughed.

Althus doubted he could beat either of them in swordsmanship, but was eager to put his hand to Thorny's sword if he was willing. He was astonished at how light it was. He had noticed how keen the blade was, but it seemed to weigh nothing in his hand compared to his own. When their contest resumed, it took some getting used to, but he soon found a new center of balance and Chess' look of amazement at his abilities pleased him very much. Althus soon stopped the session and returned Thorny's sword to him with thanks for the opportunity to experience his amazing piece of weaponry. Althus found himself a bit winded, but Chess showed no signs of exertion.

"I think," he said, "if you had a proper sword you could best us both, Althus. You have been well trained."

Althus thought of Captain Manton and Tristan and how kind the gruff captain and his son had been to him during his lonely days as a guard. He wondered how events in Anduin would affect the Captain in the days to come. It was very possible Althus would not be there to fight at his side if war came to Anduin. He regretted that, somehow, even though he never truly thought of himself as a soldier. The Captain had spent hours teaching him to use a sword and Althus might never get the chance to repay him. He looked at his sword and thought of the hours it had spent in his hand and tried not to wish for a blade as fine and light as Thorny's. He smiled at Thorny and Chess as he slid it back into his scabbard and thanked them for including him in their practice session. At the very least, he knew his wounded shoulder would still allow him to wield his sword if necessary.

Bree was by his side as they walked back down toward their camp. She showed no sign she had nearly drowned earlier that day and she laughed at Althus when he asked if he might put his ear to her chest and listen to her breathing.

"I have been accused of being a she-bear and a mother hen when it comes to *you*, Althus, but you are as much a mother hen as I," she said. He lay as close to her as he dared during the night, the brothers insisting Althus and Bree should rest while they stood watch. Althus did feel somewhat like a mother hen as he hardly slept, but listened to Bree's regular breathing through most of the night.

## Chapter Twelve

## NIGHTMARES

The next day dawned cold and gray. Soon a steady rain began to fall. Althus was dry under the Elven cloak he wore, but an errant wind would occasionally blow the rain into his face, blinding him temporarily. They pressed on, the horses tucking their noses to their chests, doggedly traveling into the chill wind and rain. They kept to the Orc track hoping the weather would keep the Orc soldiers from traveling that day. The terrain grew more rugged as they began their climb into the foothills of the Hoary Mountains. To Althus, the southern arm of the mountains seemed little closer than when they began their journey. He squinted toward them. They had seemed beautiful the previous day with the sun glittering on their snowy peaks. Now they seemed mysterious and forbidding, their heights lost in a shroud of mist. The day passed uneventfully toward nightfall with a stop at midday for rest and a meal.

Thorny, riding at Althus' side, said little, his attention on the trail ahead, only voicing concern that if the rain changed to snow, they would have to leave the trail as their tracks in freshly fallen snow could betray their recent passing to any that came this way.

When nightfall came early, they managed to find an overhanging rock with a fairly dry area beneath that sheltered them from the wind and rain. There was enough room to accommodate them all, including their horses, and there they prepared to spend the night. Chess kept first watch while Althus lay down to rest, turning his back to the fire for warmth, watching shadows cast by the flickering light chase each other across the rock wall until he slept.

He was soon dreaming of the mountains, shining in the sunlight as they appeared the day before. He stood at their very roots now, before a huge gate flanked by two stone statues, their features indistinct in his dream, vague shapes that soon faded from view as he entered the dark passage. The passage did not change, but the feeling of his dream did. Gradually, the halls descended and faces began to leer at him out of the dark recesses he passed. He found himself running now through stone halls that stretched endlessly on into the darkness, searching for Euwyn. His heartbeat thundered, his ragged breaths filled his ears as he ran endlessly. A deep pit yawned before him, the edge of it drawing him irresistibly. He tumbled over, falling for a long way through darkness before he found himself standing unhurt at the bottom of a deep pit. He saw a figure before him within a pool of light, facing away from him. Euwyn. He was certain it was Euwyn standing there. He was close enough now to put both hands on Euwyn's shoulders. As he did so, the figure spun about to face him with features that were Euwyn's, but so hideously distorted that he pushed the horrifying vision away from him. An inferno erupted behind the Wizard, casting him into sharp relief. As his face transformed to the face of the man who raised him, Althus reached for him again with both hands. Their hands came together briefly, their fingers brushing as Euwyn cried out to him. Althus screamed in horror as the Wizard fell backward into the flames. The sound of laughter echoed about him as he screamed.

Suddenly, the fire and the laughter were gone, his own cries only dying echoes. He found himself lying on cold ground with Bree bending over him, one hand on his forehead and the other over his heart. Chess and Thorny knelt beside him as well, looks of concern etched on their faces. He sat up, his heart racing beneath Bree's hand and cold sweat trickling down his back. Bree wrapped her arms about him until he could calm himself enough to speak.

"You were crying out in your sleep, Althus," Bree said. "We feared your illness had returned."

"A nightmare," he panted. "Only a nightmare."

Bree could still feel him shaking beneath her hand and continued to look at him in silence.

Althus did not want to tell them of his dream. He was almost afraid to look too closely at what it had shown him. He prayed it was only a nightmare and nothing more and apologized for waking them, offering to stand watch for the few hours remaining until dawn. He doubted he would sleep again that night. Bree and her brothers agreed after giving him a searching look. He suspected they would not sleep, but would let him feel he had taken his turn at watch to please him. The rain had ceased sometime during the night and he ventured out beyond the overhanging rock to look up at the sky. Clouds still hid the stars. Was the dream some sort of warning? His last glimpse of Euwyn's face haunted him. Was his dream telling him not to give up on Euwyn no matter in what state he found him? Was it a message from Euwyn that Althus could still save him despite what may have been done to him? He sent a silent prayer to the Creator to keep Euwyn alive.

When he looked back out into the darkness, he was startled to see yellow eyes reflecting the light of the fire behind him. For a moment, he feared his nightmare had returned. He drew his sword and backed away, putting the fire between himself and whatever creatures haunted the darkness, finding Chess and Thorny ready at his side. They stood watch together for the rest of the night, expecting an attack at any moment, but the eyes disappeared sometime before the dawn of a mist-shrouded day.

Their path that day wound between massive rounded boulders that looked as if they had been flung randomly from the mountain by giant hands. They dotted the landscape, hunched like huge gray beasts in the tall grass that struggled to survive in the sandy soil. They seemed to move like beasts, appearing and disappearing in and out of the mist that hung in the hollows about them. The mist swirled and eddied, obscuring the features of more distant landscapes. At times, from the corner of his eye, Althus thought he caught the movement of other dark shapes in the mist.

Bree and Thorny rode ahead with Chess and Althus behind them and the faithful Mars following closely. All were watchful, suspecting the beasts of the previous night tracked them. They rode with their hands on their weapons.

Without warning, the horses halted as one, crowding close to each other straining their ears in all directions and blowing great gusts of breath, testing a scent borne on the heavy air. A beast howled somewhere ahead of them in the swirling fog. Another answered from behind and then others, sounding eerily from all sides, echoing off the giant stones. The dark creatures appeared, materializing from the mist, pacing a circle just within sight, waiting.

Althus and the Elves drew their swords, Althus straining to make out the huge shapes drifting in and out of the thick air. The attack came suddenly, a concerted effort the horses met with slashing hooves even before swords were brought to bear. One beast launched itself toward Chess from atop a nearby boulder. Sand wheeled quickly on his hind legs to block the beast's leap, but the hideous creature struck Chess hard enough on the shoulder to send him flying. He landed hard, striking his head on the stony ground and lay very still.

More creatures appeared all about them, pacing the perimeter of the struggle, trailing strands of drool, ready to take the place of the slain, waiting for their share of the kill. They were foul creatures whose ancestors may have been dogs or wolves before the evil that haunted this land twisted them into their present form. Nearly as tall as the horses, they were barely more than hunched collections of bones held together by putrid, greasy pelts. Althus dispatched one by ramming his sword down its throat as Gust reared to meet its charge. Bree had drawn her bow, Thorny his sword. They were fighting for their lives a short distance away, barely holding their own, nearly overwhelmed by sheer numbers.

Althus' first concern was to reach Chess before one of the beasts did. Sand stood over his master, trying to protect him, but with his rider underfoot he could not maneuver easily. Mars stood close, doing his best to help, barely making a dent in the number of creatures drawn by the scent of Chess' blood.

Althus killed another beast springing at him from the rocks before fighting his way to Chess. He dispatched another that was trying to drag Chess from beneath Sand's punishing hooves even before he slid from Gust's back, landing in the protected area between the horses. He took Sand's place, standing over the fallen Elf. Gust guarded his back while Sand and Mars pounded quite a few more of the beasts to pulp. Althus found himself floundering in the gore that accumulated under his feet, wondering if he had made the right decision in choosing to fight on foot while still more of the creatures appeared out of the mist. The stench of the greasy, festering hides of the beasts sickened him and he was tiring, the strength of his sword arm beginning to fail. Bree and Thorny, still mounted, fighting for their lives a short distance away would soon be overwhelmed by the beasts surrounding them.

There was no way out. He glanced down at Chess, lying helpless between his feet and felt desperation begin to cloud his thoughts. He shook it away, refusing to accept that Chess might die. He could not fail. His hand touched one of the greasy creatures as he fended off its jaws with one hand, killing it with the sword held in his other. A sudden idea struck him, a dangerous gamble. If it failed, he would have spent his life stupidly and Chess and the others would die. He gathered as much courage as he could muster, moving as far from Chess' still form as he dared, leaving Sand and Mars to defend him. Lacking the time to sheath his sword properly, he dropped his trusty blade unceremoniously into the gore at his feet, freeing his hands to meet what was sure to come. Bree screamed his name in terror as one of the creatures immediately leapt upon him, pinning him underneath, its jaws seeking his throat.

Althus fended him off, stuffing his mail-clad arm between the beast's jaws. With the other hand, he stroked the beast's greasy hide and spoke words Euwyn taught him long ago. The stink of the beast increased tenfold as its greasy pelt burst into flame.

There was a moment before the beast realized its predicament, barely time for Althus to pray for the strength to hold the beast off before he found himself pinned helplessly beneath the squirming beast. He was pressed into the gore beneath him as it spun, nearly crushing him in its frenzy, snapping at the flames licking up its side. The first beast, howling in agony spun into others, setting them afire. Althus crawled to Chess, lying atop him to protect him from the maddened beasts, his Elven cloak protecting them both from the flames.

Mass confusion ensued as more and more beasts ignited, their greasy coats catching fire more easily than Althus had dared hope. Those few that escaped the flames were frightened off by the agonized howls of their companions. Even before the howls of the beasts died into the distance Althus knelt by Chess' side holding his hand to his heart and calling his name. It was difficult to see merry Chess lying still and pale, covered in blood that was thankfully, for the most part, not his own. Bree and Thorny knelt close as he tried to revive the unconscious Elf. He was relieved beyond words when Chess finally stirred and opened his eyes.

"What is that *stink*?" were the first words he spoke. "Have I missed something?" He sat up, holding his head and looked about him in amazement while Althus laughed with relief.

"Leave it to you, Chess to sleep through all the excitement," he said. "Let us get away from this reeking mess and find somewhere to clean ourselves. Chess was a bit unsteady on his feet, but Sand was at his side to support him. When they found a place to rest by a nearby stream, all of them, horses and riders alike, were found to have sustained a few minor wounds. Althus' arm was bruised beneath his mail, but the skin was not broken. Chess' head bore a lump and a gash that bled a bit, but Bree pronounced his head as sound and hard as ever. Thorny and Bree were not seriously wounded. Bree treated the horses for some gashes, but they also escaped the attack without serious harm. When the ever-efficient Bree had examined and treated them all, Althus lay down on his back in the grass with a relieved sigh, intent on enjoying the sun that chased the mist from the land for a moment. Chess came to sit beside him, looking like his old self, a smile lighting his fair features.

"You saved my life, Althus, and survived your first true battle. I am deeply in your debt," he said.

"Chess, you have saved my life in more ways than one in the past few days. I do not know how I could have gone on if you had died. I would miss your smiling face more than I can say," said Althus.

Chess seemed at an uncharacteristic loss for words and simply laid his hand on Althus' shoulder, staring off toward the mountain peaks ahead.

"I love you almost as much as I love Gust." Althus added.

Althus dozed off in the soft grass to the sound of the Elves' laughter, exhausted by the battle and soothed by the warm sun on his face.

He awoke with a start, embarrassed to find Bree and Thorny had set up camp without his help and prepared a meal for him including fish from the nearby stream. Chess still sat by his side, smiling down at him when he stirred. Thorny and Bree joined them around a warm fire, eating their evening meal while stars appeared in the darkening sky.

"We are in your debt once again, Althus," said Thorny, quietly looking up at the twinkling stars. "When Bree and I saw you fall beneath that creature we both thought it would finish you. We never dreamed you would do such a thing deliberately. Once again, your resourcefulness and courage have proven you the warrior you claim you are not.

"The race of Humans seem so fragile to us. You live very short lives and are so easily killed by disease. You feel cold and heat and weariness and yet father wishes us to think of Humans as equals. I see now the hardships in your short lives make you what you are. You are in many ways hardier and more resourceful than Elves. We live for thousands of years and become complacent. Perhaps we do not use our wits as easily as you. Things are done as they always have been done. We need Humans in our lives to teach us to think differently."

Althus could not quite agree with Thorny's view of him. He had almost failed his friends until the last moment of inspiration, but he thanked Thorny for his kind words, not knowing what else to say.

Althus could only look at Thorny and at Bree and Chess, arguing over who would stand watch that night, and think how precious they were to him.

Bree, returning triumphant from her argument with Chess, came to sit between Thorny and Althus. "How much farther do you think we have to travel?" She asked. "It seems as though we should see some of the landmarks Bull indicated in the maps he sent us after he settled here in the foothills. We have been riding straight from the ford toward the third highest peak as he said."

"I cannot say for sure. His settlement is hidden in the foothills right at the root of the mountains and they still seem some distance away. There is a tributary of the Anduin we must cross called the Amberstream. After that, we are very near the valley Bull speaks of."

Chess approached with the map, holding it out for Althus to see. "Here, Althus," he said, holding it where the firelight illuminated it. "You have a head for maps. You may as well see this so you know what our path should be."

Althus eagerly looked over Chess' shoulder at the map he held. He was very interested. He had studied maps of all kinds. They lined the walls of Euwyn's gray stone tower where he had lived all his life and he had an excellent memory of all of them. Bull's map was finely drawn and matched Euwyn's maps of this region. He easily committed the few details in which Bull's map differed from Euwyn's to memory before Chess re-rolled it and returned it to his saddlebag. The valley Bull and his family called home was clearly marked, lying between two arms of the mountain in whose depths the Dwarves' kingdom of Stonehaven lay. The route seemed clear. Althus wondered how Bull and his people kept their families safe with the Dark Lord's creatures gathering so close to their homeland.

Bree stood watch that night although Althus doubted any of them slept. The memory of the creatures that attacked them that day kept him at Bree's side through the long night. She assured him the horses would alert them to any danger that approached, but seeing her alone in the moonlight drew him to her as a moth to flame. They sat companionably side by side through the night talking of their homes and people they knew and tales of their childhood.

Bree's childhood was very different from his. Hers was as filled with magic and wonder and the company of Euwyn and his teachings as was his, but she had been raised by a father and mother, surrounded by brothers. He had no one but Euwyn to care whether he lived or died.

He gathered enough courage to ask Bree how old she was and was not surprised to find she was more than two hundred years old. Very young for an Elf, he realized. He was not surprised by her age, but it still made him feel a little awed by her years of experience when compared to his.

He knew Euwyn, although young to be such a powerful Wizard was also many hundreds of years old. Five hundred years old, Althus realized suddenly, in three more days. How he hoped to be able to wish him a happy birthday when that day came. He felt very young and insignificant in light of the fact his bones would be dust before Euwyn was considered old in Wizard's years. He wondered if Euwyn and the Elves would remember him fondly. He looked into Bree's ageless face and wondered what she was thinking. Bree, on the other hand, was leaning against him, and if she did not know what he was thinking, at least she knew what he was feeling.

"You are sad, Althus." A statement, and then the inevitable question he did not want to answer, "What troubles you?"

"The anniversary of Euwyn's birth approaches." He hedged his answer in a half-truth. "I would like to think he lives to see it and that I will be with him on that day."

Bree turned away to look at the moon. "I feel his presence still, Althus. Do not despair. The feeling has grown stronger these last few days although I fear he grows weaker even as we draw closer. Tomorrow we may have Bull to guide us. He is amazingly intelligent and knows the mountains and the Dwarves who dwell there as well as any."

Althus was happy for the present with that small hope, content to sit silently in the moonlight with Bree for the remainder of the night.

## Chapter Thirteen

### ALLIANCE

Manton came out on the battlements of Castle Anduin, squinting in the bright sunlight that warmed the golden stones. He was pleased to find his quarry so quickly, fearing that a search of the entire castle would occupy his entire day and draw unwanted attention. He dared not ask the whereabouts of Gilden and Rowan openly. There was no one he trusted left in the castle save the queen herself and he could not risk conversation with her. The proliferation of Borgas' chosen in the ranks of his soldiers left his position within the castle as perilous as that of the Elves. He had no doubt that Borgas would soon find a way to eliminate him from the scene as well. Finding the Elves alone on the battlements was a stroke of luck.

He prided himself on his ability to move silently, but the sentient Elves turned toward him even before he stepped out onto the battlements. He gathered his courage and approached them, father and son, determined to win their trust somehow. As he approached, Gilden turned to Rowan who gave a slight nod to his father as if in unspoken agreement.

"Captain Manton," Gilden greeted him in his rich melodious voice, "Rowan and I have been anxious to speak with you. There are matters we would discuss with you alone." This was not only accompanied by the offer of Gilden's hand, but also by Rowan grasping his other hand and placing a hand over his heart. Startled by the strange gesture and vaguely aware that the Elves were powerful in countless ways, he feared his life was in jeopardy, but he felt no untoward sensations save the warmth of Rowan's slender hand.

Their startlingly blue eyes held his for a long moment before they abruptly let him go. Rowan hopped up to sit on the battlements grinning broadly at his father who returned his smile. The captain looked on, somewhat perplexed by the strange greeting, but relieved to find himself none the worse for it so far.

"One cannot be too careful these days in Castle Anduin, Captain Manton," Gilden said, turning to look past Rowan and over the battlements to the distant mountains.

"Lord Gilden," began Manton, moving to stand by his side and choosing his words carefully. "I have come to report some disturbing news. First, I assume young Althus has not returned unnoticed from his quest to find our missing Wizard. I must report I have caught sight of the men who accompanied him on his mission. They were in town, brazenly carousing at the Leaping Hare Tavern. I fear they may have slain Althus at the order of their master, Borgas. Obviously they have returned to Anduin without him."

"You are observant, Captain," said Gilden. "The cowards did not have the courage to kill him themselves, but led him into an Orc ambush within the borders of my kingdom. They will pay dearly, both for drawing the foul Orcs into my forest and for their part in the plot to kill Althus."

Manton's face turned ashen beneath his beard and he slumped to the stones his back to the wall, his head in his hands.

"Do not despair, Captain," Gilden reassured him, sitting beside him on the stones. "Althus was gravely wounded, but rescued by the Elven patrol and healed of his wounds. Even now, he nears the Hoary Mountains accompanied by three Elven warriors who have no equal in our land. They are likely to succeed where no one else can."

Manton managed a brief smile at this news, the first smile to cross his face in many days. "I hope they are as good as you say, Lord Gilden. There are many dangers in the wild lands. I fear there are more now than ever before."

"They are, Captain, if you will excuse my boasting. You see, I am inordinately proud of all my children. I fear for them and young Althus, still, but I can think of no better chance for Althus to succeed. They will join with my foster son at the foot of the mountains. He knows the mountains well and will guide them from there."

Manton was stunned to learn the Elven lord had sent his own children into danger to aid Anduin and a king that obviously had no love for the Elves. Here were two Elves who had once saved King Allen's life at great risk to their own, fighting beside him to rid Anduin of a great army of Goblins. Manton shook his head at the memory. What made Gilden risk his life and that of his people for the kingdom of Anduin? Manton had been Althus' age then, a lowly foot soldier in the king's army. He remembered watching Gilden on his great roan stallion, fighting bravely against the Goblin armies on the battlefields at the borders of Anduin. Gilden had fought his way to a younger King Allen's side, bringing an Elven army to aid Anduin in its time of need.

Manton hoped it was a matter of practicality. The king certainly had not proved himself worthy of such friendship. If Anduin fell, it would certainly pose a great danger to the kingdom of the Elves to their west. As fierce as the Elven army was, their numbers were not great. Manton recalled with a shudder the thousands of Goblins who had descended from the mountains in the northwest and swept across the borders of Anduin. His wife, Elinor, had traveled in the wake of the Anduin army, caring for the wounded, Human and Elven healers working together. She had cared for Gilden then, gravely wounded during the final victorious battle. It was she who advised him now to seek out the Elves and make his loyalties known. Gilden continued to sit beside him on the stones looking at nothing, lost in thought. His next question caught Manton quite off guard. "Captain Manton," he asked, "do you have a wife? I have met your son. You must have a wife."

Manton nodded, telling him of Elinor and their meeting on the battlefields of the Goblin wars when Manton sustained a relatively minor wound. Manton wondered where the conversation would lead. "You are indeed fortunate, Captain. I will never forget Elinor and her kindness to me. She is a lovely and compassionate woman."

Gilden sighed sadly, sitting in silence for a while before he spoke again. "I miss my wife, Linden, and my home in the Dark Forest. My children and I are scattered to the four winds. I have been gone from my kingdom in the Dark Forest much too long, but cannot bring myself to leave the kingdom of Anduin to its fate. Rowan is a great comfort to me and I am fortunate to have him at my side, but I wonder if I will see my other three children and my wife and the city of Borias again."

He changed the subject abruptly. "Captain Manton, if you are willing, I would have you help us bring the families of the outlying farms within the gates of the city. Rowan and I have no authority among the people of Anduin, but if you and some of your trusted men would accompany us, I believe we could bring them all safely within the protection of the city walls before the enemy can overrun the countryside. We still have time to organize the defense of the city."

"The only men left I can trust have been sent to watch our borders," said the Captain, "but the timing may be lucky for us. They will return to the castle to warn us of the enemy's approach. They are the men to then accompany us to the outlying farms as they will have first hand knowledge of the enemy we face."

Gilden nodded, "I see you have acted wisely to protect the men remaining loyal to you. If we do this, Captain, you realize we will stand accused of treason. Our lives will be in grave danger."

"I do not see how I can do any less than what you have proposed for my own people. In any case, I fear my days as captain of the guard are ending. Most of my men have been replaced by those hand picked by Borgas. My most trusted men have simply disappeared without a trace. I only hope the men I have sent on patrol return without incident. They were sworn to secrecy as to their destination and they are those few left I would trust with my life."

"Timing in this matter will be crucial, Captain. We cannot move too soon else the king will have time to countermand your orders and send the people back to their farms before the enemy is at our gates. I fear, as you do, there are more traitors within your ranks than loyal men. Tell me, Captain," Gilden asked, "have you any clues to the whereabouts of your missing men?"

"Two have been discovered dead beside the roads outside of the city walls," the Captain answered. "I went to identify the bodies. They were my men all right, or what was left of them.

"They were butchered, Lord Gilden, cut to pieces. When I say I went to identify the bodies..." Captain Manton swallowed hard, rubbing his hand across his mouth. "Only pieces of them were found, heads with their brains removed, parts of limbs. Borgas said it was the work of wolves. No wolf could do what I saw. These men were cut with blades, not rent with sharp teeth. I said as much to the Wizard. He laughed. Standing there, looking at was left of two of my best men, he laughed." Manton's jaws worked angrily. "If I find out who killed them, I will see them dead. I think the Wizard had a hand in it, but I have no proof."

Manton gave a bitter laugh. "Listen to me! Proof!" he said. "What good is proof when there is no one to see it, no one who cares for the truth. The king is lost to us. He will not listen. Borgas rules Anduin now."

Gilden had no comfort to offer. They spoke privately for a while longer in anticipation of the evacuation of the outlying citizens of Anduin and then parted for separate destinations agreeing to meet at the same time each day.

Manton was satisfied with the result of his meeting with the Elves. It seemed they accepted him as an ally with little effort on his part. He would have been amazed to learn the Elves had plumbed the depths of his heart with a mere touch.

Φ                    Φ                    Φ

Elinor was concerned for her husband's safety in the uncertain atmosphere of Castle Anduin. Tristan seemed relatively safe compared to his father, who faced the dangers that lurked within the walls of the castle. She felt Manton's growing frustration at the loss of his men and the king's betrayal of his people.

Elinor, never one to back away when her small family's happiness was at stake, began to ask herself where the missing men might be, turning the puzzle over and over in her mind. She kept her ears open while attending to her duties in the castle infirmary, hoping to learn something from the newly acquired troops, a clue to the fate of the men they had replaced. Alive or dead, so many men could not remain hidden for long. Sooner or later, she would find some trace of them.

It was true the men that served under her husband were often rough and sometimes downright uncivilized, but these new soldiers seemed a treacherous lot by comparison. She doubted some were even fully Human. They bore some startlingly Orc-like traits. They argued and fought among themselves so frequently there were always wounds to dress. They leered at her and made crude comments as she tended them. She never approached them for any reason without Edmund, the castle physician present and even brave Edmund feared them.

Manton's men had always shown her the same respect they reserved for their beloved captain. She missed the gruff bantering that always erupted when she tended to the wounds of those injured in training. Two or more of his fellow soldiers, greatly concerned for their comrade's welfare, overseeing all aspects of his care always accompanied a wounded soldier. Very few of those men would raise a hand against their comrades. Now the king's guardsmen fought among themselves like a pack of wild dogs over a kill. They hated each other as much as they hated the enemies of Anduin. Perhaps, Elinor thought with a shudder of fear, they were one and the same and they would soon fight over the carcass of Anduin.

A chance meeting with the castle cook gave her some insight. She encountered the portly cook at the infirmary where he had come to have a nasty burn tended to. Her friendly smile and tender, caring ways made all who knew her spill their troubles in her willing ears. The cook complained about the extra food that he had been required to cook during the past weeks, innocently remarking that the present troops seemed to eat almost twice as much as the men they had replaced. Elinor wondered if they were actually eating twice as much or if the cook was actually feeding twice as many. Were the missing men still in Castle Anduin? If there was extra food taken from the kitchens, were the missing men still alive?

She meant to find out if they were alive or dead. The extra food must be delivered somewhere to the missing men. She reasoned the food must be delivered by Borgas' chosen. The cook and his servants would not be trusted with that task. She wondered why Borgas would be keeping the men alive unless he hoped to win them over to his side in time. Perhaps he could enchant them somehow, but would need some time to accomplish it. She puzzled over this while she waited for some sign of their whereabouts. Had the men found dead outside the city shown some resistance to Borgas' powers?

With only the cook's word to go by, she spent as much spare time as she dared between her duties at the infirmary and the rare moments when Captain Manton was off duty, lurking about the scullery, trying to catch one of Borgas' chosen favorites among the guard carrying food to unusual areas of the castle. She struck up a closer relationship with the cook, feigning concern over his burn, offering to lend a hand to the overworked kitchen staff to explain her presence. Fortunately, the scullery was close by the infirmary and the guards she watched were not overly intelligent. She hoped her actions did not arouse suspicion.

She knew Manton would not approve of her taking such risks so she did not tell him of her suspicions. With his concern for his missing men eating at him constantly, Elinor needed to feel she was doing something to help. Her advice to him concerning Gilden had proven sound. She remembered the Elf lord as fondly as he remembered her and hoped, with the Elves as allies, Manton would find a little hope to cling to in these dark times.

Her patience was rewarded one morning when a dozen particularly vicious looking brutes appeared in the kitchen demanding a large quantity of food. They made off with it in the direction of the castle dungeons. She knew Manton would have access to the dungeons and would have already searched there for his absent men. Still, she followed in the wake of the evil looking men, staying out of sight, hoping to discover their destination.

They stopped briefly to light torches before entering an unused area of the dungeons. Her heart nearly failed her when Borgas himself materialized from the very blackness that ruled there, as if part of the stinking darkness. She nearly turned back, sheer desperation the only force that drove her on. She crept silently, keeping to the darkness near the wall, praying the deep shadows thrown by the torches the men carried would hide her. When they reached the deepest dungeons of Castle Anduin Borgas stopped, facing a blank wall. The passageway turned to the right, but he faced the wall before him and uttered a few words, moving his hands upon the stones before him. Elinor watched in amazement as an arched opening appeared in what was once solid stone. Borgas waited as his men preceded him into the darkness beyond. He stopped the last two and took their burden from them.

"Someone has followed us," he said. "Find them and kill them."

The guards grinned and nodded as they took the torch Borgas held out to them. Elinor stood in the shadows, her heart pounding. Should she run? They would certainly hear her. She doubted she could outrun them. There was nowhere to go but back the way she came or on past her pursuers. She shrank against the wall, praying they would pass by without seeing her.

Her hand, resting against the wall dislodged a bit of loose mortar. As the two guards approached, she tossed it as far as she could beyond the shadows where she stood concealed. They broke into a run, the sound drawing them past her hiding place while she moved in the opposite direction, slipping around the corner and into the utter darkness beyond. She let her right hand brush against the wall to guide her, beginning to hope she might escape. Eventually she would find a way out. She needed only to keep turning to her right and she should reach the first passageway once more. Then, a turn to the left should bring her to the stairway that led upward to freedom. She only needed to keep her wits about her and avoid the guards who searched for her.

Unfortunately, she stumbled over something in the darkness. Still, she did not make much sound, not enough to reach the ears of the guards until she put her hand down to push herself up from the floor. She felt another hand beneath hers, a dead, cold hand, slimy with decay. She stifled her first scream with her hand. Her second scream when she found the hand severed from its owner now clung to hers as if grateful to have finally found a sympathetic friend in the darkness of the passageway, could have awakened the dead man who lost it.

She shook the thing loose and stumbled onward, but it was not long before she heard the sounds of pursuit. When one of her pursuers sprinted past, blocking her way, she tried to turn back. The other guard blocked her escape in that direction, grinning at her as he shifted from side to side. One grabbed her by the hair and shoved his torch in her face.

"Hey, Bert," he cried. "It's that nurse lady. This will be better sport than I thought. We can have a little fun with her."

Bert pushed his face close enough to Elinor's that she began to think she might pass out from the foulness of his breath. "We kin have some fun and then we can eat her. She looks nice and tender," he said, poking her in the ribs.

He pushed her against the wall, holding her hands above her head, laughing as she struggled to escape. He bent to kiss her or take a bite of her. Either seemed too horrible to contemplate. Elinor turned her face away and began to sob. Before Bert could do either, the other guard struck him from behind.

"My turn," he chuckled as Bert slumped to the floor, out cold. The second guard licked his chops like a dog contemplating his supper as he grabbed Elinor and drew her close. She closed her eyes and began to scream as he opened his mouth to tear at her throat. He jerked and grunted, pressing her against the wall. When his arms went slack about her and fell away, she opened her eyes reluctantly, whimpering with fear, expecting to find another guard waiting to take his place. Instead, she found Rowan, bloodied sword in hand, peering anxiously into her face.

"Elinor, did they hurt you?" he asked.

She could not answer. She stared at him, afraid he would melt away and she would find herself once more at the mercy of Borgas' guards.

He did not melt away. He continued to stand before her, solid and beautiful. He held his arms open and she found herself sobbing and shaking against his chest.

Gilden and Manton appeared soon after. She vaguely remembered Manton carrying her back to their rooms with Gilden and Rowan following after, keeping them safe.

She awoke some time later to find the captain pacing about the room, running a hand through his graying hair.

A look from him brought the story of her misadventure spilling out.

"What are we going to do, Manton?" Elinor asked. "I would think at least some of your men are held prisoner down there, but only the Wizard can get to them, it seems."

"First of all, Elinor, I want you to promise me you will never risk your life in such a way again!" He shouted. "What were you thinking of, woman?"

She stood before him, at a loss for words until she found herself in his arms. He kissed her and held her tightly to him. "Thank the Creator Rowan had a sudden desire to see you. He was talking to Edmund in the infirmary when he heard you scream. Edmund heard nothing, but took it very seriously when Rowan drew his weapon and took off running toward the dungeons. Edmund came to find me. Even Rowan was shaken when we found you. He said he was almost too late.

"I wish you were far from this place, Elinor. Our world seems to be crashing down around our ears and there is nothing we can do about it. Perhaps I can persuade Gilden and Rowan to leave Anduin and take you with them to the safety of the Elven kingdom."

"Manton, after thirty years together, I cannot leave your side no matter what happens in Anduin," she said softly. I cannot live without you, and Lord Gilden does not seem inclined to leave Anduin. I wish he would send his young son home, though. It seems unfair to have them both embroiled in our troubles."

"Gilden has tried to send Rowan back to Borias, but he will not leave his father's side," said Manton, remembering the desperate look in Gilden's eyes as he told Manton of his efforts to send his heir to the relative safety of the Dark Forest. "It seems the quiet Rowan has a stubborn streak as prominent as yours, Elinor."

She laughed softly. "I met Rowan years ago when I cared for his father as he lay wounded. I remember once the battle was over, he came to stay by his father's side until he was recovered. I think Rowan and I have a lot in common. We love two men whose hearts rule their heads."

"Perhaps we will all pay dearly for our loyalty to the kingdom of Anduin," he sighed, "But as for the men who may be imprisoned below, we cannot risk trying to release them, not until the time is right. Any attempt to break through the passage wall would take far too long to go unnoticed. I fear if Borgas discovers you have escaped his guards and know of their whereabouts, he will kill them all before we can find a way to set them free. Rowan has hidden the guards' bodies. We will hope no one misses them. My men will have to stay where they are for now. If Borgas is feeding them, he must be keeping them alive for some reason. I would wager he has some foul plan in mind for them. Perhaps one Wizard can be pitted against another if young Althus can rescue Euwyn from whatever holds him."

Elinor saw the doubting look that crossed her husband's face at his own words, but she hoped that somehow the young soldier and his Elven friends would succeed.

## Chapter Fourteen

## BULLROAR

Kestrel's sharp cries drew Althus' attention as he descended to Bree's shoulder from the brightening sky. The sun was just peeking over the horizon casting long shadows over the stony landscape. The little hawk had made his presence known to them periodically since they had left the Dark Forest. He followed them from the air, occasionally descending to sit on Bree's shoulder, sharing her meals when they made camp. He seemed agitated this morning. Bree's sharp eyes soon found the cause.

"Eagle!" she cried shading her eyes as she looked into the eastern sky against the light of the rising sun. "He has been waiting for us. He must bear a message from Bull."

The huge bird soon stood before Bree, allowing her to take the message he carried from about his neck. It was a short message, but a welcome one.

*Dearest Little Bree, Thorny and Chess,*
    *I will meet you at the ford of the Amberstream. Wait for me there. You will not find our hidden valley without my guidance.*
                                        *Your Brother,*
                                        *Bullroar*

Bree penned a reply. When she had inserted it safely into his container, Eagle soared back toward the mountains. It seemed their journey was almost over. They ate a simple breakfast and packed their gear, eager to reach Bull's valley before nightfall that day. Once on their way, Althus rode alongside Thorny.

"We have been fortunate on our trip through the wild lands to have encountered neither Orcs nor Goblins," Althus said.

Thorny's face was troubled, "You would think I could feel grateful for that. It makes me uneasy. It is as if the Orcs and Goblins have finally completed their gathering. I fear they are no longer crossing the wild lands in small bands, but have now assembled into a vast army, an army that will soon march northward if it does not do so already. If Stonehaven has fallen to whoever commands the Orcs, the Dwarves would have the skill to equip them. From there, such an army could strike through Craglith pass at my people, or more likely, yours. I think we will find that army in Stonehaven. No one will be safe if such an army marches out of Stonehaven, not even the Elves of the Dark Forest, if Anduin falls."

Althus shuddered at the thought of an army of Orcs and foul creatures marching against Anduin. His homeland lay unprepared and unguarded. If

Borgas still had the ear of King Allen, the evil army would slaughter the people of Anduin.

Φ         Φ         Φ

They reached the Amberstream by midday, splashing through its shallow, stony course without incident. Their path ended abruptly at this point. They faced a sheer rock wall that soared far above their heads and ran between them and the destination marked on the map as far as the eye could see. The trail they followed ran along the base of the cliff eastward to the main gates of Stonehaven. Outcroppings of stone topped the heights of the escarpment. Between these jagged boulders, the Amberstream cascaded in a broad waterfall.

Thorny and Chess rode downstream for a short distance to see if they could find a way up from the bed of the Amberstream. Bree waited at the ford, thinking Bull would be most likely to look for them there. She reluctantly agreed Althus should cross the stream once more and ride south along the rock wall for a short distance to see if he might discover a path up the escarpment in that direction. Mars, having attached himself to Gust's side for the moment tagged along with them. Althus rode until he could see clearly that the sheer rock wall swept far into the distance toward the Hoary Mountains.

He had turned about and headed back toward Bree when Gust's ears swept to attention. Althus dismissed his excitement as eagerness to rejoin the other horses until someone hiding behind a stone outcropping suddenly snatched from behind and dragged from Gust's back. He found himself face to face with a Black Giant, his feet dangling far above the ground, the front of his shirt firmly clutched in the Giant's meaty hand. His face was inches from the Giant's huge dark eyes as the Giant shook him like a dog with a rat, shouting in a strange language with a voice that threatened to deafen him. His Elven mail was choking him and he grabbed at his collar in a vain attempt to find some room to breathe. The Giant abruptly began to speak in Elvish as if it were his native tongue and Althus could now understand his words even though he did not have enough air in his lungs to answer.

"What have you done with my little sister!" he roared. He shook Althus until his teeth rattled. Althus caught sight of Bree approaching at a gallop from behind the enraged Giant and tried to warn her to stay away. All he could manage was a few strangled sounds. At least this made the Giant stop shaking him and regard him in puzzlement. "I cannot understand your speech little man," he growled, "but I will get the truth from you." Althus wondered if the Giant could make the dead speak as some Wizards and priests could, since he certainly would soon be dead if the Giant continued to question him in this manner.

Bree's voice rang out from behind the Giant. "Bullroar!" she shouted, causing the dark Giant to turn about quickly, the force causing Althus to swing like a rag doll in the hands of an overly enthusiastic child. "Put Althus down! Put him down *now!*" The Giant dropped Althus as if he had suddenly burst into flame. He landed unceremoniously on the rocky ground where he coughed and wheezed, desperately trying to draw air into his lungs.

"Bree!" the Giant roared, opening his arms as if to embrace her.

Dismounting, she ducked his embrace shooting him a look that could melt stone as she ran to Althus' side.

"What were you thinking, Bull?" she scolded, as she knelt with her arms about Althus' shoulders as he struggled to draw breath. The huge Giant, fully twice Althus' height and four times his weight, stood sheepishly wringing his hands before her.

"I thought ... I thought ..." he stammered.

"You were *not* thinking at all!" she shouted at him. Althus was amazed to feel pity welling up in his heart for the beleaguered Giant, evidently the foster brother, Bull they had traveled to meet.

"I thought he had to have harmed you. He was riding an Elven horse. He had two Elven horses, in fact. No Human rides an Elven horse. I thought he had stolen them," Bull tried to explain. "I feared he had harmed you and your brothers."

"Althus is our friend, Bull. He has survived an Orc attack and risked his life to save me and to save Chess, and *you*, who are supposed to be an ally, nearly killed him." She paused to draw breath before continuing her tirade, at which point Althus had gained his feet and drawn enough air into his lungs to intercede on the unfortunate Giant's behalf.

"I am all right, Bree," he said, struggling to make his voice sound normal. "No harm has been done. He was only thinking of you and your brothers."

"See!" said Bull, brightening visibly at Althus' defense of him. "Althus is not hurt." The Giant moved as if to put a hand to Althus' shoulder, causing Althus to back away from him hastily. At this point Thorny and Chess returned from their scouting and, following Bree's tracks, found their sister chastising the unfortunate Giant.

Their reunion was a joyful one, the Giant engulfing each brother in his huge arms while Bree stood glaring at them in consternation. Althus was at her side, smiling broadly by now, marveling at the dark Giant who was the fair Elves' adopted brother. His expectations had been far from the mark. The Giant was very handsome with eyes as dark as night in a noble face. His smooth skin was the red brown color of rich earth and his black hair braided close to his head and down his back in an uncountable number of slender braids.

"Bull," Chess laughed, "have you made Bree angry already? You have an unusual talent for getting into trouble with your little sister."

"I know, Chess," the contrite Giant admitted, "but she is right, as usual. I have let my heart rule my head once again and nearly killed your Human companion. It was merely a misunderstanding. Althus has forgiven me, but Bree is not so kind." Bull followed this pronouncement with such a sad look in Bree's direction that Althus and her brothers burst out laughing. Bree could not help but smile as well, although she muttered angrily under her breath as she stalked past her brothers and the Giant to take Moon's reins in her hand. Bull gave Althus a sheepish grin and tried to gather Gust's trailing reins for him, but Gust snapped viciously at his hand and he drew it back quickly. Althus chided Gust for his display of ill temper, but could not hide his smile from Bull.

"I guess I deserved that, and I do apologize for attacking you in such a manner. If Gust and I had not been old friends, he would have warned you before I had the opportunity to grab you from behind. He thought of me as an ally, no doubt, and did not expect me to attack you as I did. I have made a mess of our meeting and now Bree is angry with me before I have even spent a moment in her company. It was ever so even when we were children. I was so much larger than the other children and Bree always had to protect them from my clumsiness." He sighed, "Gilden and his family and, indeed, all of the Elves were very kind to me, but I am more at ease here among my own people than I ever was among the Elves."

"Well, Bull," said Althus offering the Giant his hand, "Let us at least be friends. We got off to a bad start, but we will start again as if nothing had happened between us." Bull's smile as they started back toward the waterfall, dazzling in his dark face, was one of sheer joy. Bree turned to look back at them and could not help but smile at the huge Giant and the young Human half his height, walking side-by-side, deep in conversation.

"You and the Elves will soon meet my family. My wife is the most beautiful and intelligent Giantess who ever lived," he stated proudly "and my two children the most beautiful and intelligent children. You will soon see." His obvious love for his family touched Althus deeply.

"It is difficult to imagine you are married and have become a father, Bull," said Thorny.

"It *is* a difficult thing to imagine," Chess said, laughing. "Who would marry this huge brute and allow him to sire her children? I could not believe it when we received the message he had taken a wife. Then there came a message he was going to be a father. Now he has two children! It is beyond belief!"

"Oh, he is not so bad to look at I suppose," Thorny said. "Perhaps Liddy married him out of pity."

"Liddy tells me I am the most handsome Giant she has ever met," Bull replied.

"She is a blind woman, then?" asked Chess.

"You see what a difficult life it is with these two as brothers, Althus. I cannot imagine how they persuaded you to travel in their company," Bull said.

"He had little choice in the matter," Chess laughed. "He tried to get away once, but Bree made us drag him back"

Thorny and Chess laughed, but Bull noticed Althus was blushing and Bree looked at her brothers in the same manner as she had lately looked at him.

Crossing the Amberstream once again, they stood facing the waterfall cascading over the escarpment wall. Bull spoke two words in the language of the Giants. To Althus' amazement, the water ceased to flow over the wall's face and two huge doors, hidden by the cascading waters, swung slowly open. When he asked the Giant what craft had fashioned the doors he was surprised to learn the Dwarves had cut the passageway through the solid rock and Euwyn had enchanted the doors centuries ago. They would open only to two words in Giantish spoken by a true Giant. Bull told him proudly that the enchanted doors had kept the evils infesting the wild lands from entering the valley of the Dark Giants, sending them northeast instead, traveling around the escarpment to the gates of Stonehaven.

The passageway was truly a marvel to Althus. It was broad and smooth enough for them to ride the horses three abreast. Bull led the way with Althus and Chess on either side of him. Bree and Thorny, with Mars between them, brought up the rear. The ceiling was higher than the Giant, allowing him to walk comfortably upright without fear of striking his head. The doors, enchanted so long ago, gave testament to Euwyn's good works that reached far beyond the borders of Anduin.

Althus did not wonder that the king had replaced Euwyn with the hated Borgas years ago. Euwyn was never content to dance attendance to the king of Anduin, but spent much of his time seeking out those who needed his help in other lands. Borgas, on the other hand, seemed fond of the comforts of Castle Anduin and seldom ventured beyond the castle walls.

The tunnel sloped steadily upwards for some distance and Althus was grateful when they could finally see the end ahead of them, brilliant sunshine flooding through the unguarded opening. There were no doors to block the upper end of the tunnel. They emerged to stand staring across the bowl shaped valley spreading below, struck by the simple beauty that lay before them. The entire valley was a patchwork of square stone walled fields dotted here and there by gray stone houses and barns. Placid sheep and cows grazed peacefully in the warm sunshine. There was an air of contentment about the valley that belied the evil that lurked close by in the mountains in whose arms the valley nestled.

Bull led them down a road that led straight across the valley. They could see the entire length of it to where it ended at the foot of the distant mountains. As they traveled its length, other Giants paused in their labors to watch them pass. They encountered some Giants who were traveling the road with goods to sell. Most smiled and nodded in greeting. Some stared in silence at the unusual company as they made their way across the valley.

"They are all goodly Giants," Bull said, nodding back to those they passed along the way. "All would defend this valley to their last breath, but I fear we have been isolated from the other lands far too long. My fellow Giants consider me most eccentric. I was raised by Elves, after all, and I still possess the great sword that was Gilden's gift to me. They think me a wild and untamed man with strange and violent ideas. I have spoken to the great council of our people. I hoped to convince them to take up arms against the dark force gathered in the bowels of Stonehaven. They regarded me as if I had lost my mind as I expected they would. I wished to give them the opportunity, at least, to do the right thing before it is too late and the enemy discovers our valley with no one left in the lands to aid in our defense. I would rather fight them in the mountain where they are now gathered than when they enter our beloved valley to threaten the lives of our wives and children."

"Perhaps they will see the truth of your words in time, Bull," Chess tried to reassure him. "Let us hope so. Your secret gate will not remain a secret very long if the Dwarves that fashioned it are held captive by whatever evil lurks in the mountains. Perhaps the secret has already been revealed." Everyone was silent at the disturbing thought the evil army might already know of the protected valley of the Giants.

"Then we must find our way into Stonehaven and hope the Dwarves have not joined with the forces of evil, but are held captive and may be freed," said Bull. "I cannot think the proud and fierce Dwarves would willingly serve such a master, whoever he may be. No matter what our differences, I cannot think they would openly attack those with which they have lived peacefully, more or less, for many centuries. They are stubborn, bull-headed, obstinate, and intractable at best, but they have always dealt fairly with our people when all is said and done."

"If they are such fierce warriors as you say, Bull," asked Chess, "What kind of force could possibly overcome them and hold them captive in their own underground realm?"

Bull shook his head sadly. "Some time ago there were rumors of a gemstone of great size and value the Dwarves unearthed in their deepest mines. Those Dwarves who spoke of it seemed to my eyes overly taken with its beauty, with an almost obsessive worship of it," mused Bull. "It was soon after when the Dwarves ceased to leave their stronghold to trade with us. Up until then, they were always eager to trade the metalwork completed during the winter for food we put away during the previous summer and fall to replenish their stores. We saw them seldom in any case, but we should have seen some sign of them by now.

Some of my people say the Dwarves hide within the mountain, jealously guarding their new treasure, and trading their wares with their new master, but they must still eat no matter how great the treasure they guard and our valley is the closest source of food. Perhaps their newfound treasure has attracted the attention of something or someone they could not defeat. A great number of Orcs, Goblins, Trolls and other creatures too foul to describe have recently entered the gates of Stonehaven. It troubles me to think how powerful a force it might be that keeps the Dwarves in their mountain holes and gathers such an army to its call. It troubles me that the Dwarves know so many of our secrets. They know the location of our valley and where to find the tunnel serving as our valley's entrance. They do not know the passwords, and if they did, they are not Giants and so it would do them little good. Still, if the Orcs know where our valley lies, the evil that controls them will know soon enough. If this evil, whatever it may be, can control such numbers of fell creatures, our valley is certainly not safe.

"I am glad you are here, my brothers and sister, and you, Althus. I do not know what evils lurk in Stonehaven, but I mean to find out. Perhaps with you four at my side it will not be as difficult as I feared."

## Chapter Thirteen

## LULLABY

Just as the sun sank below the horizon behind them, they reached the sheer walls at the foot of the mountain where Bull's farmstead nestled amid well-tended fields.  Lights shone from the windows where his family waited to greet them.  Bull settled the horses in a lush pasture that offered them access to a stone shelter and clear water from a stone trough and the company soon stood upon the flagstones of the farmhouse porch.  The doors flew open and two children came tumbling out to wrap themselves about Bull's sturdy legs.  His wife, Liddy, greeted her guests with genuine delight, her dark eyes dancing in her beautiful face.  She wore her hair as Bull did, her braids strung with beads of turquoise and silver, lithe and graceful despite her great size.  She was a head shorter than Bull, but still stood much taller than any man Althus had ever encountered.

"Welcome to our home," she said, her voice rich and deep. "I have prepared a meal.  Come refresh yourselves and then sit down while I set it on the table."

The children clung shyly to Bull as he took the traveler's cloaks and showed them where they could wash the dust of the road from their hands and faces.  Althus judged the children to be equivalent to five and two year old Human children although he did not know how quickly or slowly Dark Giant children grew to adulthood.  The older child was a little girl as beautiful as her mother and nearly as tall as Althus.  The younger was a boy also nearly as tall as Althus and twice as heavy from the look of him.  He gazed at his small visitors, smiling at them from behind a thumb stuck solidly in his mouth.  Althus had to admit he had never seen two more beautiful children and understood Bull's pride in his growing family.

Bull introduced Althus and the Elves to his wife and children.  The children were named after their foster grandparents, Linden and Gilden, but their parents called them Gil and Lin to the amusement of the Elves.  Lin spoke some words in the Elven tongue, but was not nearly as fluent as her mother.  Gil did not speak many words at all of any tongue, but seemed to make his wishes known as easily as any Human toddler.

The eight of them sat around a huge table piled with huge amounts of food.  Bull gathered books for Althus and the Elves to sit on from shelves that seemed stuffed to overflowing with them and they ate until they could hold no more.  Liddy insisted they rest from their travels as she cleared the remains of their supper.  They retired to huge chairs that faced a warm fire blazing in the stone fireplace.  Lin helped her mother in the kitchen while Gil, in true toddler fashion, proceeded to look for mischief.  The exasperation in Liddy's voice drew Althus back to the kitchen where Gil was pulling various items from the cupboards as Lin tried to distract him with a variety of toys and Liddy tried to deal with the growing chaos in the kitchen. Althus had little experience with children, but he had been one, once upon a time, and remembered Euwyn entertaining him with some of the simple spells Althus later learned to perform for himself.

When he could catch Gil's attention, he held his hands out before him. With a few words, he produced a bubble on each hand that grew in size until they lifted from his hands and floated upward. Gil and Lin watched with rapt attention as the bubbles reached the ceiling where they burst, releasing a shower of multicolored sparkles that disappeared into thin air as they reached the floor. The children laughed and danced in circles trying to catch bubbles and sparkles alike as Althus produced a multitude of floating spheres from his outstretched hands. Liddy looked on in amusement as she finished her kitchen duties unhampered and dried her hands on a towel.

Althus was concentrating mightily on the formation of the last bubbles when Gil, entranced by Althus' skill made his way unsteadily across the kitchen floor and promptly fell on him, ending the bubbles and pinning Althus helplessly to the stone floor. Liddy's dismayed cry brought Bull and the Elves to the kitchen door where the spectacle of Althus spread eagle beneath Gil, now squirming mightily to right himself and nearly crushing Althus in the process, caused much amusement.

"I should have warned you about that," said Bull, lifting his son off Althus and helping Althus to his feet. "Walking is a new skill to him and he is still a bit unsteady."

"I guess I should have thought of that myself, Bull," said Althus, "but I do not have much experience with one as young as Gil. I was too intent on my spell to see him coming."

"You are truly amazing, Althus." Liddy smiled at him making him suddenly conscious everyone was standing about and looking at him curiously. He excused himself as graciously as he could and stepped outside to stand in the moonlight and gaze up at the mountains towering within a half league of the farmhouse, shivering in the cold night air.

Inside the Elves were telling Bull and Liddy of the events leading up to their arrival, only confirming their feeling Althus was much more than he appeared at first glance.

Bree eventually joined him outside in the moonlight.

"I know something is troubling you, Althus," she said softly. "You know you cannot hide your feelings from us. Will you tell me what worries you?"

"I am feeling unworthy of their admiration," he sighed, unsure himself of exactly what troubled him. "I have tried to explain all I know are a few silly tricks. Spells that are so simple Euwyn could teach anyone to perform them.

I fear you expect more of me than I am capable of. I fear I will endanger all your lives if you depend on my skills as a Wizard or a swordsman."

"Do not worry, Althus," Bree assured him, "Chess and Thorny and I are Elves. We have been battling the dark forces since before you were born. Perhaps we will battle them for eternity. We live or die by our own devices, and all we expect of you, you have already given us... your friendship and loyalty. We ask no more than that. You have already proven you are a brave and loyal friend. Do not worry, Althus, you will not disappoint us no matter what we face in the mountains or what the outcome of our quest. Besides, we Elves possess some magic of our own."

Althus had a great desire to kiss her there in the moonlight as she turned to him. He fully intended to do so, but Chess poked his head out of the door at that moment to ask if they were going to spend all night standing out in the cold when warm beds awaited them inside. Althus laughed and headed for the warmth of Bull's home, wondering to himself if he really would have kissed Bree if Chess had not interrupted them at that moment. Perhaps it was just as well. What was he thinking? He was sure Gilden would not approve of his interest in his only daughter. As kind as Gilden was to him he was sure Gilden would not want a Human and a bastard as a son-in-law. He turned to look at Bree as they approached the open door and wondered if the look he saw on her face was one of disappointment or relief.

He missed entirely the angry look Bree gave Chess as she passed through the door behind him or the sheepish look of apology Chess gave her in return.

Liddy was herding the children toward their beds when they entered the house, but at Althus' reappearance, they both broke away and rushed toward him. Althus, wise to Gil's unsteadiness dodged him neatly and stood ready to retreat when he prepared to make another pass in his direction. Liddy scooped him up in her arms before he could complete the attempt and amidst his tears and lamentations bore him off to bed. Lin, on the other hand, lingered to ask Althus if he would come and say goodnight when they were ready. Althus agreed, thinking that whether they succeeded or failed in their quest, he might never see Bull's children again.

Liddy soon called him to the children's room where Lin, shyly, in Elvish words obviously provided by her more fluent mother, asked that he sing them a lullaby. The request took Althus off guard. He was prepared to tell them a story, but dutifully searched his mind for a suitable song. In its deepest recesses, he found a song Euwyn used to sing to him as a child. He sat on a stool between their beds, his feet dangling a foot from the floor and did his best to remember the tune and the words once so familiar to him.

Suddenly, as he sang, the room about him swam out of focus and, in his mind's eye, he saw Euwyn singing the familiar song, his face sunken and pale, his face bearded, and his hair dirty and unkempt. He felt the Wizard reaching out to him as if he were nearby, but weak. The connection failed quickly. Althus nearly cried out to him, but the room came back into focus just as suddenly and he sat looking at Bull's children sound asleep in their beds. He pulled his knees to his chest, clasping his arms about them and put his head down on them trying to bring his racing heart under control.

When he returned to the fireside and the rest of the company, Bree was the only one who seemed to notice his troubled look, but she made no comment. Liddy thanked him for indulging her children and Bull announced they should all retire for the night since they would have a strenuous day ahead of them. Althus was glad to retire to the privacy of his room and the huge bed within it to sort out the turmoil caused by his fleeting contact with Euwyn. He assumed Bull and Liddy sought some private moments as well in which to say goodbye to each other. He knew Bull had joined with them as much to protect his family and his people as to rescue the imprisoned Wizard. Still, it did not make sleep come any easier when he entertained the possibility the two beautiful children sleeping in the next room might lose their father. The forces gathering in the mountains threatened them as well and they would not have Bull to protect them if the attack came while their company was in the mountains. He tried to contact Euwyn once again, singing the lullaby softly to himself as he lay in the middle of the huge bed. He lay awake, staring at the ceiling, unable to still his churning thoughts, but there were no more visions, no further sign of the Wizard's presence.

## Chapter Sixteen

### ASCENT

Althus was up and dressed in his Elven uniform before first light, eager to distract himself from his doubts and fears. They had come so far. He was determined to find his missing father in the mountains and to rescue him or die in the attempt. He found the Elves with the horses, each saying farewell to their mounts. Gust pushed his hard head into Althus' chest and sighed deeply as if he understood he might never see Althus again. Althus gave him a last pat and turned away to face the mountains. The rest of the company soon joined him. Althus and the Elves carried light packs of food and soft, light coils of Elven cord over their shoulders but little else. Bull carried ropes and spikes slung about his waist and shoulders, his face still wet with tears from his farewell to Liddy.

The upper reaches of the mountains blushed pink with the first rays of the sun as Althus and the Elves stared upward to where the sheer mountain wall ended some two hundred feet above their heads. They were wondering how they would begin their ascent while Bull, unconcerned, wandered back and forth at the base of the cliff muttering to him self in Giantish and scrabbling about in the undergrowth that grew against the rock wall. He straightened suddenly with a satisfied grunt and laid both his huge hands against the rock wall before him. Two words in Giantish produced a door in the wall that opened to a narrow set of stairs winding upward into the solid rock face.

"This will take us to the top of the cliff," He informed them as they all regarded him in amazement.

"Why did you not tell us there was a stairway," said Chess. "It would have saved me worrying all night about how we were going to scale this blessed cliff."

"Oh, Chess," said Bull, unabashed, "You never worry. Remember, I know you better than that. Besides, I was not sure if I could still find the hidden door. The Dwarves and the Giants built the stairway to provide easier access to Stonehaven, but the trail upward was never entirely finished. The stairs and the secret door protect us as does the tunnel beneath the Amberstream, but no one but me has used it in quite some time. Not since the Dwarves have ceased their trade with us."

Thorny gave his brother a hearty shove toward the stairs. "Quit complaining you ungrateful Elf. Bull has found us an easy way up. Just be happy you do not have to dangle from this cliff while we haul you up."

"You haul *me* up!" Chess scoffed. "I would have been first to the top. I would have been hauling *you* up the cliff." This turned into a lively discussion that ended only when Bull informed them no one was likely to be able to haul his weight up the cliff so he would have been the one likely to haul them *all* up. Since that was the case, they would be taking the stairs.

"I would not mind hauling Bree and Althus up, but I would be too sorely tempted to let go of the rope if you two dangled from the end and started one of your silly arguments," he informed them.

"You are the world's most heartless brother," said Chess as they entered the narrow passage and began to ascend the steep stone stairway. Althus· could not help thinking that was far from the truth.

With a word from Bull, the stone door shut behind them and they stood for a moment in near darkness. The faces of the Elves were faintly visible, but gave no illumination to the surrounding passageway. Chess and Thorny drew their blades, which glowed faintly, lighting the stairs dimly, but with a few words, Althus produced a glowing orb in one hand that lit the tunnel clearly and they pressed on once more. Bull smiled at him as Althus moved past him to take the lead, but made no comment. The stairs ascended straight and steep until they reached a blank wall where, with a few words, Bull produced another door and they stepped out of the darkness onto a broad cliff. They looked down upon the Giants' valley below, glittering with dew in the morning light, mist lying in the hollows, and then upwards to the rugged mountain towering above them.

"Where are we headed, Bull?" Althus asked, noting that two paths diverged at this point, one headed downward and to their left and the other almost straight up the side of the mountain.

"The downward trail leads to the main gates of Stonehaven. They are heavily guarded," answered Bull. Our destination is the back door, high on the side of the mountain. I am sure it is also guarded, but I hope not as heavily. They will not be expecting us to ascend the mountain to attack them there, or at least they will not expect a large force to show up at their back door. Perhaps the fact no one has yet to challenge them will have made them less wary and that will certainly work to our advantage."

They all gazed upwards save Althus, whose attention was drawn in the direction of the main gates. He saw a number of huge, dark shapes appear around the side of the mountain from that direction, flying ponderously with great wing strokes. He grasped Thorny's arm and pointed toward them, needing the Elf's sight to confirm what he feared.

"Hide, quickly," Thorny shouted. "I fear something foul from the depths of Stonehaven approaches from the air."

They sprinted for the shelter of some tumbled rocks that lay against the mountain wall. Following Bree's example, Althus readied his bow. Had the enemy detected them already? That did not bode well for their mission. All eyes turned toward the approaching threat. Bull produced a sling and quickly proceeded to amass a pile of suitable stones, but the flying horrors passed over their heads and disappeared around the mountainside with a rush of leathery wings. They appeared to be perversions of the carrion birds that inhabited the mountains, some as large as a man, some larger, with no visible feathers, but a leathery hide which made their wings look much like those of a bat. From Althus' vantage, their beaks and talons appeared unusually sharp. He was thankful they were not their intended victims until he turned to Bull and saw the patent horror etched on his face. It was not until then that he realized the valley below was their target.

As one, without a word, the company left the concealing rocks, swiftly and cautiously following the path of the foul creatures around the mountainside. They were relieved to find they had not immediately flown into the valley, but were perched on the edge of the cliff overlooking it. There were twenty of the creatures, croaking loudly and peering down into the unprotected valley, waiting, watching for some unsuspecting giant to appear in the valley below. Althus thought of Bull's children. They could not afford to let any of the creatures escape. He hoped his skill with a bow and arrow would prove adequate. He knew Bree would be deadly. Bull's eyes were riveted on the creatures, his hands holding his loaded sling. Althus wondered how effective he could be with such a primitive weapon.

Following Bree's lead, Althus drew back his bow and sighted on his target praying his aim was worthy of Rowan's craftsmanship. Bull wound up with his sling, the sound of it, whirring through the air a testament to the Giant's strength. When he released it, Bree and Althus loosed their arrows. Each hit their target and three of the creatures tumbled from the cliff. Before the rest of the creatures could react, Bree and Bull had accounted for two more apiece, and Althus had killed another. They had reduced the flock by almost half before they were able to lift their ponderous forms from the cliff. Althus gave a silent prayer of thanks that they did not flee into the unwary valley below, but turned to attack them as he and Bree accounted for two more of the creatures before they drew too near for arrows. Bull drew his huge Elven blade as Althus dropped his bow and stepped in front of Bree, drawing his sword. Thorny and Chess already stood with their blades drawn to meet the approach of the remaining creatures. They dove at the company with razor sharp talons leading, the wind from their approach nearly blowing Althus over before he could bring his blade up to meet them. Their flight was powerful, but ungainly, lacking maneuverability. The agile Elves easily sidestepped the first onslaught, beheading two of the creatures as they passed.

One creature landed before Althus, grabbing him by the shoulder with its sharp beak, only his mail keeping it from tearing his arm from his body. The pain nearly brought him to his knees, but he managed to twist out of its grasp and run it through with his blade.

There was sudden quiet. Althus saw that Bull had accounted for two of the creatures, his huge blade and great strength slicing them neatly in half. The surviving four were circling about to make a second pass. Althus was winded, but prepared for another go, noting that Chess and Thorny seemed unfazed by their brush with the huge creatures. They stood ready, their bloodied blades grasped easily in their hands. The bird-like creatures were more wary this time, circling over their heads before diving once more to attack.

Bree stood atop a boulder, sheltered by an overhanging cliff. Althus watched in admiration as she loosed two arrows, both hitting their marks, sending two more creatures tumbling through the air, but Bree's face wore a look of horror as Thorny, unable to dodge one of the careening birds was knocked over the sheer cliff. The rest of the company echoed her anguished cry as Thorny disappeared over the edge. Chess stood, sword in hand, a look of stunned disbelief on his face as the two remaining creatures swung about to aim their sharp talons at his unprotected back. Bull was too far away from Chess to reach him in time. Althus knew he could kill at least one of the creatures. He sprinted toward Chess, pushing him out of the bird's path as he passed. He leapt at the creature. Meeting it in mid-air and tumbling to his back as it struck him full force. He held its beak off with his mail-clad arm as its talons raked at the Elven mail protecting his torso. The creature had him pinned helplessly to the ground, his sword beneath him.

Croaking and beating its leathery wings, the creature attempted to take off with Althus clutched in its talons. There was a whistle of feathered pinions and a wild cry, as a shadowy form struck the beast from above. Althus dropped back onto the ledge, battered and winded, but unharmed. He rolled to his feet, searching the skies for the two remaining creatures only to find that Eagle had flown to his defense, battling two foes in mid air, his wild cries echoing from the cliffs as he outmaneuvered the huge beasts, trying to knock them from the sky. With a heavy heart, Althus turned to the edge of the cliff to see where Thorny's body lay. To his amazement, he was met by the sight of a female eagle, wings flapping madly, rising slowly over the edge of the cliff, Thorny followed, firmly gripped in her talons. Bull reached his long arms out to pull the Elf over the edge of the cliff. Once relieved of her burden, the female eagle flew off to join her mate. Althus turned, taking up his bow once more. He and Bree managed to end the battle with two well-placed arrows as the eagles pressed the evil looking birds close to the cliff.

The battle over, Bree, Chess and Thorny turned to where Bull stood looking out over his valley expecting to find Thorny close by. There was no sign of him until Althus heard his clear voice repeating Bull's name and with each repetition, sounding a little more desperate and a little more winded. Chess reached the Giant's side first and found him desperately clutching Thorny to his chest, while Thorny, becoming more annoyed by the moment with his big brother, begged Bull to release him. Chess gained his release by reminding the Giant that Bree would not approve of his crushing her brother to death any more than she had his rough treatment of Althus. The threat of Bree's anger brought Bull to his senses and he gently put Thorny down, straightening his clothing and inspecting him for any damage. Thorny, still a little ruffled by his experience informed Bull he did not appreciate being mangled by a ham-handed Giant. Bull was too happy to see him safe to take offense. They all stood upon the ledge, embracing Thorny with relief, catching their breath as they surveyed the carnage about them. The eagles flew down and stood regally accepting their praise before flying off into the mountains with a wild cry and a rush of wings.

"What was it like, Thorny?" asked Chess, his eyes shining with excitement. "What was it like to fly with an eagle?"

"First of all, Chess," said Thorny rubbing his bruised shoulders, "being plucked up in mid air by an eagle with very sharp talons is only a little more pleasant than falling to one's death. Secondly, I was afraid she would not be able to lift me over the edge of the cliff. I would much rather she had set me down below where I could take the stairs up again if need be. Still, I am truly grateful they happened along at the right moment."

"They know about our valley," Bull said sadly, gazing out over the cliff. "These creatures were sent to attack my people. I fear the danger to our once peaceful valley has only begun."

"Bull," said Bree reaching up to gently place her hand on his arm, "if you feel you should go back down there to your family we will all understand. We will find our way. Perhaps you can draw a map to the Dwarves' back door." Althus, Chess and Thorny nodded in agreement, each of them thinking of Bull's wife and children in the valley below.

Bull shook his head. "If we do not stop this menace that threatens us in their mountain lair, then they will be free to attack us again and again until they find a way to defeat us. My path lies with you and I cannot turn back. I hope the slain creatures lying at the base of the cliff serve as a warning for my people, but I must do what I can to aid your cause. It is the only way my people can be truly safe again. If we start upward now, we will reach the back door by nightfall." This said, Bull picked up his gear and strode up the mountain trail, Althus and his companions hurrying to catch up with his huge strides.

The path up the mountain soon dwindled to nothing and they were glad for Bull's guidance. There was no indication of where their path lay from then on. Bull led them across the mountainside at times. At times, they climbed almost straight upwards, relying on Bull's great strength and size to lift them to higher ledges and his sturdy rope and spikes which he drove securely into the solid rock with a few swings of his hammer. The Elves seemed to climb without tiring, graceful and sure-footed. Althus felt clumsy in this unfamiliar terrain and was glad that Bull, sensing he struggled, kept close to him, lending him his huge hand when necessary. With Bull's help, they made good progress, and when late afternoon found their side of the mountain in shadow, he motioned for them to stop, gathering them all at his side.

"The entrance will be visible when we pass around this jutting rock," he informed them. "We still have a deep chasm before us that we will cross, but we will be visible from this point on to any that may guard the opening."

Bree held her hand up to silence them for a moment, turning her head to listen intently. "I hear something from the direction of the entrance," she whispered, causing them all to strain their ears to hear over the constant whine of the wind.

Thorny nodded in agreement. "Voices," he said. "Orcs and someone or something else. It cannot be good for whatever other creature we hear. The Orcs seem to be amusing themselves at another's expense."

Silently, Chess moved to peer around the jutting rock face, the others following him closely. He turned back to them, a look of anger marring his usually placid countenance.

"I counted only two Orcs," he whispered. "They have a young Dwarf by the ankles and are holding him out over the chasm, letting him have a good look before they let go of him, I would imagine."

Bree and Althus did not wait for Chess to continue, but fitted their bows and stepped around the abutment of rock to stand side by side. The Orcs were intent on their victim, who was swinging his short arms futilely and cursing at them as he hung head down over the deep chasm. They did not look up from their game to see their peril.

"What are we going to do?" whispered Bree. "If we shoot them, they will drop him. If we do not, they will drop him. Either way he is as good as dead. We will have to wait and hope they bring him back in over the ledge once more before they release him."

They held their breath and waited, but it seemed the Dwarf was ill fated. With one last shake, the Orcs let go and he plummeted headfirst into the rocky chasm. Bree and Althus' arrows found their marks and the two Orcs followed immediately after, but it was little consolation to the pair. Althus held Bree gently as she wept on his shoulder, fearing the sight of the Dwarf, dropping to his death and his short cry of terror would stay with him forever.

A commotion from below drew their attention over the edge. They found Bull on a ledge just below them and across the chasm with the wriggling Dwarf held firmly in his arms. Bull was trying to calm the Dwarf's angry cries, but the little Dwarf was putting up quite a struggle. Bull tucked the Dwarf under his arm, clamped a hand over his mouth and made his way back to where Althus and the Elves awaited them. They gathered around as Bull set the little Dwarf on his feet, his hand ready to cover his mouth once more, warning the Dwarf with a finger to his lips to speak quietly.

"Me Dad," he sobbed, "They hit me Dad. I think they killed 'im."

Bree knelt before him wiping his angry tears with the hem of her cloak.

"Tell us your name, little one, and we will help your dad," she said softly.

"Me name is Mica," he sobbed, "and me dad is Granite. The Orcs caught me feedin' the Wizard and they was goin' to throw us both into the crack fer it."

At these words, the company looked at each other, sharing grim smiles all around.

"Perhaps," said Bree, "we can help each other."

## Chapter Seventeen

## GRANITE AND MICA

"Where did you last see your father, Mica?" asked Althus as he walked beside Bull, looking up at the young Dwarf perched on Bull's broad shoulder.

"He was layin' in the tunnel just inside the door. They was gonna fling him over after they had their fun with me. He wasn't movin' at all. I think they killed him." The Dwarf began to sob once again.

"Do not assume your father is dead," said Bull. "I know him well and he has a head that matches his name. We will find him when we reach the tunnel."

They approached the tunnel with weapons drawn, but it appeared the two slain Orcs had been the only guards on duty. Mica informed them he had not seen any others guarding the door. Daylight was fading quickly as they warily approached the entrance to Stonehaven. They found Granite lying in a heap by the entrance as Mica had predicted and the young Dwarf threw himself upon his father crying lustily. Bree, kneeling to turn Granite on his back while the others stood watch, laid a hand on Mica's shoulder begging him to be still before he brought the entire mountain of foul creatures upon them.

"He is still alive, Mica so hush now and help me," she said softly to him. "We cannot stay here for long. Is there somewhere we can hide until he regains his senses?"

Mica turned about to look helplessly about for a place to hide, but Bull, more familiar with the outside of the mountain, was the one who directed them to a shallow cave, hidden from view, where they took Granite. Bree tended to a deep gash on his head, administering a draught that soon had him showing signs of consciousness. Mica fairly danced with delight as his father sat up, gingerly putting a hand to his wounded head. He squinted up at the company in the fading light and blinked in confusion. "Ooo me head," he moaned. "I must've been hit hard indeed. I'm seein' Elves and Giants and good King Allen, young again."

"Well, yer not seein' things, Dad. It's Elves and a Giant although I dunno who King Allen is. This is Althus, Dad, and they've come and rescued us from the Orcs just in the nick o' time."

His son's voice brought him fully to his senses then and he came quickly to his feet, embracing his son, dancing him about and shouting with joy. Bull quickly hushed him and while Granite's eyes still shone, his voice fell to a level quiet for a Dwarf.

The Elves introduced themselves formally to the Dwarves, giving their names and their titles. Granite and Bull had met many times before in trading sessions. Granite shook his hand, welcoming him back to his home as if he were not a gaunt shadow of his former self. He was filthy and dressed in rags, but behaved as if he were dressed in his best and inviting Bull to a feast in his honor. Bull looked at him quizzically, but not with as much puzzlement as Althus.

"Sorry, young man," rumbled the Dwarf, taking Althus' hand in his and shaking it roughly, "I wuz a little befuddled there for a while. You look so much like the king of Anduin I mistook you fer him, although he would be a much older man now. When I last saw him he wuz askin' me ta forge a set of armor for his soon to be born child an' hopin' it'd be a boy. I'd say he were about yer age then. Mebbe a few years older. Be you a relative o' his?"

Althus shook his head uncertain of what he should say. "The Wizard Euwyn is the only father I have ever known, Granite," he said simply. "We have come to rescue him from the forces in Stonehaven."

Granite regarded him with narrowed eyes, the long shaggy beard that nearly covered the entire front of his body moving as his jaws worked their way around his reply. "Well, that's a tall order for a Human, three Elves and a Giant, even with two Dwarves to help 'em, but we're game if you are. C'mon, I hafta show you somethin' that might help us." He beckoned for them to follow him, leading them out of the shallow cave and climbing to a point above it. Night was falling and they looked down into the deepening dark to the foot of the mountain where the main gates lay.

Althus' breath caught in his throat as he looked down upon a stream of moving torches. An army was on the move below him, the army Gilden warned them of. The march to Anduin had begun and he had not yet rescued Euwyn. He had not even entered Stonehaven. He was helpless to aid Anduin in its time of need. Even if they could find and rescue Euwyn the next day, they would never reach Anduin in time. His thoughts were with Gilden and Rowan, Queen Maris, and Captain Manton and his men. He had failed them. He had failed all of them. His only consolation would be to free Euwyn and he was determined to rescue him or die in the attempt.

Granite and Mica were only too happy to see the bulk of the forces occupying their home leaving for parts unknown to them. It would help them, but Althus found little comfort in it.

The others headed back to their concealing cave, but Bree, after a few brief words with her brothers, beckoned Althus to follow her even farther upwards to a ledge where she sat down cross-legged and sent her imitation of Kestrel's call ringing down the mountainside.

"Kestrel will help us," she said when the bird appeared in a few moments. "He cannot follow us below ground, but he can carry a message to Rowan for us and warn Anduin the army is on the march and will soon be at their gates. They will be glad to hear we have reached this point and have found Bull and

Dwarf allies to guide us."

Althus, still troubled by the army massing below, took some comfort in the thought that those he cared for in Anduin would not be caught unaware. Bree spoke to the bird for a time and then kissing him between his fierce eyes, she threw him into the air. He immediately disappeared into the night sky.

"He will reach Anduin more than a day before the army does," said Bree, looking off into the night sky. "At least Father will have a chance to gather the people within the gates of the city. It is possible we can reach Anduin in time if it falls under siege before the true battle begins. Let us hope our mission here does not fail." Althus again had a great desire to kiss her as she turned to look at him, an unquenchable light in her eyes that gave him hope all could still work out well for the people of Anduin. He controlled that urge, feeling it would be a betrayal of Gilden and settled for an embrace instead. The warmth of her slender body against his did little to calm his racing heart, however, and when they parted, she gave him a knowing look. Only then did he remember his feelings were no longer secret when he touched the sentient Elf. He blushed deeply, glad the dark hid his embarrassment from the rest when they returned to the shallow cave.

Thorny was watching the Dwarves devour some of their rations while Bull and Chess stood watch. He was asking the Dwarves some pointed questions. Althus knew they would have to answer them honestly with the Elf's hand casually resting on Granite's shoulder. He and Bree joined Thorny to learn what they could of the conditions within Stonehaven.

It had all begun with the discovery of a stone, as Bull had suspected, but Granite believed the stone was left for them to discover and not dug from the deep mines, as he had first believed. Granite described the stone as a huge moonstone, shaped as if it were a drop of clear liquid. It seemed lit at times by inner fires that caused the stone to glow with a greenish light.

The stone enchanted the Dwarves. At first, their innate appreciation of beautiful things seemed to explain their preoccupation with the flawless white stone. At first, only a few seemed obsessed enough to fight amongst themselves for possession of it, then more and more fell under its spell. Gradually, the stone became an obsession few could resist.

When Orcs and other foul creatures began to move into the more isolated regions of the underground kingdom, the Dwarves were so engrossed in their internal squabbles for possession of the stone they took little notice. They would oust the intruders when they settled the issue of the stone's ownership. By the time they awoke to their peril, it was too late. All had fallen under the spell of the stone and none had the will to oppose the occupation of their once hallowed halls by a collection of the foulest creatures imaginable. To their abject shame and misery, they discovered their youngest children, their most prized treasures, had been taken from them and hidden in some unknown corner of Stonehaven. The captain of the evil horde, one who called himself Magool the Chosen threatened a slow, painful death to every child if the Dwarves refused to cooperate.

Thus had begun the five years of their captivity. During those five years their captors drove them to the point of exhaustion, forcing them to forge weapons and armor for the growing army and to serve them in other ways too vile to speak of. Many Dwarves died of starvation or were slain by their captors for minor offenses. Dwarves were thrown into the chasm nearby nearly every day now.

Althus assumed Euwyn had secretly entered Stonehaven, bent on freeing the Dwarves, and had fallen captive as well. Granite was not sure exactly when Euwyn had fallen under the stone's spell. The surviving Dwarves, some thousand or more of them, by Granite's estimate, noticed a gradual lessening of the stone's power in the last few months and hope grew they would break free of its effects, find their children and overcome their captors. Mica, slipping away unnoticed from his assigned duties had discovered the Wizard trapped in the deepest pit of Stonehaven, his mind held captive by the power of the stone.

Mica piped up at that point eager to clarify something for the group. He did not feel the Wizard was completely under the stone's control, but was engaged in a mental battle with it. He felt that better explained the lessening of the stone's effect on the Dwarves.

"We could feel it," Mica said, his wide green-eyed gaze focusing on Althus as if for confirmation of his estimation of the Wizard's powers. "It wuz as if they wrestled back and forth while the stone's hold on us weakened. We hid it from the Orcs, waitin' fer our chance. We hoped he'd live long enough for us to free ourselves and him, too. So, I started sneakin' him some of my food when I could. It wuz disappearin' although I never saw him eat it, but now all he does is sit before the stone rockin' hisself and singin' bits of some lullaby. I'm fearin' his mind has failed him and we are in fer it again. I can feel the stone gainin' power as our Wizard friend gets weaker. Then I wuz caught feedin' him. Ya gotta do sumthin' Althus. He's dyin' down there in that pit and if he dies, so do the Dwarves."

Mica looked at Althus and his friends with a look of desperation. Thorny put his arms about the young Dwarf. "You may rest easy, Mica. He reassured him. "We are here for exactly that purpose and we will do all we can to accomplish it."

Althus was struck by the contrast between the two races. Mica was almost as wide as he was tall and even without his father's full beard, he looked incredibly scruffy beside the handsome, shining Elf who held him gently, trying to comfort him.

They would give Granite and Mica a night of rest before they entered

Stonehaven.  The Elves, needing no rest, stood watch as Bull and the Dwarves snored in contentment on the stone floor of the cave and Althus spent half of the night staring at the rough ceiling.  What if Euwyn's mind was gone as Mica feared?  Althus knew the strength of the Wizard better than anyone.  Could a mere stone defeat him?  How could Althus free him if such a power existed?  What hope did Althus have to defeat it if Euwyn had fallen victim to it?  In his mind, he searched through the wealth of knowledge Euwyn had given him, looking for some insight, finding none.  He closed his eyes tightly and sighed in frustration and for a moment Euwyn's face was before him looking as he had when Althus sang to Bull's children.

"Althus," he said in his deep resonant voice, and Althus could feel the deep love his foster father felt for him in the way he spoke his name, "find the staff, my son."  He was gone then, but Althus knew what he had to do when he entered the kingdom of Stonehaven.  He would find Euwyn's ebony staff and take it to him.  He closed his eyes and slept until dawn with that purpose set firmly in his mind.

## Chapter Eighteen

## STONEHAVEN

At first light, Althus stood with his friends before the entry to the underground kingdom of Stonehaven, wondering if they would live to see daylight again. They were now seven in number. He hoped they would soon be eight. Today was Euwyn's five hundredth birthday. He prayed it was a good omen.

They entered Stonehaven with their weapons drawn, encountering two Goblins whose duties were probably to guard the entrance. They were far from their posts, arguing over their ration of raw meat. Bull dispatched the first with a stone. An arrow from Bree's bow took the remaining goblin as it stood staring stupidly at its fallen companion. Althus wondered aloud if no one had missed the two Orc guards they had dispatched the day before. They had certainly not increased their guard. If anything, they had replaced the larger Orcs with the same number of smaller Goblins.

"They're a disorganized lot at best," growled Granite. "They spend more time squabbling over their meals than they do at their posts. I doubt two Orcs would be missed with the main force leavin' by the big gates. I s'pose Magool has left his lieutenants in charge while he goes off to war. That gives us the advantage cuz they aren't nearly as devious as Magool."

Granite relieved the Goblins of their swords, handing one to Mica, pushing their bodies over the edge of the gorge. He was already grinning in anticipation of the battle to free his people. Althus looked to Bree as she followed him into the darkness, noting Bull, crouching to avoid bumping his head on the tunnel ceiling, traveled by her side. She was essentially unarmed. She bore only her bow which was of little use in such close quarters. Althus asked Granite if he knew where Euwyn's staff could lie hidden. The Dwarf brightened after a moment of thought.

"I don't know fer sure, Althus," he said. "But I know where it *might* be kept and it might just be a good idea fer us to visit the place I'm thinkin' of in any case."

Granite led the company forward. Althus was amazed to find the narrow tunnel opening out into a larger and smoother one within a hundred yards of the entrance. Bull was no longer required to crouch to avoid hitting his head. Althus noted also that the passage was lit well enough when their eyes adjusted to the semi-darkness.

"Rock light," Granite said. "It isn't nearly as bright as when we wuz free ta maintain it proper."

Althus marveled at the Dwarves' stone craft in evidence all about them. The halls of Stonehaven became broad and high and the floors smooth and level. They moved along as quickly as they dared, their swords drawn in anticipation, led by the sturdy Dwarf toward their first destination, a place he lovingly called the treasure room.

"Ye can bet it'll be guarded," Granite growled. "We'll hafta battle our way in. After that, they'll soon know we're here. We'll have to move fast if we're gonna rescue Euwyn and our children afore the Orcs get to them. I'm thinkin' to arm as many Dwarves as we can find from the weapons in our treasure horde and I'm hopin' to find some battleaxes there since swordplay ain't our way, if ya get my drift."

They began to encounter larger and larger halls with gigantic fluted columns that supported ceilings soaring beyond their sight. Bree fitted an arrow to her bow once more. Althus had some difficulty preventing himself from gazing upwards as he walked, his mouth agape in wonder at the beautiful carvings lining the walls as far as the eye could see.

The stench of Orc permeated the beautiful halls, making Althus wish he had seen Stonehaven at the height of its splendor. The Orcs had no regard for beauty. Many of the beautiful carvings had been defaced, hacked beyond recognition by the uncaring horde.

Althus also wished he could travel in absolute silence as the Elves did. His steps seemed to echo back to him magnified a thousand times to his straining ears. Fortunately, Bree, Thorny, and Chess had sharper hearing than he did, and the Orcs and Goblins they attempted to avoid made enough noise to wake the dead.

When the company encountered troops of guards moving about the halls, they escaped detection by stepping into the shadows and drawing their Elven cloaks about them. Althus shared his cloak with Mica who he found ever close by, proudly carrying his Goblin sword. He smiled at the Dwarf and he grinned back, his teeth shining whitely in his dirty face. Mica had great confidence in his new friends. Althus hoped he would not be disappointed.

Granite led them on through countless chambers and tunnels until Althus feared they would spend eternity wandering through Stonehaven. After what seemed like hours to Althus' fraying patience, Granite abruptly signaled them all to a halt, stepping forward to peer around the next corner. He motioned for the rest to look. They faced a huge door covered with runes, guarded by four huge Orcs.

"We cannot afford to let any of those guards escape to sound the alarm," Thorny whispered.

The rest nodded. Althus readied his bow, he and Bree prepared to eliminate two of the guards. Bull readied his sling to take care of the third. Granite was eager to account for the last with Thorny and Chess to back them up if any failed to hit their mark. With a shout, the company leapt into the open, three of the guards falling dead before they could react.

With a roar of rage, Granite fell upon the fourth, cutting his legs from under him, hacking him to death before the startled creature had taken more than two steps.

"Remind me not to get in his way, Thorny," Chess muttered softly, helping him drag what was left of the dead Orc out of sight. They stood before the huge doors, waiting expectantly while Granite and Mica lifted the huge bar that held them shut. Granite's eyes gleamed in anticipation.

"I hope they've left our treasures alone," he growled, swinging the huge doors open. "A lot of it's Elven stuff we traded fer that burns 'em if they touch it, so I'm hopin' most of it's still here." They stepped through the huge doors, closing them behind, hoping they would have enough time to find the items they sought before the Orc guards discovered them. When Althus lit a globe and held it aloft, the entire company gasped in wonder. The chamber was full of uncountable treasures glittering in the soft light. Where would they begin to find Euwyn's staff if it were even here? Granite was searching already, tossing items here and there, throwing battleaxes into a pile, muttering to himself. Mica wandered quietly among the treasures, looking more carefully than his father, as if with some other item in his thoughts. Granite paused in his search to carry a sword across the room to Althus. He offered the hilt to him with a smile and a bow.

"This should be yours," he said. "'Tis the sword forged by the Elves as a gift fer the king of Anduin's son. We traded fer it some years back thinkin' if the king ever had another son he might come for the armor, and the sword would be here to sweeten the deal. Guess that's not gonna happen. You may as well have it."

When Althus hesitated, Granite shoved it into his hands. "You saved me son's life. At least take the sword as a token of my gratitude."

He stalked away when Althus took the sword from him, muttering to himself once again as he rifled through the piles of weapons in search of axes to add to his growing pile. Bree, Chess and Thorny were scattered about the room, looking for Euwyn's ebony staff. Althus took a moment to examine the fine blade Granite had presented to him. It shone with an inner light when his hand closed about the smooth hilt. Written on its shining surface, an integral part of the chasing that decorated the blade was an inscription in the Elven tongue:

$$αρψον\ Ανδυιν$$

"Prince of Anduin." He thought with regret of the tiny prince of Anduin who died in infancy. What right had he to carry a blade with the royal inscription on it? It would be wrong to claim the blade as his, but to please the Dwarves, he would wear the blade for now. He would carry it in defense of Anduin, in memory of the true prince, and then present it to the queen when his task was over. It felt light in his grasp. Warmth seemed to flow from the jeweled hilt into his hand. The blade was as beautiful and as light as Thorny's, but Thorny's felt cold in his hand. Lost in admiration, he was startled to find Thorny at his side, studying the blade closely, a hand resting lightly on Althus' shoulder.

"The blade I carry warms to my hand as this one does to yours. This blade wishes to be yours. Take it, Althus. Father forged this blade with his own hands and only parted with it because it held painful memories for him. I know he would wish you to keep it."

Knowing Gilden had forged the blade gave him the courage to draw his own heavy sword and scabbard from around his waist and fasten the Elven blade about him. He noticed Mica looking at him with a wide grin on his face and he offered his Anduin blade to him. Mica accepted gleefully, tossing the inferior Goblin blade aside and buckling Althus' trusty broadsword about his ample middle. Althus prayed it would not trip him as it hung almost to the floor.

He joined the search for the staff, but for an agonizing hour, they found no sign of it until Mica, puttering about amidst a pile of chests and boxes in a corner, came across a box that did not seem to belong in a room full of glittering wonders. It was a plain, gray leaden box, long enough to hold a sword or staff. It opened easily and, to his delight, Euwyn's twisted ebony staff topped with its clear gemstone lay inside. He called to Althus, as he reached to touch it. Suddenly, Mica found himself flying through the air, blue fire dancing through and around him. Althus and Bree rushed to where he landed against the wall, covered with soot, his hair dancing wildly about his head.

Althus knelt before Mica, patting at patches of his clothing that still smoked. "Mica, what happened?"

"I think I found the staff!" he shouted a huge grin showing whitely through the new layer of soot coating his already grimy face. They all gathered about the box lying where Mica had dropped it. Althus cautiously reached into it, pulling the staff free.

Bull looked from Mica to Althus who held the staff safely in his hands. "Is it Euwyn's?"

"Yes."

"Well, I guess it recognizes a friend in you, Althus," said Chess as they all started for the door. "It seems you alone can safely carry it."

Mica ran back to grab up the leaden box, now shrunk to a much smaller form, tucking it securely under his arm.

"What do ya want that box for, son?" Granite asked him, slinging a bag of axes over his shoulder nearly as big as he was and heading for the door where

Bull awaited them, carrying an even larger sack of weapons.

"I dunno, Dad," he shrugged. "Somethin' just tells me ta take it."

Granite nodded in resignation. There was no time for a debate over the wisdom of lugging a heavy box that served no purpose, but Mica often had strange ideas for a Dwarf and his father had the wisdom not to waste time arguing.

Good fortune was with them. The hallway outside the treasure chamber was still deserted. Once more, they found themselves warily following Granite through the dim halls of Stonehaven. They traveled ever downward now, both Granite and Mica leading the way, Mica proudly bearing Althus' sword. As they descended into the depths of the mountain, they encountered more Orc patrols, most in charge of small groups of Dwarves headed to their duties in the forges and mines of Stonehaven. Althus wondered how long they could travel the same corridors undetected.

Althus asked Granite to stop for a moment as a thought came to him. "Granite," he said, "we must find a way to arm the Dwarves if they are to be freed. Do you have a plan in mind?" Granite shook his shaggy head in answer to the question.

"I wuz thinkin' I would help you with rescuin' Euwyn and then think about meself and mine after," he said, looking longingly back in the direction of the forges and mines where his kin worked as slaves.

"Maybe we should split up and let Granite arm his people," Bull said. "It is doubtful we can free Euwyn and still remain undetected. There will be little time to waste. We will have to find the Dwarves' children and free them before the Dark Lord's creatures can carry out their threat to kill them.

"I will go with Granite to the forges. Mica knows where Euwyn is held captive. He can show you the way."

"I will go with Bull and Granite," said Bree. "My bow will be more useful in the open spaces of the mines and forges than creeping along these passages."

Althus was reluctant to see Bree leave his side. Still, she was no safer with him than she would be with Granite and the Giant and so, he held his tongue. He could not resist a parting embrace during which he whispered in her ear, "Be careful,"

"We will be back at your side before you know we are gone," she answered.

"I didn't get no hug, did you, Bull?" was Granite's comment to the dark Giant as the three of them strode away toward the outer reaches of Stonehaven. Mica led Althus and the Elves onward, descending toward the deepest pit.

## Chapter Nineteen

## THE FORGE

Granite pushed onward eagerly, anxious for battle. Bree wore a grim look on her face Bull remembered from his years with the Elves, fighting by her side in skirmishes with the dark forces that from time to time invaded their beloved forest. Bull was more of a warrior than his fellow Giants, having witnessed the savagery of the dark forces when they attacked his parents' caravan far from their home. Bull, little more than an infant at the time, was the only one left alive.

The Elves had arrived upon the scene too late to do anything but bury the dead. They found Bull wandering amidst the corpses of his people. Mercifully, he did not remember much from that time. For a year, he spoke no words, in fact made no sound. All but Bree thought his mind irreparably damaged by his experience. Bree never left his side during that time. Eventually, he began to speak to her and then to his Elven family and eventually, aside from his increasing size, he became as one of them. He became deadly with sling or sword and had killed many fell creatures during his years with the Elves. However, he still could not say he was eager for battle. He would have been happy to live in peace for the rest of his days if that were his lot. He was still a Giant, after all, and they were dedicated to peace and learning, but the danger to his people sent him onward, determined to free Stonehaven for the sake of his own people as well as the Dwarves.

Granite drew them into a small storeroom when they neared the forges. There, they could discuss their strategy before entering the huge hall. They could already feel the heat of the giant fire pit dominating the center of the room. Dwarves had not created the fiery furnace. It emanated from the very bowels of the earth. Pots of ore, lowered by a system of chains and pulleys hung near a pool of seething lava, to be raised again to fill the molds when the ore was melted. It was hot and dangerous work and, since their captivity, their enemies kept the Dwarves at it almost continuously. Many had collapsed at their stations, too exhausted to continue, only to be thrown into the fiery pit by their merciless captors.

Granite proposed he attempt to join a group of Dwarves entering the forge, just another Dwarf bound for his workstation. Bull and Bree, obviously un-dwarflike in appearance, would remain hidden until they heard Granite's shout and the sounds of battle within the forge room. Until that time, Granite would arm as many of his fellow Dwarves as he could before the enemy discovered him. Bull would deliver the rest of the gathered weapons and then join Bree in holding the guards at bay as long as possible.

It seemed like a foolhardy plan to Bull, but he had no other to offer and agreed readily, relying on its simplicity to provide them with at least some measure of success. There was little time for discussion. A group of Dwarves accompanied by a guard of Goblins soon approached their hiding place. Bull and Bree were glad to see Goblins rather than Orcs in charge of the group. Although Orcs were not the brightest of creatures, Goblins were incredibly stupid. Bree wondered how Granite would explain the heavy sack he bore, but, with luck, the Goblins would not even question its presence. They held their breath as Granite slipped from their place of hiding to fall in step at the rear of the group of Dwarves. The Dwarves on either side of him gave him quick, astonished sidelong glances, but no one gave any other indication of anything amiss. The Goblins, oblivious to the events unfolding under their ugly noses, arguing loudly among themselves, marched along without pause while Granite slipped axes from his sack to every Dwarf within reach. The group of Dwarves began to mill about him to hide his actions and to make sure each was able to slip a weapon under his or her ragged tunic. Bull grinned, as Bree looked up at him, amazed at the Goblins' stupidity. Obviously, matters had become very lax since the bulk of the army had departed from Stonehaven. Bree doubted Magool would have entrusted Goblins with such duties.

They slipped from hiding to stand near the entrance when Granite's group had passed out of sight, readying their weapons for the impending battle. There were a great number of Orc guards within the great chamber. The central fire pit bathed the room in a lurid red light, all features within silhouetted against the glow. It would be a difficult place in which to do battle and they prayed they would not fail at this first step in the liberation of Stonehaven. A sudden shout alerted them Granite had been discovered. They burst through the doors and into the swirling chaos of the forge. The newly armed Dwarves were giving a good account of themselves, hacking at their captors feverishly, the desire for vengeance and their innate fierceness giving them a savage strength that astonished even the Giant.

Bull killed two Orcs with his sling before the Orcs and Goblins closed on him. He drew his huge sword, cutting the enemy down as if they were wheat at harvest. He fought his way to Granite's side where he threw down his sack of weapons amid the Dwarves who had gathered there, those who were armed on the outside protecting those who were not. Bree leapt from anvil to worktable, shooting arrows into the enemy throng with deadly accuracy. She deftly kept just ahead of those who sought to close on her as she tried to aid those she saw to be hard pressed. As the armed Dwarves wielded their battle-axes, others took up the blades of their fallen enemies. It was not long before all Dwarves had armed themselves with some sort of weapon. The battle raged back and forth for a few moments, Bull cleaving madly with Granite at his side, wounded and bloodied, but hacking at the enemy, a mad grin on his grimy face. With the strength of desperation and rage on their side, the tide turned in the Dwarves' favor. The battle became a scattering of skirmishes.

Bull, temporarily bereft of enemies to slay, looked about in search of Bree and sighted her at the edge of the pit, her slight frame standing out against the glow, contrasting with the sturdy Dwarves fighting about her. She had abandoned her bow for a Goblin sword and was menacing a group of Goblins with it. Bull started for her side, hampered by milling Dwarves desperately searching for enemies to slay. He shouted a warning as an Orc approached from her right, but she faced the Goblins trying to force her over the brink of the pit and could not hear him over the din of battle and the roar of the flames behind her. A Dwarf, wildly swinging a battleaxe, swept the Orc's feet from beneath him. The Orc tumbled towards the edge, reaching out at the last moment, grasping desperately at anything to keep himself from falling into the fires below. His hand closed about Bree's ankle and with a wild cry, his momentum took them both over the edge of the pit. Bull watched her disappear, roaring in horror and rage, scattering Dwarves and Goblins alike as he flung himself forward. He landed on his stomach, his head over the edge, but the sudden heat and light dazzled his eyes and for a moment, he could not see. He lay staring in disbelief at the molten lava swirling below. She was truly gone. His beloved sister had perished in the fiery pit below him and there was nothing he could do to save her.

The battle won, Granite found him sitting at the edge of the pit with his head in his hands, sobbing as if his Giant heart were broken. Granite had seen the Elf fall, cursing his own inability to save her. Tears made grimy tracks down his cheeks as he stood with his hand on Bull's back.

"C'mon Bull, we have more ta do," he said gruffly, rubbing at his eyes with a rough and bloodied hand. "There's nothin' we can do for Bree now and she wouldn't want us ta give up before the children are safe."

Bull nodded and climbed wearily to his feet. The look in his eyes made even the savage Dwarves shy away from him. Granite almost pitied the next enemy soldier who crossed their path.

They abandoned all thought of stealth as Granite led Bull and a force of nearly three hundred Dwarves toward the mines where more Dwarves waited for freedom. Speed was of the essence now. They had to free as many Dwarves as they could before word of the rebellion spread and the enemy carried out their threat to kill the captive children. Any troops they encountered along the way were quickly defeated, most simply mowed down by the charging Giant, wielding his sword without thought for his own safety as if his reason had fled. Granite hoped his single-mindedness would not be his undoing as they neared the mines and the next major battle for Stonehaven. Many Orcs fled for the mines when faced with the raging Giant and the horde of Dwarves pelting along behind him. The number of their enemies within the mines was increasing. There was no thought of a surprise attack now. The Orcs and Goblins would be prepared to meet them head-on.

Granite tried to stop Bull before they turned the last corner, but his efforts were of little use. Granite resigned himself to the dangerous and direct course the Giant had chosen, staying close to Bull's side as they burst through the mine entrance without pause, running head on into a force of Goblins massed to bar their entrance.

Fortunately, the Orcs had chosen to stay back from the doors, sending the more expendable Goblins to serve as fodder for the initial attack. The Goblins were well armed, but not well disciplined. Granite gave a brief prayer of thanks as half of the Goblins broke and ran in the face of such a large force rushing headlong at them, led by the huge Giant. They gained the entrance to the mines without incurring as many casualties as Granite feared and Bull was fighting on with no more than a few minor wounds from his foolhardy charge. Granite feared the Giant might run right off the edge of the huge pit formed by the mining of ore and gems from the bowels of Stonehaven. With Granite's help, he did succeed in driving a good number of Goblins over the edge before him.

Granite watched as the Dwarves, laboring in the pit below, wielding picks or shovels or dragging carts of ore up the many ramps that criss-crossed its vertical sides, stopped to stare upwards as Goblins and Orcs began to rain down from the entrance level above. A great shout arose from the depths as the Dwarves turned their tools against their guards.

Bull and Granite and the Dwarves from the forge fought their way through the Orc forces and down the side of the pit, the Dwarves below them disarming the dead thrown from upper levels, discarding tools in favor of more traditional weapons. The battle for the mines was even more savage than the previous one, but when all was over, the Dwarves were victorious and few of the enemy escaped with their lives. They held no hope their victory would go undetected or unpunished for long. Granite, now accepted by all as their leader, stood before the cheering Dwarves in the very depths of the mine, and with a shout, brought them to an uneasy silence. He broke them into groups of fifty or so and sent them out to find their missing children. Soon, he and Bull were alone outside the entrance to the mine, wearily sitting against the wall, side by side, silently contemplating the task left to them.

"We hafta find Thorny and Chess and Althus now," said Granite. "We hafta tell them about Bree." He paused for a moment to steady himself. "Maybe they've freed the Wizard by now."

"Yes," said Bull rubbing his hand across his face, calmer now that their battle was ended. "I almost wish we had another battle facing us. It will be a difficult thing to tell them. I would put it off if I could."

Smiling sadly at Granite, the dark Giant rose, offering his hand to help the weary Dwarf to his feet. They ran in the direction of the deepest pit to join the rest of the original company, now missing a member very dear to them.

## Chapter Twenty

## EUWYN

Mica soon led Althus and the Elves to the deepest pit of Stonehaven. Putting a finger to his lips, Chess went ahead of them, neatly dispatching the lone guard at the door before the Orc could make a sound. Althus marveled at how deadly the deceptively mild Elf could be. Thorny dispatched a Goblin who had the misfortune to be standing just inside the entrance with equal skill and they were inside. Althus shivered even though the room was warm, heated by the inner fires of the mountain. Mica directed his gaze to the very center of the pit's floor where a lone figure knelt before a round gemstone the size of a Giant's fist. No other guards were present. Althus feared no guards were needed.

"Tis a played-out mine," Mica informed them as they gazed in amazement at the huge excavation before them. "No one comes here. I dunno what made me come. I jest wanted some time alone ta think, I 'spose. When I got here, there he wuz pacin about there on the floor of the mine. Not as bad off as he is now, but not in his right mind, either.

"I think the stone knows him fer its enemy. I went too close once. Sneaked down there, I did. I never knew it could defend itself like that. It was as if Euwyn was makin' it angry. It didn't want me near to it, I kin tell ya that.

"I kin get ya down there safely, Althus. I know the way, but I'd be wary of the stone if'n I was you. Don't get too close to it. I'll go to him with ya. He kinda knows me in a way although we never spoke. He looked at me once. Thot I saw a glimmer of somethin sane there once upon a time."

Mica looked at the figure below. He shrugged and looked back at Althus. "Mebbe not," he said. "There ain't no other way in or out. If we're caught down there, If we can't get back the way we came, we're done fer. We need the Elves ta guard the door."

"We will see that your escape route remains open, Althus," said Thorny. "Take care down there. If you give Euwyn back his staff and he still remains as he is, he might be capable of anything."

"In my nightmares, my greatest fear is that I might have to kill him. I guess it would be more likely he would kill me," said Althus. "It seems funny somehow that possibility did not cross my mind. Whatever happens, I wish I could find the words to tell you how much your friendship has meant to me. If I do not leave this pit alive, remember I came to think of you as brothers."

No more words passed between them. Chess and Thorny each embraced him briefly before Mica led Althus down the rough stairs that took them to the bottom of the pit. When they were safely down, Althus turned to Mica.

"I want you to stay here and guard these stairs, Mica. Do not come any closer," he said.

Mica began to protest and then thought better of it, promising not to move from where he stood.

Althus started across the floor of the mine towards the figure bathed in the sickly greenish light cast by the stone. If the robed and hooded figure kneeling before it was Euwyn, there was no evidence of the Wizard's former power. He sat rocking back and forth, softly singing snatches of the old lullaby Althus had sung to Bull's children on a night that seemed ages ago, the night before they entered the Orcs' mountain lair.

Althus grasped Euwyn's staff tightly for courage. It gave a faint vibration in response as he crossed the floor of the pit to stand just outside of the pool of light. Althus studied the figure kneeling before him, as afraid to find it was Euwyn as he was to find it was not.

The figure slowly raised its face to him from under its concealing hood and Althus' courage nearly left him. The sight made his heart lurch uncomfortably in his chest. It was Euwyn, or what was left of him. The dark eyes Althus knew so well stared wildly in his direction, as if looking through him at some horror taking place behind him. Euwyn was always slender, but the face he beheld was skeletal. The singing and rocking ceased, and Althus thought he saw a look of recognition fleetingly cross the Wizard's face. He steeled himself for what might come and stepped into the pool of light to offer Euwyn his staff. The force of the stone hit him like a sword through his heart. Emotions whirled about him like vultures circling a kill, no single emotion settling in his mind for any length of time. He felt fear of Euwyn overwhelm him and then anger that the Wizard had left him behind in Anduin. Shame seemed to settle in his mind like a carrion bird and began to feast on him. He heard Gilden's voice calling him a bastard. Bree mocked him for thinking she could care for one such as him. Euwyn's voice shrieked at him that he had come too late.

Through the physical pain that accompanied his mental anguish, he barely felt Euwyn tear the staff from his grasp. With his mind reeling, he did not see the Wizard swing the heavy staff at his head. His knees buckled just in time to avoid a blow that would have certainly killed him. The hold of the stone loosened and he was able to dodge the second swing more easily. Euwyn was obviously weak, but was he still there? Was part of him fighting on Althus' behalf, wrestling with the stone's focus? Althus' nightmare flashed through his brain. Euwyn appeared mad beyond redemption. Was the dream meant to warn him Euwyn still lived on in the ravaged creature that sought to kill him or was it a warning to stay away? Althus began to inch his way out of the pool of light surrounding the stone, hoping to lure Euwyn after him, gasping for air, as the horror of Euwyn's state and the emotions awakened by the stone threatened to defeat him. He reeled backwards, stumbling over the roughly hewn floor of the pit. He stumbled again, avoiding one of the Wizards wild swings. Suddenly, he was lying on the floor, stones digging into his back, Euwyn's staff pointed at his heart. Althus knew the Wizard had recovered enough to kill him with his magic, concentrated through the ebony staff. Althus could not bring himself to draw his sword against Euwyn. It would do him no good in any case.

They had passed out of the circle of light thrown by the stone, but the Wizard's face still held no sign of recognition. Althus could hear the Wizard's power building with a low hum as he continued to point the staff at his heart. He prepared himself for death. The word "father" escaped his lips more as a farewell than as a plea for mercy, uttered in sadness, a barely audible whisper, but it stirred something in the Wizard's face. His eyes shifted from their mad stare to a look of confusion and back again.

Althus saw the blue fire dance about the Wizard's hand and down the staff where it crackled in protest as if begging for release. Still, Euwyn hesitated, shifting his grip on the staff, a look of recognition lighting his face and then, a look of horror. The Wizard shifted his grip on the staff again, more surely, causing Althus to cover his face with his arm in apprehension. Above the hammering of his own heart, he heard the staff crackle as it arced through the air above him. He rolled into a defensive ball, his hands over his head, tensed for the final blow. "Father!" he cried in desperation.

He heard the staff connect with something, astonished to find himself still drawing breath. He opened his eyes to find Euwyn had knocked the stone to the floor and had just finished dropping his tattered cloak over it. When that was accomplished, he dropped to his knees at Althus' side and pulled him into his arms. Euwyn felt so insubstantial pressed against him Althus feared the Wizard's bones would crumble when he returned his embrace.

"By the Creator, Althus, it is truly you. You should not have come here, my son. I could have killed you. I have not injured you, have I?"

Euwyn held him at arm's length and looked him over anxiously while Althus smiled with relief. Euwyn then embraced him again so tightly Althus feared his own ribs would crack. He was too overjoyed to hear his father's voice and see his face again to care. They held each other at arm's length again and Euwyn laughed at him, shaking his head in wonder.

"Evidently you have left the Anduin guard for the service of Gilden's Elven patrol since I last saw you."

"Well, father," Althus said, climbing to his feet and helping Euwyn to his. "I left the uniform of Anduin in the Dark Forest when the Orcs filled it with holes."

Euwyn opened his mouth as if to say something and then held Althus close again, sighing deeply. "I suppose you have been through many perils on your way to find me, but we must leave this place before you tell me of them."

Althus was surprised to find Mica standing close by, having left his place by the foot of the stairs.

"My young friend!" cried Euwyn. "The Orcs did not kill you as I feared they would."

"No, sir," chirped Mica grinning as if his face would split. "Althus saved me."

Euwyn laid a hand on the Dwarf's head. "You were very lucky, then and I am indebted to you for the food you left me. I would have been dead of hunger if not for you."

Mica's grin grew even wider as he stood looking up at Althus and Euwyn.

"How do we destroy the stone, father?" asked Althus as they stood looking to where the stone lay, still covered by Euwyn's Elven cloak.

"We cannot destroy the stone yet, Althus. We must carry it to Anduin if we are to free the king from its influence," said Euwyn. "But I would dearly like my cloak back. It was a gift from Gilden when I lived with his family years ago."

Althus smiled, remembering the story behind Euwyn's time with the Elves. He had learned much about his father as well as the Elves in the past few days. He had much to tell Euwyn when they were safely out of the mountain.

"Here, sir," Mica said, offering the leaden box to Euwyn. "This box might hold the stone safely."

"Clever young man," Euwyn remarked to Althus. "Perhaps you should ask him to stay at your side. We will need all the good help we can find in the days ahead."

Mica blushed mightily. He bent to scoop the stone into the box from beneath Euwyn's cloak and stood to present it to the Wizard. Euwyn took the box and sealed it shut magically, handing it back to Mica when he was finished.

"You seem less affected by the stone than most, Mica. Would you carry it for us?" Euwyn asked.

"Yessir!" Mica said, proudly taking charge of the dangerous item.

The ascent from the pit seemed difficult for Euwyn. He stumbled often, leaning heavily on Mica and Althus when the way was broad enough. Althus was disturbed to see Euwyn so vulnerable. He was always possessed of a sinewy strength and grace Althus envied. It seemed wrong to find he was the stronger of them now.

Euwyn was astonished to find Chess and Thorny helping him up the last leg of his climb, greeting them with obvious delight. They waited a moment while the Wizard caught his breath and then followed Mica who led them quickly toward the area where their friends fought to free the Dwarves.

"You had us fearing for Althus' life for a while, Euwyn," said Chess. "I guess Thorny was right, though. He said you had to work it out between you and would not allow me to interfere. Thorny said you would never harm Althus."

"I would like to think he was right, Chess," Euwyn said softly. "I am more thankful than I can say I did not."

"Bree has become very fond of him," said Thorny. "I would hate to return to her without him."

"Bree is here also?" asked Euwyn. "I would like to set my eyes on the lovely Bree once again. Where is she?"

"We separated from Bree and Bull and Granite. They set out to free the Dwarves working at the forges and in the mines," Althus said. Euwyn did not miss the worry in his son's voice or the reverent way he spoke Bree's name.

Euwyn smiled, shaking his head in wonder as they hurried off to discover the fate of the rest of their company. He had been snatched from despair so abruptly he was not altogether sure it was not another trick of the stone that held him prisoner. Althus seemed real enough. Chess and Thorny's hands were warm against his arms as they supported him from either side. He could not read them as they could read him, but they seemed real. The improbability of it all lent a surreal quality to their flight through the halls of Stonehaven. Euwyn decided to enjoy the sensation, trying not to test the reality of it too deeply.

Mica led them upward once again, toward the forge room and the mines where they hoped to join Bree, Bull and Granite in their quest to liberate the Dwarves. The first group they met was composed of Dwarves armed with axes and pilfered swords. They detained them long enough to learn they had liberated the forge and the mines and troops of freed Dwarves were searching even now for their children and any Orcs unfortunate enough to remain within the halls of Stonehaven. They were a grim looking group, worried for their missing children and gaunt from years of toil and captivity. Althus and the Elves did not wish to delay them longer, but the looks of dismay on their faces when they asked them if their friends were somewhere behind them gave Althus a feeling of foreboding he could not dispel no matter how he tried. They met Bull and Granite not long after, headed toward them, weapons drawn, walking side by side with haggard faces.

Althus' smile of recognition faded from his face as he noted Bree's absence and Bull's tear streaked face. Granite, rubbing his reddened eyes with a filthy sleeve, was finding it difficult to keep his voice steady as he tried to tell them what had happened to Bree.

Bull was sobbing now, his huge hands covering his face as he repeated over and over, "I'm sorry, I'm sorry..."

"There was nothin we could do fer her," Granite growled. "It all happened so fast and we was too far away. She fell into the burnin' pit. She was a good fighter. There was nothin' we could do." His voice trailed off as he looked helplessly at Bree's brothers and then at the grieving Giant.

Althus found himself supported by Euwyn who wore a strange look on his gaunt face as if bewildered by the scene unfolding before him. Concern for his father's mental state gave Althus the strength to stay on his feet. Chess startled everyone by viciously swinging his sword to strike the wall, showering them with a hail of sparks and then turning away to stare at nothing. Thorny moved to comfort the Giant, assuring him it was not his fault as tears coursed silently down his own cheeks.

"Bree was always one to step into dangerous situations, Bull," said Thorny softly, his voice clear to all who now grieved for the fallen Elf. "She risked her life willingly and you know she would want us to finish what we started here. Come on, Bull. We cannot tarry here another moment. Let us make sure the children are safe. Perhaps they have been found by now and we can leave this hellish place."

The look Althus saw cross his face as he turned away and motioned them to follow, striding back the way they came made him realize Thorny was not as calm and accepting of Bree's death as he would have them believe. Althus looked back toward the forge room, hesitating to leave without some final sign of Bree, but the Wizard whispered enigmatically as if as much to himself as to Althus, "She is not there."

Althus was not sure what his father meant. Was there no trace left of her? Did he mean she had gone to be with the Creator? Althus, stricken by her death, did not ask. Chess walked by their side looking ahead, a look on his face Althus could not bear to see. He turned to look back at Bull and Granite walking behind and saw that Mica had rejoined his father. Granite walked with his arm about his son's shoulders as Mica quietly related their experiences in the deep pit where they had rescued Euwyn.

Althus took some comfort in their good fortune. They, at least, could still survive this day and live in freedom once again within their mountain. He hoped they would restore it to its former splendor and remember Bree who gave her life so they might be free.

## Chapter Twenty-one

## THE CHILDREN

Captain Manton stepped out of the spring sunlight into the cool, dimly lit interior of the stables where he was to meet Gilden and Rowan. His eyes adjusted slowly to the relative dark within, but he soon spotted the father and son together beyond Rowan's iron gray stallion standing patiently in the aisle. A brush lay abandoned on the cobbled floor. This seemed unusual to Captain Manton when the box in which it was usually kept sat atop a bench within easy reach of anyone working in the aisle. He had never seen the Elves so careless with their possessions, even those as humble as a curry. He stepped past the sturdy horse and found Gilden facing his son, holding him by the shoulders, a look of deep concern on his face. Rowan was biting his lower lip as if in pain, his head thrown back and his eyes tightly shut.

"Is it Bree?" Gilden asked, worry evident in his voice. Rowan merely nodded, taking a shaky breath as if to steady himself.

The Captain stood close by, uncertain whether to interrupt, waiting for the Elves to notice him there. Gilden glanced at him, nodding in acknowledgment of his presence, his attention returning immediately to his son. Rowan soon opened his eyes and stared at his hands, his expression changing from intense pain to a worried frown. There were tears in his eyes. The Captain wondered if they were tears of pain or of grief or both.

"Can you tell me anything more than what you felt?" Gilden asked. "What is happening to her?"

"I think she has been badly burned, father. More than that, I cannot tell you. I wish I could."

Captain Manton could see that Rowan was badly shaken.

Gilden turned to him while Rowan retrieved the dropped brush and returned it to the box where it belonged. "Children," he said. "Twins. They feel each other's pain, especially when they are in danger. It is a wonder to me they do not drive me mad with worry."

The Captain did not know what to say in the face of such an amazing and horrifying thing. To know one's child was in danger in some far-off land and yet be unable to help them must be a great burden. It made him think of his son, Tristan, sent off to watch their borders for the forces that threatened them. He wished he could put his arms about his son once more before the evil forces stood at their gates. At least he could hope the greatest danger Tristan faced was a night out in the cold, sleeping on hard ground.

"I have a message from Bree that concerns us all, Captain," Gilden continued, dismissing his troubles for the time being. "They entered the mountain stronghold of Stonehaven this morning, if all went according to plan. Of even more concern to the people of Anduin, she sends word they observed a great army, consisting of some three thousand Orcs and Goblins and various other foul creatures, leaving the main gates of Stonehaven last evening, heading for the Craglith pass. My people will delay them as long as possible, but my small army of Elves will not be able to delay a force of that size for long, if they dare enter the Dark Wood at all. Your men will probably sight them as they cross our mutual borders. By then, I will also have word of their passage through our lands. With luck, your patrol will be back in time to assist us in the gathering of the outlying families of Anduin. Before the king is aware of what we have done, the enemy will be at our gates. It will be too late for King Allan or Borgas to turn them back out from the safety of the walls then. I wanted to keep you informed, as I have informed the queen of what I know, so you would be prepared to feed and house your people as the time draws near.

"How do you know all of this?" asked Manton. "Do Bree and her brother communicate words as well as pain to each other? That is truly amazing."

"They do communicate in a way that is unusual, even for our people," said Gilden. He turned to Rowan who produced an amazing imitation of a hawk's cry. A small sparrow hawk appeared, as if out of nowhere, to light on Rowan's shoulder. "This small hawk is their link. They send messages to each other through him."

Φ       Φ       Φ

Bree was unsure whether to count herself lucky or unlucky. Her light weight and the intense updraft from the heat of the boiling lava below had blown her against the wall of the pit, her slide downward towards the molten lava below halted by a narrow, protruding ledge. She was not sure whether her fate was any better than that of the Orc who had perished the instant he hit the boiling lava below. A quick death might have been preferable to being broiled alive by the intense heat as she clung desperately to the wall of the pit. Her Elven cloak and her clothing would protect her temporarily from the heat, but her hands were burned by the hot rocks of the wall, her vision seared by the heat and light. Through her tearing eyes, she thought she could see a crack in the wall to her left and she gingerly edged her way to it. It was wide enough for her to wriggle into, affording her some relief from the heat, but where could she go from there? She could not climb the wall in the intense heat even if her injured hands would allow it.

Her only chance was the crack. She wriggled farther into it and found to her relief that, rather than narrowing, it began to widen considerably, running some distance into the rock wall. Still blinded by the heat of the pit, she inched her way along the left wall brushing against it with her shoulder, using the hot air at her back to direct her as she moved in total darkness. She paused once to hold her hands before her face, relieved to see them glowing faintly before her, giving her hope she would soon recover her sight.

She encountered a wooden door with a barred window at the end of her journey. She could see light filtering through the window, but the door was locked.

She sank to the floor to rest and contemplate her predicament, leaping to her feet again at a sound that set her heart beating in fear. There was a shuffling in the room nearby. With her sight returning, she could see countless large eyes staring directly at her through the darkness. She stood in near panic for what seemed an eternity, not daring to move, but knowing whatever inhabited the room could probably see her very clearly in the dim rock light that existed everywhere in the Dwarves' domain. The next sound that reached her ears allowed her to relax considerably. She heard plainly the sound of a child crying and others trying to quiet him. She sat against the door once more in an attempt to look less threatening, waiting for one of them to make the first move. She hoped the increasing volume of the child's crying would not bring the guards before she had their escape organized. She would escape this place somehow and she would not leave the children behind.

She waited for what seemed like an eternity during which her eyesight returned enough for her to see the children. They appeared very young, the youngest about four years of age and the oldest only nine or ten. She realized most of these children had probably spent the last years of their lives as captives in this crude cell. As they grew, they would replace those who became ill or injured in the forges and mines of Stonehaven. They would be the next generation of slaves who worked to provide weapons and armor for the Dark Lord's army. They were too young yet to work effectively, but made the perfect hostages. She remembered Granite saying their children were their greatest treasure.

It was not long before curiosity overcame one of the older children. She approached Bree cautiously, standing within an arm's length of her, staring intently into her face.

Bree stared back at the bedraggled little figure. It was impossible to determine the color of the tangled curls that fell nearly to the child's knees. She was covered in filth from head to toe. Only the color of her eyes was still discernible. They reminded Bree of Mica's emerald green eyes.

"My name is Bree. What is your name?" asked Bree softly, hoping her voice would not send the little Dwarf back to the safety of the group huddling at the rear of the cell.

"Opal. Me name's Opal," replied the child. "Are ye a magic fairy, Bree?"

"No," replied Bree, "I am just an Elf, but I have come to set you and the others free from this place."

The excited murmurs that followed made Bree hope desperately she could keep her promise. The rest of the children, encouraged by Opal's example, soon clustered about her, touching her hair and her face in wonder and inspecting her as if she were the most exciting thing they had ever encountered. Bree realized with great sadness that she was probably the only adult other than an Orc or Goblin they had encountered in years. It was a testament to the strength of their race so many still survived.

There had to be at least fifty children living in the rough cell. They all looked as if their captors fed them barely enough to keep them alive. Their faces should have been round and full, but their cheeks were hollow, their eyes dull in the dim light.

Bree moved to sit in the center of the cell, facing the door. She readied her bow with her injured hands, hoping she could aim with enough accuracy and fit enough arrows to kill the enemies she knew would soon come. The battle in the forge room and the battle she hoped had been fought successfully without her in the mines would bring the Orcs to kill the Dwarves' children soon enough. Even so, it seemed an eternity before she heard angry shouts from the other side of the door and the turning of a key in the lock. She stood to meet the Orcs head-on.

She felled the first Orc that came through the door with an arrow through its eye. She managed to fit another arrow, taking the second Orc through its throat. By the time she fit the third arrow, her hands were bleeding badly and the bowstring slipped from her hand before she had pulled it back entirely or aimed it properly. The third arrow buried itself shallowly in the third Orc's chest. Before she could slip past him, the Orc had his hands about her neck and was slowly choking the life from her. She could not take her eyes from his face, grinning evilly, inches from her own as her life slipped slowly away. She was barely conscious enough to see his expression change from one of intense pleasure to one of total surprise, but his hands slid from her throat and she found herself on her hands and knees. The Orc had fallen backward through the door, his companion's blade thrust upwards through his heart. Opal stood by her patting her gently on the back.

"I kilt him fer ye, Bree. He can't hurt ye no more. When can we go away from here?"

Bree shuddered at the child's emotionless voice and climbed unsteadily to her feet.

"Now," she said. "We have to leave now."

She shepherded the children through the halls of Stonehaven, choosing the ways that seemed to lead downward, hoping to find her companions or a group of freed Dwarves before they met any more Orcs. She could do little to save the children now. Her hands were nearly useless. She left droplets of blood behind her as she pushed her small charges onward. It touched her to see the older children comforting the youngest, taking turns at carrying them on their shoulders. Opal traveled by her side, looking up at her silently from time to time as if for reassurance. Bree hoped her trust was not misplaced as she led them in what she guessed might be the right direction.

Her keen hearing soon detected the sounds of pursuit. Amid the sounds of the booted footsteps of the Orcs and the slapping of goblin feet, she heard something that made her drive the children on as quickly as she dared. A howling reached her ears, echoing eerily through the halls of Stonehaven.

They were hunted.

She frantically sought a means of defense that would give them some hope of reaching the Dwarves before the beasts overtook them.

She had encountered the wolf-like beasts before, during their journey to the mountains. She would attempt to use her bow to slow their attack, but her aim would be shaky at best without the full use of her hands. Could she buy the children enough time to escape? Surely, the free Dwarves would be scouring the passages and halls of Stonehaven for their missing children by now. She prayed they would find them in time when she had to send them on without her. She readied her bow as they ran, knowing the blood from her hands would make it difficult to draw without it slipping through her fingers. When the sounds of pursuit drew nearer and she feared they would soon be within sight of the wolf creatures, she sent the children running down a side passage. They needed little urging, the hideous howling of the beasts driving them onward as fast as their feet could carry them. Bree slowed momentarily, hoping to draw the beasts after her by allowing them to catch sight of her. The sight of her and the scent of fresh blood dripping from the tips of her fingers would send them after her and buy the children time to escape.

She could smell their foulness long before she could see them. A mixed troop of Orcs and Goblins accompanied them, but she could not be certain of how many, as the huge wolves blocked most of them from sight. Their hideous cries became a deafening roar as they caught sight of her, their gaping jaws lined with an impossible number of razor sharp fangs. She turned and ran, hoping none would turn aside to pursue the children, lost from sight down the curving side corridor. She stopped once to shoot an arrow into their midst, but her aim was not true and it only enraged them further. She ran straight on for as long as she could, putting as much distance between them and the children as possible before she began to turn down side passages in a vain attempt to lose the pursuing beasts. She dared not look behind her.

Without the children to slow her, she could almost match her pursuers in speed, but she could not run forever. They were close enough now she could feel their hot breath at her heels. She awkwardly fitted another arrow to her bow, preparing to make a last, desperate stand.

## Chapter Twenty-two

## THE FINAL BATTLE

Althus, Euwyn and company soon encountered one of the searching bands of Dwarves. The Dwarves gathered about Granite and Mica, their faces haggard in the pale light. The desperation on their faces was echoed in their voices.

"Where could they be holdin 'em, Granite? They'll kill em before we kin search all o Stonehaven," one fierce-looking Dwarf said.

"We'll hafta get ourselves organized," Granite answered. "We'll search all the most likely places until we find 'em. I dunno what else we kin do. Me friends and I will go to the lower levels. Shale, you take yer group ta the great council chamber and search from there up ta the forge level. We can't stop lookin fer 'em jest because there's lotsa places ta search. We might get lucky."

Granite's words seemed prophetic when the children came pelting headlong down the passageway, barreling into the arms of the astonished Dwarves before the echo of his words died.

They were all speaking breathlessly, laughing and crying all at once. There was a spontaneous melee as adults and children sorted themselves into fathers and sons, mothers and daughters. The result was total chaos.

Althus stood pressed against the wall. He wondered what miracle had freed the children, wishing with all his heavy heart that Bree could have been here to see them united with their parents. He knew that some children would not find their parents alive and some would not find their children among those that had survived their long captivity. Tears slid unheeded down his face.

He found one tiny child pulling at his sleeve, looking up at him with an earnest little face.

"Sir? Sir, please," she said, begging him to hear her. Althus wiped the tears from his face and knelt down to speak to her above the tumult raging about them.

"What is it, little one?" he asked.

"Me name's Opal," she said. "I think somebody should go help the lady. The big wolves and the Orcs and Goblins was after her."

"What lady?" Althus asked, "Are there more Dwarves behind you?"

Althus was not prepared for the answer he received from the little Dwarf.

"The Elf lady, Bree, she's back there," she said, pointing back the way they had come. "She saved us from the fearsome wolves, but she's hurt bad and I'm afraid they'll eat her up."

Opal burst into tears as Althus gaped at her in disbelief. He stood there for only a split second before he was off down the passage, drawing his sword as he ran without a thought for his companions.

Mica, Granite, Chess, Thorny, Bull and Euwyn looked at one another in astonishment before sprinting after him, the Elves drawing their swords as well.

Althus trusted to his instincts for a time, knowing that if the wolves were in pursuit of her, he would not find Bree where the children parted from her, if she still lived, but probably somewhere beyond that point. He soon stopped at a meeting of four passageways, unsure of his direction, desperate to find Bree in time. He could not lose her again. He was not sure he could bear it. The others soon caught up with him. He found Euwyn at his side, the Wizard's hand grasping at his arm, preventing him from darting down another passageway.

"Hold a minute, Althus. Where are you bound?" he asked softly as if Althus might have taken leave of his senses.

"Bree," he gasped. "The child said Bree freed them and whatever pursued them still pursues her. We have to find her! We cannot lose her again!"

Euwyn understood his son's desperation, but his hand still held Althus where he stood. He did not have much strength left, but he knew Althus would not disobey him.

Bree's brothers, hearing that she might be alive were as desperate as Althus to find her. Bull, Granite and Mica, hearing the news, danced with impatience to be off.

"Wait!" Euwyn commanded, and this one word held them there while he drew a silver chain from beneath his ragged clothing. It bore a pendant on it, graven with the image of a small hawk. He held it in his hand, closed his eyes, and took a deep breath. When he opened them again, he started down the passageway to their left, beckoning for them to follow, his staff held before him and the pendant still clasped in his hand.

The company followed close at his heels.

Φ Φ Φ

Bree found herself in a large hall with a stone table at its center and there she chose to make a stand against the evil forces at her heels. She leapt upon the table, drawing her bow as best she could, shooting arrows into the pursuing horde. With luck, she hoped to thin their ranks before they caught and killed her.

The Orcs and Goblins stood back, letting the wolves have their fun, watching in anticipation, feral grins pasted on their ugly faces. The wolves circled the table, drooling in anticipation. They soon closed in too near for her bow. Bree used her remaining arrows to stab at them, the touch of the

Elf-crafted arrows burning the evil creatures and driving them back temporarily. She watched as they gathered again for a concerted attack.

She felt the hawk pendant that always hung about her neck, Euwyn's parting gift to her many years ago, grow cold against her skin. She wondered what that might mean, but she had no time for puzzles now. She wearily prepared herself for their final charge, kneeling atop the stone table, shuddering as she realized it was a table meant to hold the dead while they lay in state before burial. She lowered her gaze to the stone surface, unwilling to look into the jaws of the beasts as they closed about her.

A surprised yelp made her raise her eyes just in time to see the beast closest to her fall to the floor, writhing in agony. Bull stood behind the unwary Orcs, his sling in his hand and a look at once joyful and fierce on his dark face. She turned at the sound of another wolf in agony to find Althus, bow in hand, standing a few paces to the right of Bull. Euwyn's staff lit the room with a bolt of blue fire and the remaining beasts lay dead about the stone table, a putrid smoke rising from their rank carcasses. Thorny and Chess were already wielding their blades, easily outmaneuvering the clumsy Orcs, dealing out death with every thrust of their swords. With Bree's immediate danger averted, Althus and Bull drew their swords as well, joining Mica with his sword and Granite wielding his huge battleaxe.

Althus was an amazing swordsman, even with his own heavy broadsword, but with the sword of Anduin in his hands, he was every bit as deadly as the Elves. The few remaining Orcs and Goblins did not stand a chance against their combined force and Althus, Chess, and Thorny in turn were soon embracing Bree amid the carnage as she sat on the edge of the stone table. Althus was the first to notice her ravaged hands. He stood before her, gently holding her hands in his, palms upward, examining them carefully. Bree leaned her forehead on his shoulder, and drew a shuddering breath. He could not say whether he wept with joy at seeing her alive or with distress at her obvious pain.

Euwyn stepped in to take her hands from him, examining them closely as well, speaking softly to her alone. She kissed his cheek in greeting, but shook her head, trying to pull her hands away. He persisted, however, and in the end, she sat quietly while he held each blistered and torn hand in turn, moving his staff above them, chanting in the language Althus knew he reserved for his most powerful and difficult spells. The company stood close, guarding them while Euwyn worked. They looked on in wonder as Bree's hands became whole once more with only a faint pinkness to the skin remaining.

By the time Bree's healing was complete, Althus stood close behind the Wizard. When Euwyn collapsed, he caught him neatly and lowered him to the floor.

"Ye've done this before, Althus," Granite said.

Althus nodded, his eyes never leaving Euwyn's face as he knelt at his side, his fingers touching the pulse at the base of his neck. "He has very little strength left, but it is of no use to ask him to spare himself when someone is in need of healing, especially one he cares for as much as he cares for Bree," he said.

Bree knelt at Euwyn's side as well. "I tried to tell him I could wait. He would not listen," She sighed. "He is as stubborn as ever."

Euwyn was breathing evenly and his pulse was strong. Bull stepped in and scooped the Wizard up in his arms as easily as if he were a small child and stood ready to carry him wherever the company needed to go.

"Bull," said Thorny, "I think you should take Euwyn and Bree out of Stonehaven through the main gates and wait there while the rest of us make sure the Dwarves get their children out safely."

Bull looked at Euwyn resting in his arms and Bree standing at his side and reluctantly agreed with Thorny. He knew they would miss his strength as they traveled Stonehaven's dangerous ways, but he knew also they entrusted Bree and Euwyn's lives to his care and, to them, that was no small thing.

"Mica, you kin be their guide ta the main gates," said Granite, placing a rough hand on his son's shoulder. "We can't be sure there aren't any of the enemy lurking outside the gates and they may need you to protect 'em."

Mica was ready to protest at having to leave the battle before it was finished, but his father's final words made him realize he might be of more use at the Giant's side than within the mountain stronghold.

Althus held Bree close and placed a hand on Euwyn's shoulder where he rested in Bull's arms. Chess and Thorny each embraced their sister before Mica led Bull toward the gates and Granite led Althus, Chess and Thorny deeper into Stonehaven.

Althus could not help but look back after his friends as Mica led them off, wondering if he would see them again. Bree was even more precious to him now that he had thought her lost to him, and he could barely think of losing Euwyn again after struggling so hard to free him. He glanced at Thorny and Chess and from their grim faces, he knew they were feeling the same. Many Dwarves lay dead in the forge and mines of their home, having given their lives so their people could live in freedom. They could not let the children be recaptured or the fortress be retaken no matter what the cost.

Althus gripped the Sword of Anduin resolutely as Granite led them back in the direction thry had come, seeking to rejoin the children of Stonehaven and their Dwarf escort. They found them safely making their way toward them, on their way to the gates and escape from the mountain. Another company of Dwarves, moving in the same direction, trying to keep ahead of a company of Orcs and seeking a place to set up an ambush, had overtaken them. The joined company had taken the children on their shoulders, the second group temporarily abandoning their battle plans.

Thorny and Chess sent them onward, preparing to face the following band of Orcs and buy them the time they needed. The Dwarves not burdened with a child stayed behind to stand with them.

Althus and the small band of Elves and Dwarves positioned themselves as best they could in a corner of the dimly lit corridors and soon engaged the pursuing company of Orcs. They were outnumbered by at least two to one by Althus' count, but the agility and skill of Thorny and Chess and the fierceness of the Dwarves and the fact that the much larger Orcs were hindered by the close quarters made up for their lack of numbers.

The company held their own and even seemed to be gaining the advantage until a mixed company of Orcs and Goblins emerged from a corridor behind them. They found themselves surrounded, greatly outnumbered, their company facing in two directions at once and fighting for their lives.

Thorny bore a deep gash in his thigh from an Orc sword he was too crowded by the fighting about him to dodge effectively. Chess' golden curls were stained with blood from a glancing blow he had taken above his left eye and the blood dripping from his wound was obstructing his sight. Althus tried not to worry about his companions, attempting to concentrate on the battle around him. His breath was coming in ragged gasps as he dodged Orc swords and Goblin clubs in an attempt to penetrate the enemy's defenses. He had killed more of the enemy than he cared to count and still they kept coming. He wondered how many more Orcs and Goblins could be left in Stonehaven. How many would they leave for the Dwarves to deal with when their dwindling company had drawn its last breath and the force they now battled overran them to fight on in the corridors of the mountain?

Althus noticed Granite and six of the Dwarves that had joined them were still standing, but hard-pressed. They did not have the protection of his Elven mail. Only their fierceness and their skill with their battle-axes kept them standing this long.

How long would Thorny and Chess hold out? They would probably be the last ones standing. Even wounded, they showed little signs of tiring. He was nearly exhausted and more than thankful he bore a light Elven sword instead of his heavy broadsword, and thankful for his light Elven mail, but even so, he could barely keep his head clear in the chaos that reigned about him. He was relying on pure instinct now to keep himself alive. He prayed Euwyn, Bree, Bull and Mica were safe from the dangers within the mountain and had not encountered any enemy forces beyond the gates. Althus thought longingly of the open sky and wished he could see it once more before he fell.

## Chapter Twenty-three

## PROPHECY

Mica led Bree and Bull, bearing the unconscious Euwyn, unerringly to the great gates of Stonehaven. They traveled in silence, worried about those left behind. Bree reached up to touch Euwyn often to be certain he rested quietly.

Upon reaching the gates, they stood in awe at the great statues flanking the opening, images of past Dwarf leaders, kings of the mountain stronghold, their great battle-axes resting at their feet. At least three times the height of the Giant, they glowed red in the sun lowering toward the western horizon.

Bree could not help but look back the way they had come and wish her brothers and Althus were standing by her side to see the Dwarves' handiwork and the open sky.

"Our brothers will need my help, Bree. I must go back," said Bull, laying Euwyn down gently in the grassy meadow beyond the gates. The Wizard did not stir. Bull brushed the tangled hair from the Wizard's lean face and stared down at him. "I will bring your son out of Stonehaven alive or die in the attempt, Euwyn. That is a promise I will keep, although you do not hear me make it."

He was turning back toward the gates when Eagle's cry drew his gaze upward. Another cry brought a smile to his dark face.

Liddy and three other Giants were descending from the mountainside.

It was only moments before Liddy flung herself into Bull's arms. The three Giants with her, armed with pitchforks, stood by grinning broadly while Liddy and Bull kissed fervently.

"I could not wait for you at home, Bull," said Liddy when they parted. "We saw the creatures at the base of the cliff and I was afraid for you. When I found my brothers returned from their journey, I left the children with sister Althea and persuaded them to come with me."

"Liddy, I am more glad than I can say to find you here."

He turned to Bree and Mica, "Did I not tell you she was the cleverest most beautiful wife ever?"

Bree smiled. "I never doubted it at all, Bull," she said.

Liddy introduced her brothers Gabriel, Apollo, and Gideon to Bree and Mica.

"I see you have found Euwyn and added a Dwarf to your company, Bull. Where are the rest?" she asked, concern showing in her dark eyes.

"We have added two Dwarves, Liddy, but one remains with Chess and Thorny and Althus. In fact, we have freed nearly all of the Dwarves, and their kinsmen will most likely be free before this day ends. If all goes well, some of them should soon be following us out of the mountain with their children. I am thankful your brothers have secured the gates for their escape," he said, turning to Liddy's brothers, "but I must enter Stonehaven once more to help Althus and the Elves to safety if I can. The halls of Stonehaven are still infested with Orcs and Goblins."

"Lead on," said Apollo. "We have lain in wait here long enough, slaying Orcs that tried to leave through these gates. We have been dragging them out of sight so our presence remains undetected, but it is slow work and we would enter Stonehaven to help you slay even more of them if Bree and Mica are willing to take our places here."

Bree and Mica readily agreed. Bull, smiling at the unexpected presence of Liddy's wild and roving brothers, motioned them to follow him. Before they had regained the gates of the mountain, the Dwarves, bearing the children on their shoulders, reached the entrance. They turned about as well, following the Giants into Stonehaven, leaving their children under Bree and Liddy's watchful eyes, heading back to where Althus and the Elves fought to cover their escape.

Φ        Φ        Φ

Althus found himself fighting with Thorny and Chess at his back, having lost sight of the fierce Dwarves moments before as the Orcs overwhelmed them. The strength of Chess and Thorny encouraged him to fight on, even though their efforts seemed hopeless in the face of the overwhelming number of Orcs left standing. Althus thought he heard Bull's voice through the clash of swords and axes and the cries of the Orcs. He hoped the Giant had not come alone to die needlessly in an attempt to reach them.

He fought on doggedly and again thought he heard more than one Giant voice and the voices of Dwarves and sounds of clashing axes as well. A spark of hope began to grow within him. He hoped Chess and Thorny heard as well.

The force of Orcs and Goblins standing between them and the gates appeared to be thinning. Moments later, Althus was startled to see a Goblin rise above the fray as if it had gained the ability to levitate. It was only when he noticed the tines of a pitchfork protruding from its chest that Althus caught sight of the Giant behind it. The Giants were tossing Orcs and Goblins over their shoulders with their pitchforks as if they were pitching hay to cattle. The ranks of the enemy left standing between Althus and the Giants and Dwarves thinned to nothing. Bull and his company continued forward, tearing into the force beyond Chess and Thorny without pause. They left Chess, Thorny, Althus, Granite and two other Dwarves, the only surviving Dwarves of the original six, to catch their breath and count themselves lucky to be alive.

The Giants and their company of Dwarves soon returned to report the enemy slain and the corridors secure as far as the eye could see. They all turned as one and headed wearily toward the main gates and the open sky.

Althus thought he had never seen a sunset so beautiful as Bree and Liddy, surrounded by the Dwarves' children, ran to greet them. He had not even the strength left to sheath his sword, embracing Bree with one arm as he held his sword in the other.

Bree led them all to where Liddy had made camp, hidden in a grove of trees at the base of the mountain. There, a small stream trickled down the sheer mountain wall into a pool below. It was not far from the entrance to Stonehaven, but hidden from the confusion at the main gates. She and Liddy sat them all down and washed and tended their wounds. Chess and Thorny's injuries would need careful tending, but Bree assured Althus they would soon heal. Althus had escaped relatively unscathed and Bull and the other Giants were similarly lucky. Euwyn still lay unmoving where Liddy had laid him on a soft pallet in the shelter of the tent they all shared.

"You *are* truly amazing, Liddy," said Bree. "How did you get all this over the mountains so quickly?"

"We used the hidden stairs and many hands to carry all of it here. All of the Giants gave anything they could spare," said Liddy. "Once it was delivered, most of the Giants returned to the valley to make sure it was defended, but my brothers and I stayed here to secure the gates. The appearance of the creatures lying slain at the base of the cliffs at the head of our valley gave the Giants something to think about. They finally realized they were not safe in their isolated valley and if no one came to the aid of the Dwarves, save Bull, what would come next if he failed? Certainly, the master of the Orcs and Goblins now knows of our existence and more trouble is sure to come our way unless we do something to stop it. Bull is the only giant truly trained in the use of a weapon. The Giants decided it was best to aid him in any way they could. It seems to me that for a small investment of supplies and a little effort, they have gained much in one short day. We Giants should be very grateful to all of you for risking your lives when most of us were unwilling to do so."

The Dwarves chose to remain nearer to the gates to await their kin who had yet to find their way out. The ever-resourceful Liddy had brought enough supplies for all. Her brothers distributed food and medicines among the grateful Dwarves while she and Bree made sure there were enough healers among them to tend their wounds.

Althus went to sit by Euwyn's side. The Wizard lay as still as death, his gaunt face ghostly pale against the dark hairs of his beard. Althus laid a hand on the Wizard's shoulder, relieved to see him open his eyes. Euwyn reached up to grasp Althus' hand studying him closely, his dark eyes questioning.

"Happy birthday, father," said Althus smiling down at him, overjoyed to see Euwyn smile in return.

"It was not all a dream, then. You are truly here beside me and I am free of that cursed stone. I cannot tell you how I have missed you and how good it is to feel the air move about me," he said, pausing to consider a moment before adding with look of amazement on his face, "Is it really my birthday? I would be five hundred years old. You have never forgotten my birthday since you were old enough to take note of such things."

A worried frown crossed his face as if a sudden doubt had struck him. "Where are Bree and Chess and Thorny?" he asked. "I do not see them here. Where are they?" he said, trying to rise.

Althus pushed him down, "All of our friends are well enough, considering. Your health concerns us now. You must rest."

Euwyn laughed, "I must be a sad sight, judging from the way you are looking at me."

"You are free and that is something to celebrate," Althus said. "The Dwarves are free as well."

Althus told him of the last battle in the corridors of Stonehaven and of their rescue by the Giants. "Many Dwarves died in the battle to liberate Stonehaven." he said when he had finished. "Still, the remaining Dwarves and their children are free to live their lives as they were meant to within their mountain stronghold."

"I should have been there to help them," Euwyn said. "I could have saved more of them."

"You are only one man, Euwyn. You cannot keep the entire world safe from harm. We should all be required to help ourselves at times. It was necessary Bree should be healed, but you must learn to trust us to take care of ourselves."

Euwyn was looking at him intensely now. "There is something you have not told me, Althus. Are Thorny and Chess badly injured?" he asked. "I could help them. I feel rested."

"You have not listened to one word I have said to you!" Althus cried in desperation.

Fortunately, the Elves arrived to reassure him before Althus was forced to physically restrain him.

Bree bent and kissed him on the cheek, "Happy Birthday, Euwyn," she said. "I see you have recovered enough to make Althus angry with you. Let me guess. You have decided you are well enough to care for the wounded."

Althus could not help but laugh, his anger forgotten. Euwyn held Bree's hands in his, examining them to make sure they were thoroughly healed.

Chess and Thorny stepped closer. They each wished him a happy birthday as well. Althus could see Euwyn inspecting them from head to toe, evaluating their wounds carefully even though they were invisible to Althus, Thorny's hidden by a clean pair of breeches and Chess' hidden by his thick, curly hair. Thorny walked with a slight limp and Chess seemed a little paler than usual. Althus knew Euwyn saw all of it, but he seemed satisfied they would heal without his assistance.

"I have called the horses, Althus." said Thorny. "They will join us tonight. As for you, Wizard, if you wish to ride with us tomorrow, you must rest and eat."

"Yes, you look terrible," said Chess. "I wonder if Mars will know you. You do not even smell like yourself."

"Chess!" Bree cried.

"He is right, Bree." Euwyn laughed. "I must bathe and make myself otherwise presentable so Mars will know me. I cannot greet my old friend looking like a wild man."

"You will rest and eat first," Thorny said. "The horses will have to leave the Giant's valley the way they came in and then follow the escarpment to reach us. They will not arrive for hours yet."

"Then," he said softly, "there is time to tell Althus things I have kept from him for far too long. Things I would have told him long ago, but for a promise I made to his mother."

Bree and Thorny turned as if they would leave them to speak to each other in private, dragging Chess with them.

"Please, stay and hear what I have to say," Euwyn begged as they turned away. "You have earned the right to know the truth and it concerns your people as well as Althus and the people of Anduin." The Elves returned to sit quietly while Euwyn told his tale.

Φ　　　　　　Φ　　　　　　Φ

Althus was suddenly afraid to hear what Euwyn had to say. How could the story of his birth concern the people of Anduin or the Elves of the Dark Forest? Why had Euwyn kept it secret for so long? Who was his mother and was she still alive? What had Euwyn promised her? His mouth felt dry as dust and his heart pounded in his chest. He still wanted what he had always wanted, to travel by the Wizard's side wherever he went and share whatever dangers he faced. Somehow, he was afraid what he was about to hear would change all that. It all seemed unimportant now, who he was or where he had come from, but he sat obediently at Euwyn's side as he began his tale.

"I do not doubt," he said, "that when you overhear people calling you a bastard, you believe what they say. They could not be more wrong, Althus. You are the son of King Allen and Queen Maris of Anduin."

Althus stood at Euwyn's surprising announcement, a look of doubt clouding his face.

"Father, the only prince of Anduin has been dead these many years. You are still confused by the strain of your captivity. Bree will give you something to make you sleep and we will talk in the morning when you are more yourself."

Euwyn shook his head. "Althus, you are the child everyone thinks died in infancy."

When Althus began to protest once more, Euwyn motioned impatiently for him to sit. "I will explain it all to you if you will sit down and listen to what I have to say."

The Elves drew closer as Euwyn began his tale once more.

"It all began with the appearance of the Wizard, Borgas, in Anduin. In those days, I was court Wizard, as you know. I must admit I was not the best court Wizard. I would not spend my days amusing the king and his court, but spent much of my time as I do now when in Anduin, traveling here and there, associating with commoners and leaving the amusement of the court to jesters and such. Borgas appeared as if out of thin air and soon wormed himself into the king's good graces. I must admit, I could have easily prevented it with a little more attentiveness to the court's wishes, but I found I did not really care for the job of court Wizard. The Creator did not give me the power to heal only to benefit those of royal blood.

"If I had foreseen the result of Borgas' installation in my place, I would have found a way to keep that position. It affected you, Althus, most deeply of all.

"The trouble began when it was announced the queen was with child. Had I suspected the power Borgas wielded over your father, King Allen, perhaps I could have prevented what transpired prior to your birth. By then, however, I had ceased to visit the castle entirely, having been relieved of my duties there and feeling my presence was more important elsewhere. When the queen realized what was happening and came to me for help, Borgas had already poisoned the king's mind against you."

Euwyn paused as a look of anger crossed his face. "I still cannot understand how a father could sentence his unborn son to death. It was a callous and incomprehensible act and totally out of character for the King Allen I knew. We had our differences, but I would never have expected such a cruel thing of him. I did not find out until recently how completely, and by what means, Borgas gained control of the king's mind. The King requested that Borgas make a prophecy regarding the unborn child, as tradition dictates. To the dismay of all, the prophecy stated this:

*'The firstborn son of Anduin will bring death to the kingdom.*
*The true ruler of Anduin will lie at his feet, slain by his hand.*
*He will stain the throne of Anduin with blood.*

*The dead will walk the halls of Anduin and come to rule at his side.'*

"Upon hearing this prophecy, the king sentenced you to death. Borgas created such a fear of you in his mind and heart he would not see you live even for the span of a single day. He would not even hear the pleading of Queen Maris, who once was dearer than life to him. She begged him to spare you until they could be sure of the prophecy. After all, how could an infant harm anyone? However, the king would not have Maris become attached to her ill-fated son. As if a mother, who carried a baby in her womb for even a day would not care for it as much if it were born or yet unborn.

"So, the queen came to me, desperate for any chance to save you. She begged me to do something, anything. I used a spell to make everyone but the queen believe you were dead, stillborn. I have such powers, although it pained me to use them. It made me feel as if I was no better than Borgas. Still, I had to save you somehow, and it seemed the only way. It was a dangerous spell to use on one as young as you were. Borgas was there at your birth. His intention was to kill you. I cast my spell, a spell that only made you appear dead, in a manner that shielded you from him. I prayed you would survive it. You were very ill for many days after. So ill, I could not give you up as quickly as I planned.

"The king was satisfied that you were stillborn, fooled into thinking you dead and buried. All I had to do to convince the king of your death was to convince Borgas of it and that was easy enough. He was present at your birth to make sure of it.

"The queen sent you to me by way of her nurse, Elinor, and, to be safe, I convinced her when you were safely in my arms that she had merely delivered a package of books, so even she could not reveal our secret. The queen and I alone knew you still lived and so it has been until now. Even you were not trusted with the knowledge of who you really were."

Here Euwyn paused to smile at Althus fondly. "You were such a dear child. I must admit I found the prospect of raising a child frightening to say the least. I did not intend to raise you myself, but you were so ill for the first few days I could not leave you in another's care. By the time you were well enough for me to find suitable parents, I had become very fond of you. It was foolish of me, but I decided to raise you myself. You survived my bumbling attempts at parenting and I am more proud of you than I can say. You have some Elven blood, you know, as your mother is half Elven. I am glad you have met Elves, so you can know something of the people whose blood runs in your veins."

"Ha!" cried Chess. "I knew you were part Elf! Did I not say you were?"

Bree shot him a look. Chess sat back once again, still looking very pleased with himself.

Althus sat silently, trying to make sense of Euwyn's story. It explained the queen's attentions, but how could the king, his father, sentence him to death before he even laid eyes on him? It was contrary to everything he felt a father should be. Everything Euwyn was to him.

"How could King Allen believe this prophecy? Why would he place more importance on the words of a man like Borgas than the life of his own son?" Althus asked. "My life would have been taken from me on this man's words alone?"

At the look Euwyn gave him, he fell silent.

"I saw the same prophecy when the queen asked me to look into your future," Euwyn said gently. "I kept it to myself, but I can no longer hide from you the things you have a right to know, Althus. The queen asked me to watch you carefully for any signs of anger or ambition that could bring you to murder your father, but I cannot see any treachery in you. I have never known any deception in you, even as a small child. Perhaps it is the Elven blood in you. Elven blood is more potent than that of other races. To be even one-quarter Elven as you are, makes you more Elf than Human. I do not think you are capable of deceit and I am proud of you for that more than any other thing. Still, the prophecy remains.

I would have told the king, had he cared for my opinion, that prophecy can be a dangerous business. It is always the truth wrapped in a shroud of things unsaid. We may hear the prophecy as it is given to us, but not see the true meaning of it. I have enough faith in you to know we cannot trust what this prophecy tells us. Do not trouble yourself over what it may seem to foretell. If it means what it seems to at first hearing, why would Borgas have been so eager to see you dead? Why would he want to prevent it from coming true? Certainly, the death of King Allen would be to his advantage. The people of Anduin would be unlikely to support an assassin upon the throne. I would not be surprised if they soon found Borgas ruling the kingdom if that came to pass."

"Father, it said the dead will walk the halls of Anduin and rule by the prince's side," Althus said quietly, unable to hide the shudder that ran through him. "What can that possibly mean?"

"I cannot tell you," Euwyn sighed, running his hands through his dark hair. It seems even more unlikely than the first part, but all may come to pass in time and I trust it will not happen as Borgas would have us believe."

Euwyn's assurances meant much to Althus, but he could not help worrying over what the prophecy seemed to foretell. If he did not return to Anduin, the prophecy could not come true, but his heart was with the people of his homeland and he could not stay away when he knew the danger they faced. He would have to risk fulfilling the chilling prophecy and return to Anduin to do what he could to save his kingdom. The thought made him pause. It was truly his kingdom if Euwyn's tale were true. The people who lived there were his people and as their prince he was sworn to protect them. By tradition, the prince of Anduin was commander of its army. He drew the Sword of Anduin and turned its blade to reflect the light, reading once more the words written on the shining blade.

"The Sword of Anduin," said Euwyn admiring the shining blade. "It is your sword and only you have the right to wield it, Althus. It has already served you well."

"I would like to tell Gilden how grateful I am for his wonderful blade," said Althus.

"You can tell him when we reach Anduin," said Bree. "He will be pleased to learn it has found its rightful owner."

"Speaking of reaching Anduin," said Euwyn. "Perhaps the horses will arrive soon and I would greet my old friend, wearing a little less filth and a little less hair."

Althus was reluctant to let Euwyn leave his bed, but was overruled by the stubborn Wizard, who insisted he was entirely well enough for a bath and a shave. He invited Althus to join him in the nearby pool. Bree and her brothers, having already washed away the grime of battle, went to search out Liddy and some fresh clothes for them.

Euwyn heated the icy pool of water to steaming with a word. He and Althus soaked for a time, letting the warmth ease their sore muscles. Althus was shocked to see how thin Euwyn had become, evidence of the ordeal the Wizard had endured in the last few weeks. Even as painfully thin as he had become, and even if he seemed a little less steady on his feet, his smile and the light in his dark eyes had returned. Washed and clean-shaven with his thick black mane of hair put in order, he looked more like the man Althus remembered as his father.

"Well, Althus," he said when they stood together beneath Liddy's tent, Althus in his Elven uniform and Euwyn in the clean breeches and shirt Liddy had produced by some miracle known only to her, "I have told you all I know of the events that brought you to me as a child. You have not told me what you are thinking. How do you feel about the things I have told you?"

"I am still turning these things about in my mind. I cannot quite see myself as the prince of Anduin and certainly not as its king. All I want now is what I have always had. My life seems destined to change whether I wish it or not, but I cannot ever think of King Allen as my father. He may have sired me, but you will always be my true father and that will not change. I realize the king may have been under Borgas' influence when he called for my death, and I may forgive him, in time. But, I cannot forget his actions. As for the prophecy, I will trust your judgment concerning such things. I have no wish to harm King Allen and no desire to sit on the throne of Anduin. I only wish to free Anduin from the evil that threatens its people and that I cannot do unless you and I return there."

Euwyn nodded in agreement.

"To Anduin, then, and let events unfold as they may. Together we will see what we can do for the people there. As for your future as prince of Anduin that, too, will wait until the fate of its people has been decided."

As they left Liddy's camp, Althus felt a great weight lifted from his shoulders. With Euwyn by his side, all things seemed possible. The Wizard's arm about his shoulders and deep voice in his ear helped him set aside, for a time, the daunting task that still lay before them. The sound of small creatures, chirping in the warm night air of late spring, filled the moonlit meadow as Chess, Thorny and Bree joined them in anticipation of the horses' arrival.

Liddy had sent her brother, Apollo, to gather the rest of their possessions and carry them to their camp by way of the secret stairs. She assured them Eagle would deliver a message to the Giants guarding the secret passage behind the waterfall. They would open the gates there and let the horses free. Althus was amazed to think Thorny could call the horses from such a distance.

"I do not have the focus of Rowan," admitted Thorny. "I cannot think of anyone that does. He is much better than I am at reaching a state of total concentration. As hard as I try, I cannot shut out the things that happen about me and so I cannot reach them from as far away. Still, I can usually reach them if they are close enough."

Bree came to stand next to Althus and eventually drew him apart from the others, leaving Thorny and Chess to speak with Euwyn. His hands sought hers as they stood facing each other, bathed in the light of the full moon. Mist, rising from the warm ground into the cooling air, swirled and eddied about their knees in the light breeze moving across the meadow.

He could not find the words he sought to tell her what she meant to him. If she was touching him, she knew what he was feeling, but he wished for the courage to put it into words. She smiled at him as he desperately tried to think of something to say, but the desire to kiss her sent his mind reeling. He knew he should not be here with her alone. He was weary beyond all reason and knew his resolve to keep her at arm's length was quickly fading. He took a deep breath, trying to steady his whirling thoughts, but her scent, drawn in with that breath, only made him want to kiss her even more. He was about to throw caution to the wind when he realized the sound of his heart beating in his chest was not the only sound throbbing through his head. They turned as one to see the horses, moonlight glancing off their glossy coats, pounding across the meadow.

Moon led the way, her gray coat shining in the moonlight like a beacon.

They ran close together, their manes and tails streaming in the wind of their passing, moving gracefully through the tall grass like water surging in a swift stream. The horses made an entire circuit of the meadow at full gallop before each sought their rider, rearing briefly on their hind legs before them in salutation and then each pressing their heads to their rider's chest in greeting.

Althus was overjoyed to see Gust before him, safe and sound. He rubbed his ears, speaking his name with affection. He could see Euwyn with his arms about Mars and Thorny and Chess greeting Ochre and Sand with the same show of affection. Moon and Bree were touching foreheads as Bree stroked the mare's face with both hands. Althus felt their company was now complete, thanking the Creator they had all survived the liberation of Stonehaven. He turned to rejoin the others, but Gust moved in front of him, barring his way. He gave Althus a hard shove with his nose, causing him to stumble into Bree. Their lips were so close. He took a deep breath and took her into his arms, pressing her against Moon's warm shoulder while he kissed her. She kissed him back just as passionately. He held her as long as he dared, standing in the mist-shrouded meadow, hidden by the horses.

"I thought I had lost you, Bree," he whispered into her hair. He found he was shaking and took another deep breath to steady himself. "What would I have done without you?"

"I almost lost you, too, Althus. But, we are both safe and we are together and everything is all right. That is all that matters. Euwyn is rescued and will soon recover completely as will Chess and Thorny." Gust chose that moment to stuff his head between them. Althus shoved him away, shaking his fist at him. "Enough of your interference, you scoundrel. What makes you think you know so much?" To which Gust merely snorted loudly and shook his head, undeterred by Althus' scolding.

"He has truly bonded with you if he can sense what you are thinking so easily," laughed Bree.

"I suppose any Elf, two legged or four could know what I feel if they tried. I feel it so deeply," Althus sighed. "I am so tongue-tied around you I can scarcely speak and when I speak I cannot seem to find the right words."

"Words are not necessary between us, Althus. I can sense what you are feeling now, even without touching you."

Althus shook his head in wonder as they moved on to join Euwyn and her brothers. What now? In a moment of weakness, he had done what he had been determined not to and now Bree could read him so completely he could never hide his feelings from her. What of Gilden and her brothers? Chess seemed to know, but seemed amused by it rather than angry. Did Thorny suspect? He sighed deeply, too exhausted to worry about it for the moment. They needed to find Bull and Liddy to thank them and they needed to find Granite and Mica as well to see if anything further was required of them before they left for Anduin.

## Chapter Twenty-four

## PARTING

Euwyn and the rest made their way to the area where the Dwarves were setting up a makeshift camp. Liddy and Bull and her brothers still moved among them, handing out supplies to those who needed them. Those who had the heart to re-enter the ruined halls of the underground kingdom carried out more supplies. The dead would be removed, those of the enemy as well as the Dwarves who had given their lives. Only then would all of the surviving Dwarves re-enter the halls of Stonehaven.

They found Granite and Mica in the middle of all, keeping order among their people as others handed out food and supplies. Another Dwarf, one Althus recognized as one of the three who survived the last fight was staying close to Granite's side.

Granite greeted them with a grin that nearly split his face in two, a grin that repeated itself on Mica's face as he caught sight of their approach. Mica's wide green eyes wandered over each of the horses in turn, his admiration and awe plain on his face.

Granite threw a brawny arm about the third Dwarf while he introduced them.

"This is me wife, Beryl," he said.

Althus had to make a conscious effort not to let his mouth hang open in astonishment. Beryl wore a beard like Granite's. Perhaps her beard was softer and curled more beautifully, but Althus could hardly separate her in appearance from the two males standing by her side.

"Yeah, this is me Mother," said Mica, tearing his gaze from the horses and smiling at Beryl with obvious pride.

Althus looked at the five hundred or so Dwarves settling in near the gates wondering how many women had fought and died by his side. He could not remember thinking any one Dwarf less fierce than another. Euwyn did not seem at all surprised to find Dwarf females so similar to their male counterparts, but he did comment on the addition of a plain gold band about Granite's forehead.

"Granite, are you the ruler of this kingdom?" he asked.

"Yeah, me dad was ruler when the Orcs took over. He was one of the first ta be tossed ta his death from where ya rescued me and Mica. Guess that makes me king now. The others seem ta think so."

Granite did not seem too impressed by his own title, but he was impressed when Chess informed him Althus was the real prince of Anduin and, most important to Chess, had real Elven blood running through his veins. Althus was embarrassed to find his bloodlines of so much concern to others. He wondered why his heritage was so important to them. Chess and Thorny were princes in their own land and Bree certainly was a princess, if that was what one called the sons and daughters of rulers in the Dark Forest. Althus never heard Gilden called anything but Lord Gilden, but he was ruler of the Elves and had been for centuries.

When he posed the question aloud, Thorny said, "I think it is because Anduin lies at the heart of our lands and has always been the key to the safety of the lands about it. If Anduin falls, it is said the rest will follow. Much rests on the shoulders of the ruler of Anduin and lately, the state of the ruler of Anduin has been in question. You give us hope for the future of Anduin and so the future of all of the realms about you. To be sure, you are only one man, but you have made a great difference to those here and powerful allies in the short time since you have left Anduin.

"Perhaps the evil that drives the army sent against Anduin foresaw this, and therefore planned your death before you traveled much beyond Anduin's borders. Their plans have worked against them. It brought you to us and then to the Giants and the Dwarves. If you had passed through our realm safely on your way here, we would not have joined with you and learned the truth of who you are. You may have been killed by one of the creatures we encountered before you were able to rescue Euwyn or we might have been killed in an attempted rescue without your aid. You must admit, Althus, you saved Bree and Chess from death."

Althus nodded, embarrassed by the stir Thorny's speech had caused among the Dwarves. They all gathered about to hear what Thorny had to say. When Thorny fell silent, the Dwarves began to cheer for their liberator, the crown prince of Anduin.

Euwyn looked at Althus with astonishment. "You really must tell me of your adventures while we travel tomorrow, Althus. I am filled with curiosity to know what you encountered while I languished in the bowels of Stonehaven. For now, I would settle for something to eat."

Althus was relieved when Euwyn's hunger caused Dwarves and Giants to scatter in all directions in a quest for food for him and his companions. Granite guided them to a fire where he invited them to sit and warm themselves while their meal was prepared. Liddy appeared, bearing more food than they could possibly eat, giving Euwyn a look of concern as she heaped his plate full.

"Easy, Liddy," he protested. "So much food after eating almost nothing for such along time will certainly make me ill."

"Eat what you can," she said. "You look as if you have not eaten for a year."

Euwyn nodded in resignation and did his best to do justice to what was set before him. Althus was close to dozing off, trying with all his might not to fall face down into his plate. Granite, claimed to know a secret route that would take them through the heart of the Hoary Mountains standing between Stonehaven and Anduin and brought out a map, motioning them all closer to examine it. Euwyn produced a glowing orb that hung over their heads as they gathered to see the route Granite was so eager to show them.

"See here, he said pointing to a symbol on the map spread before them. It's a path that'll take ya right through the mountains directly south of Anduin. All ya gotta do then is cross the river and yer nearly there. Ya might even beat the Orcs and Goblins there if ya don't find any trouble along the way."

"I have lived near these mountains all my life, Granite, and I know of no passes through them safe for a man on foot let alone one on horseback and I, for one, am reluctant to leave the horses behind. We will need them when we reach Anduin. With the Orcs about we cannot risk sending them back alone through the Craglith pass." Euwyn said.

"No, no," said Granite shaking his head. "I'm not makin' meself clear somehow. I'm speakin of a tunnel through the mountains, not a pass through the mountains. The entrance is well hidden and hasn't been used in centuries. Some foolish talk of monsters dwellin' there, but monsters wouldn't be any problem fer you lot ta deal with at any rate."

Althus wondered if his hearing was failing. He thought he heard Chess and Thorny agree monsters would be no problem if, indeed, the tunnel would be a shorter way through the mountains. Althus decided he must have misunderstood the part about the monsters. He must have dozed off again and missed some of the conversation. Granite was assuring them the tunnel would be suitable for travel with horses. The Dwarves excavated it long ago, hoping to send caravans of goods through the mountains to trade with Anduin.

"I can give ya the map and the passwords and ye'll be in Anduin afore ye know it."

Mica's green eyes shone with excitement as he looked at his father. "Dad, you showed me the entrance ta the tunnel long ago, remember? I could go with 'em and then they'd be sure ta find it easy. It might be hard ta find, even with the map."

"Well," growled Granite, "I guess ya could go if they'll be havin' ya along. Ya could at least take them to the door this side of the mountains and then come back here if ya want."

Euwyn nodded. "We would be honored to have the prince of Stonehaven as our guide." Mica's face beamed with pleasure as he ran off to prepare his gear for the trip.

Granite sighed, "I don't think Mica wants ta go back into the mountain yet. He's spent a good part of his life as a prisoner in the halls of Stonehaven.

Perhaps some day he'll see it different, but fer now I'll let him go his own way and hope he'll return ta us in time. I don't doubt if ye'll have him he'll go with ya all the way ta Anduin. He's a brave young lad and good with sword or battle-axe."

"We are honored to have your son by our side, Granite," said Althus. "I will look after him and bring him back to you safely as soon as I can."

"I have no doubt ye will, Althus," Granite said gruffly, laying his hand on Althus' shoulder before leaving them to their own thoughts.

Euwyn and the Elves continued to study the map. For once, Althus was too weary even to take a second look. He dozed off to the sound of their voices and did not wake until he felt himself lifted from the ground. Chess and Thorny carried him off toward their camp, laughing merrily at Althus when he demanded they put him down.

"Do not think we will be easy on you now that we know you are Prince of Anduin," Chess laughed.

"It is time for all little princes to go to bed," said Thorny.

It was not that Althus did not wish to go to bed. He had wished for a nice soft bed all evening, but finding himself carried there by two laughing Elves was a little embarrassing. They did not stop at carrying him to his bed, but insisted upon stripping him to his small clothes when they got there. They reminded him forcefully of their strength as his struggles to escape them gained him nothing. Even wounded, they showed little sign of weakness or weariness. He escaped them once, but was summarily dragged back to his bed and soon found himself dressed in a clean shirt in addition to his small clothes. By the time they were finished with him, he was laughing as well and more tired than ever. When they left, he vaguely remembered being grateful they did not leave him lying naked when Bree came to say goodnight, kissing his forehead as if he were a small child.

Φ                    Φ                    Φ

Sometime during the night, Euwyn, the Giants and the Elves all joined him under the huge tent. Althus awoke to find them all stirring about him. Chess was in the act of pulling his shirt over his head, smiling at Althus when he found him awake.

"Come on, Althus," he chirped, throwing Althus' clothes at him. "You do not want to miss Liddy's breakfast. We should be on our way soon. Get your gear together. We ride for Granite's secret way through the mountain."

Althus dragged himself upright, wondering how Chess could be so wide-awake and evidently feeling no ill effects from the previous day's battle. Every muscle in Althus' body ached as he hastily pulled on his uniform, fearing Chess, who was nearly dancing with impatience, would offer to help him. He remembered his experience from the night before and wanted to avoid another such encounter.

He followed Chess to where Liddy and Bree were piling food on plates. He looked about for Euwyn and was happy to find him looking even more himself than he had the night before. He engaged the four remaining Giants in what seemed to be a heated discussion, not far from where breakfast was served. Althus smiled to see the Giants nodding at whatever Euwyn said to them. They towered above the Wizard like trees and yet Euwyn looked as if he were more than holding his own with the Giants in whatever debate they were engaged. When Euwyn caught sight of Althus and Chess, he left the Giants and came to join them. Liddy sized him up as if he were a prize pig she would fatten for market and set a plate of food before him that would have been too much even for one of the Giants. Euwyn eyed the plate warily while Liddy stood over him, spoon in hand as if she dared him to refuse it. He looked at Althus, Chess, and Thorny who joined him and sighed deeply.

"I must get away from her soon," he moaned softly when Liddy had gone back to her cooking. "If I do not, Mars will be unable to carry me as far as Anduin."

Althus and the Elves tried their best to look sympathetic, but Euwyn's dark, sorrowful eyes barely showing over the mounded plate soon had them laughing at his plight. He complained of their callous disregard for his welfare between bites. The Giants soon joined them, and when Gideon complained the Wizard had left nothing for them to eat, merriment erupted once more at Euwyn's expense.

When Liddy's back was turned, Euwyn transferred much of the contents of his plate onto those of the Giants with a few words and a gesture, startling Gabriel and causing him to spit his drink at Bull. Liddy, who happened to see her brother's actions, but not Euwyn's, scolded Bull and her brothers for behaving like young wolves at the table.

Althus greatly enjoyed their last meal together at Liddy's camp. He forgot the plight of Anduin for a time and the burdens he would have to shoulder as a prince of that country. He was happy to sit in peace, sharing their company in the dappled shade of the grove and enjoying the laughter and smiles that surrounded him. Their time together was over too soon. By mid morning, their gear was packed and they mounted their horses, ready to depart. There were many tears when they bid farewell to the Giants and Althus promised to return if he could.

They headed for the gates of Stonehaven to say farewell to Granite and the rest of the Dwarves, finding Mica first, as he wanted to be sure they did not leave him behind. He carried Althus' sword at his hip and a small pack on his back. Althus wondered what Granite thought of his son bearing a sword instead of the more traditional battle-axe.

Granite soon joined them, handing the small leaden box containing the powerful stone to Euwyn who strapped it securely in his saddlebag. Althus could not help but worry at having the stone in their possession, especially so close to Euwyn, but the Wizard assured him its effects could not escape the leaden box and it was imperative it accompany them to Anduin.

A pile of Orc and goblin corpses and carcasses of creatures Althus was unable to identify was growing in the meadow far beyond the gates, but the hundreds of shrouded forms arranged in lines close by held Althus' attention. He felt tears sliding down his face as he beheld the great number of Dwarves who had given their lives in order that others might be free. He estimated nearly a third of the adult population of Stonehaven lay dead and wondered how many more would be carried from the halls of the underground kingdom before the day was through. Granite drew him from his thoughts, reaching up to place a rough hand over his.

"Don't grieve fer my people, young prince. They died willin' enough ta free their kin. They couldn't have lived much longer with the shame of captivity. At least they died fightin' fer their people and not cowerin' in the dark. We'll clear the halls of filth and bury our dead and by this time tomorra we'll be on our way ta Anduin ta fight the foul army that waits fer ya there."

Althus shook his head. "No, Granite, there are too few of your people left as it is. I cannot ask you to risk what you have left to save Anduin. We will find a way to save ourselves. I cannot live with the thought more of your people will die."

"Besides," said Euwyn, "I have already forbidden the Giants to follow us. I think secrecy will be our best path for now. It will be difficult enough to enter Anduin unnoticed without a company of Giants and Dwarves at our back. I fear the master of this evil has infested the palace where the king of Anduin holds court with one of his servants and that is where the first battle must take place. If we cannot free those within the castle walls, there will be little hope of victory over the evil forces beyond the walls no matter how great an army we raise."

Granite nodded in reluctant agreement, but Althus saw a stubborn look cross his face before he hid it behind a rueful smile. "Mebbe yer right, Euwyn," he said. "Who am I ta argue with a Wizard?"

Their second round of tearful goodbyes took somewhat longer. All the Dwarves wanted to shake their hands and thank them for their freedom. Althus could not help but think the Dwarves had brought about their own victory and his company's part in the events of the previous day was minor compared to their sacrifices.

Their goodbyes having been said, and Granite and Beryl having said a gruff farewell to their son, they turned the horses north, Mica happily perched on Moon's back, behind Bree, pointing the way.

## Chapter Twenty-five

### EUWYN'S TALE

They traveled through the rugged valley that ran between the northern and southern arms of the Hoary Mountains. The meadow that surrounded the entrance to Stonehaven soon gave way to a rocky land dotted with tufts of coarse grass, rising gradually as they rode toward the mountains ahead. Althus was glad to leave the dark halls of Stonehaven behind and despite the danger ahead could not help but enjoy the sun on his back and his horse beneath him as they traveled the rugged landscape.

Euwyn traveled by his side, gazing about as if he could not see enough, occasionally turning to smile at Althus. Mars seemed a different animal with Euwyn astride his broad back. His step seemed lighter, his neck arched proudly as if he had waited many years only to carry his chosen rider once again. Althus and Euwyn rode in near silence at first, occasionally commenting on the terrain or the weather. Althus wondered how the stone had ensnared the Wizard, but he was reluctant to ask questions that would bring unpleasant memories and so he decided to let them rest for a time.

They stopped briefly in a small copse of stunted trees to eat their midday meal, hoping to reach the foot of the mountains by nightfall. To everyone's delight, Kestrel appeared out of a cloudless sky to alight on Bree's shoulder. She lifted him gently and held him between her hands briefly, staring intently into his fierce eyes. By then everyone had gathered about to hear the message the little hawk brought.

"Father and Rowan worry for our safety," she said. "I will tell them of our success in freeing the Dwarves and Euwyn, and that we are all safely on our way to Anduin. They have received our message the enemy is on the march and await further word from the Anduin troops stationed along the border. I will tell them of our secret way and our hope to reach them before the enemy is at their gates." Bree soon released the little hawk into the blue sky. Before he had flown from sight, they were mounted and on their way once again. Althus noticed Bree looking at her hands and asked if they still pained her. She blushed, pausing to run a hand through her short, tousled hair before replying to Althus' question. "No," she said softly, "I have felt no pain in my hands since Euwyn healed them, but father asked me about my hands. I fear I have caused Rowan some pain."

Althus regarded her curiously. "Do you mean to say Rowan felt your burns? All the way to Anduin?" He was dumbfounded at the thought of it.

"Yes, I am afraid he may have felt it, although briefly. That is sometimes the way between twins. Rowan is especially sensitive to my pain. Whenever I am wounded, he knows somehow. I feel his pain sometimes, but not as deeply or as often." She sighed and stared off toward the mountains ahead. "He is so dear to me, Althus. I hope he is safe in Anduin. I hope father is safe as well. Rowan will not leave father's side and each would give their lives to protect the other. Still, we know they were safe not long ago. They sent Kestrel to us and he travels swiftly."

"We will soon be in Anduin if Granite's tunnel takes us through the heart of the mountains as he says," Althus reassured her. "We will reach them in time."

He wished he were as certain as he pretended. He hoped Euwyn had a plan in mind for their arrival in Anduin. He had little idea what their first move should be. He had a few miles to think about it. Getting there would have to be enough of a challenge for now. He maneuvered Gust so he and Bree traveled beside Euwyn to ask the Wizard a question that had occurred to him.

"How did you find Bree so quickly in the tunnels of Stonehaven, father?" he asked. "I saw you holding the medal you wear about your neck. Did it help you find her somehow?"

Euwyn nodded, looking a bit embarrassed. "Yes, I prayed you still wore one of the pendants I gave to you and Rowan when I lived with you in Borias, Bree. I never told you they held some magic. I did not want you to think I was foolish for worrying about you and wanting to protect you. You were at that age when you valued your independence above all else. I almost forgot about them. It was so long ago that I gave them to you. The medallions are linked. One can enable me to locate the others if I hold it in my hand and think of the one I am seeking."

"I felt the pendant about my neck grow icy cold when I faced the wolf creatures in Stonehaven," Bree said. "I had little time to puzzle over it. Rowan and I have grown to adulthood since you gave us the small medallions and we never knew they were more than a simple remembrance of you, Euwyn. Rowan still wears his as well. We have never taken them from about our necks. Thank the Creator you had the foresight to give them to us or I would have been one of those who died in Stonehaven."

Althus shuddered at the thought of Bree lying beneath one of the shrouds he saw before the gates of the Dwarves' kingdom. He pulled a pendant from beneath his tunic. His bore a pattern of a continuous band woven in an intricate pattern that had neither beginning nor end. Euwyn pulled a leather cord from beneath his tunic as well and Bree followed suit. Euwyn's held three pendants, one that matched the one hanging about Althus' neck and one to match Bree's. Her pendant bore the image of a standing hawk above a tiny red stone. Althus knew the third would bear the image of a tree to match the one on the medallion he had seen about Rowan's neck. They both regarded Euwyn in silence.

"I would only use them if I felt you were in danger," he said, sounding like a child caught in some mischief. "All right, I apologize for marking you. Perhaps it was taking things a bit too far." He looked so guilty Bree and Althus could not help but laugh at him.

"You are such an interfering old Wizard," said Bree. "I think we are all most grateful for that."

Euwyn smiled. "I am not so old," he said. Bree and Althus tucked their pendants back beneath their clothes.

"Perhaps we should tag Chess and Thorny as well," laughed Bree. "Then he can spy on all of us at once."

"No, please," laughed Euwyn. "No one should be burdened with keeping track of those two. They would wear me out keeping them from trouble."

Althus looked at the two brothers riding ahead of them, engaged in some heated discussion beyond their hearing, wishing he could always keep them near. He wondered how long they would be together. If they survived the next few days, the Elves would return to the Dark Forest. Would they see each other again or would he be tied to the kingdom of Anduin? He shook his head. Such thoughts were premature. They had to survive first. He would worry about the future later when he could be sure he had one.

Euwyn asked to hear the tale of their journey from Anduin to Stonehaven. Althus and Bree entertained him with the tale while they rode ever nearer to the jagged peaks ahead and the entrance to the ancient passage marked on Granite's map.

They were soon climbing the shoulder of the mountains on a stony trail that rose in switchbacks. They could see the entire valley just crossed, spreading out behind them in the fading twilight. A column of black smoke rose into the sky where the Dwarves burned the dead of their enemy near the gates of Stonehaven. The last rays of sunlight found them facing a narrow wooden bridge spanning a tributary of the Amberstream. It was a small, rocky stream running the length of the valley, originating from the point where the northern and southern arms of the Hoary Mountains joined not many leagues to the southeast. The narrow bridge swayed slightly in the mountain wind, suspended from ropes as thick as a man's arm with closely spaced wooden planks forming its floor. The rushing stream ran far below in a chasm cut deep into the rocky foot of the mountains by its swift waters. Mica assured them the Dwarves kept the bridge in good repair up until the time of their captivity and the timbers should still be sound enough for the horses to cross safely. He pointed out the gates they sought as well, barely visible across the wooden span in a shallow bay in the mountainside, a ledge smoothed by Dwarven stone craft providing a gathering area before them.

With the light failing, they decided to make camp this side of the bridge and cross it the next morning. They found a sheltered area among the rocks of the mountainside and built a small fire to ward off the chill. After they had eaten, Althus could no longer resist asking Euwyn some of the questions he had kept to himself.

"You have heard our tale, Father. Tell us how you became a prisoner of the stone," he asked.

Euwyn moved to sit cross-legged across the fire from Althus. The dancing firelight illuminated his face, but cast his eyes into shadow as he began his tale. "I will tell you what I remember of it. I fear I was careless and somewhat conceited in my approach regarding the stone. Entering Stonehaven was not a difficult task. I merely made myself appear as a stupid Goblin. If any Orc questioned my presence in places where I should not be... well, I was only a stupid Goblin after all.

The stone had enslaved the Dwarves by intensifying their love of beautiful things, especially those that come from the earth itself such as gold and silver and gemstones. It played upon their greed and their pride until they hopelessly pitted themselves against one another in a struggle to possess the stone. I imagined myself immune to such emotions since Wizards, as you know, are usually happy with very few possessions. We are generally a nomadic race, sometimes staying in one place for a time, but never for very long. The number of possessions we keep are limited to those things necessary for the practice of our craft. We keep nothing for the sake of beauty alone. Even the desire for power does not afflict many of us as it does most other races. Perhaps that is because we are the most powerful of all races.

I did not realize how treacherous the stone could be. I found the stone in the depths of Stonehaven and thought I was well prepared to do battle with it. I was so sure I could defeat it. It was foolish of me to assume I knew all the stone was capable of. It soon found my weakness. I thought I would go mad. Perhaps I did go mad for a time. At least I shielded the Dwarves from the stone's influence while it concentrated its powers on me. Perhaps I could have overcome it in time. Perhaps not. Could I succeed if I challenged it again, now that I have faced it once and escaped? It may come to that. I am stronger now than I was when you came to my rescue, but I am not eager to risk the stone again. I may have to." Euwyn's voice trailed off as if he said the last only to himself. They sat in silence while he stared absently into the fire.

Althus wondered what horrors the Wizard had faced during his encounter with the stone. He had the look of a man who had come face to face with death or worse. He did not reveal what weakness the stone found in him and no one had the courage to ask. Althus decided a change of subject was in order.

"Did the Dwarves unearth the stone in the mines of Stonehaven?" he asked. "How did the stone come into their possession?"

Euwyn gave Althus a startled look before answering as if he had forgotten where he was.

"The Dwarves did unearth the stone somewhere in Stonehaven, but I suspect it was buried there shortly before it was discovered. Someone meant for them to find it. Somewhere, I fear, there lurks an evil beyond imagining whose sole purpose is to rule our world or destroy it. That evil gathered the army of foul creatures marching toward Anduin and that army needed the skills of the Dwarves to make armor and weapons. We have cut their supply, but the force gathered and armed in Stonehaven is already marching fully equipped. I learned a few things while I roamed the halls of Stonehaven in relative freedom, before I faced the stone.

Other armies will arise to march against all the races of the world if we cannot discover where the power behind these forces lies hidden and destroy it. I doubt Stonehaven will ever again serve as a refuge for those forces now that the Dwarves are free and alerted to the dangers they face, but I fear other stones lay waiting for discovery in other kingdoms. Perhaps even in the Dark Forest or in the realm of the sea Elves. The bird-like creatures the Orcs call Myoti and the wolf-like Nasua and creatures like them are bred somewhere deep in the mountains. I fear the Dark Lord that Gilden and his people and the other Elven races drove from our lands more than a thousand years ago has returned. If so, all the people of our land face slavery or death at the hands of his evil hordes. I heard the Orcs refer to their "Great Lord" often enough, which leads me to believe we have not encountered the true power behind the evil army as yet. I fear this Lord of theirs lurks even deeper in the Hoary Mountains than any of us have ever traveled.

"Perhaps we have become enough of a thorn in this Dark Lord's side that he will take notice of us. I hope, for now, his attention is directed toward his army and Anduin, but we must move cautiously. I must face him sooner or later if I can, but I would feel safer facing this evil master if I knew Anduin was not in enemy hands"

"I will not be left behind again, Father," said Althus. "I have had enough of being left behind while you face whatever threatens us all. It is madness for you to be traveling alone in these perilous times when I could be at your side."

Thorny nodded in agreement. "If Anduin falls it will serve as a stepping stone to conquer the lands that border it, including the Dark Forest. It seems the fate of the Elves is bound to that of Anduin. Obviously, that is father's belief as well or he and Rowan would not be in Anduin now. We cannot let you deal with this evil master alone, Euwyn. The Elves will be at your side when that time comes."

"As for your traveling with me, Althus, until now the queen has forbidden me from exposing you to needless danger," said Euwyn. "I suppose she will have to loosen her grip on you. I am not sure what persuaded her to let you leave the castle even now. Perhaps she realized the castle was no safer for you than the open road when my power to disguise you from Borgas and the king began to fail. I do not flatter myself she felt your life worth risking for mine if she felt she had any other choice. Still, you are a grown man, after all, and will take your rightful place as the prince and protector of Anduin if I am to aid in its defense. I will not have it otherwise. Maris will have to let you make your own decisions. The secrets and lies have gone on too long and you see what the result has been. The people of Anduin are undefended. The king no longer shows any regard for them, and those loyal to Borgas have replaced the men who were loyal to the king. I fear Borgas is in league with this Dark Lord.

"He controls King Allen and thus he controls the kingdom of Anduin. He is the one we must defeat first and at any cost. If I can destroy the stone we carry within the influence of the stone hidden somewhere in Anduin, I believe I can destroy both stones. If they are all parts of the one stone I am thinking of, there is a resonance that connects them. If I can bring them close together and find the resonance of one, others close to it will shatter as well. I am familiar with the resonance of the piece of the stone we bear. I felt it in the very marrow of my bones as it sought to control me. Perhaps I can shatter it if I regain enough of my power before we reach Anduin."

"Stones," Althus said.

All looked at him, questioning.

"The stone in Anduin is not hidden," he continued. "Somehow it has been separated into smaller stones and they hang about the necks of those loyal to Borgas or those controlled by him. King Allen himself wears a stone about his neck. The men who traveled with me from Anduin wore them also."

"A new twist to the stone's use," Euwyn said. "Borgas' control over Castle Anduin is as complete as I feared it might be. Let us hope the stone we carry can be destroyed and that, through its destruction, we can destroy the rest that lie within the kingdom of Anduin. All of our hopes hang on this."

## Chapter Twenty-six

## THE BRIDGE

They awoke the next morning to a cold fog that obscured the far end of the bridge, coating everything with fine droplets. The company stood wrapped against the chill in their Elven cloaks, surveying the short stretch of the bridge still visible to them through the seething mist. The planks that formed the floor of the bridge were slick with moisture. Fortunately, there was only a light breeze. At least the bridge would not sway except from their crossing of it. They would cross the bridge one at a time. Euwyn was the first to cross, leading Mars, who stepped cautiously behind the Wizard, eyeing the floor suspiciously as it tilted under his feet. Euwyn was soon hailing them from the other side. Bree and Moon followed, reaching the other side safely. Thorny and Ochre followed and then Chess and Sand.

Althus looked at Mica still standing at his side, somewhat surprised to find he had not followed Bree and Moon. He realized then Mica had not moved since the company started to cross. He was not fond of heights himself and did not relish dragging a reluctant Dwarf across the narrow bridge. He handed Mica Gust's reins and placed his cloak about his shoulders, asking him if he could lead the horse across while he guarded their backs. Althus did not know what he would say if Mica asked what he was guarding their backs from, but it seemed to set the stocky Dwarf in motion. Gust allowed Mica to lead him onto the bridge, keeping his head close to the Dwarf's shoulder. Althus smiled to see him grasp Gust's mane with his free hand as they made their way slowly across the bridge. He followed close behind, hoping the safety of the far side was not as far away as it had looked the day before.

They were somewhere near the center of the bridge, both ends of it lost from sight in the mist when the first sign of trouble came. Althus felt the span jerk suddenly as the harsh cry of Myoti rent the air around him. He shouted at Mica to get off the bridge. Gust hesitated for a moment until Althus repeated his warning, swatting him across his rump to get him moving. Mica was hauling on Gust's reins for all he was worth, frantically trying to get him off the bridge so Althus could follow. With a final look over his shoulder, Gust allowed Mica to lead him on, his hooves slipping on the wet planks as the Myoti struck the bridge once more, causing it to sway crazily. Althus heard Gust's hooves strike stone just as the Myoti severed one of the ropes holding the bridge. He barely managed to grab the remaining rope before the floor of the bridge gave way beneath his feet.

He heard an arrow slip past and a harsh cry as it found its mark. The Myoti were attacking the supports at the end furthest from where his friends stood. To strike even one of the Myoti from such a distance in this fog was an amazing feat of marksmanship. Bree was evidently able to see the Myoti flying under the cover of mist much better than he could.

He was too frightened to think, thankful the mist hid the long drop to the shallow, rocky stream beneath him. He began to inch his way along the rope toward the far end, hoping the creatures would not sever the rope he clung to so desperately before he reached the safety of solid ground. The rope held, but his luck did not. He felt a rush of air as one of the Myoti dove toward him and a searing pain as its talons fastened about one of his legs. As the Myoti tore his hands from the rope, his head connected solidly with the planks of the bridge. He swung head down, unconscious, as the creature lifted him into the air.

Bree dropped her bow and covered her face with her hands as Euwyn's arms came about her. Thorny and Chess stared after the Myoti as it bore Althus southward, deeper into the mountains. Another lingered only long enough to sever the remaining rope holding the bridge before winging after its companion. Mica struggled with Gust, leading him away from the edge of the chasm. Bree and Euwyn had slain three of the creatures before they plucked Althus from the bridge, but neither was willing to kill the one carrying Althus, even though his death was certain either way. They stood trapped on the ledge before the doors guarding the mountain passage.

They stood in stunned silence long after the creatures had flown from sight. There was no way for them to follow, no way down and no way to turn back. They could only continue toward Anduin. Euwyn was the first to move toward the doors. He soon had them open and stood staring into the darkness of the passage, unmoving.

"We cannot go on without trying to save Althus!" Chess cried. "How can you leave him to such a fate?"

"Chess!" Bree cried, her face streaming with tears.

Euwyn spun about to face them. The look in his dark eyes drove Chess back a step.

"Do you think I can fly, Chess? Do you think if there was the least chance I could go after my son I would not have thrown myself from this cliff in an attempt to follow? I would gladly give my life for Althus. If you think I love him less because he is not my own flesh and blood, you are wrong!"

"I am sorry, Euwyn," said Chess as tears began to stream down his face as well and Bree came to put her arms about him.

Euwyn turned towards the passage once again, but did not enter. "What can I do?" he said more quietly. His voice echoed into the darkness. When Mars came to stand beside him, he grasped his mane in one hand and they stepped into the passage together. The rest followed at a distance.

At this end of the passage, the floor was smooth and even. It was more than large enough for two of them to walk side by side even if they had been leading horses laden with packs. The sound of their footsteps and the horses' hooves on stone echoed eerily about them as they moved along the passage. Mica's voice trembled as he called forth rocklight to illuminate their path. No one had the heart to speak beyond that.

Gust was giving Mica some trouble as well. For the first hour or so as they traveled the passage he stopped numerous times to gaze behind him as if expecting Althus to appear from that direction. Mica dragged him onward as best he could and Gust eventually followed the Dwarf without stopping, his head hanging nearly to his knees.

Mica almost wished the horse had not given up. Now Mica had time to think of the reason he found himself leading a riderless horse. Everyone pulled their cloaks closely about them as if the air chilled them, each buried deeply in their own thoughts. Mica sniffed and sobbed as he pulled Althus' cloak close.

Mica was sure their minds were as troubled as his. Althus would not die an easy death. He tried to think of anything to keep his mind occupied. He could only imagine Althus torn apart while he still lived, gutted by the sharp beak and talons of the hideous creature as he screamed in agony.

Euwyn's thoughts ran about his head like a mouse in a box. What could he have done to save his son? How *could* he turn toward Anduin when the Myoti carried Althus to certain death in the opposite direction? The passage was the only way. When he reached the other side, what could he do? It would take the better part of two days to travel through the mountains. If Granite was right, they would not reach the gates at the far end until tomorrow evening. Althus would almost certainly be dead by then. He would certainly be dead by the time they could find him. It would take months to search the southern reaches of the mountains. It would be insane even to attempt it.

Their only logical course was to continue toward Anduin. He wanted to turn back southward as soon as he cleared the passage, but he knew that was a foolish thought and a useless course to take. That knowledge did not make him want to take it any less. He sighed deeply, rubbing his chest absently. There was a painful knot there that might never leave him, but he knew Anduin would remain his destination even without the offering of a prince to lead them.

He looked at Bree who had moved forward to stumble along at his side. Her eyes seemed to stare ahead without seeing. They looked as empty as he felt. She did not even turn her head to look back at him. Chess and Thorny walked ahead with their hands to the hilts of their swords. Chess still rubbed at his cheeks with his sleeve and Thorny rested a hand on his brother's shoulder speaking softly to him as they traveled farther down the dim halls.

The first day of their journey passed uneventfully. The passage continued, gradually sloping downward. Eventually, narrow channels cut on either side of the passage appeared and began to run with water, keeping the footing dry as they continued along their way. They appreciated them even more when they stopped for the night at a point where the passage widened for that purpose. Stone benches lined the walls and there was a pit for fire delved into the floor with wood stored nearby. They sat in near silence about a fire that seemed cheerless after a meal no one seemed to want. Bree was the first to break the silence.

"I should have killed him," she whispered. Her voice raised the hair on the back of Mica's neck.

"You killed the creatures you could see, Bree," said Thorny. "You did the best you could."

"Not the creatures, Thorny," she said, turning to face her brother. "I should have killed Althus. I could have made sure he did not suffer. I could have done that easily. I could not do it, Thorny. I failed him when he needed someone to help him."

Thorny put his arms about his sister and held her while she cried.

"I could have done the same, Bree," said Euwyn softly. "I could have done it as easily as you. If you failed him, then I did also. I do not think Althus would have wanted you to live with the knowledge you killed him with your own hand. He was not a coward. Perhaps a bit innocent, but never a coward."

Euwyn sighed and rubbed a hand across his chest. "I wondered if I had done the wrong thing in taking him in as a babe. Wizards are not meant to have families. They are not supposed to have any one person more dear to them than others. We are meant to serve all good people equally without the ties of family or friends. I allowed myself to become too close to Althus. It has made me less powerful than I could be. Less powerful than I *should* be.

To my everlasting shame, that is what enabled the stone to hold me. It lured me with images of Althus. Once it held me, I could not escape. He was tortured before my eyes in a thousand different ways. I could not help him. I could not look away. I knew the images must be false, but I could not turn my back on them for fear they were true after all and I would miss something that would enable me to save him. I fear for all of those who are dear to me and there will come a time that will cloud my judgment and make me hesitate to do what is the greater good for all people. Perhaps this is my punishment for wandering from the path I was to take. May the Creator have mercy on me. I am a poor excuse for a Wizard."

The Elves all stared at him in dismay while he gazed desolately into the fire.

"I do not know of any other Wizard who has done more for others than you, Euwyn," Bree said softly. "I cannot think of a people within your reach you have not touched in some way, and you are young for a Wizard. Rowan and I would have died as children if not for you. Perhaps I will not prove to be worthy, but I know Rowan will lead our people well when the time comes. You did our people a great service by saving his young life and I am more than thankful you saved mine as well.

Without you, the Dwarves would still be held as slaves within their own halls. You diverted the stone's power so they could free themselves. Even the Black Giants are kept safe by your spells that still hold their secret ways hidden from those who would invade their peaceful valley. You have spent years serving the people of Anduin. These are only the things I know of and each time we travel beyond our borders, we find more. That is enough for me to know you are a great Wizard." She reached out a hand to turn his head so his eyes met hers. "You are too hard on yourself by far. What you see as your greatest weakness, others see as your greatest strength. Perhaps we should be thinking of what Althus would want us to do now he is gone. Let us both stop doubting ourselves and go on."

Euwyn turned his head back toward the fire, but his dark eyes held a fierce look that was not there before. He gave a small nod and smiled grimly. "I will at least have my revenge on that bastard, Borgas, or die in the attempt," he growled. "Thank you, Bree. You are right, we will go on."

Bree watched him absently rub his hand across his chest again, pulling his cloak closer about himself as if he were cold or in pain or perhaps both. She felt empty as well, but she would go on to Anduin. If for no other purpose than to watch over Euwyn and to help Rowan and her father in whatever way she could.

They all sat in silence for a while until Chess suddenly sprang to his feet. They all looked up at him in surprise as he began pacing about the fire. "Wait... wait!" he said. "What about the prophecy? Althus has not fulfilled the prophecy yet! He cannot be dead! Not until he fulfills the prophecy!"

Thorny looked at him in dismay. "Chess," he said gently as if he were trying to settle a madman, "Chess, stop being an ass and sit down. You are not helping at all."

Chess looked a little abashed, but he would not give up. "Well, I will not believe he is dead until I see with my own eyes."

"I wish you could be right, Chess. I do not see how it could be possible, but I will not say you are wrong to feel as you do," Thorny sighed.

They rested a while longer while the horses ate their ration of grain and then pressed on, suddenly longing for open sky over their heads. Bree's heart was heavy, but her concern for Euwyn kept her attention focused on him. At first, he had seemed to shake off the effects of his captivity as soon as they rescued him from Stonehaven. Even though he seemed gaunt and pale, he was the same man they remembered from their childhood. Since the loss of Althus, he had lost that spark. He walked in silence with Mars striding at his side.  He seemed weary, occasionally rubbing his hand across his chest in a gesture Bree found disturbing.  No matter what Euwyn said, Bree could see the loss of Althus weakened the Wizard much more than his presence ever had.  Perhaps he was a different breed of Wizard.  Perhaps he needed to love in order to be strong.  When she wrapped an arm about him as they walked side by side, the emotions she drew from him frightened her.    Still, somewhere deep in him she felt a desire for vengeance.  She hoped that would keep him going until they had done what they could to save the people of Anduin.

The channels to either side of the passage gathered more water the deeper they traveled into the mountains, but the floor of the passage remained dry and their journey was an easy one.

"Where are the monsters your father promised us?" Chess asked Mica.

Mica shrugged his broad shoulders.  "Sorry, Chess.  Mebbe they're dead and gone.  Mebbe they starved ta death when no one came along ta serve as their dinner."

Thorny and Bree assured him no apologies were necessary.

By the time they finally stood facing the lower entrance of the passage, the water had gathered into a huge lake occupying a cavern of immense proportions.  The broad, dry floor they traveled continued uninterrupted across a stone causeway, right up to the massive, carved gates that marked the end of their underground journey.  They paused to admire the mirror-like surface of the lake at its mid point.  Gazing upwards at the stalactites glittering in the rocklight they did not see the tentacles sliding from the water and across the causeway, reaching for the unwary travelers.

"Do you smell something foul here?" asked Chess.

Thorny turned to answer him in time to see a tentacle wrap itself about one of Gust's hind legs.  The sturdy horse's hooves grated on stone as something dragged him toward the water.  He began to kick fiercely as Mica grabbed his bridle and hung on for dear life.

Thorny was the first to react.  He drew his blade and severed the tentacle just as Gust was about to be pulled from the roadway.  He then  hacked away the writhing tentacles that had fastened themselves about his own legs, freeing himself just in time to see Chess' golden head disappear beneath the water.  The terror in his brother's eyes froze him to the spot long enough for Euwyn to jump in after the disappearing Elf before Thorny could do so himself.  Bree caught him by the arm before he could follow.  An awful silence followed.  Mica watched the surface of the lake, his green eyes wide with fear as he tried to keep Gust quiet.  The water became nearly still.  Bree and Thorny held their breath while the moment seemed to stretch into an eternity.

Suddenly, the entire lake erupted into the air with a loud boom, throwing Mica and the Elves to their knees and setting the horses leaping about in confusion. The lake settled back into its bed momentarily before its level began to drop rapidly as if it were a tub of water with its drain plug suddenly removed. Euwyn was the first to emerge from the swirling waters, turning about to drag Chess over the edge of the roadway, gasping for breath and covered with an evil smelling layer of slime. Chess' mood seemed as foul as his smell when he regained the ability to speak.

"You *would* save the horse first," He sputtered, "while the foul monster proceeded to swallow me whole. If it had not been for Euwyn, I would have been dinner for that stinking beast!"

"Well, Chess," said Thorny, backing away as Chess came near, attempting to escape the stench that came with him. "You wanted to know where the monsters were. You found your monster. I did not wish to interfere."

Chess glared at him for a moment and then turned to find Euwyn standing nearby, dry as a bone and looking off toward the gates.

"What was that creature?" Chess asked.

"I am not sure. It seemed to consist mostly of tentacles with a very large mouth and stomach thrown in for good measure. I was sorry I was forced to kill it when it swallowed you. It may have been the last of its kind. The blast I used seems to have blown a hole in the beautiful lake as well. It is a pity," he said casually, as if he had just climbed out of his bath. "Perhaps we should leave this place before we meet any more of Granite's surprises."

"Wait," said Chess, "my deepest thanks for rescuing me, Euwyn, but could you dry me off as well and rid me of this monster's stink?'

"If I dry you now, Chess, the stink will only cling to you more determinedly. Perhaps you can wash the beast's remains from yourself after we have left this place behind."

Chess grumbled as they all headed for the gates. Everyone gave him a wide berth, including the horses. Even Sand did not seem anxious to walk beside his master. When Chess waited for him to take his usual place at his shoulder, the beast regarded him from five paces away with his one blue eye and would not come any closer.

Euwyn soon had the gates open. They were grateful to step out into the narrow, rugged valley that cut its way between two peaks. It would be a relatively easy journey down this valley into Anduin. Chess immediately immersed himself in the stream that ran down the valley. No one had the heart to tell him the stream issuing from the draining lake only smelled a little less foul than he did. Euwyn dried him easily when he crawled out of the stream, but he had done little to lessen the smell. When they were out of Chess' hearing, Bree asked the Wizard if he could do something to tame the aura still following Chess like a faithful hound, but Euwyn regretfully told her it would have to wait until they made camp for the night. Until then they would have to keep their distance and hope for the best. They would make camp soon.

The valley widened before them as they traveled in the gathering twilight. Bree shaded her eyes with her hand, studying something very large moving up the valley toward them.

## Chapter Twenty-seven

## ANTARES AND SOLOMON

Antares banked slowly, circling above the thick clouds shrouding the mountains below. The sun, just rising above the horizon, glittered on his scaled hide as his sinuous body made a graceful arc. The cold air at this altitude cooled his anger, but he held on to it as best he could. To lose the anger would uncover his underlying despair. Dragons were not supposed to feel such emotions. The foul Myoti he had spied from a distance had given him something else to think of for a time, but they had ducked below the clouds before he could overtake them. He circled lazily, wishing his hatred for them would keep the other thoughts from his mind as he waited for them to reemerge from the heavy mist that blanketed the cold mountain valleys.

His thoughts were free again to think of the things he would dearly like to forget. Solomon! How he wished he had never met the man! He would not be a part of his madness, but how could he abandon someone like Solomon? Brother Augustine, head of their powerful alliance had entrusted him, the most powerful of the allied Dragons, with the task of watching over Solomon since he had left the halls of the Brotherhood, but how was he to keep the man from harming himself? He had done well so far. He had kept Solomon alive through the brutal mountain winter. How long could he keep watch over him? He had taken to the air this morning in frustration, intending never to return, but he was already having second thoughts. Solomon was still of the Brotherhood, no matter how strangely he behaved.

If he intended to die this night, he should at least have stayed with him during his last hours. He supposed he owed his lost friend that much. The very least he could do was to take care of his remains, cremating them with Dragon fire and scattering his ashes to the mountain wind as was the custom of the Brotherhood of Dragon Riders. Perhaps it would be for the best, after all. Antares was weary of watching him suffer. He could not interfere. It was not for Antares to decide the worth of Solomon's life.     Brother Augustine would mourn his favorite Rider for a time, but he would get over it. There was too much death and danger in the mountains of late to allow the Brotherhood's attentions to be drawn elsewhere. Antares would find another Rider. He was a Dragon, after all. Dragons did not feel love for their riders. A certain respect and loyalty, perhaps, but not love.

He could not explain what he felt, really. He had not felt this way before. He had had many riders in his lifetime. He was proud to say most had retired from service. He was big and powerful, even for a Dragon, and had taken care of his riders well. Only two had been lost in battle. He had regretted losing them, but this time it felt different somehow. Perhaps because

Solomon had once been the best Rider of the Brotherhood. Antares would have given half his scales to see him smile again. The sound of his laughter, even the sound of his voice, was only a dim memory now. He roared in frustration, preparing to turn southward, back to the high meadow where Solomon had spent his last days.

Two of the abominations he had been chasing reemerged from the clouds and he gratefully turned his thoughts to their destruction. There had been five, but these two would serve for now. He needed an outlet for his pent-up rage and they would do nicely. He closed in, intending to turn them to cinders before they could duck back into the clouds, but one of them carried something that made him pause, hovering in mid air with a grunt of surprise. It was a man. Of what race he could not tell. It occurred to him Solomon might be distracted from his intentions by someone needing his skills as a healer. He could not detect any signs of life in the forlorn figure hanging from the ugly creature's talons, but he was in the mood for some sport. This made the kill a little more challenging. He would take their prey from them as he killed them.

He caught the unburdened one quickly and watched with satisfaction as it plummeted toward the earth, its dark, leathery form engulfed in flames. That was too easy. The second dove for the cover of the clouds, its bat-like wings folded close to its body, but Antares was now close enough to follow without losing sight of it. The flight of the Myoti was slow and lumbering compared to that of the Dragon. Antares cut through the air like an arrow, easily keeping his prey in sight. He slid beneath it, forcing it to rise back above the clouds and into the sunlight. He kept after it even then, chasing it ever higher until he could see it beginning to tire. Enough sport for now. He should end it. Every moment he toyed with the creature increased the chance that the prize the bird held was damaged beyond healing.

Before the Myoti could react, he was above it. His talons fastened about its neck and strangled the life from it. The man dropped from its claws and Antares dove for him, snatching him up just before he disappeared beneath the clouds. He winced in sympathy, forced to grasp the man by the shoulders rather roughly. Oh well, better injured than dead. He was pleased to find the man still alive, protected by a fine coat of mail. At least he would only have to deal with some bruises and the wounds the Myoti had torn in his leg. Antares shifted his burden about so he cradled him in his talons and turned back to where he hoped he would find Solomon.

He found him easily enough. He had not moved from where Antares had left him, sitting atop a rock and staring vacantly across a stony alpine meadow toward a cluster of ruins. Antares landed before Solomon as gracefully as he could on three legs, blocking his view of the ruins completely. He laid his prize gently on the grass and gestured as if the inert, bloody figure was a rare treasure. Solomon recoiled, staring at the man curled on his side in the grass as if Antares had laid a venomous snake at his feet. When Antares roared at him, "Move, man, he needs healing!" he ran.

Φ           Φ           Φ

Althus woke slowly to find a curly head bending over him, silhouetted by the sun shining through white canvas. Why was Chess bandaging his head? Where were Bree and Euwyn? He closed his eyes and tried to gather his wits about him. What had happened? His head was throbbing.

"Chess? Is everyone all right?" he asked. Events were coming back to him and he was more than amazed to be alive. He opened his eyes again, concerned that Chess did not answer him. The face moved so the light illumined its features and he knew immediately it was not Chess, kneeling beside him and tending his wounds so skillfully. The gentleness of the hands that tended him seemed echoed in the youthful face that turned toward him. He looked into a face framed by a halo of light brown curls. The golden eyes that met his for a moment, their pupils rimmed with black, were striking, disturbingly familiar. They regarded him levelly for a moment and then lost their focus, looking through him as the man gently fastened the bandage about his head. The man stood abruptly and stepped away to empty a bowl of water on the ground outside the tent and Althus studied him carefully.

He was bare to the waist, clad only in buff colored breeches, a number of scars making light streaks across his back. When he turned to face Althus again, he saw that more scars ran across his chest. Even more startling was the man's size. He was less than five feet tall. Perfectly made for a Human, or perhaps made more like an Elf. He was definitely not a child. His shoulders were broad and there was hair on his chest. Somehow, the blocky Dwarves seemed less startling than this Elf in miniature.

"His name is Solomon, or Sollie if you wish to be more familiar, although he has not the manners to tell you so," said a deep rumbling voice from somewhere behind his head.

The voice was so deep it made Althus' chest vibrate. Solomon did not react at all to the voice, but kept to his task. Althus tried to turn his head far enough to see the man who spoke, but the pain in his shoulders forced him to change his mind. He studied the things he could see without moving. He lay beneath a white tent on a soft pile of furs. There was little else to see. Someone had stripped him to his small clothes. He was relieved to see his mail, bow and sword lying within reach. Evidently, he had not fallen among enemies. His clothing was piled nearby as well, except for his breeches, which hung from a tent pole, evidently recently laundered and mended. Solomon was brewing something that smelled like Bree's willowbark tea.

"Please, could you tell me who you are and where I am?" he asked. "I remember being torn from the bridge by a Myoti, but that is the last I know." He fingered the bandage about his head. "I must have struck my head on the bridge. Are the rest nearby? Is everyone else safe?"

"As for the rest you speak of," said the deep voice. "I saw no one else. I killed the Myoti with great pleasure and brought you here to Solomon to be healed. It is my goal to kill them all. You were merely something I brought home to amuse Solomon. I am Antares. Welcome to our mountains. What is your name, large man?"

Solomon came to help him sit up while he drank the tea he had brewed. Now Althus could see a number of neat stitches closing a series of wounds the Myoti's talons had torn in his thigh and realized Solomon had not only set the stitches in his leg, but also cleaned and mended his breeches. Althus lowered his head, trying to look into Solomon's eyes as Solomon gazed silently at the cup he held out to him. Golden eyes, ringed with black. Suddenly he knew where he had seen such eyes before. They were not unlike the eyes of Bree's fierce little hawk.

Althus took the cup, deliberately trapping Solomon's hands against it with his own. He only wished to know Solomon understood him when he thanked him, but Solomon froze, taking a sharp, shallow breath as if in fear, his eyes never leaving the cup. Althus released him and looked to where the deep voice originated, hoping for more response from that quarter. Had he possessed more strength and Solomon less, he would have been sent running, injured or not. He barely stifled a yelp of fear and nearly spilled the drink Solomon held as he stared into the face of a huge Dragon. The size of the beast was beyond his wildest nightmares. It stood outside the tent, its head filling the entire open side. The Dragon's golden eyes regarded him more directly, but no less placidly than Solomon's.

"Well, son, do you *have* a name?"

Althus opened his mouth twice before he found his voice. He had been speaking the Dragon, not the large man his mind had conjured.

"Althus," he finally croaked. "My name is Althus." His wits seemed to have left him, but he managed to stammer a sincere thank you to Antares for saving his life before he fell silent, waiting for his heart to stop pounding before he spoke again.

Suddenly, he remembered Euwyn's tale of the Dragon Riders. Althus had been twelve or thirteen at the time and had expressed a fervent desire to be as tall as Euwyn. The Wizard, shaking his head, sat him down to hear their tale. Euwyn informed him they were so small in stature they grew to little more than half the height of most Wizards. Euwyn knew little of them except they called themselves the Brotherhood of the Dragon and they were sworn to help those in need traveling the dangerous paths deep in the Hoary Mountains.

They dwelt far to the south, according to Euwyn, deeper in the mountains than Euwyn had ever traveled. The Wizard had seen a Dragon only once, and then from a great distance, as it caught the sun, turning away southward from where the Wizard stood. If the tale was true and if Solomon was a Dragon rider, then this Dragon was his ally rather than a threat to him.

Althus looked at Solomon curiously. Euwyn had described the Dragon Riders as fierce warriors. He had not mentioned anything about them not speaking. Solomon moved about his tasks as if his mind were elsewhere. There was a disturbing sadness and weariness about him. He looked as if he had not eaten well in a long time. Was Euwyn wrong about the Dragons and their Riders? Was Solomon a prisoner of the Dragon? Althus did not think so. Solomon seemed to ignore the Dragon, not fear him. There was something wrong here.

Althus wondered how far away his friends were now and whether he would ever see them again. They must think him dead in any case. He thought of Bree and his distress was plain on his face.

Antares tipped his head, regarding him closely. "Do not worry, Althus you are not a prisoner here. When you have rested, we will return you to your friends. Sollie and I will take you as far as the northern edge of the mountains. We do not travel beyond the safety of the mountains according to our oath, but I expect your friends cannot be far from there." He turned his head to look at Solomon his eyes narrowing. "Sollie will accompany us. Tomorrow."

Althus could not help thinking he would agree to anything if the Dragon looked at him in that manner, but Solomon only looked off toward the ruins and did not answer.

"Very well, then, Sollie," Antares roared, causing Althus to duck his head and cover his ears. "Do what you must! Break your vows to the Brotherhood! I will find another rider! Perhaps Althus will take your place! He cannot be as big a fool as you!"

Solomon seemed unmoved by the Dragon's tirade. He gathered a bucket in each hand and walked off across the alpine meadow leaving the Dragon staring after him.

Antares swung his head back to glare at Althus, causing him to flinch away involuntarily. He dropped to his belly with a disgusted sound, his eyes losing their fire as he said, more quietly, "I hoped your presence here would change his mind. He seemed as if it might. He certainly did a fine job stitching your leg. He cared enough about you to watch over you until you woke and we knew you would live. You lost a lot of blood, you know. Perhaps if you were to take a turn for the worse." Antares eyed him speculatively before he continued. "No, I could never lie to him. It would be unfair. He cannot lie to me and you have a smell of Elf about you. You probably could not lie to him either, even if his life depended upon it. Perhaps it is best to let him do as he wishes. He knows I will see you safely back to your friends without him if I must. Damned Elf." The Dragon heaved a sad sigh and fell silent.

"Elf? He looks much like an Elf I know, but he is not nearly as tall as Chess and his kin. Is he really an Elf?" asked Althus, too intrigued now for fear of the Dragon to keep him silent.

"The Brotherhood of the Dragon are Mountain Elves, the most ancient Elven race. Your friend must be a Wood Elf if he resembles Solomon. Sea Elves are more like you in appearance. All have common ancestors. You appear to have some Human blood in you. Yes?"

Althus nodded, astonished at the knowledge of the races the Dragon possessed. He wished Euwyn were here to speak to Antares. The Wizard would have some interesting questions to ask such a learned beast.

"What can I do to help Solomon?" Althus asked. "Is there an enemy that threatens him? I would like to repay him for his fine care. I am skilled with the sword and the bow. Will he let me help him? Can he speak? I have yet to hear him utter a word."

"Whoa, young warrior," the Dragon laughed, a sound like distant thunder. "You are in no shape for fighting yet. In any case, although there are enemies in abundance in our mountains of late, Sollie's enemy is Sollie himself. Come, Althus, I am sorry to have called you a mere amusement for Sollie. I thought perhaps I could get some reaction from him," said the Dragon, snorting a small gout of fire from his nostrils and looking after Solomon, a small figure receding into the distance.

"He will be going as far as the falls for water. We have time to talk before he returns. Sit with your sore shoulders against my side and I will tell you Sollie's tale while the heat of my body eases your torn muscles. I am responsible for those injuries, I fear. You are fortunate you were wearing such a marvelous coat of mail when I was forced to catch you in mid air."

Althus could not help but think he was more thankful he was not conscious during the experience. He limped over to sit against the Dragon's side. It was like sitting with his back against a forge. Solomon's tea and the Dragon's warmth eased his sore shoulders and when he leaned his aching head back against the Dragon's side, it eased that as well. He grinned when he thought of what he was doing. No one would believe him.

Now that he was less fearful of the Dragon, he was able to admire his beauty. His scales were as green and as glossy as finely cut emeralds, each edged with bands of gold and red.

The smallest were palm sized and the largest big enough for both of Althus' hands to fit side-by-side. Brilliant red whisker-like barbels hung from his ears and his broad muzzle. Althus was surprised to find Dragons had ears. They made him look even less the lizard-like creature Althus pictured when he imagined what a Dragon might look like. They were dog like, sticking straight out or folding against his head, or assuming any position in between as they reflected his mood. His eyes were golden and slitted like a cat's. Beyond the confines of the tent, Althus could see along the entire length of the Dragon. Antares was as long and sinuous as a serpent with huge, leathery red wings folded at his sides. It would take ten horses standing head to tail to match his length. Althus tried to picture him knifing through the skies with Solomon astride him, scanning the lands below for Orcs or the skies above for the Myoti for which Antares seemed to hold a special hatred. He was unaware he had closed his eyes until Antares asked him if he was weary. He assured the Dragon he was wide awake and Antares began Solomon's tale.

"I will not start too far in the past as Sollie grew up in the usual manner, a child of the Mountain Elves from a village much like that whose ruins you see across the meadow. Orcs killed Solomon's mother when he was very young and he grew up in the Hall with his father, a Dragon Rider and another child named Joseph who lost his entire family in the same raid. Jonah, Solomon's father, took Joseph in and raised them as brothers. Solomon and Joseph joined the Brotherhood of the Dragon as many young men do who are brave enough, following in their father's footsteps. I remember Solomon well as a young man in training. He laughed often and smiled always. I would give much just to see his smile again.

"I was bound to Brother Augustine at the time. He is the head of our order and I was last bound to him. Sollie and I spent much time together, patrolling the mountains with Joseph and his Dragon, Procyon. Augustine was intending to retire soon from active duty and I was free to carry Solomon. Sollie soon became the best and bravest of the Brotherhood and became Second Rider, second only to Augustine. He would have been bonded to a Dragon, any Dragon who would choose to be his life's partner. I think it was Augustine's wish that Solomon be bound to me, although he never said so aloud. We are free to choose our own Riders.

"That never came to pass. Solomon met a woman from this village whose ruins you see before you and fell in love with her. This is not forbidden, mind you. Many of the brothers are married and many children roam the Halls of the Brotherhood. We all rejoiced in Sollie's happiness.

Her name was Bess. I met her once. Sollie brought her especially to meet me. She was a pretty little thing, I suppose, if you consider Elves pretty. They seemed happy in each other's company, and to me it seemed as if they shared every thought in their heads. A year ago to this day they were to be married.

"If we had only suspected what lurked near this isolated, north most village we could have prevented what happened here." Antares paused to look at the ruins in silence before continuing his tale. "If the Orcs and Goblins had descended on any other day, perhaps they would have been detected, but wedding plans were on everyone's mind. It seems no one in the village thought to carry weapons to a wedding. We had not been troubled this far north by such creatures for a hundred years or more. They descended upon this village a thousand strong, an unprecedented number of creatures, against less than a hundred villagers.

"They killed everyone in the village and burned it to the ground. Sollie was the only survivor and he would have died soon after the others had the Brothers not arrived for the wedding celebration. The Orcs and Goblins were no match for armed Dragon riders. We soon killed them all, but it was too late for Bess and the rest of her village. We found Sollie, his limbs broken, bleeding from dozens of wounds, beaten nearly senseless, still trying to reach her side. He killed a good number of the enemy with his bare hands before they overwhelmed him. In retaliation, they made him witness the death of everyone in the village, men, women, and children alike, and none died an easy death. He wore the uniform of the Brotherhood and was truly his father's son. They made him pay dearly for it. I suspect somehow the evil that controls these creatures knew of the celebration to take place that day and it was not coincidence that brought them here. I hate to think it, but there may be a traitor among the ranks of the Brotherhood.

"Joseph carried him back to the Hall of the Brotherhood. He was soaked in Sollie's blood before they reached it. We did not expect him to survive the trip, but he did. I did not expect him to live through the night, but Brother Augustine and the rest of the Brothers would not give up on him. He lay near death for nearly a month before he slowly began to heal. I can hardly believe he is as whole as ever in body, if not in mind. He bears scars, but they are fading.

"Brother Augustine loves him still, no matter how the events of a year ago have changed him. When Sollie left the Brotherhood, Brother Augustine released me from my bond to him so I could follow Sollie and keep him safe until he recovered.

"If he had not, Joseph would have followed Solomon, despite the fact Solomon has not spoken to Joseph or even met his eyes in the past year. We could all see this was destroying Joseph as well. Augustine felt it best to separate them. He keeps Joseph busy, tending to his duties, and I am here, guarding this mad creature who cannot recover.

"Augustine still does not give up hope. He comes to see Sollie often and now that Sollie has settled here for a while, he brings food and supplies. Joseph was allowed to come only once. It was a mistake. It was as if Solomon was blind to him. I do not think Solomon knew he was before him until Joseph touched him. Solomon was frozen with fear then, as he was today when you touched his hands.

"Joseph backed away as if he had been struck. Solomon screamed in his sleep that entire night. I could not wake him. It was as if he were punished for touching another. He called Joseph's name, but Joseph was not there to hear it. I do not think it would have comforted Joseph much to know it.

"Perhaps he will be punished for touching you. Perhaps he feels it does not matter since he will take his own life tonight," Antares shook his head. "No, he would have cared for you even if he suffered for it. That is the kind of man he is, the kind of man that is now lost to the Brotherhood."

Antares heaved a gusty sigh. "At least Sollie has supplies enough to take care of you, even though he himself has been living little better than an animal. He has not spoken a word in a year except when he cries out in his sleep. If not for that, I would wonder if he *could* speak. His dreams are so troubled, he seldom sleeps now, but what is worse, I think he sees them dying when he merely closes his eyes. It is as if something or someone still holds him. I think the Dark Lord's wraiths did something to his mind that day, something that will not allow him to forget.

"He seems weary. I am weary from watching him suffer. I am a Dragon, after all. He will not ride and I cannot stay earth bound forever. He is a Rider still, and could return to his post in the Brotherhood if he only would consider it. When I encountered you, I had made up my mind to leave him before he took his own life tonight in the ruins.

"I know that is what he intends. I can see it in his eyes. He holds his father's knife, staring at it as if it will help him do what he feels he must.

"In the end, I could not leave him. I would have turned back even without you, but when I rescued you, I hoped you would serve as a diversion from this madness. Well, you needed saving and those creatures needed killing, so the effort was not all loss."

Althus gazed at the ruins. He tried to imagine what it would be like to see the people of an entire village, people you knew and loved, tortured to death while you looked on, helpless to save them. When he reached the point where he imagined he could hear the screams of the dying, he tried to think of something else.

Sollie returned soon after Antares concluded his tale. Althus could not help looking at the small Elf in a different light. He was a warrior, clearly more experienced and skilled than Althus. Second in command to a force as ancient and powerful as any in the world, but captive to the horrors of the events of one single day.

Althus found himself desperately wanting to help him in some way, but if Antares had failed and Joseph could not reach him, what was there for him to do? Perhaps the Dragon was right. Perhaps a decent end was all Althus could offer him. He was determined to accompany the small Elf wherever he went tonight. If he could not prevent him from taking his own life, at least he would not die alone.

The mountain air grew cold as the sun neared the western horizon. After looking closely at his wounded leg, Solomon helped Althus into his clothes and wrapped a fleecy blanket about him. He himself still wore only breeches, but did not seem to notice the cold.

Althus wondered what spark still remained that made him aware Althus might suffer from it. Somewhere in his troubled mind, he still thought as a healer would. Was Antares wrong? Maybe Solomon would not take his own life tonight as the Dragon feared he would. How could the Dragon be so certain if Solomon never spoke? Althus was determined to watch over him through the night.

Solomon brewed him another cup of tea and Althus drank it eagerly, thinking he would need something to deaden his pain if he intended to follow Solomon as far as the ruins. Too late he realized the tea contained more than something to ease his pain. He fought sleep desperately, but the little healer knew his business well and Althus was soon fast asleep on his bed of furs.

Althus awoke with a start some hours later. He struggled painfully to his feet, knowing somehow that Solomon was already gone. He found Antares lying not far from the tent, his eyes intent on the ruins.

"You did not stop him," Althus said more as a statement than a question.

"No," the Dragon replied without turning his head, "I could not. I will truly miss him. Riders come and go, but he was special."

"You have made your choice, then, to let him go," said Althus.

"It was his choice. When he left, I thought I saw a moment of indecision. He made sure you rested comfortably before he went. He stood looking at you for a long time, his hands clenched at his sides as if he would have embraced you in farewell if he dared. This touching thing is important to Elves. I do not understand it myself, but I am told it is so. I hoped he would stay to see you returned to your friends safely, but in the end, he left as I feared he would."

Althus did not waste any more time on words. He started for the ruins as quickly as his wounded leg would allow.

"Be cautious, Althus," Antares called after him. "He is as deadly with his bare hands as he is with a blade and if you cross him or he does not know you, he would kill you easily, even if you were armed."

Althus shuddered at that thought. He considered going back for his sword, but knew he would not use it against Solomon even if he had it in his hands.

The moon bathed the meadow in pale light, but he still stumbled over rocks buried in the tall grass that he could not see. He did not risk casting the spell that would illuminate his way. He was afraid of what Solomon would do if he saw his approach. He reached the ruins and began searching as silently as he could for some sign of Solomon. He was shivering, not from the cold, but from the eerie feeling the ruined village watched him as he disturbed the silence had reigned there for a year. His footsteps echoed off the tumbled gray stones that once formed walls protecting the families who inhabited this place. His imagination conjured up the sound of children laughing as they chased each other through the streets of the village. There were dark stains on the ground. In the moonlight, he could not say for certain whether they were bloodstains or something else entirely.

He came upon Solomon near the middle of the ruined village, still alive, kneeling before a half-burned archway adorned with dead remnants of vines and greenery. Althus recognized it at once as the place where Solomon and Bess should have pledged their lives to each other a year ago. Solomon held the point of a knife to his heart. It glittered in the moonlight. Antares' last words came to him again. Althus stood only three paces away, uncertain of what he should do next. He opened his mouth to speak, but his voice caught in his throat. Another voice, whispering across the ruined courtyard made his blood run cold.

"Solomon," it whispered, a woman's voice like the wind through tall grass. "Solomon, do not do this."

"Bess?"

Althus was startled, realizing the answering voice was Solomon's, barely more than a whisper. He began to see the figure of a woman standing before Solomon, the moonlight shining through her as if she were made of mist. More figures appeared behind the first and Althus could hear more than one voice now, repeating Solomon's name. Solomon dropped the knife and covered his face with his hands.

"Look at me, Solomon," Bess whispered. "We are at peace. We have been at peace for a year. Can you not find peace, Solomon?"

"I see it," Solomon said, dropping his hands from his face and reaching toward Bess, the horror plain on his face even in the moonlight. "I see it again and again. I hear the screams. I see the children die. I cannot forget. I cannot forgive myself. I see your deaths each time I close my eyes. I cannot go on. Please, Bess, help me. My resolve weakens." Solomon's voice faded to a whisper again as he spoke the last words, but Althus heard them and clung to them. There was a part of Solomon that did not want to die.

"I will help you, Solomon, but not in the way you ask. In the dark days to come, you will be needed here," Bess said as the figures behind her moved toward Solomon. Each figure walked past Solomon where he knelt, speaking his name in soft, echoing voices, passing a hand through him before disappearing into thin air. The tiniest of them leapt straight through him. Althus thought he could hear them giggling as they did. Bess touched him last of all, speaking words to him Althus could not hear before she walked away. She did not disappear as the others had, but appeared before Althus. He was too startled to do more than bow his head in greeting. He had not seen her approach. She was suddenly there before him, her eyes looking at him gravely.

"Care for him tonight, Prince Althus. The coldness in his heart will kill him if you do not. The Dragon cannot help him. A Dragon's heart is forever cold. It is their nature. Your heart beats as hot and fierce as Solomon's. Your futures are bound together. If he dies, your cause will fail." Her last words echoed into silence and she was gone as suddenly as she had come.

He found Solomon lying on the ground where he had knelt. Althus laid his hand on his shoulder and called his name, but he did not answer. Frost coated his skin, frost colder than the mountain air about them. Solomon glittered as if the stars had fallen from the skies to cover him.

Althus took his coat off, wrapped it about Solomon and gathered him into his arms. It was like embracing an armful of winter snow. He was thankful the Elf was small. Althus' battered shoulders ached before he had stumbled more than a few steps, but there was no fuel for a fire here. Everything that would burn had been turned to ash a year ago. He made his way out of the ruins and stopped at the edge of the meadow. There was nothing to burn here, either. He would not let Solomon die now if he could help it. He started doggedly across the meadow, his eyes on the ground before him, trying not to fall on his face. A sudden rush of air pushed against him, nearly bowling him over, and Antares stood before him blocking out the moonlight.

"I came," he said simply. "I did not want you to carry his body far with your wounds. I will cremate his remains as a final service to him."

Althus stood gaping stupidly at the Dragon for a moment. He clutched Solomon tightly as if Antares might cremate him before Althus could tell him he was still alive. He finally recovered his wits enough to inform the Dragon that Solomon was not dead.

Althus was shivering without his coat. Antares ordered him to sit and curled his massive body around them, extending a wing over them to shield them from the cold night air. The Dragon was better than a fire. He tucked his head under his wing, adding his hot breath to the heat of his body. Althus leaned Solomon against the Dragon's side and sat beside him, holding him close. He could not think of anything more to do for him. He wrapped his arms about him and hoped it was enough. Solomon stirred during the night, shivering in the manner of Elves as he recovered. Antares said he seemed at peace and Althus did not try to wake him. He wondered if Euwyn had felt the same when she held Althus as a child. He felt strangely drawn to the little Elf, but when he laid a hand on Solomon's curly head where it had come to rest in his lap, Antares spoke to him softly.

"Do not make the mistake of thinking of Sollie as a child, Althus. Even though he is as small as a child of your people, I have seen him kill an Orc many times his size with his bare hands. He is as dangerous a warrior as I have ever seen, even unarmed. Few warriors of any size would equal him when he is armed with blade or bow."

"I will not leave him here alone, Antares. I know you would care for him, but I want to be here with him when he wakes. Besides, he has my coat and it is too cold out there to wander about in my shirtsleeves."

Antares laughed softly in the dark. "You are much like him, you know. At least, like he once was. Up to now, he still seemed to know friend from foe, but I cannot say what state he will be in when he wakes. He has been growing worse of late. I hope his journey to the place where he was wounded has not unhinged him totally. I never thought I would have to warn another such as you against him. He has always been a compassionate little fellow. Perhaps that was his downfall. He could not recover from the death of Bess and the people of her village."

Althus looked at the small Elf huddled against his side and tried to take Antares' warning to heart, but it was hard to imagine Solomon harming anyone. His clear voice as he spoke to Bess in the village did not seem like that of a man gone mad. He was overwhelmed with grief and guilt over what had happened to her and her people, but he did not seem mad. Althus could not imagine surviving to live on if Bree and her family suffered such a fate before his eyes.

He tried to stay awake in light of Antares' warning, but his mind wandered sleepily. He wondered where Bree was now. He hoped he could introduce Bree and Solomon to each other. Was she thinking of him? He supposed she must be.

Antares' words came back to him. It was true of the Elves he knew. They touched each other often, a hand to another's arm when speaking, an arm about another's shoulders. At first, he had thought it a gesture between family members, but he was subject to the same gestures. It was a way of communication for them as important as speaking, perhaps more important and more direct. He realized how truly isolated Solomon had become, separated from those he called his brothers. Antares believed Solomon could not touch another without punishment. How had he endured it?

Althus soon slept as well, dreaming of the children he and Bree might have, while Antares watched over both of them.

## Chapter Twenty-eight

## DRAGONFLIGHT

Althus awoke the next morning to find Solomon missing. His own coat lay across his lap, the small knife lying upon it. He shuddered to think Solomon still had it in his possession as he lay by his side. When he crawled out from beneath Antares' wing the little Elf was nowhere in sight. Taking advantage of Althus' exit, Antares uncurled himself, stretching his great red wings and yawning wide enough to show his broad tongue and a shocking number of sharp teeth in a display Althus could have appreciated if he were not driven frantic by Solomon's absence.

"Where is he, Antares?" he shouted, turning about to take in the surrounding terrain, hoping to see the Elf somewhere within sight.

"He left," said the Dragon.

"Where did he go?" Althus was really beginning to feel frantic now.

"Do not worry," the Dragon said on the verge of another yawn. "He left early this morning. He said he would find you some breakfast. I *hope* he finds you some breakfast. You must be hungry. All this hopping around, chasing about in the dark. Waste of energy." He yawned once more. "You should stop jumping about before you open that wound in your leg. Sollie was most concerned to find you had been wandering about the meadow in the cold and dark last night. He told me to keep an eye on you. You do not want him to think me untrustworthy, do you?"

Althus stopped suddenly, his mouth falling open as the Dragon's words hit him. "He said...? He told you to keep an eye on me? He spoke to you!"

"I wondered when you would catch on," Antares said. "You are not nearly as intelligent as you look. What happened in the ruins last night? What did you say to him to change his mind?"

"I did not say a word to him. There were spirits in the ruins last night, Bess and the rest of the people from her village. They did something to him. I do not know what, exactly. Maybe Solomon can give us some answers."

"Well," said Antares, sounding skeptical. "Spirits, you say. Hm. Well, Sollie said to meet him at the falls. Brother Augustine left Sollie's gear there when he realized where we were headed in hopes he would come to his senses and wear the uniform of the order once again. Thank the Creator he left a tent and Sollie's medical supplies as well, for your sake. I am hopeful we will find him suitably clothed for once and not running around half naked like a mountain savage."

Althus laughed at the Dragon's obvious disgust for Solomon's lack of decorum.

"Come, Althus, you have been on that leg too much and I suspect your head wound might be troubling you. Spirits, indeed! Climb up and I will carry you to the falls."

Althus looked at him doubtfully.

"Do not worry, Althus. I will not leave the ground with you. At least, not yet," Antares assured him.

With a boulder nearby and some help from Antares, Althus was just able to scramble up to perch behind the Dragon's head. They wandered across the meadow, the warm sunshine turning the damp grass to a sea of diamonds. Althus began to wonder if the last day had been a dream produced by the wound to his head and he would wake to find Solomon and Antares were products of his imagination. It was not that his head did not feel much better this morning, but it all seemed so improbable. If Antares held to his promise, he would soon be back among his friends and would press on from there to Anduin. They could reach Anduin tomorrow or the next day. He prayed fervently that his companions had made their way safely through the mountains. With Euwyn to guide and protect them, he felt it was most likely they had.

Across the meadow, Althus could see a thin stream cascading down from a rift high in the mountainside. Antares made straight for it, his huge strides covering the distance in a very short time. Solomon was there when they arrived. He now wore a handsomely cut red coat embroidered about the collar and cuffs with golden Dragons and black leather boots over his breeches. He no longer looked through Althus, but took his hands in greeting. Althus looked on, grinning as Solomon stared at their clasped hands, reluctant to let go. He did release Althus eventually, returning Althus' delighted grin with a steady look.

"I am sorry. Where have my manners gone? Sit, Althus," he said. "Eat something before I tend your wounds and then we will be on our way."

Althus thought the words rather ordinary for what Solomon had been through, but the sound of his voice was enough. It was an Elf's voice. It rang clear like the voices of the other Elves he had met, no lighter or less melodic despite his small size. Althus found himself waiting eagerly for him to speak again, reluctant to say more than a few words himself. Still he could not refuse when Solomon asked him to tell them of the mission that had brought him and his companions into the mountains. They sat in the shade of a small grove of trees, enjoying the music of the falling water while Althus told them his tale from beginning to end, leaving out nothing except his title, Prince of Anduin. A look that passed between Solomon and Antares made Althus wonder if he should have told them of his claim to the throne of Anduin.

"Your tale is amazing, Althus. It seems we are destined to fight the same foes in different lands," said Solomon. "The Brotherhood will be much interested in your story. The enemy seeks to gain a foothold farther north than we imagined. Perhaps we will have to extend our influence beyond the mountains. When we have seen you safely back to your friends I must report to the Hall and Brother Augustine and make my apologies to him. I hope to reclaim my post as his Second. Perhaps Antares here would consent to a bonding with me. I owe him much. Perhaps he is sick of me." He looked to the Dragon for an answer.

"You have been difficult lately, Sollie. However, I suppose if you have become yourself again and the Brotherhood agrees, I would consider it," said the Dragon.

Somehow, Althus knew it was already done.

"Tell me, are all Dragon riders healers as well?" Althus asked as Solomon redressed his head wound and his leg.

"Yes, we all study healing to some degree. Some are more skilled than others," he answered. "It makes our lives more balanced, according to Brother Augustine. He is our greatest healer. Killing and healing are opposites, it seems. We often heal the victims of the creatures we kill if it is not beyond our skills to help them. Some we take to the Halls for healing by the elder Brothers. I suppose that is why Brother Augustine no longer rides into battle. He is too valuable as a healer to risk losing him.

"You will not need his skills, Althus. It seems you are on the mend already. It is a long flight to the northern edge of the mountains, but I think you are fit enough to travel. We will arrive by nightfall if the weather holds."

Althus tried to imagine flying over the mountains on Antares' back. He hoped he would not embarrass himself. He was glad the Dragon was intelligent. At least Althus hoped he would fly carefully with a novice aboard.

When the time came to leave, Solomon leapt up easily to sit astride the Dragon. He offered his hand to Althus who scrambled up to sit behind him. They stopped at the tent to gather Althus' weapons and mail. Solomon dismounted and mounted the huge Dragon so easily, his small hands and feet finding purchase among the Dragon's glassy scales, while even with Solomon's hand to help him, Althus had found it difficult to scramble up the Dragon's sleek sides. His wounded leg and sore shoulders hindered him, but he still did not think he could manage the climb without the small Elf's hands to help him, even without his wounds. Althus smiled to himself. This was certainly what Solomon was born to do. He wore a bow and sword now, similar to the ones Althus carried, but crafted in a size to suit Solomon. They seemed a part of him. It was not difficult to imagine him, as small as he was, leading the Dragon riders to war against evil forces invading the mountains of his homeland. His eyes scanned the skies as if they were home to him.

With a short run and a powerful stroke of his wings, Antares was airborne. Althus clung to Solomon as the Dragon left the ground. The meadow below receded at a frightening rate as the Dragon gained altitude. Solomon looked over his shoulder and Althus grinned at him, happy to be on his way and fascinated by the terrain passing beneath them. It was not as frightening as he feared. It was easy to pretend he looked at a very detailed map and not the unforgiving boulders of the mountainside passing leagues below. Althus only gave a small gasp when Antares paused momentarily in mid air before diving down one mountainside and soaring up the next.

Solomon smacked him on top of his scaly head. "Stop showing off, Antares. If it is your wish that I wear my uniform once again, you cannot cause Althus to leave his breakfast all over it."

Antares snorted, "Althus is no coward. Perhaps we can make a Dragon Rider of him."

Althus laughed, "I cannot even mount you without Solomon's help. I think I was meant to keep both feet on the ground for the most part."

The Dragon's flight was effortless. He threaded the mountain passes, knowing his route exactly. Of course, he had been this way only a day ago. To Althus, it seemed too many amazing things had happened for only the span of a day.

The morning passed quickly with Althus caught up in the beautiful mountain terrain passing below him, a different vista unfolding with each mountain ridge they crossed. Solomon seemed to radiate confidence as he gazed ahead, keeping an eye on the mountains and the skies. They stayed close to the peaks, avoiding the more frigid air of the higher altitudes. Solomon assured him they could fly much higher, but he was concerned Althus would suffer from the cold. Althus would have been glad for the cloak he had given Mica at the bridge, but the scenery below so enchanted him he hardly noticed.

Near midday, they landed in a wooded valley at the base of yet another small cascade of water, a narrow thread of white that fell down the mountainside from the snow that capped its peak. After Solomon and Althus dismounted, Antares excused himself and flew off down the valley to find a meal of fresh meat. Solomon and Althus settled themselves in a grassy glade and shared a meal of dried meat, fruit and cheese. After they had finished their meal, Solomon lay on his back on the grass, watching the sky for Antares' return. He wore such a look of peaceful contentment Althus could not resist asking him what he remembered from the night before. Solomon continued to look at the sky, but his eyes held a faraway look as if he searched for a memory already becoming unclear.

"I can remember most of it, Althus," he began. "I remember seeing Bess very clearly and the rest of the people of her village, her family and their little children. As they each passed a hand through me, I felt coldness. With each touch, I grew colder." He rolled on his side to regard Althus with golden eyes that seemed to shine with the memory. "Each one took the memory of their death from me and left a bit of their lives in its place. I do not know if I can explain it to you, Althus. I know they are dead. I remember how they died, but I can no longer see their deaths even when I try to. The knowledge is there, but not the sight of it. In its place, they each left me with a bit of wisdom they treasured when they were alive. Even the littlest child left me with some bit of knowledge... where to find the best shiny stones, where to find the sweetest berries, the best places to hide when your mother has chores for you to do. I suppose it must seem a lot of useless information to you, but I think I will carry it with me always. Sometimes the things we think most common are not common at all."

Althus nodded in agreement. He smiled, thinking of the giggles he had heard when the children touched Solomon. Solomon did not smile back, but he rolled onto his back in the grass with a satisfied sigh.

"It is good to ride Antares again. Very good."

Solomon sat up to look at Althus. "You are angry with Antares for letting me go last night."

Althus nodded. "How could he give up on you? How could he let you go there alone?"

"Do not be angry with him, Althus. I am sure I used up what little pity his Dragon heart could muster long ago. He is a Dragon, after all. They do not think as we do. They have pledged themselves to our cause, but they are not ours to command. We are partners, Antares and I. I have failed him this past year. I have not held true to my part of our agreement."

"I will forgive him, then, Solomon, but you must forgive yourself as well," Althus said.

Solomon sighed and looked away.

"You must tell me something, Althus," he said. "Why did you not tell us you were Prince of Anduin?"

The question caught Althus by surprise. "How... how did you know?" he finally managed to stammer.

"Bess told me," Solomon answered still staring placidly at the sky.

Althus remembered Bess calling him Prince of Anduin. He answered Solomon's question as truthfully as he could. It still seemed too strange to be true. If anyone but Euwyn had told the tale, he would have thought them mad.

"I see," said Solomon, seeming to mull it over for a moment. "That explains your lack of arrogance. I would expect you to be at least a little conceited if you had been brought up in a palace as a prince."

"I fear it is too late to learn to act like a prince. I am too much a peasant at heart, I fear. I was fortunate to have Euwyn to teach me so at least I do not lack education even if I am lacking in arrogance."

"Well, I, for one," Solomon said, "think you are a vast improvement over the few princes I have met."

"Thank you, Solomon. I value your opinion."

This earned Althus a nod of agreement, but Althus was disappointed when Solomon still did not smile.

## Chapter Twenty-nine

## REUNION

Antares reappeared licking his jaws after a successful hunt. After another takeoff even more abrupt than the first in order to clear the trees, they were airborne again. Althus settled himself as securely as he could and resumed his study of the terrain passing below.

The sun was lowering in the west when Antares announced they had passed the region where he had rescued Althus from the Myoti. Their path from that point would have to depend on Althus' memory of the terrain they had traveled to reach the suspended bridge from the gates of Stonehaven. Solomon informed Althus they did not often stray near the kingdom of the Dwarves, as there was no love between Dwarves and Dragons. The terrain from this point would be unfamiliar to Antares.

Althus turned them westward, hoping his memory of Granite's map was accurate and they would find the bridge by skirting the south slopes of the northern arm of the mountains. Althus almost missed the ruined bridge. Antares circled southward, retracing their route, passing over the Black Giants' valley and the peak they had scaled to enter Stonehaven's back gate. All seemed peaceful. Even the meadow before Stonehaven's massive gates was empty. Althus wished he could catch a glimpse of Granite or one of his people as he soared overhead, but they were most likely busy within the halls of Stonehaven. They had much to do to restore it to its former glory.

Antares landed on the ledge before the gates of the Dwarves' passageway where Althus had last glimpsed his companions. There was no sign of them, but he had not expected them to stand waiting for him on that forsaken jut of rock. There was no way for them to travel onward except through the passage. There was no other way to escape the ledge. They must think him long dead. He could hardly believe he had survived. Antares merely dropped off the ledge and twisted, soaring through the rift below to become airborne. Althus' stomach twisted violently as well as the Dragon left the ledge, making him feel weightless for a moment before the Dragon's powerful wings bore them upward toward the peaks above.

They headed due north while Althus tried to recall as many details as he could from Granite's map concerning the northern entrance to the passage. Antares soon flew through the highest passes that lay within the heart of the mountain range and was losing altitude in an easy glide toward Anduin.

Althus could see his homeland from here, although he could not make it out in any great detail. His breath caught on a lump in his throat when he could finally make out the massive walls of Castle Anduin in the distance. What was happening there? Would they reach it in time? A small voice in the back of his head asked what he would be in time for. Surely, a Wizard, a Dwarf, a Human and three Elves were no match for the army of thousands that approached the kingdom of Anduin. He was a poor excuse for a prince, but he could not stand by and do nothing while Anduin fell. He was all the people of Anduin had, unless the king had come to his senses.

He hoped to find his little band of friends safely through the mountains. They were all he had to give him the courage to press on. The sun was nearing the western horizon as they skimmed down the slope of the last mountain before the land opened out into the wide valley of the Anduin River. The wind howled past his ears as Antares dove earthward, gaining speed at a terrifying rate. Althus did not realize he was holding his breath until the Dragon leveled out and he released it.

"Enough of your antics, Dragon!" Solomon shouted over the howl of the wind, "You will have Althus breaking one of my ribs if you persist."

This brought a rumble from the Dragon Althus took for laughter. He was embarrassed to find he had indeed wrapped his arms about the small Elf before him like a frightened maiden sitting behind the rider of a runaway horse. He let go while Solomon could still breathe.

Antares swung in a wide circle while Althus fervently hoped none of the people of Anduin noticed the huge Dragon flying along the mountain slopes so close to their homes. They flew westward, closely following the slopes of the mountains, searching for an opening the map described between two peaks. When they found nothing that looked like the area they sought in that direction, they circled out over the valley once again and returned to the slopes to search eastward. Althus feared they would run out of daylight before they found the valley for which they searched, but Solomon suddenly bent to speak into Antares' ear and pointed ahead to a valley that fit the description on the map. Antares made another banking turn that made Althus' knees quiver, sailing through a narrow rift in the mountains that widened into a broad valley as they rode an updraft into the mountains. Antares landed at the point where the valley began to narrow once more toward the foot of the mountain, lying on his belly while Althus and Solomon slid to the ground. Althus had to lean against the Dragon for a moment before his legs would hold him without wobbling. He shivered from the cold, wishing he could lean against the Dragon's warmth for a while longer as he watched the Elf peer up the valley.

"There is no sense in flying all the way in and risking an arrow. We can go the rest of the way on foot. If your Bree is as good with a bow as you say, she could find a soft spot to stick an arrow in Antares' hide before she catches sight of you. Best to avoid that. It makes him unbearably touchy for days," Solomon remarked casually.

Althus looked at the Dragon wondering what a Dragon would be like if he were "touchy."

"Well, you know what it is like, Althus," growled the Dragon defensively, "I have seen the scars in your hide."

Althus remembered being nearly dead from the arrows in his hide, not merely "touchy." He nodded in sympathy.

"Althus!" Solomon stepped closer and grabbed his arm, pointing up the valley toward the mountainside. "I think I see them!"

Althus looked to where Solomon pointed. He thought he could just see a white speck moving down the valley that could be Bree's horse, Moon. Solomon was nearly as excited as he was. He was dragging Althus up the valley at a near run despite his injured leg before the last words left his mouth, giving Althus no time to be sure of what he was seeing. Antares gave another of his rumbling chuckles as he ambled along a short distance behind.

As they drew nearer, Althus could make out five horses of varying hues and five figures of varying sizes leading them. There could be no mistaking the golden heads of the three Elves shining in the fading twilight, the small, broad Dwarf and the tall, dark Wizard striding down the valley.

"They have made it safely through the mountains, Solomon!" Althus shouted. "Those are my friends! It must be them!"

He could not yet make out their faces, but a cry from Bree told him the Elves could see his. Althus stumbled into a run as Bree left the rest to run down the valley toward him. They met in a tangle of arms and legs. Bree kissed him roughly before he could say a word and wrapped herself about him as closely as she could. When they parted, they were both laughing and crying at once. Euwyn was close behind Bree, wrapping one arm about his shoulders, the other hand pressing Althus' head against his chest. It was unnerving to Althus to find the Wizard dampening his head with tears. He had never seen him cry. He found Mica beaming up at him, his arms about his waist while Thorny and Chess each had a hand on his shoulders. Thorny smiled with obvious delight and relief while Chess grinned from ear to ear, wiping tears from his bright eyes with his sleeve. The horses gathered about the group, Gust thrusting his nose beneath his arm, demanding attention. The first moments of shock and disbelief passed and then everyone began to ask questions at once.

"You are hurt," said Bree, touching the bandage about his head.

"You are shivering as well," said Thorny, taking Althus' cloak from Mica's eager hands and wrapping it about his shoulders. "It must have been cold, flying through the mountains without your cloak."

"Which of your wounds troubles you most, Althus?" Euwyn asked anxiously. "I will heal that injury first."

"My wounds are well tended, father. There is no need for you to trouble yourself." Althus assured him.

Althus wanted to ask why Chess reeked like a fish dead three days, but decided to save it for later.

"Where did you find the Dragon, Althus?" Mica asked quietly. Mica's question silenced them all. They turned to regard the Dragon and his rider.

When Althus ran ahead, Solomon and Antares stopped to watch, keeping some distance from the confusion. Until that moment, the only ones eyeing the Dragon were the horses. They stood at attention, ready to defend their riders.

Althus turned to introduce Solomon and Antares to his friends.

Chess strode toward the Dragon, his eyes bright with excitement. "He is beautiful! Where did you find him?"

"I found him hanging from the claws of a Myoti," rumbled the Dragon. "He *is* rather pretty for one who is mostly Human. He says he belongs to you. If he were mine, *I* would take better care of him."

Chess was so startled, he stumbled backward, landing on his backside some distance from where he started.

Solomon strode forward and offered Chess a hand. "I am Solomon of the Brotherhood of Dragon Riders. You must be Chess." Solomon led Chess back toward the others while Chess looked over his shoulder at Antares following behind.

"He talks!" said Chess.

"Yes. Unfortunately, he has a bad habit of talking too much." Solomon glared over his shoulder at the Dragon who was still laughing.

Althus introduced his rescuers to the rest of his friends. He watched as Euwyn and the Elves each knelt to embrace him and Mica thumped him on the back. They thanked the small Elf so profusely he began to turn red with embarrassment.

"I did little but tend his wounds," he protested. "Antares was his savior. Besides, it is the sworn oath of the Dragon Riders to help those we can, and he has repaid us."

"Well, Solomon," said Euwyn, noting the small Elf's growing uneasiness, "I am sure you two will have a tale to tell, but you must be tired and hungry after your long flight. We will make camp and have something to eat. Then you will tell us what you will of your adventures of the past two days."

He turned them back down the valley to where a grassy meadow offered a good place to rest for the night. Euwyn walked with an arm about Althus' shoulders, reluctant to let go. Bree was relieved to see the troubled look that worried her had disappeared the instant the Wizard set eyes on his missing son. She was no less relieved to see Althus alive and well, but she could not help but think Anduin's fate and therefore that of her father and her brother depended on both Euwyn and Althus. To have Althus back and the Wizard acting himself again seemed a promising start to their attempt to rescue the people of Anduin.

Althus and Solomon sat with Euwyn in the gathering twilight while Mica and the Elves quickly made camp and began preparations for their evening meal. Euwyn talked to Solomon of his life as a Dragon Rider, curious as always to know how other people lived and how the evil forces that threatened all the people of their world affected them. Solomon was informative and honest. He admitted he had left the Hall for a time and had not been back for many months, but would return to service now that Althus and his friends were reunited. He did not elaborate on his injuries or why he had left the Hall. To keep the curious Wizard from delving further, Althus turned to another subject.

"Tell me," asked Althus, "why does Chess smell like a three day old carp left in the sun to rot?"

"I knew it!" shouted Chess rounding on his siblings. "You said it was barely noticeable! I still smell! I will smell like this forever! It will never wash off!"

He dug a change of clothing and a chunk of soap out of his saddlebags and stalked off toward the stream that ran through the narrow valley on its way to the Anduin River.

"Someone should tell him the water in that particular stream smells as bad as he does," said Bree.

"I do not like to see him wandering off by himself and since I am the one who offended him, I will go," said Althus trying hard to hide his amusement. "You can tell us what happened later."

"Perhaps Antares and I should go also. Antares can heat water for him and dry him when he is finished," said Solomon as he joined Althus with the Dragon trailing behind. Gust was not about to let Althus out of his sight. He trotted off to place himself at Althus' shoulder, making a wide detour around the Dragon

Thorny, Euwyn, Mica and Bree watched Althus and Solomon walk away, followed by the huge Dragon who looked back at them over his shoulder and winked at them as he left. Euwyn laughed, pleased, but puzzled. "Something has happened between those two to make them such fast friends. Or should I say between those three." He shook his head in wonder. "I suppose we will hear the entire story when the time is right," he sighed. "Still, the boy gathers friends to him like Dwarves gather precious stones."

"Yeah, that's the truth," said Mica chuckling at the sight of the Dragon following Althus and Solomon like a lap dog. "Very big friends I'd say."

"He also has a knack for surviving when hoping for it seems impossible," Thorny added. "I hate to admit to Chess he was right."

"I thank the Creator he was," Bree said as they turned to their tasks.

Althus and Solomon caught up with Chess as he reached the stream. They were just in time to advise him to look for bath water elsewhere.

"It smells nearly as bad as you, Chess," said Althus.

Chess looked up the slope in the direction of the passage entrance with a look of revelation on his face. "Of course," he said. "I did not notice the smell over my own, but Euwyn drained the monster's pool when he rescued me. This water must come from there. No wonder I could not wash the smell off in this stream."

Solomon and Althus looked at each other. "Monster?" asked Althus. "Did he say Euwyn rescued him from a monster?"

"That is what I heard him say," said Solomon. "I would like to hear the tale of this monster."

"You will hear it later," said Chess.

"There is a small cascade coming down the mountain wall a little farther on, Chess, perhaps that would be better place to wash. I could heat it for you," rumbled Antares. Chess looked at the Dragon a little doubtfully, but smiled and shrugged in resignation.

"Anything to wash this stink from me."

They found a small pool at the base of the cascade as they often did below the temporary falls of water that graced the mountainsides in the spring. The narrow cascades of water fell from the snowcaps that covered the high peaks, drying up in the hot summer weather when the snowcaps had melted entirely only to appear again the next spring. The water was ice cold, but Antares heated it to steaming in a few minutes with a blast so hot Chess and Althus had to stand far back.

Althus sat nearby with Gust standing over him protectively while Chess stripped down to his small clothes and eased gingerly into the heated pool. Solomon tossed him the soap and started toward Althus, but Chess had other ideas. He had been muttering to himself most of the way to the pool about not needing an audience to bathe himself, but Althus and Solomon had followed anyway. Althus was uneasy about any of the company wandering off alone and Solomon was still feeling a little protective of Althus who had not fully recovered from his injuries.

"If you two must be here while I bathe at least one of you should be in here with me," Chess said.

"No one wishes to share a bath with someone who smells as you do," Solomon said.

Chess wore an angry and determined look in his eye as he climbed halfway out of the pool to reach for Solomon who was making his way back to Althus along the edge. Althus did not even see how Solomon did it, but he quickly flipped Chess back into the water. Chess emerged, sputtering, the gleam still in his eye, looking a little more wary, but no less determined. Solomon was grinning broadly by the time Chess leapt from the pool, reaching for him once again. Chess ended up back in the pool again. By the time he had recovered from his second face full of water, Solomon had shed his boots and coat and was leaping into the pool beside him. Chess was still undaunted. He could not believe such a small Elf could best him, and now they were both in the water he felt his height gave him an advantage. Solomon tripped him backward into the water three times, finally holding him under while he looked casually at Althus who sat nearby laughing at them both.

"Will he ever give up or will I have to drown him?" he asked.

"I think he has gotten his way, Solomon. You *are* in the pool with him and that is what he wanted, after all. Perhaps you could let him up now."

Chess was beginning to struggle as if he was running out of air. Solomon took his hands away and Chess emerged sputtering and gasping his eyes wide in astonishment.

"How do you *do* that!" he gasped. "You are so much smaller than I!"

"Ah, but I am quicker than you," Solomon replied, tossing the soap at Chess who barely caught it before it hit him in the chest.

"Can you teach me?" said Chess rubbing the soap vigorously through his hair, causing most of it to stand on end. The hopeful look and the soap dripping down his face sent Solomon into gales of laughter. Althus stopped laughing himself, just to hear it better.

"Yes, I can teach you. You *are* an Elf although a bit overgrown. You cannot be as clumsy as you seem."

"Never underestimate your opponent, Chess no matter what his size," said Althus, "and never underestimate the value of a friend."

"You are right, Althus," said Chess smiling at Solomon. "It seems we have added a fierce little brother to our company... and a big lizard."

"Lizard!" Antares snorted. The accompanying gout of fire caused Chess to take cover beneath the water. When Chess resurfaced, he found the Dragon's face mere inches from his own. "I would be careful if I were you, Chess," he growled. "No Dragon likes to be called a lizard and very few Dragons are as sweet tempered as I."

Solomon gave a snort of derision at that, but Chess took the Dragon seriously. "Yes, Antares," he said meekly, never taking his eyes from the Dragon's nostrils aimed at his chest.

"I like him," Antares said, suddenly, swinging his head toward Solomon. "He *is* amusing. I find I can forgive him for calling me a lizard since he has made you laugh, Solomon. That is something I have yearned to hear for a long time."

After repeated sessions with the soap, Althus and Solomon pronounced Chess fit to return to camp. Solomon stood before Antares while the Dragon carefully produced a small flame to dry him. Chess declined to stand as close, but Antares managed to dry him sufficiently as well. Solomon assured him the slight smell of sulfur would not remain with him long. Althus thought the whiff of sulfur smelled like roses when compared to the reeking aura that had followed Chess earlier. Much to Solomon's amazement, Althus produced a globe of light to illuminate their way back to camp. Antares rumbled with contentment as he ambled along behind Chess, snorting every so often, just to see him jump.

## Chapter Thirty

## A PLEDGE

They passed a pleasant evening together. All eyes were upon Althus as he ate. Everyone but Solomon seemed to fear he would vanish if they looked away. The fourth time he looked up from his meal to find Euwyn gazing at him, his food halfway to his mouth he assured them all he was not about to disappear. Everyone apologized and it lessened a bit, but then, Solomon could not stop laughing every time he caught one of them staring.

After they finished their meal, Euwyn asked once more if Althus would let him heal his injuries. Althus declined, assuring the Wizard he would heal well enough on his own. Sighing in resignation, the Wizard wandered off and found himself talking to Antares. A short while later Althus noticed Mica carrying the heavy box containing the stone over to join the Dragon and the Wizard. Althus shivered at the mere thought of the stone. Its evil had touched him for only a moment. He could not imagine how Euwyn had managed to keep his wits intact after his experience. Antares and Euwyn were deeply engaged in conversation while Mica sat listening, the box resting on the ground before him.

Bree came to sit between Althus and Solomon in the moonlight while Thorny and Chess entertained them with the tale of their journey through the mountain. The night was warm and pleasant for spring. Stars shimmered faintly in the sky where the moonlight did not outshine them. The horses grazed on the spare grass nearby while Althus enjoyed the musical voices of the Elves in the soft night air and wondered where the next few nights would find them. He wished this night could last forever, but he knew the morning would find them heading into the troubled valley of Anduin.

Solomon and Antares would journey back to the Hall of the Brotherhood in the mountains far to the south. Solomon already seemed to belong among them. Thorny and Chess had begun calling him "little brother" almost immediately.

Euwyn, Mica, and Antares joined them when the tale reached the point where the Wizard had jumped into the lake to rescue Chess from the monster that swallowed him whole. Chess was immediately apologetic.

"I did not thank you properly for saving my life, Euwyn. I am afraid I was less grateful than I should have been."

Euwyn merely laughed the rich, deep laugh Bree once feared she might never hear again. "You are forgiven, Chess. I was a little distracted and I should have been quick enough to prevent your being eaten in the first place."

"Perhaps it was not Euwyn that saved you, Chess," said Solomon. "Perhaps you were just too difficult for the monster to digest."

Everyone laughed, including Chess. "Whatever you say little brother. I am through disagreeing with you. I have enough bruises from our first disagreement. I am not going to seek more by picking another fight with you."

"I am sorry I treated you so roughly, Chess," said Solomon with a grin that made his eyes glitter in the firelight. "But you seemed so cocky and sure you could best me. I could not resist showing you the error of your thinking. The honor and reputation of the Dragon Riders was at stake. Even the women of the order are formidable warriors."

"Women?" Bree repeated in astonishment. "There are women in the Brotherhood?"

"Yes, but very few, in fact, only three. Two have been members for almost as many years as Brother Augustine. The third was still in training when I left the Halls. She will have become a full Brother by now. Her training was my responsibility until I was injured. When I was under Brother Augustine's care, she visited me every day, I think. I remember her being there now. She sat with me every evening without fail, I would guess.

"Holly.

"She is the only rider ever to ride a white Sea Dragon. She must have trained very hard each day and still she took the time to come to me and tell me of it. She always told me of the events of the day as she wrote them in her journal. She left her journal with me and came to write in it every evening. I can see her sitting cross-legged on the end of the bed as she wrote. I did not think of her until now. Bree reminds me of her in some ways. She is very beautiful. There were tears on her face when I left the Hall." He ran a hand through his unruly curls and sighed, staring into the fire. "Why did I not see them until now? She was a true friend when I needed one. Joseph was there often as well. All of the Brothers were."

"You will return to the Hall tomorrow, Solomon," said Althus. "They will understand and they will welcome you back."

Solomon did not look so sure. He smiled at Althus, but it was a sad, fearful smile.

"At least I have met all of you and that would not have happened had I not left the Hall of the Brotherhood. I will speak to them on your behalf. I hope to take my place as Second Rider of the Brotherhood again. Perhaps when you face the enemy at your gates, the Dragon Riders will be there to worry them from behind."

"We must face the enemy *within* our gates first, Solomon," said Euwyn. "What will happen after that, only the Creator knows. We will take on the task one step at a time. We are honored to have you as an ally."

Solomon stood to face Althus, drawing his sword and holding it so the hilt was closest to Althus. The firelight danced along the razor sharp blade from the hilt to the tip as Solomon went down on one knee and bowed his head before Althus.

"I, Solomon Goshawk of the Brotherhood of Dragon Riders pledge my hands, my sword and my bow to the service of Althus, Prince of Anduin and Commander of its forces."

Althus looked a bit stunned by the sudden formality, hard pressed not to let his mouth hang open. It was a moment before he could think how to respond. He knelt on one knee before Solomon only because to stand would have been to tower over the small figure kneeling before him. "I accept your pledge with great honor, Solomon Goshawk of the Brotherhood of the Dragon Riders. May the winds always favor your Dragon's wings." Althus was not sure where the last bit came from, but he rather liked it and it made Solomon smile. "When all is said and done in Anduin for better or worse I vow to return to your mountains to aid you in your struggle as well, should I survive to do so."

With a ring of fine steel, Chess and Thorny knelt and drew their swords. Bree now held her bow and Euwyn his staff. Mica drew the heavy broadsword Althus had given him. Solomon rose to his feet, his eyes now at a level with theirs, looking at each of them expectantly.

Thorny raised his sword to the starry sky and shouted, "Allies! In the name of my father, Lord Gilden, and on behalf of my brothers and my sister, I proclaim the Elves of the Dark Wood allied to Prince Althus of Anduin, the Dwarves of Stonehaven, the Brotherhood of the Dragon Riders, the Black Giants, the Sea Elves of the Great Seas, and the Wizards of our world."

Mica, standing in order to do so, raised his sword to touch the tip to that of Thorny's and as the Prince of Stonehaven and on behalf of his father, Granite, King of Stonehaven, made the same pledge. Althus added his blade and his pledge to that of the others, as did Solomon. Bree touched the tip of her bow to the others and Chess added his blade as well.

When Euwyn made his pledge and touched his staff to the tips of their blades, Althus felt as if his youth had fled forever. He felt fear and excitement wash through him and a strange sensation that must have come from the rest of the company. A feeling of shared emotions almost overwhelmed him when Antares came close enough to add a talon to their raised swords. They looked gravely into each other's eyes in silence for a moment before they smiled at each other and sheathed their weapons. Even the horses had drawn close, their eyes and ears attentive to the pledges made by the light of the stars.

"We have made history here," said Euwyn. "I can feel it in my bones. There are seven races named in our pledge. There is no one here to speak for the Giants and the Sea Elves, and perhaps some day there will be more, but it is a beginning. It gives me hope for the future of our world. You are all young yet and there is still time for you to have a hand in the shaping of it. But you, Althus," he said drawing Althus to him roughly with an arm about his shoulders, "you must learn to keep your feet on the ground. No more flying for you." Euwyn was smiling down at him as if he were jesting, but he knew the Wizard well enough to see the fear for him mingled with the joy in his dark eyes. He could not promise never to fly again, but he did not think Euwyn was thinking only of Antares when he asked for that promise.

He did promise to be more careful in the future.

Soon after, Bree led Althus away from the others. He found himself gazing into her eyes in the moonlight a short distance from the camp. For a long while, they stood with their arms about each other, and then, with a kiss, she sent him off to bed. He protested feebly, but his leg and his shoulders were aching and his eyes wanted to close of their own accord. When she threatened to have Chess and Thorny put him to bed, he resigned himself to his bedroll a short distance from where Antares, Euwyn and the Elves sat talking through the night. Althus slept fitfully, wondering what tomorrow would bring, but each time he awoke, the voices of his friends and Mica's ground shaking snores reassured him that, at least in this hidden valley, all was well.

Φ          Φ          Φ

The next morning found them traveling down the narrowing valley. The path, from that point, allowed them to ride the horses instead of leading them. Solomon rode Antares, taking up nearly the entire valley as it narrowed briefly before it spilled into the wide valley of the Anduin River. They paused atop a low foothill overlooking Anduin to say farewell to Solomon. He offered Mica a ride back to Stonehaven, but the Dwarf shook his head with a look of horror at the huge Dragon. "No, thank ye kindly Solomon," he said his green eyes wide as the Dragon eyed him closely tilting his huge head. "If ye'll pardon me sayin' so, Dwarves and Dragons don't get along so well, even if I was intendin' to leave Althus' side. I don't think flyin' is fer me. I'll leave that to you and Althus if ye don't mind. I'd best not be flyin' to Stonehaven on the back of one. I don't think it would be safe fer Antares or me."

Antares laughed his deep rumbling laugh and shook his head at the thought of the Dwarves harming him.

Gust drew close enough for Solomon to reach down and grasp Althus' hand in farewell. Solomon drew a small Dragon scale hung on a fine golden chain from about his neck and pressed it into Althus' hand. It was half the size of Solomon's palm, bearing a golden Dragon across its width.

"A gift from Antares and from me," he said. "It is a first scale. One of the first scales Antares shed after he was hatched and therefore as ancient as he is. Legends say it will protect you if you wear it about your neck. Even the Dragons are not sure how or from what. It is an ancient custom and much of the details are lost. Augustine wears Antares' first shed about his neck. This is his second shed and nearly as powerful, so tradition says."

"Thank you, Solomon. I will wear it always if only to remember our friendship."

"Even if I must return alone, Althus, I will return," Solomon said.

Antares was in the air while the words were barely out of Solomon's mouth. He circled over their heads in farewell, banking so sharply one wing nearly brushed the ground, and then they were off, disappearing over the mountains behind them.

Althus sent a prayer after them. There were nearly as many enemies in the air now as on the ground. He turned to his companions to find sharp-eyed Bree peering off to the west.

"There is a rider coming swiftly down the Forest Road," she said.

They all settled in their saddles atop the hill to see who the approaching rider might be until Bree flung an arm westward pointing to the sky. "Myoti!" she cried.

Althus and Gust were pounding down the hillside at full speed before the others could react. Mars shot forward with a curse from Euwyn and the rest followed nearly at the same moment.

"That boy will kill himself yet," the Wizard shouted over the pounding of the horses' hooves. "How many do you count, Bree?"

"Too many, I am afraid. The horse approaching appears exhausted. They have been pursued for some time, I fear."

She readied her bow, dropping her reins on Moon's neck. Althus, a few strides ahead did the same. They were nearly in range. Bree's first shot took one creature through the head. Althus prayed his aim was good enough. Shooting from the back of a galloping horse was very different from shooting with his feet securely on the ground. His first shot merely clipped a creature's wing, but his second brought one down at least, even if he did not kill it. Bree brought down two more before he strung a fourth arrow. The rider's face was plain now. The horse ran blindly, close to dropping from exhaustion.

The rider's eyes were wide with terror, but he did not look at the Myoti behind or at Althus and his companions, but at something over their heads. A roar split the air behind them, nearly causing Althus to drop his bow. A shadow passed over them and Antares, glittering in the morning sun dove upon the Myoti like a fox among chickens. He snapped the neck of one with his jaws and another with his talons. The rest he turned to cinders before they had time to turn aside.

Althus and his friends stood in the middle of the road, having joined with the rider and watched as Antares circled them once again, nearly brushing the ground with his wing as before. Solomon saluted from Antares back while Antares roared, "I will kill them all! Farewell again, my friends!"

Althus wished he could have ridden the Dragon into battle with Solomon. Almost. The Dragon disappeared and they turned to the rider, dismounted now, leaning against Gust while Thorny and Chess tended to his exhausted mount.

"Tristan, what on earth are you doing out here playing with those birds when you should obviously be on duty?" asked Althus.

Tristan's exhausted, dust streaked face looked up at him in consternation. "Playing! Playing! They nearly had Tarsus and me for lunch! Althus, you young dog, I have never been happier to see anyone in my life. Speaking of creatures that fly.... I thought that Dragon was going to settle us all in our graves. I take it he and his rider are friends of yours? You have been a very busy lad since I left you at castle Anduin. I worried you were not safe there. It looks as if you have not even been there for quite some time."

Althus laughed to hear Tristan taking him to task as if they were still guardsmen together in castle Anduin. "I will tell you my tale if you tell me why you are out here on the road alone, fleeing for your life."

"I was not alone when I started out this morning. Ryder was with me." Tristan looked back down the road and scrubbed a hand through his coppery hair now gray with dust. He swallowed once. "The creatures got him. They plucked him right off his horse. I thought that would be the last I saw of him, but I saw him again, or what was left of him. They dropped most of his body onto the road before me some miles back." Tristan drew a shaky breath before he could continue. "The Orc army is perhaps half a day behind. I would expect them shortly before nightfall if they travel at the pace they held when I last saw them. Ryder and I were the last two men to track their progress. We headed to the castle to warn father that the army would soon be at the gates of the city. He will be relieved to see you and Euwyn, although you would have been better off staying far from Anduin. I hope the king has warned the people of Anduin to seek shelter within the walls of the city."

"Last I knew, the king denied the approaching army existed," said Althus. "I fear the evacuation of Anduin, if it has been accomplished, has been the work of your father and the Elves, Gilden and Rowan."

Tristan looked toward the shining castle far in the distance. "If that is the case, then father could probably use all the friends he can find."

"Exactly so," said Euwyn. "We should be on our way."

Thorny and Chess had somehow restored Tarsus enough so he no longer seemed as exhausted as when Tristan dismounted. They were soon on their way toward Castle Anduin. Althus introduced the Elves and the Dwarf to Tristan and told his tale as they traveled.

When he had finished, Tristan shook his head in amazement. "And to think father told me you were to stay within the castle walls dancing attendance to the queen when I asked for you to accompany us to watch the borders of Anduin. He said the queen wanted you safe by her side. I told him you would be safer with me than in the castle. You seem to have found a more dangerous path for yourself than any of us has traveled and it seems you have found allies wherever you set your feet. I knew you were more than just the queen's favorite toy."

Althus turned to Tristan, his face turning quite red. "What? Is that what the soldiers thought?" He stopped Gust in the middle of the road. Tristan rode ahead a few paces until he found Euwyn and Mars facing him. At Euwyn's angry look, Tristan stopped his mount and braced himself for the angry words sure to follow.

"Father said it was not so, but why else would the queen take such an interest in a lowly soldier?" he stammered uneasily. "I do not think it is because he was raised by a Wizard as father says."

"She takes notice of him," Euwyn said in a voice that held the sound of thunder in it, "because he is her son and the son of King Allen."

Tristan gave a snort of laughter. Euwyn's furious countenance made him swallow the disbelieving words that would have followed.

"Please, Tristan, believe me," said Althus. "I am not the queen's toy as you call it. Whether you believe I am her son or not, I do not care. It is hard enough for me to believe myself."

They rode on in silence then, except for Euwyn muttering to himself about soldiers and gossip.

"You are Prince of Anduin, then, Althus?" Tristan finally asked looking a bit unsure whether Althus was joking or serious.

"Yes, Tristan, it seems I am. That makes me your commander, you know."

Tristan executed a salute, his fist to his heart, in Althus' direction. "I do not know what made me doubt you. It makes sense now I think of it. You have the look of the king about you and you certainly have proved yourself worthy of the crown in the last days. If Euwyn says it is so, then I suppose it must be. The good Wizard does not lie. I am sorry Althus, I mean, your majesty. It will take some getting used to."

"Please call me Althus, Tristan. I am frightened enough of what awaits me in Castle Anduin. If you call me anything but Althus it will only frighten me more."

Tristan noticed for the first time how pale Althus looked and how his hand shook on Gust's reins.

"I am your man, Althus. I will guard you until death," vowed Tristan bowing low in his saddle.

"Yes, well that *is* comforting," muttered Althus, sending Gust off at a canter to catch up with Euwyn.

"Do you want to stop at the tower, father? We should turn aside here if you do," Althus said, as if Euwyn did not know the way.

"No," he said. "No, Antares had some answers for me. Speaking with him was like having a library of books at hand. He was familiar with the stone."

Althus noticed Euwyn looked as worried as he felt. His dark eyes strayed often to the saddlebag where the chest containing the stone rode. "Did you know it is called the Dragon's Egg by some? It is not an egg, though, but a gemstone with powers of its own. The original stone looks somewhat like a Dragon's egg, according to Antares. The stone we carry is only a piece melted from the larger stone by Dragon's fire. Whenever the stone is heated by a Dragon's breath, it sheds droplets that form smaller and slightly less powerful versions of the original. That must be the source of the ones you saw set in pendants worn by Borgas and the king. All are linked to each other and the original stone. If we shatter the stone we carry, it may free the king from Borgas' influence. If not, only the breaking of the original stone will do. It must be destroyed in either case, before there are even more of its offspring unleashed upon our world."

Euwyn drew them all into a copse of trees beside the road before he continued. "Antares fears the original stone rests somewhere in the mountains close to the Brotherhood's territory. He suspects it is hidden where the Myoti and the Nasua are bred.

"The Nasua are part wolf, twisted by evil to make them as you see them. The Myoti, on the other hand, are part Dragon and therefore even more powerful than the Nasua. So, you see why Antares hates them.

"Somewhere in the mountains lies the original Dragon's Egg and the breeding place for these creatures. Most likely in the same place, since Antares feels it is unlikely they hold more than one Dragon as captive... or ally. It is uncertain which, although Antares seems to know which Dragon they might hold.

"I am afraid even if we succeed here in Anduin, my task is not finished. I must also return to the mountains and search out this Dragon's Egg and destroy it and every piece taken from it. I must find this Dark Lord, the Great Lord the Orcs and Goblins speak of. He will not rest until he has conquered all the lands. I must find him and find some way to defeat him."

"We" said Althus.

"We" growled Mica.

"Remember, we are sworn allies now, Euwyn," said Bree. "You cannot go without us."

"If my prince goes, then I go also," said Tristan.

Euwyn smiled sadly. If I could do as I wish, I would send you all safely back to your homes. However, I must think of what is the greater good for all of the people of our world.

"*We.* I guess I must get used to saying it. The last few weeks have shown me it will require more than one Wizard. The next few days will not be easy ones, but all the lands depend on us to make a start. If we die in the attempt..." The Wizard did not finish.

Bree watched him rub his hand across his chest in a way she had not seen since Althus had returned to them. It made her shiver under her cloak as if a bitter wind had found its way beneath, to realize powerful Euwyn was as frightened as they were. Thorny and Chess looked grimly at the castle looming closer. Mica, peering at the castle from where he sat behind Bree, kept his hand on the hilt of his sword. He looked surer than any of them and fiercer, but he was a Dwarf after all and his people were known to be fearless in battle

"We will not enter the castle through the main gates," said Euwyn. "I will disguise the rest of us as some of Tristan's fellow soldiers and we will hope no one realizes there are too many of us to account for the soldiers left outside castle walls. When we enter the castle grounds, Tristan will do the talking for all of us. We will have to risk someone will question the horses we ride as I cannot spare the power it would take to disguise them also."

## Chapter Thirty-one

## CASTLE ANDUIN

Even before they crossed the bridge over the Anduin, they could see Gilden and Manton had been successful in evacuating the outlying farms. There was not a soul to be seen working the fields or traveling the roads. No one stirred beyond the gates of the city. Watchmen stood guard atop the walls in great number. Anduin looked like a city prepared for a siege.

The sturdy soldier who stopped them before the gate recognized Tristan and, after a curious look at his companions, allowed them to enter. Tristan spoke a quiet warning in the guard's ear of the army approaching almost at their heels. The guard did not hesitate. He sent a runner at once, passing the word to those atop the walls.

Althus knew at a glance that their numbers were too few to face the army approaching Anduin.

"If we fail in our first task, Althus, the numbers atop the wall will not matter," Euwyn said. "The Dark Lord's army will dig themselves in and wait for the gates to be opened for them from the inside before they risk losing some of their number in battle. Their commanders certainly know they have allies within the castle walls. That is where we start, within the walls of the castle. We have to reach the king and defeat Borgas before he welcomes our enemies inside and allows your people to be slaughtered."

"I hope if we battle these creatures we can find enough men for that task," Tristan said. "Many have disappeared as if into thin air to be replaced by men I would not trust to guard a dead goat. If only the men we lost would magically reappear. At best, we would still be outnumbered three to one, but we might have a chance of holding them off for a while."

"If only I had that power, Tristan," Euwyn sighed, regarding Althus whose eyes were on the throng of people milling about them. "Althus is more powerful than I in that regard, although he does not see it yet. Perhaps he will bring us help from unexpected places."

Althus, occupied by the faces of the people about him, did not hear Euwyn's words. There was a general look of despair about the people within the walls of the city as if they held no hope for the future. Most of them had so little to begin with and they seemed about to lose even that. Many of them would lose their lives. Most of them would if the approaching army breached the gates of the city. They held no hope King Allen would protect them if it came to that. He would not raise a finger in defense of them until the enemy was at the gates of the castle itself. Althus feared not even then.

He recognized many people Euwyn had healed in the sea of faces milling aimlessly about them. He wished they could see Euwyn for who he was.

That would be something to which they could cling. Perhaps it was a small thing. He did not like seeing the people of Anduin so frightened.

Euwyn watched him as his jaws clenched and his eyes flashed in anger and nodded to himself. Althus would be a great king some day if the Creator granted him the time.

Their journey through the city was slow as they made their way through the press of people jammed within its walls. Althus wondered how Gilden and Rowan and the Captain had managed such a thorough evacuation of the surrounding countryside. Surely, there must have been some who would refuse to leave their farms and everything they possessed on the mere rumor of an approaching army. He admired their thoroughness. How had they managed it? Suddenly, his ears caught a snatch of conversation that made him smile.

"A Dragon," someone said. "A huge Dragon flying against the mountains. I saw it with my own eyes I tell you, and I was not the only one. Our enemies have Dragons to use against us!"

Althus was not pleased to have been the cause of his people's panic and to have them think of Antares and Solomon as enemies, but he smiled to think they had aided in the evacuation of the farmers of Anduin. There would have been no chance of prying some of them from their farms otherwise.

They eventually made their way to the gates that would admit them to the stable area where most small bands of soldiers chose to enter the grounds of the castle. Althus was startled to find the guards there looked hardly Human. They eyed the company as if they were a roast at supper. Althus' hand strayed to the hilt of his sword as they passed through the gates, forced to turn their backs to them. He was glad he wore his mail. His wounds itched as he remembered the feel of arrows burying themselves in his back. Gust rolled his eyes and snorted uneasily as if he felt the same, moving beneath Althus like a coiled spring, his ears flicking back to catch any threatening sound from behind. How would they reach the king if these beasts had replaced all the castle guard? Even Tristan would not be safe within the walls of the castle.

They led their horses into the stables farthest from the castle proper, relieved to find them deserted. Althus doubted many horses would tolerate one of these beasts as a rider or a groom. Only three horses stood in the building they entered. Chess smiled as Rowan's iron gray stallion reached out to nose him when he led Sand into the stall beside him.

"Hello, Argent," he said, stroking his neck. "Can you tell us where Rowan and father are? If you could speak you might be helpful, but I fear you know as little as we do of what is occurring within these walls."

Argent regarded him placidly, offering no insights.

They settled their horses into stalls alongside Rowan's gray stallion and Gilden's blue roan, Slate, and a horse Althus recognized as the queen's black mare, Raven. With Tristan in the lead, they left the stables and entered the castle by a servant's entrance, avoiding the barracks entrance where they expected to find more of Borgas' men.

Euwyn gathered them just within the entry, hidden from the guards nearby. He quickly changed their appearances. They now looked as hideous as the guards they tried to avoid.

"Keep together or we will end up killing each other. Remember, Borgas will see us as we truly are. He will not be deceived. At least, not long enough for it to be of any use. I will only be able to keep us concealed until we reach the throne room and then I will need all of my strength for what I must do there."

Mica was watching the Wizard, his green eyes serious and steady as he held the lead box before him. Euwyn gave him a thin smile as Tristan led them onward. A troop of guards, swords drawn, came rushing through the doorway they had just left. They halted abruptly at the sight of the company a short distance down the corridor. One of them shouted in a language unfamiliar to all except the Wizard. Euwyn answered them in the same guttural language, pointing away from the company and down the opposite passageway. With much shoving and grunting and what Althus took to be cursing, the troop moved off in the direction Euwyn had pointed them. At everyone's questioning look, Euwyn said, "If we see us, our orders are to kill us. Meanwhile, we went that way."

They continued moving in the opposite direction.

"What language was that?" asked Althus, looking back toward the retreating guards.

"Orc" said Euwyn.

"Where are we headed, Tristan?" Chess asked as Tristan led them through the halls of the castle, peering cautiously around corners despite the spell that made them appear as just another troop of the half Human guards.

"I think I know where we might find someone who can tell us what is happening within these walls. If only she is where I hope to find her."

They crossed more corridors and Tristan finally led them to the door of the large open room that served as an infirmary. He waited for a few moments until the physician and a young nurse occupied themselves with a patient at the far end of the room. When a middle-aged woman with a few strands of gray showing in her red hair passed by, he quickly stepped through the door and pulled her into the corridor. Her eyes went wide with fear and he clapped his hand over her mouth to stifle her frightened cry.

"Tristan, what are you doing?" hissed Thorny. "You will frighten this poor woman to death. She thinks you are one of the guards!"

"Oh. Yes. I am sorry, mother. It is me, Tristan."

When Euwyn removed the spell, her eyes widened in amazement.

"It *is* you. Oh, Tristan," she cried, throwing her arms about him. "Thank the Creator you are safe! You have brought Euwyn back with you. This must be Althus, and these must be Gilden's children, and a Dwarf. Oh, Tristan. It is not safe here in the castle for any of you."

Mother, I came here hoping to find you. We need to know what is happening here in the castle."

"Tristan, all of the castle guards have been replaced by these creatures. Borgas discovered that your father and Gilden were preparing Anduin for war against the king's wishes and now Rowan and Gilden and your father are confined somewhere here in the castle. I do not know where, but they are to appear before the king today, in less than an hour's time. Your father arranged that the guards who accompanied you to the borders be stopped at the city walls and word sent to the castle from there. They are safe, for now, stationed atop the outer walls. There are no Humans left in the castle except the king and queen and a few of their staff Borgas would not allow to leave. The lords and ladies of the court left the castle long ago. I suppose they are still within the city gates, but there is no one here to help you. Unless..."

She fell silent, a speculative look in her eyes as she turned towards Euwyn.

"The soldiers!" she said. "I think I know where the missing soldiers are. Perhaps Euwyn can free them."

"Lead on, mother," said Tristan. "Show us where they are."

By the way," said Tristan as they followed in Elinor's wake, "Do you know Althus is the prince of Anduin?"

"Yes, I do," she replied casually.

They all stopped moving and stood staring at her. She stopped as well and turned to face them.

"I was the nurse who gave him into Euwyn's care. I kept the queen's secret because it was important to her and the safety of her child. Thanks to the spell Euwyn felt it necessary to put on me, I did not remember what happened that night until a few years later. You could have trusted me then, Euwyn. I would not have put Althus in danger. Even Manton does not know."

"I am sorry, Elinor. I felt it was necessary."

"I suppose I must forgive you," she sighed. "You have done a fine job of raising him and he has mellowed you, as well, in the years he has been by your side. I remember you as a frightening sort of Wizard."

Euwyn responded with a small bow and a smile.

"Well, in any case, by the time I remembered, no one thought to ask any more questions of me. Not even Manton, although I think he suspects the truth or at least part of it. He told me Gilden thinks Althus bears a striking resemblance to the king as a young man. I do not think either of them suspects Althus is the queen's son as well."

Althus' face reddened at the realization Gilden and Manton both thought him the king's bastard son.

Elinor gave Althus a solemn look. "I am sorry, Althus. I could have at least set Manton straight in the matter, but it seemed safer to let them think what they would. You must realize neither of them thinks any less of you."

Althus nodded silently. He had never liked the term bastard, but it hardly seemed to matter any longer. He had more important matters to worry him now.

With Euwyn's spell back in place, they followed Elinor downward into the deepest reaches of the Castle Anduin, encountering patrols obviously searching for them at nearly every turn until they reached the lowest levels. She led them to a blank wall and as they stood before it she looked back at the Wizard, an expectant look in her eyes. "They are here," she said. "Behind this wall. At least the guards were taking a great quantity of food through here. I saw Borgas make an opening in this wall."

Tristan gaped at her as if she had taken leave of her senses. "Mother, this wall is as solid as the rest. There is no door here and even if there were, why would they be keeping our men as prisoners down here? Why not kill them and be done with it? It does not make sense."

"I cannot tell you why. I can only tell you what I saw. There is something behind this wall!"

Euwyn stepped to the wall and laid both hands against the smooth stone. "Have you never heard the saying that an army travels on its stomach, Tristan?" he asked. At Tristan's puzzled look he added, "There will be an army of three thousand at our gates soon if it is not already there. To an Orc, any meat is acceptable and the meat of a dead enemy is considered a special delicacy. There will be others to feed as well, creatures foul beyond any you can imagine."

Elinor's hands flew to cover her mouth and the rest looked as if they would like to relieve themselves of the contents of their stomachs.

Euwyn's hands continued to search the wall. Thorny and Chess kept watch, their swords drawn for any guards that might be patrolling the area. Moments passed and blue veins of light began to radiate through the stone from Euwyn's fingertips. Suddenly the stone evaporated leaving an archway in the stone wall wide enough for all of them to walk through at once. Tristan, Thorny, Chess and Euwyn moved through the opening while Althus and Mica, swords drawn, waited with Bree and Elinor.

The sounds of many Human voices soon began to echo from the darkness beyond the opening. They were rough voices, cheering and weeping all at once amid the sound of Tristan and the Elves begging them to move quietly. The lost soldiers of Castle Anduin began to file out of the darkness.

Althus inspected them carefully as they stumbled out of the darkness, squinting from the light, even in the dimly lit corridors. They were a sorry sight, filthy from head to toe, their uniforms nearly unrecognizable, but even those bearing poorly tended wounds smiled fiercely when they emerged from their prison, a good many of them supported by their comrades. Almost all nodded in recognition when their eyes met those of Althus.

They knew who had freed them. Althus did not know how they knew. Elinor and Bree saw what the soldiers saw as they filed past.

Althus stood with the sword of Anduin drawn, the Elven blade reflecting the flickering torchlight, his sapphire eyes assessing the troops he would command. Even in the uniform of the Elves, he looked ready to lead them. They formed ranks as orderly as the corridor would allow, their attention completely on Althus.

Althus was astonished at how many men the sealed chamber held.

"We must arm these men somehow," Althus whispered to Tristan. "How will we manage that?"

"There is an old armory on this level. The weapons may be old and rusty and I do not know if there will be enough, but once some are armed, we will take weapons from the enemy," Tristan replied.

Althus looked doubtfully at the sorry looking men still stepping through the opening to crowd the hallway about him. They spoke in hushed voices, but all wore determined looks on their grimy faces.

"Do what you can, then Tristan. I will leave it to you. Euwyn and I are bound for the throne room where Gilden and Rowan and your father are soon to face a charge of treason. As the Prince of Anduin, I will have a say in the matter. Elinor, will you allow us to escort you back to the safety of the infirmary?" he said, offering her his hand.

"No, my prince," she said smiling at him. "Some of these men have wounds that need looking after. I will have to make do with what little I can find, but I can be of use here, and here with my son I will stay, if it please your majesty."

Althus cringed at the titles she threw at him so easily. To him, they only threatened to separate him from the companions he valued. He looked sadly after Elinor as she and Tristan trotted his newfound troops off toward the armory.

As Althus, Euwyn, Mica and the Elves headed back toward the more populated areas of the castle, Althus prayed Tristan and his men would reach the armory safely. While the disguise Euwyn wove about Althus, Mica and the Elves enabled them to move about the castle in relative safety, the spell not longer protected Tristan. He and the men who accompanied him would have to rely on luck and skill to make their way.

"How many men do you estimate were held down here, Althus?" asked Chess.

"I would estimate close to seven hundred. I cannot imagine how so many survived this long in such conditions. They are a tough lot. I do not think I appreciated that fact as much as I should have when I was one of them."

"You are their commander now," said Chess. "You will have plenty of time to show your appreciation when all is said and done."

"Perhaps," said Althus, "if I do not get them all killed by day's end and you and your family and little Mica in the bargain."

"We are all here by choice, Althus. We are here to rescue our father and brother. Mica is here because he chooses to be as well. Whatever happens, we chose our own fates. Remember that, Althus," said Chess.

Althus did not find Chess' words comforting at all. He seemed all too willing to accept the fact he might die at Althus' side that day. Cold fear crept through him at the very thought that any of them might not live to see the sun set.

## Chapter Thirty-two

## TREASON

Gilden, the first to face the charges leveled at the three conspirators, gazed defiantly at King Allen. Two of Borgas' half Orc guards shifted uneasily on either side of him and he found some satisfaction in the fact they seemed more afraid of him that he was of them. Captain Manton and Rowan stood somewhere behind him, waiting for their turn before the throne. He studied the king closely as Borgas read the list of charges against him. The entire list amounted to one word... treason, if the term treason applied to one who was not a subject of this particular kingdom.

It did not matter. Borgas, overly fond of the sound of his own voice and the exercise of his authority, droned on and Gilden was absorbed in his study of the king. Borgas also glanced in the king's direction more often than usual. King Allen's eyes met Gilden's directly for the first time in years. He did not seem to be attending to Borgas' list of charges any more than Gilden was. What was happening here? Something was different in the king's face.

Queen Maris stood at his side. She looked down at him, her eyes widening with astonishment when he reached up to take her hand. Gilden had seen no signs of affection pass between them since he had arrived at Castle Anduin days ago. Was something weakening Borgas' hold on the king? He could think of only one man who might wield that kind of power. Euwyn. Had the Wizard returned? Was he somewhere within the castle, casting his enchantments within its walls?

Gilden waited in anticipation as Borgas finally wound down. Borgas paused expectantly, looking to King Allen for his judgment, finally bending to whisper urgently into the king's ear.

King Allen seemed to struggle for a moment and then, almost in a whisper, he said, "I cannot."

Borgas' mouth gaped open in astonishment for a long moment while Gilden stood looking at him, still hoping and wondering what might be occurring before him.

With or without King Allen, Borgas was determined to pronounce sentence and execute the Elf lord here and now. It did not really matter if he was losing control of the king. His men occupied the castle entirely. The king had no power here any longer. His pronouncements were merely a formality, even less than that now. They were merely amusement for the benefit of his men, a mere show of control now that the castle was his. Soon, the entire kingdom would be his and with the death of Gilden and his son, he would deal a severe blow to the kingdom of the Elves. Once the population of Anduin submitted to his will, he would march on the Dark Forest. That would be his greatest conquest. The other kingdoms would fall easily once they knew the Wood Elves had fallen.

"The king has declared all three of these traitors will be put to death, here and now," Borgas announced in ringing tones for the benefit of those present.

The queen gasped in disbelief as King Allen leapt to his feet. "I have said no such thing! This man is like a brother to me!" he shouted.

Borgas sent him to the floor with an offhand gesture as if he swatted an offending fly.

No one was more astonished than Gilden to hear such words from the king's mouth. King Allen had done nothing but heap abuse on his head since his arrival. Somehow, it made his decision to stay by the king's side almost worth the price. Nothing could be worth the loss of his son, however. As quick as light, he disarmed one of the guards flanking him and slew both of them before either of the slow-witted half Orcs could react. He was in mid stride toward the guards next closest when the force of the Wizard's spell struck him. He was pinned where he stood, rooted to the floor. Rowan and Manton had taken his lead and also disarmed and killed their guards. The Wizard held them in place just as easily.

Borgas cackled with delight, rubbing his hands together. "I will kill your son first, Elf. He will die by my hand so you will learn to respect my powers before you follow him. He raised a hand toward Rowan and made a grasping gesture with it, releasing Rowan from the spell binding him so all could watch him struggle.

Borgas was unprepared to have Rowan gut another guard with the sword he still held, but the guard was a small loss to Borgas when compared to the pleasure of watching Rowan struggle to breathe, as the spell he cast wound about his throat, depriving him of air. He could not decide whether it was more pleasurable to watch the dying Elf or the face of his father as Rowan slowly fell to his knees and then sank to the floor, his hands at his throat, his eyes wide with pain.

The queen sank to the floor beside the fallen king, weeping into her hands. Tears slid down Manton's face as he watched Rowan die. Gilden's face was dark with fury.

The sight of it turned Borgas' smile a trifle sickly for a fleeting moment until he remembered who was in charge of castle Anduin. Watching the Elf die was pleasurable, but over much too soon. Who to execute next, he wondered to himself and what would be the most entertaining way to do it? He rubbed his hands together in anticipation. He was tempted to add the king to the list of possibilities, but he might find further uses for him before the entire kingdom was his.

Perhaps Captain Manton's wife should witness her husband's execution. That would be worth the time it took to summon her from the infirmary. Why was she not already here? He puzzled over her absence for a moment and then sent a guard to bring her.

Φ              Φ              Φ

Althus knew the castle well from his duty as the queen's guard. They were soon nearing the throne room at the heart of Castle Anduin. They moved at a run now, as they neared their goal, depending on the Wizard's skill to conceal them. The halls were nearly deserted in any case. Only a few of the castle's servants seemed to be about and they scurried in the opposite direction at the sight of a troop of what appeared to be castle guards, hurrying toward the throne room. Suddenly, Bree went down, clutching at her throat and gasping for air. Althus was kneeling before her in the moment it took him to stop and turn about.

"Bree, what is it?" he asked as she clutched at his shoulder and tried to catch her breath. "Are you hurt?"

For a moment, she could only shake her head, only adding to her companions' confusion until Thorny asked, "Is it Rowan?" Bree nodded, tears sliding down her face. "He is dying, Althus. Please, you must find him! I will be all right."

Althus rose to his feet, pulling Bree with him. Mica moved to lend his sturdy shoulder to lean on. "Go ahead," he said, drawing his broadsword. "I will keep her safe until she can go on." He handed Euwyn the lead box with the stone inside. Their eyes met over it for a moment and Mica gave the Wizard a grim smile. "Ya don't need me ta carry this any more. Ya know what has ta be done and I know ya have the will ta do it."

Euwyn returned his smile with an uncertain one of his own before they sprinted on toward their destination. Althus felt the fear tighten about his chest another notch as they left Bree behind. The doors to the throne room stood open and they entered at a run. Euwyn held their disguise until they stood before the throne, surrounded by castle guards.

Althus saw that a few were no longer among the living with grim satisfaction until he saw Rowan's body lying there as well. Chess seemed to come apart at the sight of his fallen brother. He collapsed in a heap over his body, weeping loudly. Althus felt as if he could easily do the same. Borgas sneered in contempt at the unseemly display and turned his attention to Althus, Euwyn and Thorny.

"Why, Gilden," he said, "I believe there are a few of your children I have not put to death as yet. How convenient of them to deliver themselves to me."

"Let Gilden and Captain Manton go, Borgas," Euwyn said, his voice steady and commanding. The guards stepped back fearfully, as if they would leave this fight to the two Wizards.

Borgas cackled as if he were watching a jester capering before him. "What can you possibly do, hedge Wizard, that would persuade me to do such a foolish thing?"

As if in reply, Euwyn opened the lead box and removed the stone from its depths.

Borgas suddenly looked less than certain. "Where did you get that?" he hissed.

"Let us say the Dwarves let me take it as a token of our friendship. You see, we have freed them from its influence and they have driven their enemies out of Stonehaven."

Borgas' eyes shifted uneasily. "You lie! You cannot harm the stone. It will destroy you!"

"You are wrong, Borgas. I have spoken with the Dragon Antares. He has assured me I *can* destroy it," Euwyn said, raising the stone over his head, holding it with both hands.

Althus watched as Euwyn raised his eyes to look deep into the stone. A deep humming that set Althus' teeth on edge emanated from the Wizard while the stone bathed Euwyn in its sickly green light. Althus stepped away from without thinking, remembering its touch all too well. Thorny stepped away as well, raising his sword, ready to protect the Wizard at all costs.

Without warning, Borgas appeared at Althus' side. A hand at the back of his neck held him rigid as if encased in stone while Borgas held his other hand to Althus' chest.

"Hear me, Wizard," Borgas snarled while Althus felt Borgas' hand burning its way through his flesh. "I can pluck his heart from his chest and show it to you while it still beats. Give me the stone and I will release you and your young bastard. I will guarantee your safe passage anywhere you desire. If you oppose me, I will kill him and be assured, I will make him suffer the torments of hell before I am finished with him."

Althus struggled against the searing agony of the Wizard's hand against his chest. He could barely turn his eyes to where Euwyn stood. He tried to hide the fear and pain he felt, but his face refused to obey him.

Euwyn's dark eyes turned toward his as if he beheld all the sorrows of the world before returning to gaze into the depths of the stone, trembling as if the weight of the stone sought to crush him. His eyes did not leave its depths again. The humming never wavered. Thorny was dancing everywhere at once, seeking to reach Althus, but unwilling to leave the defenseless Wizard to the guards who had gathered enough courage to approach with their broadswords drawn. Borgas seemed to struggle, his hand against Althus' chest, his eyes bulging from his head as he sought to penetrate.

Pain washed over Althus as the Wizard pressed his hand against his heart. He imagined himself in the dark corridors of Stonehaven once more, struggling in vain to outrun the darkness, all sounds drowned out by his heartbeat, as it slowed until it stopped altogether and darkness overtook him.

Borgas let Althus' body slide to the floor with a last look, just as a crackling sound split the air. The stone exploded with a roar and a flash, a cascade of smaller blasts echoing about the room as it took the smaller stones with it. In the silence that followed, a fine dust settled over Euwyn where he lay bleeding on the floor. The guards stood staring uneasily at the Elves standing shoulder to shoulder between Euwyn and Borgas. Rowan stood supported by his brothers, a little paler than usual, but very much alive. Borgas shrieked as if the sight of Rowan standing before him, or perhaps the shattering of the stones had driven him mad. "You are dead, Elf! You are dead!" He raised his hands as if to cast another spell, but his eyes went wide with shock, his hands trembled, arrested in mid gesture. Althus had run him through with the sword of Anduin from where he lay at his feet, rising to his knees to drive the sword to its hilt beneath Borgas' ribs and through his heart.

Althus rose to his feet, now face to face with the evil Wizard. "Neither of us are as dead as you might hope, Borgas," he said to the Wizard's staring eyes. "You will never trouble the people of Anduin again." His voice echoed his certainty throughout the hall.

Althus had pulled his sword free of the Wizard's body, the Elven blade smoking faintly, and was wiping it on the dead Wizard's robes when Tristan and his troops burst through the door.

Pandemonium reigned for a time as the clash of swords and pikes rang out, accompanied by the shouts of men and Orcs. Tristan waded in, his red hair marking him as he fought. Gilden and Manton, released by the Wizard's death, joined the fighting while Rowan and Althus embraced over Borgas' body and tried to stay out of the fray. Althus could not stop grinning at Rowan. He looked a bit confused, but returned Althus' smile with one of his own.

Thorny and Chess appeared out of nowhere, shoving them roughly away from the Wizard's corpse, standing between them and the Wizard while a black, oily mist oozed from beneath and spread itself across the floor. The surrounding battle turned into a rout. The stones were shattered, the Wizard dead. For the moment, there was nothing holding Borgas' men to their original purpose. Tristan and his troops chased after the surviving half Orcs who made a break for the main gates of the castle.

Gilden and Manton carried Euwyn away from the spreading darkness while it gathered itself about its source and rose from the floor, winding itself into a twisted column that writhed and shifted, as if struggling to maintain its form. There were moments when it resembled a twisted version of Borgas, but the shape lost its definition quickly. A voice, rasping like a snake slithering over dry leaves filled the hall while many pairs of eyes seemed to glare out of the darkness.

"Althus, Prince of Anduin. I have marked you now. I will seek your death with all the powers of hell. My army sits before your gates. You cannot defeat me so easily. I am a wraith bound to the Lord of Darkness. You cannot destroy me. Behold. Your death stands before you." A low moan that accompanied the specter rose to a shriek that drove them all to cover their ears as the darkness twisted and rose to disappear from sight.

Silence reigned again in the throne room until Chess spoke. "Hmpf," he snorted, "big talk for a puff of dirty smoke."

Gilden soon had his arms about Rowan and Chess and Thorny each in turn. Althus was relieved to find Bree at his side, sharing her father's embrace with him. Gilden looked as happy to see Althus as he was to see his own children. Manton was helping Euwyn to a chair while Elinor fussed about him, gently removing shards of the stone from his hair and face. Shards of the stone still glittered on his dark clothing as he moved, his hands and face laced with cuts.

The Wizard caught sight of Althus moments before he reached his side. It was all Elinor could do to keep him seated. She squawked at him like a mother hen while he smiled at Althus through the blood that left trails down his cheeks. They embraced each other while Elinor continued to dab gently at the Wizard's bloodied face.

"You did it, father," Althus said, "Mica was right. You destroyed the stone."

"I was afraid I would pay dearly for it, Althus. I was certain Borgas had killed you. Forgive me, Althus. I could not give him the stone even to save your life."

"You did what you had to do. You did what was right. You could never have ransomed the lives of the people of Anduin for mine," Althus said.

Euwyn thought of how close he had come to doing just that.

Althus lay his hands on the Wizard's shoulders, inspecting Elinor's handiwork as she moved on to inspect the Wizard's hands. "I think a few more scars will make you look more like the dangerous Wizard you are. You are far too pretty for a Wizard," he said.

Euwyn laughed, and then gave Althus a searching look. "What kept Borgas from killing you, I wonder."

Althus still felt a remnant of the burning sensation in his chest. Elinor caught his grimace of pain as he gingerly felt about under his mail and sternly ordered him to strip to the waist. He wondered what happened to the "your majesty" she had thrown his way earlier that day. The coat of his uniform, his light mail and his linen shirt beneath were soon lying across a nearby chair while Elinor inspected the burn that decorated the center of his chest. It was the exact shape and size of the Wizard's hand with a deeper burn in the shape of the green and gold Dragon's scale Solomon and Antares had given him to wear, even to an impression of the golden Dragon dancing across the center of it. The burn was deep and painful, but when Euwyn laid his hand over it, whispering a few words, it nearly disappeared. The tiny golden Dragon continued to dance across his chest however, as if the metal had permanently melted to his skin. The burning sensation was gone completely and that was good enough for Althus.

"I must remember to thank Solomon and Antares when I see them next," Euwyn said. "The Dragon and his rider have become your guardians, Althus, even when they are far from your side. Perhaps it would be wiser in the future, however, to wear their gift on top of your mail instead of next to your skin."

Althus nodded, fingering the scale and thinking of the small Elf. Solomon would be pleased to know the role his gift had played in protecting Althus' life.

The Elves gathered about them, their looks of concern for Euwyn turning to smiles when they found he would recover. Chess prodded the golden Dragon on Althus' chest, admiring it.

"It seems the little Elf has put his brand on you, Althus. He will have you riding a Dragon yet."

Bree put her hand upon it to see if it caused Althus pain, unwilling to take his word it did not. Her warm hand on his bare skin made him feel a bit dizzy. When his eyes met hers, she kissed him, and his knees nearly failed him. He was afraid to look at Gilden, but heard his laugh among the others when Chess said, "Leave him alone, Bree. He has been through enough for one day." When his head was clear enough to think, he asked Rowan what had happened to him.

Rowan could tell the story clearly enough until he lost consciousness, but then he seemed a bit unsure of whether the rest he remembered was real or some wild dream.

"I thought at first that I woke with Chess' mouth on mine as if he were kissing me. Then I imagined he told me you taught him to do it." Rowan looked from Chess to Althus and back to Chess again. "I must have been dreaming."

"No, Rowan. You did not imagine it. That is how Althus brought Bree back to life when she was drowned," said Chess, anxious to tell his older brother how cleverly he had saved his life. "Althus said anyone could do it and Bree was not really dead, and it seems he was right when he said anyone could do it although I must say I doubted it at the time."

Chess' enthusiasm for the subject was huge. "I must say you looked truly dead to me. It was not hard to pretend I was overcome by grief so I could try Althus' cure on you. I have never seen anyone look more dead than you,

Rowan. Well, maybe if you had been covered in blood as well."

"*Enough*!" cried Gilden covering his ears. "Enough. I do not wish to hear more about any of my children looking dead." He glared a warning at Chess. "It seems I owe the lives of my children to Althus as he has saved each one of you at one time or another if your stories are true. I thought you would take care of him. It seems he has been taking care of you instead."

"Well, Euwyn saved me once as well, although if he had been a little quicker about it he could have saved me a day of smelling like a dead fish," said Chess.

He was prepared to elaborate, but Gilden held up a hand to silence him.

"Save your story, Chess. There will be time for stories later," he said.

Euwyn had escaped from Elinor and was kneeling at King Allen's side. Queen Maris watched anxiously as he worked over the fallen ruler of Anduin.

Gilden joined Euwyn at the king's side. "In the end, he found he could not sentence me to death as Borgas wished," Gilden said. "The Wizard's influence on him seemed to be weakening. Perhaps our friendship was stronger. I thought I saw the King Allen I remembered before he fell."

"You must remember, Gilden, this is Althus' true father. This man sired him. You knew him as well as I did before he became Borgas' puppet. He was a good king once and perhaps he will be again." Euwyn said as the king began to stir.

King Allen opened his eyes. They strayed from Gilden to Euwyn. He grasped Euwyn's bloody hand. "You must help us, Euwyn. This Wizard, Borgas is evil incarnate. I did not see until it was too late."

"He is dead, your majesty. Your son has killed him." Gilden said gently.

Tears trickled from the king's eyes. "You are confused, Gilden. I have no son. My son is dead. I sentenced my unborn child to death."

"I would not allow such a thing, your majesty," Euwyn said. "Your son is here on behalf of his people. You will acknowledge his claim to the throne of Anduin when you are feeling more yourself. For now, you will rest and think of your son and what you will say to him when you meet."

Euwyn left the king abruptly, satisfied he would recover. Gilden followed. The Wizard was angry, the king's words a reminder of what he had been capable of under Borgas' control. Gilden looked at his own children, now gathered safely about him, and wondered how such a thing was possible.

Mica stayed at the queen's side until Edmund, the castle physician and another nurse appeared on the scene and took the king to his rooms. Althus was surrounded by the Elves, helping Elinor bandage Euwyn's hands when Mica and the queen stepped into their midst. He was a little ashamed to have turned his attention so totally to the injured Wizard and not to the woman he now knew to be his mother, but she seemed not to notice or at least she seemed to understand his deeper concern for Euwyn. He turned to face her, resting a hand on Mica's shoulder when the sturdy Dwarf came to stand by his side.

"I want to thank you and your friends for what you have done for our people today," she said, as she stood before Althus, clasping her hands together tightly as if to keep from reaching out to him.

"I could not stand by and see Anduin fall to such evil without trying to stop it," said Althus. "I have always loved the people of Anduin and if what Euwyn says is true, I am responsible for their safety as their prince and therefore the commander of Anduin's army. This is especially so when their king has failed them for so long."

"So you know the truth now, Althus. Euwyn has told you. I am pleased that at least you still care for Anduin even though you must hate your father and me for denying you your right to grow up here in the castle as Prince of Anduin," she said, her eyes shining with tears.

"I could never hate you, Queen Maris. You did what you thought was necessary. It must have been difficult for you to see me grow up as someone else's child and yet, you have always been a part of my life as long as I can remember. As for King Allen, I cannot say I will soon forgive him or that I will ever trust him.

"I was happy with Euwyn in the stone tower. At least I grew to understand my people and know the pain the king's betrayal caused them. I know more of the lives of the people of Anduin than I would have otherwise. King Allen will never understand his people as I do and I cannot imagine growing up within these walls."

She embraced him then and he returned the gesture. It felt a bit strange to be so familiar with a woman he had thought of as his ruler for such a long time, but tears trickled from her eyes as she drew back to smile at him. "I am so proud of you, my son. You have become a fine man and you will be a great king some day."

She did not seem to notice the look of near panic that crossed Althus' face at the idea of becoming King of Anduin or his look of anger when, turning away to follow the king and his attendants, she promised to call him to the king's side when he recovered. She did not understand him at all. Did she think he was here to establish himself as Prince of Anduin in hopes of some day becoming Anduin's king? He only wanted to do what he could to save the kingdom from the enemy at its gates or, more likely, die in the attempt. His greatest wish was to return to the tower with Euwyn if they survived the coming conflict.

He found Euwyn's reassuring hand on his shoulder and sighed in resignation as he watched the queen depart.

"I suppose I cannot avoid a meeting with the king," he said, "at least, not forever, but I must see to the defense of Anduin and to that purpose I must see the enemy we are facing. I suppose they must be at our gates by now. That is where I should be, not here dancing attendance to a man who would be happier if I were dead."

He turned abruptly, striding toward the main gates of the castle with Mica trotting along at his side. The Elves and Euwyn followed as well with Manton and twenty of his men taking up positions from which they could protect him if the need arose.

Althus strode through the gates of the castle, across the open drawbridge and into the streets of the City of Anduin without stopping. The troops surrounding him kept pace, clearing the way as he headed for the walls surrounding the city. A murmur arose as he strode through the streets. Many of Anduin's citizens recognized Euwyn and his young son from Euwyn's works as a healer among them. A few people began to shout the Wizard's name as they entered the streets of the city. By the time they reached the city's walls, it became a hopeful chant. A crowd followed them to the walls and then spread itself about the base of it as the entire company climbed the narrow, winding stairs to its top.

Gilden and Euwyn appeared at Althus' side as he took his first look at the great army seething like a dark ocean about the city's outer walls. No one spoke as they watched the forces of Orcs and Goblins settling in about the walls just beyond the range of the bowmen standing nearly shoulder to shoulder along the battlements. Althus recognized a good many of them as farmers from beyond the walls and craftsmen from within. Some were young men with wives and small children. Some were too old to be soldiers, but they were here upon the wall, waiting to defend their families as best they could against overwhelming odds. Althus wished he had some hope to offer them. He was proud of these men who were willing to fight for Anduin even when the situation seemed hopeless. Their forces, even bolstered by the citizens of Anduin, could not number much more than a thousand. There were at least three thousand outside the gates with all the time they needed to prepare for the assault to come.

The sight of Euwyn brought a smile to many faces. Whether they counted him as a healer or a warrior among them, Althus could not tell. Either way, the people knew him as a friend. The Wizard had not been called to battle on Anduin soil since the Goblin wars, but Althus knew little of his role in that conflict. He remembered the fire the Wizard had called forth against the creatures in Stonehaven and the amazing way he had destroyed the stone that was part of the Dragon's egg and wondered how powerful a weapon the Wizard could be when fully rested.

Perhaps they would have a few days to prepare as the surrounding army laid siege to the castle, hoping to weaken Anduin's resistance. They would be disappointed when Borgas and his men did not open the gates and welcome them with open arms. They would have to fight their way in if they hoped to take Anduin. He had freed the true soldiers of Anduin and thus taken their rations from them. That was something, at least. His soldiers would die fighting for their people and not as fodder for the Dark Lord's army.

He did not dare hope there was enough food within the walls of Anduin to feed its people for long. Perhaps the enemy would launch an assault as soon as they were gathered, but Althus expected they would stay encamped about the city walls for a time. They would wait, hoping their allies would admit them and then, when they failed to do so, waiting for the population of Anduin to run out of food.

Waiting would be difficult for his people. Not knowing their enemy's intentions would drive many within the gates of Anduin mad with fear. Althus counted on the servants of the Dark Lord driving these forces and the Dark Lord himself finding some amusement in that. He needed a few days at least to prepare and to hope Solomon would return with the Dragon Riders.

## Chapter Thirty-three

## REPAIRS

Antares was soon above the mountains, gliding south through the last passes of the northern range. Solomon sighed as he watched the rugged landscape slide away beneath him and rested his head in his hands, elbows atop the Dragon's broad head as they left the kingdom of Anduin behind.

"Do not worry about them so," said Antares. "We will return in time with more Riders. Augustine will not let Anduin fall."

"Perhaps," was all Solomon would say.

"What are you fretting over, little warrior?" the Dragon asked after a moment's silence. "The Dragon Riders will welcome you back."

"I suppose Augustine will, but what of the others? I have failed them this past year. My place was with them, fighting the evil that infests our land, not wandering the mountains like a lunatic."

The Dragon snorted, "I am a Dragon and do not understand much of the feelings of Elves, but it seems you had some cause to be lost for a time. You seem to forget how gravely injured you were. I do not think many would have survived the injuries you suffered to your body, let alone survive with a sound mind. You needed a year to recover. Few would have recovered at all. Forget the rest."

"Still, it is a weakness I am not proud of and it worries me that it may happen again when I should be keeping my wits about me. Do you think I am fit to be Second among the Dragon Riders? If *I* doubt it, how will the others feel? If I cannot convince them I am fit to lead, will Augustine still send Dragon Riders to Anduin?"

"You think too much, Sollie. That has always been your problem. In addition, you care too much for those people who are not our concern. Dragon Riders are fierce warriors, fighting for your own people and the occasional members of other races that wander into our mountains. You would take us beyond our boundaries. Even now, you have allied yourself with this Human and the Wizard and the Elves and the Dwarf in a cause likely to fail. I see the coming battle in Anduin as a place where we can strike back at these forces breeding in our mountains and causing harm to your people, but as for the Humans, they are frail creatures. They live such a short time and their lives are often lived in suffering and misery. It is their nature. Do you really think winning this battle will make a difference to the race called Humans? You have known them all such a short time. You put yourself in danger again of losing these people you care for. You should try to be more like a Dragon. Do what you must, do not care for others so deeply, and do not waste your time on worry or guilt or regret. That is what will drive you mad in the end if you allow it."

"I will try, Antares," Solomon laughed, "but I cannot be as uncaring as you pretend to be. You are nearly as bad as I am, even though you cannot admit it. As for Althus and Euwyn and their friends, I think they will help us in turn when the time comes. Think of our friendship as an investment in the future of our people if you cannot see it any other way."

The Dragon gave another derisive snort and lapsed into silence as they glided through the last pass and out of the northern arm of the mountains.

Far below, Solomon spied the severed bridge and signaled Antares to circle closer. Gathered about the southern end was a well-armed army of Dwarves.

"I think Mica's people are trying to reach Anduin as well, Antares. Let us see if we can help them repair the bridge," Solomon shouted over the roar of the wind from their rapid descent.

"Are you mad, Sollie? You know how Dwarves feel about Dragons. The greedy little stumpers will decorate my hide with battle-axes before you can say a word to them," Antares growled.

"Well, if you fear them that much, Dragon, then set me down out of range and I will speak to them alone."

"You *are* mad if you think I fear them," said Antares. "I just do not trust Dwarves."

"Mica is one of them, Antares," Solomon reminded him. "You seemed to spend a lot of time with him for someone you did not trust."

"Mica was different," Antares said simply.

"Very well," the Dragon sighed. "You will not rest until I give in to you, even if you risk life and limb in the attempt. We will approach these Dwarves if you wish. Let it be on your head if they riddle us with their axes."

Antares landed a short distance from the Dwarves. Solomon quickly dismounted as angry shouts began to spread through their ranks. Axes appeared in every hand as the Elf approached. A sea of angry faces soon surrounded him. They took him roughly by the arms and forced to his knees. He heard Antares growl angrily from somewhere behind him, but he stayed where he was as Solomon had asked. Solomon did not wish to start a fight with the Dwarves, but only to find a way to speak to their leader before they silenced him permanently. He knelt on the stony ground and tried to appear as unthreatening as possible while the Dwarves about him jostled each other for a better look at their captive. Solomon could easily overpower a few of them, but had no hope of escaping the large army of heavily armed Dwarves with his life if they decided he should die. He was relieved when a red-haired Dwarf with Mica's green eyes and a circlet of gold about his brow forced his way through the crowd, shouting at the black bearded Dwarf that held Solomon so roughly. Solomon bowed his head before the fiery looking Dwarf as he approached.

"Ease up, Shale, ye got no cause to handle the little Rider so rough," the burly Dwarf shouted. "Haven't ye learned anythin' in the last few days? He's an Elf and a shirttail relative to those that jest freed ya. Let him up, I say!" With much grumbling and shoving, the Dwarves let go of Solomon, making a space about him and the red haired Dwarf. The Dwarf held a hand up and the other Dwarves fell nearly silent. A few grumbles still sounded in the ranks, but the Dwarf with the circlet was obviously in charge of the unruly army. Solomon thought of all the tales he had heard concerning the ferocity of Dwarves and wondered if it would not have been wiser to continue on their way and leave the Dwarves to solve the problem of the severed bridge in their own way.

"What is it you wish of us, Rider?" growled the Dwarf in charge. "We do not have time for idle chatter. State your business and then be on your way with that lizard you ride."

Solomon took a deep breath, still kneeling where he was, hoping to get the words out that he needed to say before they tossed him into the chasm for being as bold as to offer help to a Dwarf. A sudden inspiration hit him.

"I thought my friend Mica would want the bridge repaired before I continued on my way to the Hall of the Dragon Riders. If you would permit us to help you, we could save you some time." There, he thought. He had not insulted them by suggesting they could not repair it and Mica would certainly want the bridge repaired, even though the young Dwarf had not said so specifically.

The face of the Dwarf who stood before him changed from anger to wonder to a huge smile in a fraction of a second. "Mica wasn't on the bridge, then, when it fell? You've seen him? Are the rest all right? There were three Elves, a Wizard and a Human with him. Where did you see him?"

"Only Althus was on the bridge when Myoti severed it, and he was rescued by my Dragon, Antares. I saw Mica beyond the gates at the other end of your passage when we returned Althus to them. They were all safe and well when I left them this morning and should be in Anduin soon if they are not already," Solomon said, looking up into the wide green eyes so much like Mica's.

The sturdy Dwarf grabbed his hand and shook it vigorously, dragging him to his feet. "I'm Granite, king of Stonehaven. Mica is me son. Ye've given me some peace today, Elf. I wuz just fixing' ta send someone down ta look fer me son and me friends at the bottom of the gorge."

"I am Solomon and the Dragon is Antares," he said. "It is an honor to meet you, King Granite. Your son, Mica, is a fine young man. You must be proud of him."

"That I am, Solomon, and I'm grateful to ye fer word of him and his friends," Granite said. "I'm fixin' ta take the army of Stonehaven through the passage to Anduin ta fight the creatures there. How do ye propose ta help us fix the bridge?"

"I think Antares and I can raise it if you have the materials to repair it," Solomon replied.

The Dwarf seemed to consider this for a moment, and then nodded in agreement.

A deep voice spoke from behind Solomon. "My brothers and I can hold it while it is repaired if the Dragon can only raise it."

Solomon turned to find himself facing the knees of four Black Giants standing behind him. They had approached so silently he did not know they were there until they spoke.

"I am Bull and these are my wife's brothers, Gideon, Gabriel and Apollo. I grew up as Bree, Chess, and Thorny's brother so I, too, thank you for news of their safety."

Solomon had hastily backed two steps away from the Giants when he turned to find them towering over him, but Bull squatted down to offer Solomon his hand in greeting. The small Elf watched apprehensively as the massive hand engulfed the one he offered in return. Even squatting, the Giant was more than twice as tall as Solomon was. Nothing could have been gentler, however, than Bull's hand holding his. He looked at the dark, smiling face of the Giant and could not help but smile back.

"Come on, Bull," said Granite gruffly. "Enough chatter. Let's get the bridge fixed an' be on our way. I'm sure the little fella didn't stop jest ta talk. He and the lizard want ta be on their way as much as us."

The Dwarves soon produced a length of heavy rope, standing at a distance while Bull helped Solomon load it onto Antares' back. Bull insisted they take the time to introduce him properly to the Dragon before doing so. Antares seemed very cordial toward the Giant and his kin, but the looks he sent in the Dwarves' direction kept them watching from a respectable distance away.

With a leap and a powerful thrust of his wings, Antares was soon gliding down through the rift toward the free end of the bridge that dangled halfway down the opposite face. As long as it was, it still ended far above the rushing cataract below.

"This is not going to be easy," growled the Dragon. "How do you propose to tie a rope to the end of this bridge when it is dangling in mid air? I cannot promise I can hover steadily enough or close enough to the wall without the currents in this rift driving us against it."

"We will at least attempt it, Antares," said Solomon. "You do not want the Dwarves to think you are frightened, do you?"

Antares snorted in reply. "You will break your foolish neck and mine in the bargain to impress a bunch of scruffy Dwarves! I am not afraid and you know it, but if you are killed how will you help Althus?"

"You would go on without me, Antares, and finish what we have started. Besides, if we can help the Dwarves reach Anduin more quickly and survive the attempt, we will have accomplished much more than we set out to. We did pledge ourselves allies to Mica and the Dwarves, after all. Have you forgotten already?" he asked.

Antares did not reply, but Solomon knew he was thinking of the events of the night before. The words they had said to each other and the pledges they had made seemed to sit in Solomon's heart like a live coal. He would sooner die than forsake his friends and they all were equally important if their world were to survive the gathering darkness.

Antares reached the dangling end of the bridge and hovered as close to the severed end as he dared while the Dwarves lined the edge of the chasm, their craggy, bearded faces peering anxiously over the distant edge. Solomon grasped the end of the thick rope in one hand, stretching his other hand to reach the last plank attached to the bridge, intending to tie one end off and carry the other back to the waiting Dwarves. There was no reaching the dangling end from where he sat behind the huge Dragon's head. He decided to change tactics.

"Here, Antares" he said, tossing the end of the rope over the end of the Dragon's broad snout. "Take the end of the rope and pass it to me when I am ready. I am going to jump onto the bridge from your back."

"You are *what*?!" roared the Dragon. It was too late for Antares to protest. Solomon was already in mid air, leaping for the bridge. He caught the last plank easily enough, just before it broke in half with a crack. Solomon plunged toward certain death on the rocks below. Antares was in motion before the sound of the breaking plank died. He plummeted after the Elf like a rock while the Giants and the Dwarves above held their breath. If the chasm had been a span shallower or Antares' neck a hand shorter, Solomon certainly would have been killed. The Dragon caught the Elf in his jaws just before he hit bottom. He flew a short distance to where a gravel bank gave him room to land and spit the Elf unceremoniously onto the ground.

"Sollie, are you hurt?" he cried, nosing the Elf who lay on his side, rolled in a defensive ball.

Solomon unrolled himself and lay on his back, breathing heavily for a moment, his golden eyes wide with relief before he sat up and casually inspected his person for damage.

"No," he said, "you did not even rip my uniform. You are as gentle as a mother cat, Antares."

"Hey, you dropped the rope!" he cried suddenly. "I hope you know where you left it." Solomon turned about looking for the errant rope while Antares gaped at him.

"The rope!" he sputtered. "The rope? You are concerned about the rope?

You are certainly are not going to try that again! I will not be a part of it!"

Solomon looked up at the bridge, considering. "Perhaps if I can find the rope, I can climb up from here," he said, starting back upstream in the direction they had come. "It must have fallen close by somewhere."

"Wait! Sollie! I forbid you to climb up there!" Antares tried to look menacing as he intercepted the Elf before he ran out of solid ground, but Solomon's familiar look of determination told him there was no use in trying to dissuade him. The end of the rope lay upon the edge of the bank, a good part of it immersed in the stream. Solomon pounced on it and drew it out of the water, looping the wet coils about his shoulder.

"Sollie, please do not try this again," Antares begged, hoping a pathetic look would work where threats would not.

Solomon laughed and patted him on the snout. "Well, you sad old Dragon, are you going to help me get up there or do I climb? You do not want the Dwarves to think we are cowards, do you?"

"They cannot call you a coward, but they will certainly think you are mad." Antares said with a sigh as he bent down for Solomon to remount.

Their second attempt was more successful. Antares tested the planks for soundness with claws and snout before Solomon leapt onto the bridge and with only a little trouble caused by the weight and slipperiness of the wet rope, the Elf was able to tie the end to a solid plank. He drew the loose end up and tossed it to Antares, prompting a short argument with the Dragon over whether he would ride the Dragon or the end of the bridge back to the rim of the chasm. Antares again gave in and flew off to where the Dwarves waited, the end of the rope held firmly in his jaws. He landed safely and the Giants took the rope from him, carefully drawing the bridge back into position.

When Solomon scrambled to his feet and leapt from the bridge to the safety of solid ground, Bull was there, reaching out with two huge hands to catch him. The Giant held him up briefly for inspection before setting him firmly on his own two feet. Bull's dark face wore an expression of profound relief as he squatted before the Elf.

"I thought you were finished when you fell into the chasm," he said. "Thank the Creator you have such a wondrous friend as Antares to save you."

"He is a friend beyond price, Bull. He has saved my life more than once and I fear I make his life difficult. It is a wonder he puts up with me since Dragons cannot feel love for anyone," Solomon said with a grin in Antares' direction.

Antares snorted, startling the few Dwarves foolhardy enough to stand close by, but made no comment.

Bull's deep laughter echoed against the rock walls across the chasm as he and Solomon stood next to the Dragon and watched the Dwarves and Bull's brothers secure the bridge and replace the missing plank. A lone Dwarf crossed the bridge to inspect it for soundness and Solomon was pleased to see Antares watching closely, prepared to spring into action if the bridge proved unsound and the Dwarf's life was in danger. His words had touched the stubborn Dragon somehow, even though Antares would never admit it. The bridge proved to be sound, however, and the Dwarf returned smiling and bowing to Antares and Solomon as he strode past them to join the rest of the troops waiting to cross.

Granite appeared at their side after his own inspection tour.

"I would like ta thank ye fer yer help, Solomon," he said. "It woulda taken us a whole day ta climb down this side o' the chasm an halfway up the other to reach the free end o' that bridge."

"Antares and I have pledged ourselves allies to your son and his people. We would be poor allies indeed if we turned our backs when our first chance to aid his people presented itself," Solomon offered, waiting anxiously for the Dwarf king's reaction to his son's pledge.

Granite's mouth hung open for a moment as his green-eyed gaze traveled from Solomon to the huge Dragon and back again.

Antares' eyes narrowed dangerously as he waited for the explosion to come.

"And I suppose Mica has pledged our people allies to you and yer Dragon in return?" Granite growled.

"Yes, your majesty," Solomon answered. "He has."

Granite seemed to chew on this bit of information as his gaze returned to the bridge and the gates beyond. He muttered to himself for a while, shaking his head as he considered his options.

"Allies, ya say?" he asked again, considering the possibilities. "I don't know what the rest o' them will think o' this turn of events. Dragons and Dwarves don't get along as a rule. Too much alike, I think. Still, yer riders would be powerful friends at that, an' Mica *is* the Prince of Stonehaven. Mebbe he should have a say in who we count as our friends... Well, Elf, I guess ya can say we're allies if it pleases ya ta say so. We'll give it a go fer now."

Solomon had held his breath as Granite made his decision. His sigh of relief made Granite chuckle.

"Ya haven't asked the rest of the Riders if they want ta be allied to a bunch o' Dwarves yet, have ya?"

"No, your majesty, I have not," Solomon answered. "I am on my way to the Hall of the Dragon Riders to ask them to aid Anduin in its war against the Orcs and Goblins and other creatures that will, I fear, reach the city of Anduin by nightfall. This army of foul creatures has been bred somewhere close to our lands in the mountains, driven by some unknown evil, perhaps the Dark Lord returned, to spread their misery to the lands beyond. We must stop them somewhere, somehow. We may as well begin with Anduin. I hope to convince the other Riders of this as well."

"Well put, Solomon," said the sturdy Dwarf. "It seems my people have played a part in armin' the nasty beasts while we was their slaves. I guess we feel the same as you. Might as well start our fightin' in Anduin. We'll end up fightin' em at our own doorstep soon enough if we don't. Besides, I think if we all stick together we might stand a chance o' comin' out all right!" he said, slapping Solomon on the back and nearly knocking him to his knees.

## Chapter Thirty-four

## HOLLY

Solomon and Antares were soon winging their way southward once more after seeing the Dwarves off across the bridge. They could not hope to reach the Hall before nightfall now and would spend the night in the mountain meadow near the waterfall where they had breakfasted with Althus the previous morning. It would be another day of flying before they reached the Hall of the Dragon riders where they would present their case before Brother Augustine, the leader of their order. Solomon, trying to decide how best to present his case on behalf of Anduin, was deep in thought as they approached the meadow. Antares circled the meadow before landing in order to draw Solomon's attention to the scene below.

"Look, Sollie," he rumbled. "It seems a visitor has arrived since we left."

Curled up in the grass below was the white Dragon, Polaris. A small figure wearing red and gold sitting on a boulder below would have to be the Dragon Rider, Holly. A sudden bout of panic seized Solomon. He considered flying on to spend the night elsewhere, but he knew Holly and Polaris would have seen them by now. A Dragon the size of Antares would be impossible to overlook. As they descended, he could see Holly marking their approach. They landed smoothly near to where Polaris stood waiting. Solomon took a deep breath to steady himself before sliding to the ground. He had not spoken to another Rider in a year. He did not remember seeing another Rider since leaving the Hall months ago.

Holly had been his student for a very short time and a friend to him when he could no longer be her instructor. What did she and the other Riders think of him? If only she did not hate him for what he had become in the last year. He was not sure he could survive if the Riders turned against him. He could return to help Althus without the others, but he would always be an outcast. He could turn back toward Anduin now if he must, but the Riders were his family. Holly would tell him truthfully how she and the rest felt about him.

It took a gentle nudge from behind by Antares to set his feet in motion. He bowed in greeting to Polaris whose red eyes regarded him closely before he started across the meadow to greet the Rider running toward him. They met in the middle of a sea of waving grass, standing three paces apart, watching each other cautiously. Holly saluted him, fist to heart and stood before him, her blue eyes searching his. Did she seem almost hopeful?

Solomon remembered her better now. The blue eyes and smooth, fine featured face that almost never betrayed the emotions beneath. She bore a large journal tucked under her arm with a quill closed within its pages. He remembered her holding her journal, writing the events of the day in it in a firm, clear hand. He *did* remember seeing it. He saw her again in his mind's eye, sitting cross-legged at the foot of his bed, reading the events of each day from its pages.

He returned her salute and stood looking into those serene eyes while the wind whipped her red gold hair about her face and the few moments he could remember of the past year ran through his head. She had been there for him. His mouth went dry. What could he possibly do or say that would show her what that meant to him? She stood at attention, her eyes searching his until he spoke.

"I am sorry, Holly," was all he could think to say to her. "I hope you can forgive me for treating you so callously. You were a good friend to me when I was recovering from my injuries. I am afraid it was a thankless task for you."

A smile lit her face. "It is true, then," she said. "The Creator has sent you back to us. Augustine said if I found you here, still alive, you might have come to your senses. I did not dare hope it would be so. When I found no sign of you, I feared the worst, but here you are, wearing your uniform, riding Antares and speaking to me like the man I remember from the first days when you undertook my training. It is what we all hoped for after the months you spent apart from us, sir. Certainly, no apology is necessary."

Solomon meant only to take her hand and thank her for her friendship, but he found himself drawing her into his arms as if suddenly he needed more from her. He had missed the Riders he commanded.

It was as if Holly's words lifted a great weight from his heart. Even if she were the only friend he had among them, at least she was willing to accept him. The Brotherhood sent her to find him, so Augustine also wanted him back. He would endure whatever the next days had in store for him if only he could count on Holly and Augustine and his brother , Joseph to stand by his side.

"Please call me Sollie," he said to her when he drew away, still resting his hands on her shoulders. "You are a real Dragon Rider now, not one of my students and therefore my equal in the Brotherhood. You cannot know how happy I am to see another Rider. Especially one who can tell me so much of what I have missed in the last few months. Augustine must have chosen you to search for me for that very reason. I hope you have written it all in your journal and will consent to read it to me," he said, eyeing the large tome she carried hopefully.

"Of course, sir .... I mean Sollie. I have written all the events of the past year in my journal and it would be my pleasure to read them to you. It is not often anyone besides Augustine takes an interest in my writings. I had supposed no one else would read them for at least a hundred years or more. You may be sorry you asked," she said.

"I doubt I could ever be sorry to hear of the everyday lives of the Riders, as boring as they might seem at times."

"Our lives have not been quiet in the past year. Your unfortunate experience was by far the worst that happened, but only the beginning," Holly sighed.

"Well, I have a tale to tell as well, but it is much shorter than yours as it only involves the past three days. I will entertain you with my tale and in return you will read to me from your book."

They soon faced each other across a small fire. The two Dragons curled about them, lying contentedly with their heads together, sheltering the two riders from the cold wind that blew through the mountains, listening to the tales told over the fire in the fading twilight. Holly's head bent over her journal as her quill flew across the pages, recording Solomon and Antares' tale exactly as they told it. Antares' tale began with his rescue of Althus. When he reached the part where he laid the unconscious prince at Solomon's feet, he let Solomon tell the rest. Solomon left nothing out. He told Holly of his state of mind when the injured Althus arrived and his intention to die by his own hand in the ruined village that night. He felt he owed her a true accounting of himself if she was to judge his fitness to return to the Riders.

The tale of their journey to the northern fringes of the mountains to meet with the rest of Althus' company was much easier to tell. Antares, who still seemed to think Solomon had taken a foolish risk when he stopped to help the Dwarves and the Giants, interrupted the story of their return and the broken bridge often.

Solomon could not see Holly's face. It was hidden from him, shadowed by her hair as she bent close to the journal in her lap. The flickering firelight made it difficult to see the page, but she seemed determined to make a thorough account of Solomon's tale. What would she think of an alliance between the Dragon Riders and the Humans of Anduin? Would she see it in the same light as he did, as an alliance that could ultimately be for the good of all races, or would she see the Humans as Antares did, an extra burden requiring too much of the Riders' resources? It would have been easier to plead his cause if the wood Elves of the Dark Forest were the ones asking for help, but if Anduin fell, the Dark Forest would be next to feel the power of the evil forces. Their task would be even more difficult with the resources of Anduin added to the dark army.

He waited for her to look up from her writing. She seemed preoccupied for a time, making diagrams of the bridge and sketching rough maps in the margins. She read over what she had written and asked him a few questions, adding more details and drawings until his patience was wearing a bit thin. She finally noticed that he was waiting for her opinion, but she still seemed at a loss for words.

"Sollie, you have been lost to the Brotherhood for months now," she began, choosing her words carefully. "Surely you know we needed to have a Second Rider to lead us, especially now that dark creatures are now bred at our very doorstep somewhere here in the mountains. They have raided many of the mountain villages, killing our people and ransacking their storehouses. The mountain passes are no longer safe for our people to travel unguarded. We are sorely pressed to keep the evil at bay."

"I have been replaced, then," Solomon said softly. "I should not have expected otherwise."

"No, you have not been replaced in the hearts and minds of the Riders. Not permanently," she assured him. "Augustine would not allow it until we were sure you would never return. That is why I was here looking for you, Sollie. We had to know what happened to you. We cannot wait any longer for you to come back to us." She shook her head and ran a hand through her hair, pushing it back from her face. "Marcus has been acting as Second Rider since you were injured. Do you remember that from when you still were with us, too weak to leave?"

Solomon shook his head. "I remember very little from the past year. Some has come back to me in the past few days. You were the first of my memories to return. I remembered you sitting and reading to me each evening. I cannot tell you what you read, but only that you were there when I needed someone. I think I owe you my life. You would not let me sink so deep within myself that I could let go. I know it was probably a task Augustine assigned to you, but you were very kind to spend the hours when you could have been resting or studying in such a thankless way."

"I read to you each evening for nearly a month before Augustine knew of it," she admitted. "Joseph came to sit with you each night as well. Joseph persuaded you to eat and drink. He and I became good friends during that time.

"When Augustine found us out, I was afraid he would be angry. We were disturbing you when you should have been resting, but he seemed pleased to know someone was there keeping an eye on you, even if you did not know it. He said we could continue as long as we wished. He warned me at that time you might not live much longer. He was afraid to say this to Joseph. Somehow, you proved him wrong." She paused to clear her throat and rub her hand across her eyes.

Solomon asked her if she were tired. For some reason he could not understand, she laughed at him.

"No," she said, "and we have wandered far from the important things we were once discussing while you thanked me for something I did because it pleased me to do so."

"Oh, yes, Marcus." Solomon tried to drag his mind away from Holly's odd behavior and back to the subject that should have been of more concern to him. "I remember him of course. I did not know he was acting as Second Rider, but he would be the logical choice. He would do well as Second Rider."

The look Holly gave him made him wonder if she did not have a different opinion of Marcus, but she went on before he could ask. "He has done well as Second Rider. He is a capable enough leader, but I fear he does not care for his fellow Riders as much as he cares for his own position within the Brotherhood. He certainly will not care much for the fate of Anduin and possibly not even that of the Elves of the Dark Forest. Marcus will not be happy to see you return as Second Rider. I am afraid he would rather you did not return at all. He will not step aside without protest. I think there will be a vote taken and he has had an entire year to plant the seeds of doubt in the minds of those who could be persuaded to vote against you."

"It may be best if the Brotherhood freely chooses between us," Solomon mused. "Perhaps he is the better man. If I am accepted once again as a member of the Brotherhood, that will be enough. Maybe it is more than I should expect."

Holly shut the huge book in her lap with a resounding bang. Both Dragons raised their heads in surprise as she leapt up to stand glaring at Solomon.

"*No!*" She shouted, "It is not for the best if they choose the wrong man because he has spoken against you when you were not there to defend yourself! I do not know if I can remain as one of the Brotherhood if he is to remain as Second Rider! I cannot believe Augustine would allow it!"

Solomon looked at her in alarm. He had never seen her angry. He did remember her clearly from the first month he had served as her instructor and her unruffled calm always impressed him, even when training was going badly for her and she was battered and sore to prove it.

He waited for her to regain her composure. She picked up the book she had uncharacteristically dropped to the ground in her haste to rise and dusted it off carefully before resuming her seat across the fire from him.

"Tell me why you dislike the man so," he asked.

She sat staring at him as if she were reluctant to tell him. He could not help hoping she had not changed so much in the last year she would dislike the man with no cause.

"He came into your room when you lay helpless," she said with a faint shudder. "I was reading to you as I did every evening, but he had ordered Joseph to guard duty. Marcus laughed at me. He said I was wasting my time. I could have forgiven him for saying that," she continued quickly, cutting Solomon off before he defended Marcus. "He was not the only one to feel that way, although he was the only one to say it openly. It was the next thing he said that I will never be able to forgive. He said we would be better off when you were dead. He did not say you would be better off dead, which I could not agree with, but I could understand it if he were saying you would be better off if your suffering were ended. He did not even have the decency to say *if* you died. It was as if he was counting on you to die and therefore clear the way for him to be Second Rider permanently."

She went on, enlightening him a bit more. "He was my instructor after you were injured, and he wanted to be more than an instructor to me. I told him truthfully I found his advances improper, considering his position as my superior, but he was persistent. Fortunately, I think you had taught me enough to make him wary of pressing the issue too far. I spent my evenings in your room hoping to escape him for the short time each day when I was not in training or studying with the elders. Even then, I preferred your company to his. He came there only once, but it was enough to make me hate him forever for what he said that night."

"Did you tell Augustine of his behavior toward you?" Solomon asked, somehow more disturbed by Marcus' behavior toward Holly than Marcus' wish that he were dead. For some reason that seemed less of a personal affront to Solomon than the liberties he tried to take with Solomon's favorite and most promising pupil.

"Of course I did not, Sollie. Augustine has more important matters troubling him now. As members of the Brotherhood he needs us to help him protect our fellow mountain Elves, not burden him with our personal problems. I can handle Marcus more easily than he realizes. He was not half as good an instructor as you. You taught me more in a few short weeks than he could in a lifetime. He thinks he is a great warrior. While he is flourishing his sword and posturing, someone with half your talent could easily run him through."

Solomon was startled to see a look of pleasure on her face as she thought of it. "Holly!" he cried, shocked at the direction her thoughts were taking her. "You would not harm a member of the Brotherhood!"

"No. No, I could not. I admit the thought of it has given me some pleasure in my dreams, but I suppose I could not. I would not mind putting him in his place, though. Just once."

Solomon could not help but laugh at her look of serene pleasure at the thought of laying her hands on the hated Marcus. She was still smiling happily, as she turned the pages of her beloved journal back to the entries she had made when Solomon was injured. He moved to sit by her side where he could admire her simple illustrations. Many of the entries were common accountings of the comings and goings of the Riders or the gathering of supplies. Accounts of skirmishes became more frequent as the year went on. Each entry ended with the words, "read to Solomon tonight" and a few words describing his condition. Most pages bore the words "no change." Holly did not read these words to him, but he could read them for himself as he sat sharing the pages of the journal with her. There was as little mention of Marcus as possible as if he did not deserve to occupy the pages of her book. One page was devoted to a drawing she attempted to turn past. Solomon placed a hand in the book before she could lose the place and turned back to admire her artwork. It was an amazing likeness of someone he thought he should know. It took him a few moments to realize it was his face gazing back at him from the page.

"I drew that when you first opened your eyes after you were injured. I wanted to remember you somehow if... if... Well, I guess I still was afraid you would die on me. I took great pains to make it look as much like you as possible, but I am afraid I am a writer, not an artist.

Solomon stared at the drawing. It seemed disturbingly lifelike to him. He wondered what thoughts lurked behind the face as she was drawing it. The knowledge that he would never know made him shiver. He looked normal enough in her drawing, but he wondered how much of it she drew from memory. His hand still rested on the page opposite his likeness. Holly placed her hand upon his, turning to look into his eyes.

If you are worried about that time, Sollie, you should not," she said. "You were silent and withdrawn. We tried to reach you, but I think we expected too much of you too soon. You were always the bravest and strongest among us. It frightened us all to find you were not indestructible, but I think it made us more cautious and taught us some much-needed humility. We look out for each other now more than ever. We have been reminded what it is like to lose one of our Brothers.

Solomon turned the page. How fortunate he was to have met Holly here before he reached the Hall. He hoped when they finished Holly's journal that night he could begin to put the past to rest. He realized for the first time that even though he had been withdrawn from the Brotherhood for the past year, he had never been alone. Holly and Joseph had been by his side and then, when they could not be with him, Augustine had sent Antares to look after him. So much time and effort invested in his recovery. Perhaps he could resume the duty he had left behind, but he had so little time. He needed to return to Anduin. Marcus would not give up the post easily and Solomon did not have the time to fight him for it. He hoped Holly would understand.

They spent the rest of the evening with their heads together, reading the entries in Holly's book. The entries soon included graphic descriptions of the skirmishes in which Holly had taken part since the completion of her training. They were straightforward accounts without dramatics or embellishment. Mere statements of the facts and events of the day. To Solomon, the plain factual accounts of the numbers and nature of the beasts they encountered were chilling enough. Holly's illustrations only served to emphasize the evil nature of the creatures they fought. They were both yawning and rubbing tired eyes before they slept that night.

## Chapter Thirty-five

## ABDUCTION

As they flew southward toward the Hall of the Dragon Riders the next day, Solomon could not help but admire the sleek white Dragon flying beside him. She was much smaller than Antares, but from experience, he knew the lithe Dragon could knife through the skies with amazing speed and was more agile than any other Dragon of the Brotherhood. She obeyed Holly without hesitation even though he could not see how they communicated. He remembered watching them in training, amazed at the acrobatic maneuvers they could perform.

It had been difficult for Holly to convince the Brotherhood that a wild Dragon from the western seas could serve a Dragon Rider as well as the Dragons from the southern mountain regions. Polaris did not have the power of speech as Antares did, but she seemed every bit as intelligent to Solomon. Her eyes were very expressive and knowing when they were turned in his direction. She did not have slitted pupils like the Dragons with which Solomon was most familiar, but eyes that were startlingly Elven. Antares accepted her as an equal. In fact, he seemed quite fond of her, and there were not many Solomon could think of that bore that distinction.

Holly had come to the Brotherhood from the westernmost fringes of their territory where the mountains reached to the shores of the Great Sea, the lone survivor of a village overrun by a band of Goblins. The white Dragon found her hidden in the ruins of her village, remaining as her protector and companion until she left her home to beg admittance to the Brotherhood of Dragon Riders.

No one had the heart to turn her away. Solomon offered to train her and her unusual Dragon. He never regretted his decision. Holly, hardened by her experiences and with nowhere else to call home, had become a dedicated student.

She had fallen into the habit of treating him as an equal easily after their first hours together the previous evening. As a student, she had been eager to please him and a little awed by his position as Second Rider. She was now as self-assured and confident as any fully trained Rider. Her newfound assurance made Solomon feel more at ease with her. She seemed more than willing to speak her mind if she disagreed with him. An easy friendship was already forming, replacing their student and master relationship. Considering her history, he felt she understood him better than most.

The morning air was cold over the mountains, pale sunlight just beginning to burn through the mist that hung in the valleys as they passed over the first small mountain village. He could make out the faces of a few of its people turned upward to mark their passing. Here and there, a small figure would wave as they flew overhead.

Without the Dragons to carry them, the Riders would find it impossible to protect these small, scattered villages hidden in the deep mountain valleys. Trails between these villages were primitive and often impassable, skirting the sheer cliffs of the mountains and winding through the dense pine forests of the lower slopes. Without the Dragon Riders, the farmers and craftsmen of the small villages would be nearly defenseless. It was no wonder the Brotherhood of Dragons and Riders were revered and respected by the mountain Elves.

Solomon hoped he was not making a mistake in asking Riders to take part in the defense of Anduin. How many could be spared when the mountains were beginning to feel the presence of the very same creatures?

It was shortly past midday, as they approached the village of Krest, that they caught the first signs of battle. Quickly changing their course to bring them directly over the valley that sheltered the village, they found the air above it teeming with Myoti, punctuated by the glistening forms of five Dragons of varying hues. Solomon's heart beat faster at the sight of his men, the men who were once under his command, joined in battle with a band of Goblins in the village below. The Dragon Riders were outnumbered three to one, but Solomon knew the odds still favored the Riders. He and Holly were prepared to make the odds favor them even more.

With a shriek, Polaris dove into the milling Myoti, wreaking havoc among their lumbering ranks. Antares followed closely, burning two Myoti to cinders and snapping the neck of another as he dove through the milling creatures and toward the battle below. He knew his first task was to set Solomon down where he could join the Riders in the village. Once the enemy gained entrance to a village, Dragons were only used as a last resort. The huge Dragons often caused more damage than they prevented within the confines of village walls.

Six riders faced the Goblin band as Polaris dropped Holly at Solomon's side and followed Antares back to join the battle in the sky above them. As he plunged into the fray, Solomon took note of the Elves that surrounded him. Joseph and Noah stood at his right hand as they had countless times before. Matthew and Ephraim stood at his left, beyond Holly. They all seemed to be grinning for some reason he could not fathom. Joseph sported a wicked looking cut over one eye and Ephraim held one arm close to his side as if injured.

The Goblins had scattered at the sight of the two Dragons, but were advancing once more, now that the Dragons had flown off. After a brief glance at Solomon, the Elves' attention returned to the advancing Goblins.

As usual, the Goblins armed themselves with a motley assortment of weapons. They wielded clubs with skill and the short spears they carried seemed to work well for them. Others armed with heavy swords seemed more of a danger to themselves than to the Elves they faced. The only advantages the Goblins held were their numbers and their size. Their long arms and legs gave them some advantage in reach, but they were no match for the swift and agile Elves.

With howls and shrieks, the Goblins finally made their move, charging directly into the waiting Riders. Solomon made the first kill, ducking easily under the arm of a club-wielding creature and sliding his sword between the creature's ribs as its club hit the ground where he once stood. Joseph slipped past the sword-wielding goblin that had marked him as its victim and drove his sword into its armpit as it stupidly looked to see where he had gone. Solomon caught sight of Holly finishing one creature off with its own club and Ephraim, the Elf that Solomon considered the most skilled and experienced among his men, seemed to be holding his own, even though he fought with only one arm. Matthew and Noah were having similar success although Noah now showed a bloody tear in his uniform from a Goblin spear.

The battle was short and fierce. When the surviving Goblins numbered fewer than six and the battle seemed less in their favor, the creatures turned and fled, foolishly running across the open meadow surrounding the village, making for the shelter of the forest. They did not get far. The Dragons had finished off the hated Myoti and were eagerly looking for more prey. As if according to agreement, each Dragon present for the commencement of the battle picked out a goblin and turned them to cinders.

The Riders stood at the edge of the village and surveyed their work. Not one goblin or Myoti had escaped. The Dragons landed to stand shoulder to shoulder in the meadow just outside the village walls, gleaming in the afternoon sun, each watching anxiously for their riders to approach. The Dragons much preferred to battle their enemies outside the villages in which case their riders would fight while still mounted. There was some competition among the Dragons involving the length of time their riders went without injury. Battles fought hand to hand and afoot in the villages were far more dangerous for the Riders and the Dragons frowned on them.

Solomon surveyed the Dragons, noting there were more Dragons present than there were Riders. He was beginning to worry about the missing Rider when he noticed the eyes of the four riders present turned toward him. He returned their gaze as boldly as he dared, uncertain of his place among them and wondering what they were thinking of his sudden appearance. He looked at Holly for reassurance, but she was staring at Ephraim and Ephraim was looking at Solomon, his face as impassive as Solomon remembered it.

"I did not think you would return, Solomon," he said. "I did not dare hope you would." Ephraim threw his good arm about Solomon's shoulders and suddenly everyone was smiling and laughing.

"You were thinking we had forgotten you for a moment there, were you not?"

Matthew and Noah were congratulating Holly on a job well done while they took turns shaking Solomon's hand and telling him how well he looked.

"He is still the best swordsman I ever saw," said Noah.

"And I would wager he is still the best instructor to be had anywhere," added Matthew.

Solomon looked toward Joseph. He stood back from the others, watching silently as they greeted him. Solomon stepped toward him, hesitantly, wondering if Joseph still felt the same way about him after his long absence. His answer came when Joseph grabbed him roughly and wrapped him in a fierce embrace.

"I have missed you more than I can say, Solomon," he said, his voice thick with emotion. "Welcome back."

Their obvious joy at his return made Solomon feel a little awkward. He wanted to speak to Joseph alone and all of them at once. They bombarded him with questions so quickly he could barely take it all in and then, suddenly, there was dead silence. All eyes turned to the group of mountain Elves approaching from within the village and the Dragon Rider who led them, wearing the medallion of Second Rider. Ephraim's good hand on Solomon's shoulder tightened enough that Solomon thought he would wear a bruise there tomorrow.

With his men at his back, he had the courage to face anyone. Holly swung around to face Marcus as he approached. Solomon wondered why the look in her eyes did not wither him on the spot. The thought made him smile.

"So. How fortunate we are. Our former Second Rider has decided to return to us," he said smiling at Solomon and offering him his hand.

Solomon shook his hand briefly noting that Marcus did not sound as if he counted himself truly fortunate.

"As you can see, I have turned the soldiers of the Dragon patrol into a very efficient fighting force in your absence," he continued. "We no longer have unfortunate incidences in which entire villages are wiped out such as the one in which somehow you were the only survivor."

Solomon had to grasp Holly firmly by the back of her sword belt to keep her at his side. Fortunately, Marcus did not seem to notice.

"I thank you for stepping in as Second Rider, Marcus," Solomon answered smoothly. The mention of the people killed in Bess' village stung him, but he would not show it before his men. "You will be relieved to know I am now able to resume my post." He could not resist saying so, if only to gauge Marcus' reaction.

"Well, Solomon, we shall see how the rest of the Riders feel about that. I think your injuries may still prevent you from serving us as well as you might wish, but I am sure Augustine can still find you a place within the Brotherhood. He still seems to think you may be of some service to us. Perhaps you could serve with the older brothers as a healer. I hear you are as good with a salve as you were with a sword," he said with a smug smile.

Solomon was through with the war of words. "Speaking of my healing skills, Marcus, I think some of my men could use those skills before they bleed to death where they stand. They are weary as well. We can discuss the matter of my position among the Riders when we return to the Hall. As you know, Marcus, it is a matter for the entire Brotherhood to decide."

He turned on his heel and strode toward the waiting Dragons. The five Riders followed at his back, leaving Marcus standing with the villagers. After a sour look in Solomon's direction, Marcus turned to them, basking in their thanks and admiration. Holly could not help but notice as she looked back at the villagers that the majority of them were looking after Solomon and the Riders retreating toward the Dragons.

Ephraim looked angry. Holly and Matthew muttered under their breath.

Joseph shook his head as he turned to smile at Solomon through the blood running freely down his face. When Solomon smiled back, Joseph wrapped an arm about his shoulders.

Ephraim stumbled and Joseph reached out to put his free arm about the elder Elf as they went to meet the Dragons. Ephraim had been a Rider longest of all still in active duty. He was a quiet man, not given to lengthy speeches, but always willing to give advice when asked. He stood a hand taller than Solomon, but, in contrast to the solid Joseph who supported him, he was lean and sinewy with dark eyes that seemed to see right into your soul when he looked at you.

Solomon was never certain what Ephraim thought of him, but knew him to be fair and practical. If he did not think Solomon fit for duty as Second Rider he would say so, and many would follow his lead. Solomon would rather be judged by Ephraim than Marcus in any case. At least Ephraim would put the welfare of the Riders before his own interests.

Matthew, who held the post of Dragon master, went to inspect the Dragons for injuries while Solomon tended to the wounded Elves. Noah was the first to be treated. Holly dug supplies from her pack while Solomon helped him out of his coat and shirt. He thought of Althus' fine coat of mail and wished each of his men possessed such protection. It proved to be a minor wound, however, and Solomon quickly had a neat bandage in place about Noah's ribs and turned to Joseph's wound. He had Joseph stitched and was setting Ephraim's broken shoulder when Marcus finally appeared to supervise the proceedings. Matthew, having returned with his black Dragon, Sirius at his side, reported the Dragons unharmed and ready to travel as soon as their

Riders were.

"When you are done with coddling your friends, Solomon, we must return to the Hall. Darkness will be upon us soon," Marcus said, strutting about while Solomon concentrated on Ephraim. Solomon nodded absently, fully aware darkness would fall soon, but attempting, with Holly's assistance, to cause Ephraim as little pain as possible as he realigned the broken bones of his shoulder.

"Did you hear me, Solomon or are your wits wandering again?" Marcus shouted at him.

"I hear you," Solomon responded mildly, his attention hardly wavering from his task.

Vega, Ephraim's red Dragon had wandered over to be near his master during the process of setting his shoulder. Standing behind Marcus, he sneezed suddenly, sending Marcus dancing out of the way of the small gout of fire issuing from his nostrils.

"Sorry, Marcus," he growled. "Must be allergic to something here in this field."

A glance showed Solomon the Dragon did not look as sorry as he should have. A small smile replaced the pain on Ephraim's face. Solomon tried not to look at Marcus while Holly grinned at him from behind Ephraim's shoulder where Marcus could not see her expression.

Dragons were never disciplined. They served at their own choosing and did as they pleased. The Riders, however, were subject to the discipline of the officers they served. Solomon faced enough of an uphill battle without adding to the acting Second Rider's animosity toward him. Marcus did not look amused, sending a withering look at Vega, who ignored him entirely, intent on his rider once again.

They were soon winging their way through the gathering twilight toward the Hall of the Dragon Riders. The sun had nearly set, and watch fires were lit against the approaching darkness when they came in sight of their home. The Hall was actually an island on a sapphire lake within the massive crater of an extinct volcano. At first glance, it appeared to be no more than a rugged island, a weathered volcanic core, rising from the center of the lake. Warmed by the fires that drew near the earth's surface, the lake and the island at its center often disappeared in the mists that rose from the lake's surface into the cold mountain air.

Tonight, only the thinnest of mists swirled over the lake. The Hall stood clearly visible against the water, its sheer walls of black obsidian glittering in the setting sun. The only evidence that it was actually a fortress were massive gates set in the face of the sheer rock and the faint glow of torchlight that shone from narrow windows cut into its walls.

It was customary for incoming riders to land on the shores of the placid lake, outside the gates of the fortress. There were Dragons there already. Eighteen Dragons served the riders at Solomon's last count. Almost all would be present when Marcus' company landed. It was quite a sight to see so many Dragons of various hues, glittering in the fading twilight, all gathered in one place. When at rest, the Dragons tended to roost atop the fortress, their varying hues standing out against the ebony rocks like precious jewels. They gathered before the huge iron bound gates now, in anticipation of the Riders' return.

All eyes watched Solomon and Antares by the time they followed Polaris in her slow glide earthward. Marcus had taken the head of the flight as Second Rider and Solomon and Holly were the last to land. Unfortunately, for Marcus, it only served to cause more of a stir as the Dragons present on the ground and the Riders still stationed among them speculated as to the identity of the rider on Antares' huge back. All knew of Holly's mission to find Solomon and bring him back to the Hall. Even before they landed, Solomon was the name on everyone's lips.

He was barely on solid ground before the Riders were welcoming him home, shaking his hands, patting him on the back and asking hopefully if he were back for good. He was greeted by the brothers Jonathan and Samuel, short and stocky Esther and fair-haired Sarah. More riders appeared as word spread through the fortress. Joshua, Isaiah, and Timothy came running to shake his hand and welcome him back. Augustine, who wrapped Solomon in a bear hug that threatened to crush him, soon followed them. He held Solomon at arm's length for closer inspection and then crushed his bones a bit more for good measure.

There was so much commotion that Solomon was relieved when Augustine hustled the Riders back to their posts with the promise of a celebration later that evening. Augustine led him through the gates of the Hall, down its familiar corridors and into Solomon's private rooms, chatting excitedly all the way. They both paused to look at the plain, comfortable place Solomon had called home for so long. Solomon was surprised to find it essentially unchanged. Perhaps a little neater than he remembered, but his few meager possessions were still there. He wondered why Marcus had not occupied his rooms, as they were usually reserved for the Second Rider.

"Well, for one thing," Augustine answered when asked, "you were still here and very ill when Marcus took over the post of Second. I was unwilling to move you from any place you found familiar then. As time went on, we still hoped Marcus' appointment would be temporary." Augustine fell silent, looking about the room as if he were remembering those unhappy days.

Solomon found Augustine unchanged from the burly Elf he remembered so fondly. His closely cropped hair and beard were snow white and had been as long as Solomon had been his Second in Command. The familiar smile lit his brilliant blue eyes. Essentially, he had not changed since he had taken Solomon on as a young trainee years ago. Solomon was still young for an Elf at two hundred thirty years of age while Augustine numbered his years at over a thousand. Only two Dragon Riders still living at the hall were older than Augustine. Very few Riders who survived to retire remained to serve as healers as Augustine had. Most returned to the villages where they were born to offer their services to those who lived there. Healers were sorely needed in the isolated mountain villages.

Solomon watched Augustine fondly while he struggled to form the questions that he needed to ask. His eyes met Solomon's for a long moment as if trying to search out the answers there. Finally, he took a deep breath and plunged ahead.

"How are you, Solomon?" he asked. "It seems as if my prayers have been answered and you have recovered fully. You seem changed in some ways, but in ways that make you even stronger than before. I know you as well as a father knows a son, Solomon and I know you cannot lie to me. Are you fully recovered?"

"I feel as if I am," Solomon answered, "but I am afraid I cannot be sure. How can you or I or any of the Riders know if I can be trusted when I have only just returned? I cannot say with certainty where I was or what I did until three days ago, although Antares could tell you. He kept me safe while I wandered the mountains." Solomon shivered, thinking of the year he had lost, tortured by memories of the day Bess' entire village was slaughtered.

"Tell me, then. What do you remember of the past three days?" Augustine asked gently, expecting to hear a tale of Solomon slowly becoming more aware of his surroundings and Antares persuading him to return home.

The tale Solomon had to tell him was far from the tale he expected. He suspected the anniversary of the attack on Bess' village would find Solomon there, in the ruins, and he was not surprised to hear him admit his intention to end his tortured existence that night. He was astonished to hear Antares was not Solomon's only companion there. Solomon told the tale of Althus and his friends from beginning to end while Augustine listened in amazement.

The details of Solomon's story were too precise for it to have been anything but the truth. Antares would know the truth, but Augustine could not find it in his heart to doubt Solomon's story. He hoped Holly had recorded it in her journal as Solomon told it to her. She would have dug for every fact Solomon could give her and added drawings and maps to illustrate his words.

He wondered if Solomon had any idea how Holly felt about him. He thought not. Holly would not show her true feelings for Solomon until she was sure he no longer mourned for Bess. She would be a valuable friend to Solomon until then. All of the Riders would be glad to see Solomon return to their ranks. Although Augustine was not sure how many of them felt he was capable of holding the position of Second Rider again.

Solomon walked across the room to its north-facing window. It hung open in an attempt to air out the room. The hope that Solomon would return had evidently reached the ears of the women in charge. He took a deep breath and leaned on the stone sill.

"Whether I return as Second Rider or merely as a Rider or even just as Solomon Goshawk, I must return north, Augustine," he said, staring out the window at the darkening sky as if he were anxious to be on his way. "I have given my word to return to Anduin. I have returned here with a request on behalf of the Humans and the other races of our world for the Riders' help. I should be speaking on their behalf now, not of my own position here unless it has some impact on whether or not we join in the fight to save Anduin.

A force consisting of some three thousand or more Orcs and Goblins has left the Dwarven kingdom of Stonehaven and marches northward. The Dwarves of Stonehaven are freed of their captivity and now march to Anduin's defense. They are a small remnant of the once powerful Dwarf army, willing to fight for those who risked their lives to free them.

If the kingdom of Anduin falls to the dark forces that threaten it, it will only be the first of many. The fall of Anduin could mean the end of the realm of the wood Elves. It could mean the end for all the Elven races as well and the end of the other races of good beings living in our world.

Perhaps now is not the time for me to seek to return to my post as Second Rider. I do not have the time to make a proper appeal to my fellow Riders or to prove myself to them. I cannot be sure I am fit for my post or even to be a Rider again for that matter. I only know that if we let the resources of Anduin fall into our enemies' hands, their evil will spread throughout the land, growing in strength and numbers until we cannot stand against them, even with the help of the Dragons. Anduin lies at the very heart of our world. If they gain a foothold there, I fear we are all doomed."

When Solomon turned from the window, Augustine held his hands up to stop Solomon from continuing. "There will be a feast tonight to celebrate your return. We will discuss all of these matters then. Get some rest now, Solomon. A few moments of rest while I speak to Antares of these matters and perhaps find where the Dragons stand will not be amiss. I am certain he has stated your case before his brethren by now. It will not do to come before the rest of the Riders looking as if you have just come from running wild in the mountains."

As Augustine left him standing alone in his quarters he thought to himself that he had almost done just that very thing. The walls seemed to close in on him as soon as Augustine departed, leaving him to his own thoughts as he bathed and donned the dress uniform he had not worn in over a year. It fit a trifle looser, but still fit reasonably well. He could not rest easily with walls surrounding him after so many months sleeping in the open. He was still not himself and could never be the same confident young soldier he had been before, but he prayed the uneasiness he suffered now would pass.

As if in answer to his prayers, there was a knock at his door. When he opened it, Holly stood there with Ephraim and Joseph. Joseph was in the process of advising Ephraim that at his age, he should be in bed, resting his broken shoulder and Holly seemed ready to agree with Joseph. Ephraim's harried look made Solomon forget his own troubles as he drew him into the room and sat him down on the bed. Joseph and Holly followed, both talking at once, asking Solomon to back them up. Solomon silenced them both with a look and, after careful examination of Ephraim's injury, told them to leave him alone. The older brothers had strapped his arm skillfully and Ephraim seemed well enough, overall.

"He seems to think he must attend the feast in your honor tonight," said Joseph, his concern for the older rider plain on his face. "I think he should be resting."

"Perhaps so, Joseph," laughed Solomon. "He does look rather more solemn than usual, but you know we will never get an admission from him that he is in pain, nor will you make him lie down and rest if he does not wish to. Was he not your instructor as well as mine when we first sought to join the Dragon Riders?"

"Yes, Solomon," sighed Joseph, "he was, and you are right. I suppose he will do what he wants, despite what we think is best for him. We will just have to keep a close eye on him."

"Enough!" cried Ephraim. "You talk as if I could not hear you! A little more respect for your elder, young Joseph! Come on, I am hungry. And I am tired of you two clucking over me like two brooding hens."

Solomon could not help noticing that Ephraim seemed unusually anxious to change the subject. His shoulder was causing him some pain, but he obviously would not miss the evening's festivities. Solomon suspected that Holly had related part of Solomon's tale to Ephraim and he did not want to miss Solomon's telling of it.

Ephraim left abruptly with Holly at his side, leaving Solomon alone with Joseph. They looked at each other in silence for a moment before Joseph wrapped his arms about Solomon for the second time that day. This time he allowed himself a few tears. "I am sorry, Solomon. I am sorry I was so angry with you when we last met. It was stupid of me. I wanted so much to help you. You were there, keeping me alive after I lost my family. You and Jonah became my family. If not for you, Solomon, I do not think I could have survived. Somehow, I could not help you in return."

"I cannot say why that was so, Joseph. Antares feels the wraiths present that day were responsible for the state in which I spent the past year. Perhaps he is right."

Joseph considered the possibility in silence, looking deep into Solomon's golden eyes. "I did notice a difference in your eyes. When we could not reach you, they seemed paler than usual. No one else could see it. Today, they are your father's eyes once more, the eyes of the Goshawk line of warriors. If ever I meet this prince Althus, I will thank him for sending you back to us."

"If all goes as I hope it will, Joseph, you will soon fight at his side."

Φ               Φ               Φ

Riders had already filled the tables of the banquet hall. All were present. The entire company of active Riders, with the addition of Solomon, numbered eighteen in all. The only two Riders besides Augustine who were still in service, but no longer riding into battle were Anthony and Bartholomew. They still served as healers and advisors, bringing the number to twenty. Augustine, who was the First Rider of the Brotherhood of Dragon Riders and a healer as well, made their number twenty-one. Four young faces at one table wore the uniform of riders in training. Counting these, and Solomon himself, the Dragon Riders present numbered twenty-five.

As was the custom for special occasions, the wives and older children of the Riders served the food. Solomon, overwhelmed by the obvious joy with which the Riders and their families welcomed him, ran a gauntlet of hugs and handshakes and nearly tripped over some of the youngest children who capered about his feet as Holly led him to a place at the head table. She left him there feeling a bit dazed by all the commotion and relieved to find himself seated at the opposite end of the table from the brooding Marcus. He sat at Augustine's right hand. The only two seated at the head table who were not elders were he and Marcus. The Second Rider traditionally sat with the elders until Solomon had become Second Rider. He preferred to sit with the men who fought at his side. He still felt out of place among the wise and learned elders.

Four of the seven elders still rode into battle. Of these four, Ephraim sat at Solomon's right and Adam just beyond Ephraim. Esther and Sarah sat on the opposite side of Augustine, beyond Anthony and Bartholomew. There was an expectant look to the elders as if they anticipated more than a good meal from this evening. Augustine stood before Solomon could take his seat, a signal for all of the Brotherhood present to rise.

"May the Creator continue to bless us as he has this day with the return of Solomon to our Hall and the continued safety of our Riders and our allies, the Dragons," he said, raising his cup in a general toast to Solomon and all the Riders. "Solomon has quite a tale to tell us of the past few days and a request concerning us all, but first we will eat this fine feast and enjoy each other's company for a time."

The voices of the Dragon Riders filled the hall. Speculation over what Solomon might have to tell them ran rampant about the vast room. Solomon began to feel at ease when he looked out over the men he knew so well. Their laughter and friendly banter made him feel at home. Their faith that he would return to their ranks some day touched him. He knew his request for aid on behalf of beleaguered Anduin would receive a fair hearing and began to think he might succeed. Perhaps he would even find himself Second Rider once more.

When the meal was finished, his comrades dragged him from his place and hoisted him atop a table in the center of the room. Everyone, from the seven elders of the Brotherhood to the smallest child, gathered about to hear what he had to say. He hesitated for a moment. How could he tell the Brotherhood of his intention to take his own life on the day Antares brought Althus to him. He took another deep breath and looked at Holly, who gave him a smile of encouragement. He realized that she knew the whole truth. She had even recorded it in her journal and still, she did not condemn him for what he had nearly done.

He began his tale slowly, trying to make sense of that first day himself. It was only from Antares that he knew exactly what had happened that day. He remembered clearly the sight of Althus lying helpless before him and the irresistible need to help him. The rest was lost to him until he faced the ghosts of the ruined village, but he told the tale as Antares had told it to Holly. After that, the tale was easier to tell. He remembered the details from that point on perfectly.

The Brotherhood listened respectfully to his story, the deep silence interrupted only occasionally by the oohs and aahs of the children when his tale was especially exciting. The elders' eyes never left him as if they could see the truth of his story before he even uttered the words. He met their eyes directly, knowing they would play a large part in the success or failure of his mission. He finished with a plea for help for Anduin and then the floor was open for the rest of the Riders to voice their opinions. He climbed down from the table and found the comfort of Holly's arm around him while he waited for the others to speak.

"I am proud of you, Sollie," she whispered in his ear. "It took great courage to tell your tale from beginning to end."

He looked at her with a grateful smile. Her loyalty and friendship would help him face the opposition he knew would come from some of the Riders, including those he counted as his friends.

Marcus was the first to speak, eager to take Solomon's vacated place atop the table.

"Are we to believe this wild tale?" he began. "Even if we could spare a few of our number on this futile mission to save a few miserable Humans, how are we to know it is not a plot to draw us away from our responsibilities here? We cannot know where Solomon has been for the last few months. What if he has fallen in with the very forces we struggle against? How else could he have survived so long alone in the mountains?"

"You accuse Solomon of treason?" Ephraim's voice as he interrupted Marcus' oration bore an angry edge that silenced the mutters that followed. "I have never known him to lie, Marcus. What makes you think he is lying now?"

Marcus looked a bit uneasy under Ephraim's angry stare. "I am simply saying that he would have been easy prey for our enemies. If any of this tale is true, how do we know he is not under some spell such as this stone he speaks of cast on this Wizard he claims to have met?"

"I think we should consider the possibility that the enemy we face has left just enough of his evil minions here to harass us with the very purpose of keeping us from the defense of Anduin," Ephraim countered. "Where do you think they will turn after they conquer Anduin and take what that rich land has to offer? We will face the Dark Lord's army some day. I do not speak of the bands of Orcs and Goblins we fight now, but the force of thousands that presently march against Anduin. If we do not act now, will we be the only ones who remain to stand against them? With the resources of Anduin at their disposal and the resources of the other lands they will conquer, what chance will we have to defeat them? Would you have us wait until the enemy has conquered all the surrounding lands and we stand alone against them?

"I believe Solomon's story. I have heard of this Euwyn he speaks of and if the accounts I have heard are true, he is a powerful Wizard who has performed many good works in his lifetime. He has not reached his full potential since he is still young for his race and already tales of him have reached far beyond the lands he frequents. The accounts tell of an adopted son. Solomon's tale rings true to my ears."

"He cannot tell you where he has been or what he has done since he has left us!" Marcus shouted to the Riders present. "Ask him! He claims he does not know!"

Augustine intervened before the discussion could go farther. "You forget, Solomon was not alone at any time during his absence, Marcus. You are forgetting Antares who was at Solomon's side. To accuse Solomon of treason is to accuse Antares as well."

There was a general murmuring and nodding of heads at Augustine's quiet reminder.

"I have spoken with Antares," Augustine continued. "He has confirmed Solomon's story. In fact, part of the story is his tale alone, as Solomon was not part of Prince Althus' initial rescue.

"Perhaps each of us should consider the matter of Anduin and its struggles until tomorrow. We will meet with Antares and the other Dragons at dawn before the main gates of the Hall. You will be able to ask Antares and Solomon any questions that may occur to you between now and then and when Solomon has answered all questions, a vote will be taken. All will have an equal say in our decision. We will also decide whether Solomon will reclaim the position of Second Rider."

Marcus seemed unsatisfied with the outcome of the evening, but he could do little but wait until morning. The majority seemed content with Augustine's decision to let the matter rest for now. Solomon was anxious to return to Anduin, but would not leave until daylight in any case. If he could bring others with him, it would be more than worth a few hours' wait.

He was soon back in his rooms, staring out into the night sky, grateful to those who supported his cause. The Dragon Riders would hold Ephraim's opinion in high regard. He had thanked Ephraim for his support and was assured by the elder Rider that many others felt the same. Esther and Sarah had both voiced their support as well. Solomon felt hopeful.

At the same time, Marcus' accusations troubled him. It was ridiculous to think he could have become a pawn of the dark forces. Antares would have turned him to ashes if he even suspected such a thing. Solomon knew the accusations were groundless, but even the thought he may have been exposed to evil while he wandered the mountains made him uneasy. He tried to dismiss the feeling, but doubt and the walls seemed to close in on him once again now that he was alone.

As he stood at the open window, he caught sight of the white-robed figure of Augustine in the moonlight, wandering from the main gates toward the shore of the lake. Solomon quickly donned his coat and hurried to catch up with him. He would seek wise Augustine's council. Perhaps a talk with his friend and leader would set his mind at ease. Noah guarded the open gates and greeted Solomon as he passed.

Solomon's breath steamed in the cold air as he trotted along the stone path to the shore. Jagged rocks broke through the black sand beach at irregular intervals. Solomon made his way between two of these monoliths and stood uncertainly on the beach, hoping to determine which direction Augustine had taken along the shore.

A patch of white down the shore to his left, illuminated by the moon, sent him sprinting down the beach. It was Augustine, lying face down on the wet sand. He stirred and moaned softly as Solomon turned him over, clutching feebly at Solomon's sleeve. A knife protruded from his chest, slid expertly between his ribs. Blood was rapidly staining the front of his robes. Solomon removed his coat to place it under Augustine's head and ripped a sleeve from his shirt to press against the wound. Augustine continued to grasp at Solomon's sleeve.

"It is no use, Sollie. Leave me," he whispered. "Warn the Riders. There is a traitor among us!"

"Save your strength," Solomon begged. "You will tell us all later."

"No," Augustine gasped, blood trickling from his mouth, "There is no later for me. Marcus... Marcus has betrayed the Riders. He has betrayed us, Sollie. Warn them for me."

Augustine closed his eyes for a moment as if satisfied Solomon understood the message he had sought to deliver. His breath grew shallower as Solomon struggled to stem the blood that escaped despite the pressure he held against the wound.

Solomon could not leave Augustine. He was too far from the Hall for shouting. He was searching desperately for some way to summon help when he saw another Rider approaching. He could not be sure which of them strode toward him, silhouetted against the light of the moon. He shouted to the Rider to return to the Hall and fetch brothers Anthony and Bartholomew, but the figure continued to approach. A chill passed through Solomon when he recognized the Rider as Marcus.

Augustine opened his eyes once more, but his gaze traveled past Solomon's shoulder and a look of horror crossed his ashen countenance. "No!" he panted as Solomon turned, too late to avoid the blow that came from behind.

Solomon lay unconscious across Augustine's body while Marcus negotiated desperately with the goblin that had just laid him out with a blow to the back of his head.

"You say we take mighty Augustine to our master," growled the Goblin, threatening Marcus with his club. "Now he dead. What you say we do now?"

"It could not be helped," said Marcus. "You were not here when you said you would be. I showed you where to land and made you a map of how to get here. I distracted the watchmen. You were not here to help me subdue him. I had to kill him. That is your fault."

"We take other one, then."

"Yes, yes, he is a Rider. Second Rider in fact. He has killed many of your people. He is a better prize to take to your master than Augustine. Your master will be just as pleased that Augustine is dead. He will be very pleased to have this one instead."

Things were not going quite the way Marcus planned. He had offered Augustine in Solomon's place for reasons of his own. Still, it seemed too good an opportunity to let pass. He had rid himself of Augustine. Now, he would rid himself of the much-loved Solomon as well. That would satisfy the demands of the dark one who promised him powers beyond his wildest dreams in exchange for Augustine or Solomon delivered alive.

Marcus was a little worried the secret power the Dark Lord sought did not actually exist. He could not really accept the information he had accidentally uncovered as the truth. If it was true, and Solomon became a servant of the Dark Lord, it could cost Marcus control of the Dragons. If he knew Solomon, however, he would die before serving the Dark Lord. So, what did it truly matter? He almost found it in his heart to pity his rival for the post of Second Rider. His death would not come easily at the Dark Lord's hands.

Negotiations concluded quickly. Marcus received a token payment for his trouble and they bound Solomon securely and dumped him unceremoniously into a small skiff where a second goblin awaited the first. The Goblins were soon on the far shore, lugging their prize quickly to the southeast to be presented before the Dark Lord. With a small smile on his face, Marcus watched them disappear into the mists that had come with nightfall to cover the waters of the lake. When his plan to offer up Augustine as a captive had gone awry, he had thought all was lost, but things were working out well after all. He ran toward the main gates, anxious to set his new plan in motion.

## Chapter Thirty-six

## KATE

Holly sat on Solomon's bed, too stunned for more tears. She would never believe Solomon could have killed Augustine. Her anger at the accusation almost outweighed her sorrow at the loss of their beloved leader. Joseph stood at the window as Solomon had done the night before, an angry scowl darkening his handsome features. Ephraim paced the room, a look of desperation on his lean face.

"Solomon could not have done this!" he shouted. "Never in a million years will I believe the accusations Marcus makes against him. No one loved Augustine more than Solomon. What could be his motive for such an act? Antares knows Solomon as well as any of us and he swears Solomon could never harm Augustine or any other Rider for that matter."

Holly opened her journal to look at the drawing of Solomon. The soft smile and kind eyes she had captured brought tears to her eyes again.

Ephraim stopped pacing, an arrested look on his face as he gazed at Solomon's traveling gear resting in a corner of the room. He reached into the open pack and brought out a small, gleaming dagger.

"Look," he cried. "Have you ever known Solomon to possess or use any dagger but the one his father carried before he died? This dagger I hold in my hand?"

Joseph turned to look at the bright blade glinting in the light from the window. "That is true, Ephraim. You and I know it for the truth, but it will not prove anything to the other Riders. Marcus claims he saw Solomon kill Augustine with his own eyes. Solomon's bloody coat was found with Augustine's body and Noah saw him follow Augustine toward the shore last night."

"Noah said Solomon seemed himself when he left the hall, not like a man about to commit murder," Holly said. "Solomon spoke to him when he left. He certainly did not act as if he did not want to be seen."

"Marcus is still Second Rider, Holly," Ephraim sighed. "Few will doubt his word."

Holly closed her journal and stared at its cover, her mind darting here and there, looking for a way to clear Solomon's name. "I, for one, doubt every word that issues from Marcus' mouth," she said.

Joseph had turned back to the window. "I am going to look for him. He has not taken Antares. He cannot have gone far in such a short time."

He turned to look at Holly. "Will you come with me, Holly?"

She was already on her feet and moving for the door before he finished the question. "I think I know of someone who will help us," she said over her shoulder. "Someone who is not a Rider and lives some distance from here, but has skills we can use."

"Keep an eye on Marcus for us, Ephraim," said Joseph as he followed Holly from the room.

He soon caught up with her as she trotted briskly through the stone corridors.

"What makes you so sure we can find Solomon before the other Riders, Holly? You know Marcus sent every available man to search for him at dawn. That was four hours ago. They may have found him by now."

Holly stopped and faced him, a fierce grin on her face. "I spoke to Matthew just after he sent the Dragon Riders out this morning. Something he said to me just struck me as odd as I read it over in the pages of my journal. He said Marcus sent riders out in every direction but southeast. Granted, Solomon may head north toward Anduin, but then, why did he send Riders in all other directions but southeast? Marcus knows something. I do not think he wants Solomon found and I think he knows Solomon is headed in that particular direction. If he knows where Solomon is headed, perhaps he has had a hand in his disappearance. I am grasping at straws, Joseph, but it is all we have to go on."

Joseph looked at her for a moment, considering her theory. "I, too, wonder if Solomon left by choice or if he has been taken. If he is innocent, and I believe in my heart of hearts that he is, he would not have left the Hall willingly before he knew whether the Riders would fly with him to the defense of Anduin. There are many forested valleys to the southeast. If he has been taken in that direction it will be difficult to spot him from the air."

"That is why I will ask the Mistress of Hounds to help us. Somehow she must be persuaded," Holly called over her shoulder, once more trotting ahead toward the Dragons' field.

Joseph was grinning as he ran by her side.

Φ                    Φ                    Φ

Solomon struggled against the pain that gripped his head. He regained consciousness slowly, confused by the pain in his wrists and ankles and the unfamiliarity of his surroundings. He found himself lying on a bed of pine needles in a forest. He was incredibly thirsty and bound hand and foot, lying face down on the ground beneath the pines. The events of the evening before came back to him with a sickening jolt. He could feel stickiness on his hands and remembered them pressed against the wound in Augustine's chest, desperately trying to stop the flow of blood. He retched violently from the pain in his head and the realization Augustine was dead.

Rough hands grabbed him by the hair and pulled him to his feet. A hideous goblin face swam into focus, much too close to his. He closed his eyes, hoping the ugly apparition would disappear, but when he opened them, the goblin was still there, its foul breath still in his face.

It spat some words at him he did not understand and then yanked him to a nearby stream and plunged his head beneath the water. The creature yanked him back out, gasping and coughing. He had inhaled more than he drank, but he guessed the goblin was not trying to relieve his thirst. It spoke more words in its own language, but they meant nothing to him. He tried to look defiant as the goblin shook him fiercely, causing his head to throb painfully until he thought he would lose what little he had left in his stomach.

Another goblin appeared, speaking sharply to the first and it abruptly flung Solomon to the ground once more. The second goblin stood over him, looking him over with a grin that showed the creature's formidable array of pointed yellow teeth.

"You be good little Elf, eh? You be good and I not let Gorp kill you," it growled at him, grinning even more widely at Gorp, who snorted at him in disgust. "Gorp not like that you and Skank can talk and he not unnerstand. Skank smarter than Gorp. Gorp stupid."

Solomon thought from the murderous look Gorp shot at Skank that Skank was none too bright.

"We take you to the Great Lord's palace. It a long journey so little Elf must be good or we have to bash you until you sleep again. You will be Great Lord's special guest. New toy for him to explore. Marcus promise us Augustine, but you have to do instead."

The look Solomon gave him sent the goblin back a pace until he remembered the feared Rider was bound and helpless. Nevertheless, the goblin turned away and occupied himself with a chunk of raw meat he chewed with gusto, blood running down his chin onto the dirty rags that barely covered his filthy, hairless chest.

Solomon, fearing he would vomit once again, occupied himself with a study of his surroundings. There was little to see. The Goblins were traveling with little more than a club carried by Skank and a spear leaning against a tree that most likely belonged to Gorp, keeping to the heavily wooded mountain valleys. He would have to keep his wits about him and look for a way to escape. He would focus on that for now and try not to think of the Riders at the Hall who did not know there was a traitor in their midst or of Anduin whose cause now seemed doomed to failure. He was being carried even farther from the Brotherhood to a meeting with the Dark Lord that commanded these foul creatures. He did not relish meeting him, whoever or whatever he was.

They were soon on their way again, Solomon bouncing painfully on Skank's bony shoulder, his nostrils filled with the reek surrounding the unwashed creature.

Φ          Φ          Φ

Joseph admired the dwelling to which a half-day's flight had brought them. He had admired the simple but beautiful home many times as he flew over, but now that he saw it more closely, he realized how elegant the place really was. The sun neared the western horizon, painting the front of the home and the surrounding mountain slopes with a warm glow. The structure was underground for the most part, as much a part of the mountainside as it could be, a curving front made of glass panels the only part visible. Strange blackened panels of glass also lay across the front on either side of the clear glass, slanted as if to catch the sun. Joseph had never seen such large pieces of glass. The making of glass was a difficult art at best. He wondered what civilization had made such large, curving, flawless pieces of a substance was fairly rare in his country, even in small pieces. Two sleek metal windmills sat atop the structure where they would catch the winds blowing constantly here in the mountains. The structure overlooked the small expanse of mountain meadow where they had landed.

It was an inviting home, but Joseph studied it from atop his blue Dragon, Procyon, while two huge hounds greeted Holly galloping about her gleefully, their bodies curling about her with pleasure as she called them by name and ruffled their shaggy coats. They were the biggest dogs Joseph had ever seen, their beautiful dense coats mostly black with brown about their eyes and legs and white markings on chests, faces and feet. Holly finally persuaded him to dismount when the melee of their greetings had subsided, whereupon the melee began again as the creatures threatened to trample Joseph in their quest to be the first to greet him.

Procyon found his partner's predicament very amusing and Polaris looked on as if it were the best of entertainment. Antares lashed his tail with impatience.

A rich voice cut through the ruckus. A one word command from their mistress was enough to quiet the dogs and send them leaping to sit obediently side by side, their tongues lolling, looking expectantly toward the figure that approached from the direction of the dwelling. Joseph looked curiously at the woman that came toward them. This woman, Kate, was the mysterious Mistress of Hounds. Joseph had heard strange tales of the woman who lived isolated on this mountainside, far from the villages of the Mountain Elves. Holly said she came from a very distant land where machines ruled the people who lived there. She did not look unusual in any way he could see. Kate was a bit broader than Holly and a head taller. She looked fit enough, not as graceful or agile as an Elf, but there was a sturdy look to her. Joseph could see she was not Elven, but Human. Close up he could see that her short brown hair held threads of silver and her face wore a few fine wrinkles. Her eyes were the color of smoke, startling in a face darkened by sunlight in the nature of Humans. She regarded the Riders and their Dragons fearlessly as she spoke.

"Greetings, Dragon Rider Holly," she said, speaking in the Elvish tongue. "What brings you here?" Joseph noticed that she hesitated before speaking as if she formed her words first in a different tongue and then translated them as she spoke.

Holly cleared her throat uneasily. "We have come to beg your help, Kate. Our need is desperate or I would not ask."

Kate hesitated again before she answered while Joseph wondered what her native tongue would sound like and where she had learned their language. Her accent was most unusual, although she spoke their language well, aside from her slight hesitation.

"It would be very dangerous for me to meddle in the affairs of your land," she said. "It is against the rules of my profession and my homeland for me to influence the outcome of events here in your mountains. I have already broken so many of our laws merely by speaking to you."

"Please, Kate," Holly begged. "Please hear me out at least. A Rider will die if you do not help us."

"I am sorry, Holly," she said and Joseph thought she looked genuinely distressed, "Of course, I will hear you if you wish. I owe you that much for teaching me the language of your people over the past few months, but you know I am here only to photograph the plants and animals of your world. I am a scholar, a photographer, and no more than that. I really do not know how I can help you."

"Just hear me, Kate, that is all I ask," Holly pleaded.

Holly wondered if she were asking too much of Kate. The woman had always been kind to her. They had become friends. Now she would ask her friend to risk everything to help them. Should they forget Kate and the dogs she so proudly hailed as the best rescue dogs ever bred in her world? Perhaps they could find Solomon without them. She wondered if she were right to ask such a thing of Kate.

"Come, then, at least I can give you something to eat and drink. It is not often I have guests," she said, slipping an arm about Holly's shoulders and drawing her towards her home.

Joseph considered the unusual Kate as they climbed the path. Despite her reluctance to help them, he liked her eyes and the brief smile she gave him when they were introduced that deepened the fine wrinkles around them. He understood what a scholar was, but what was the other thing she claimed to be?

Holly had told him she did not belong here in their world. Her clothing was strange to him. She wore sturdy laced boots that reached above her ankles, but no further, and blue breeches of a tough looking material that covered the tops of them. Her thickly woven shirt lacked buttons, laces, or any device that would allow it to be removed. Joseph supposed she needed the thickness of it for warmth if she were truly Human. Perhaps she never took it off.

His curiosity increased as he realized he was about to see the interior of her home. She slid a panel of the strange, sleek glass aside and stepped inside, motioning for them to follow her. Joseph was able to get a closer look at Kate's glass. It was cool and smooth to his touch and he could see through it as if it were made of air. He sheepishly rubbed away the handprint he made on the smooth surface with his sleeve while Kate laughed softly at him.

She served them a cold drink that was sour and sweet at the same time with small pieces of ice floating in cups also made of glass, but tinted a beautiful blue. He studied Kate again as she spoke quietly with Holly and wondered exactly where she had come from and what other amazing things she could show him. There were things in the room where they sat unfamiliar to him, so unfamiliar he could not even guess at their purpose. Kate even set flat pieces of glass before her eyes when she brought out a map of the area. She drew a line from the Hall to a general area to the southeast she suspected the Orcs and Goblins called home. She traveled the area about her outpost extensively with her dogs and had seen a great number of Orcs and Goblins traveling to or from that general area. If they held one of the Riders captive, it would seem reasonable to assume the Orcs or the Goblins would have something to do with it and they would be taking their captive toward the place they called home. It was an area the Dragon Riders watched carefully, a region guarded by a poisonous swamp that bled noxious gases into the air above it. No one really knew what lay deep in the center of that region. So far, no one who had set foot in that area, hoping to discover the entrance to the Orcs' stronghold had returned. The wasteland was considered the lair of the Dark Lord and his wraiths and no one returned alive from that forsaken land.

Joseph found himself wandering about the curious room. Wonders lurked in every corner, forcing him to shove his hands in his pockets to avoid the temptation to touch the things he did not understand. Hundreds of images covered the walls of the large circular room, each image so true he wondered if Kate captured the subjects with some sort of magic. An image of a mountain flower was so real he felt as if he could touch it and feel its velvety petals. Kate appeared at his shoulder.

"These are called photographs," she said as he turned back to look again at the amazing images. "I take many photographs to keep a record of the things I find here."

Familiar creatures that looked as if they could step from the walls paraded before his dazzled eyes. There were photographs of the mountain Elves and their villages. There were even a few of the Dragon Riders, as they would appear as they passed overhead. Suddenly, Solomon's face was before him, so real it seemed as if he would speak. At Joseph's shout of amazement, Kate took the photograph down from the wall and held it closer to Joseph.

"Do you know him, Joseph?" Kate asked. "He is a Dragon Rider. His name is Solomon. At least, I think that is what he was saying to me. I met him in a high mountain meadow a year ago now, before I spoke a word of your language. I understand there are only a few Dragon Riders, so you and Holly must know him. I have not seen him since..." Her face paled as her eyes met Joseph's, her eyes brimming with tears. "He is angry with me, I fear. I have made some mistake. It was inadvertent, I assure you, but he would not even speak to me the last time I saw him. If you see him would you tell him I am sorry for whatever I have done?"

Joseph watched dumbfounded as the tears began to slide down her face. One moment she had seemed very self-possessed and now she was crying like a child. How did she know Solomon? Why did she find the idea he might be angry at her so troubling?

"Do not cry, Kate," Joseph said, greatly moved by her tears. "Solomon was not angry with you."

He scrubbed a hand across his face, searching for a way to explain. "He was badly injured a year ago. When he was well enough, he left us to wander the mountains. He would have been alone if Augustine had not sent Antares to look after him. Believe me, Kate, when you saw him, he was not himself. He was struggling with the memory of the death of his friends. He witnessed the deaths of an entire village at the hands of the Dark Lord's creatures, deaths so hideous the memory of them nearly killed him. He probably did not even see you."

Kate shuddered, wiping at her face, "I thought he must be furious with me when he would not even look at me as I spoke to him. When you cannot speak another's language, it is possible to be offensive without knowing it." She paused, as if gathering her courage for the next question. "Has he recovered? Is he well again?"

"He was last night, but now he has disappeared and our leader has been murdered."

Holly had come to stand by Joseph's side. "We fear Solomon has been kidnapped. If they do not kill him, I fear he will become a captive of the Dark Lord. It would be better for him if they killed him."

She could not look at Solomon's face any longer. She turned toward the fading twilight visible through the glass panels. "We should not have come here. We should have spent the daylight searching for him. If we cannot find him in time, it will be my fault. Kate cannot help us."

Joseph wrapped her in his arms to comfort her, but he also feared they had made the wrong choice. "We do not know he came this way, Holly. Perhaps the others have found him by now. He may already be back at the Hall."

"I will help you find him," Kate said softly, studying the photograph of Solomon held in her hands. "He saved my life the day I met him. This photograph was taken that day. I was being foolish beyond belief, trying to photograph a troop of Orcs and Goblins. They cornered me in a blind canyon and killed two of my dogs. I thought I was doomed to die that day until Solomon dropped from the sky to stand beside me. He and his Dragon made short work of the Orcs with little help from the two dogs I had remaining. He helped me bury the dogs that had given their lives trying to protect me and escorted me home.

He was the first mountain Elf I met face to face. The first I ever tried to communicate with. The first Rider I met until I met Holly a few weeks later. It was my encounter with Solomon and the sound of his voice as he tried to speak with me made me realize how empty and lonely I had allowed my life to become and inspired me to ask Holly to teach me your beautiful language. It has been very hard for me to stay objective since that day. He was such a paradox. At one moment, he was a fierce warrior, the next, a very gentle and caring young man. He even helped me care for the dogs the Orcs wounded. Every Elf I have met since makes me think of Solomon and his kindness to me.

"The dogs and I will help you find him. At the very least we owe him that." She laughed then, but there was sadness in it. "I am so out of place here in your world and yet, I find myself wishing so much to be a part of it. I have broken so many of the rules already. I have never been one to break rules, but as hard as I try, I cannot help but care about the Elves that live here in the mountains. Perhaps I cannot remain apart from them any longer," she sighed. "I will leave it in the Creator's hands. If I am to be punished for my actions, then I will accept that."

They decided to leave at daybreak, returning to the dense forest at a point southeast of the Hall where they hoped to pick up Solomon's scent. Joseph wondered what it would mean for Kate now that she had joined their cause. He hoped they did not trade Solomon's life for hers.

Kate spent the rest of the evening distracting them with a demonstration of the art of photography. She took their picture with a device she called a camera and, within minutes, produced an image of Holly and Joseph standing side by side that made them look at each other in amazement.

They learned that the windmills furnished power, making all of the strange devices function and that the black glass panels produced hot water and heated Kate's home. At the heart of all stood a device Kate called a computer. Joseph was amazed something so small could have such power. Kate informed him she had more than one computer to aid in her research and then showed them a device even smaller than the first that could do almost as much as the larger one. Everything was amazing to Joseph, and Kate was not reluctant to show him anything he asked to see.

She was a teacher in her own land. Joseph sensed she was an excellent one. She allowed him to hold the things he admired in his own hands, even letting him take a photograph of her and Holly with her camera. She sat him down at the keyboard of her computer and showed him how to send his image to something she called the printer. She tried to convince him she was not a Wizard or a sorcerer and nothing she did involved magic of any sort. Still, the more she showed him, the more amazing her devices seemed, even if he could make them do as he commanded, he doubted they would listen to him without Kate at his side.

He lay awake that night long after Kate had extinguished the lights with a touch of her hand and wondered about her world in the moments when he was not consumed with worry over Solomon.

Kate told them sadly that there was nothing the computer could do in their world to help them find Solomon. They would rely on the dogs and their own feet for that.

## Chapter Thirty-seven

## STORM

The Creator was with them the next morning as the day dawned warm and still, with fog hanging in the hollows, a good day for tracking. Kate gave the dogs a drug that made them sleep and they were strapped securely to the backs of Polaris and Procyon. They flew from Kate's home to a point as far southeast of the Hall as they dared without risking the possibility their quarry had taken a different path. They would begin their search in a certain narrow mountain valley. By Joseph's reckoning, if Solomon's captors had taken him southeast from the Hall, the terrain would make it necessary for them to cross this narrow valley at some point. Finding an area clear enough for the Dragons to land was a challenge. Once they had found such an area and their feet were on solid ground, they left the Dragons and followed the coursing dogs on foot through the dense coniferous forest.

Once they were sufficiently awake, Kate sent the two dogs, Buck and Rolf, searching from one side of the valley to the other, their keen noses questing for the scent Holly had given them from a shirt appropriated from Solomon's room. They searched for many hours, making slow progress through the dense pine forest while the remaining hours of daylight dwindled to less than two. Holly was ready to cry with frustration as Kate gave the dogs another opportunity to sniff Solomon's shirt and sent them off once more. They had not traveled very far down the valley and Joseph feared they had wasted another day they might have spent searching with the Dragons in hopes of catching a glimpse of something through the dense forest canopy.

Suddenly, they heard Buck's deep bark a short distance down the valley. Before they reached him, Rolf was adding his voice to his brother's. The dogs rooted about near the base of a tree where something or someone had obviously lain in the pine needles and then been dragged a short distance. They found a handprint in the dust nearby too small for an Orc or goblin to make, and Rolf nosed a few strands of hair out of the litter. A pile of rotting scraps of meat and bones nearby along with the tracks of large, spatulate feet told them Goblins had camped here recently. Kate looked closely at the strands of hair lying across Holly's palm. They were not from a Goblin. They curled their way across her palm, fine enough for her breath to stir them where they lay.

"They could be Solomon's," she said.

Holly nodded, running the few strands she held through her fingers and looking closely at the tiny bits they left behind.

"There is blood on them," she said softly.

Buck came to lean against her as she knelt beneath the tree, whining and trying to lick her face while Rolf ran off a short distance and turned back to bark insistently at them. They took the hint and scrambled after him as he put his nose to the ground and loped off down the valley. Both dogs were soon running full speed with Holly, Joseph and Kate trying desperately to stay within the sound of their baying without slowing them. When they passed through a clearing, Joseph produced a whistle from his pocket and blew a short blast up the valley. The three Dragons appeared, gliding down the valley toward them. They were soon mounted, winging their way to where the rapidly receding voices of the dogs echoed off the sheer mountain walls. Antares led, flying powerfully with Polaris and Procyon riding his slipstream, easily keeping pace with the swiftly coursing dogs.

Joseph prayed they would find Solomon alive. Why were Goblins carrying off an Elf? He had never known them to take hostages. They were much too fond of killing. Someone must have sent them to bring Solomon back. A chill ran down his spine. How far were the Goblins from their destination? If they failed to stop them before they reached it, Solomon would be better off dead. They could not let them get away.

As if they were all of the same mind, no one suggested they stop when night fell. They would trust the voices of the dogs and the faint light of the waxing moon climbing into the night sky to guide them. The air grew cold and the breath of all six turned to vapor, trailing behind them as they sped over the darkening land. Kate cast a worried look at a line of clouds massing in the distance, threatening to steal the moonlight from them. A bolt of lightening split the sky. If they failed to find Solomon before the storm caught them, there was little chance they would ever find him in time. The dogs could not track him in the rain and finding their quarry without the help of the dogs would be impossible once clouds hid the light of the moon. The Dragons followed the dogs more closely, hoping to outrun the storm.

Φ       Φ       Φ

Solomon was preparing to spend another miserable night. The Goblins dumped him without ceremony, shivering from hunger and thirst on the stony ground beneath yet another pine. He was still tightly bound, the cords digging deep into his wrists, grateful for the boots he wore that protected his ankles from the same fate. The Goblins seemed unlikely to untie him soon for any reason, being rightfully wary of giving him any opportunity to attack them, even though he was unarmed. He was losing hope and strength. He was desperately thirsty now and his head still throbbed painfully. He was not sure he wanted to reach his destination alive in any case.

He sent a silent prayer of apology to Althus for failing him, wishing he could see Holly and Joseph once more before he faced the Dark Lord. He thought of Augustine and fought the tears that threatened. He would not show his captors any weakness. Skank was muttering happily as he hacked some unfortunate creature into chunks of raw meat for the Goblins' dinner.

"We be near the Great Lord's palace now," he hissed happily. "You be his guest tomorrow night, little Elf Rider. He keep you in his best and deepest dungeon until you scream to get out. Scream, scream will do you no good. You do whatever he tells you just to see light. Any light. Torch light." Skank shrieked with laughter. "You do what he say, maybe he let you work for him like Marcus."

"I will never serve him. I am not like Marcus and I will never be like Marcus. You have wasted your time bringing me here."

Solomon could not suppress a gasp of pain as Skank kicked him hard in the ribs.

"You not make Skank look bad. Great Lord has a stone that will make you do as he say."

Solomon wished he could impart that bit of information to Euwyn somehow. The Wizard would find the location of that particular artifact of great interest.

Solomon's Elven hearing caught the sound of baying hounds long before the Goblins did. He thought of the Nasua and wondered if they would eat Goblins as readily as they ate Elves. He thought he had his answer when Skank and Gorp jumped to their feet at the sound, the whites of their frightened eyes showing plainly, as they peered anxiously into the dark forest. Solomon was almost relieved to think the creatures might kill him while he lay bound and helpless. It seemed a better alternative to what he faced if he survived another day.

Skank shouted something at Gorp and Solomon was surprised to find his legs suddenly free of their bonds. Skank bent over him with a short blade touching his throat.

"You must climb tree with us or we kill you."

Solomon laughed at the hollow threat. He was better off dead than what they had in mind for him. He stood still for as long as he dared, waiting for the feeling to return to his feet and then launched himself at Gorp, butting him with his head and sending him sprawling. Unfortunately, the pain of using his injured head in such a manner nearly made him pass out. He was still staggering, shaking his head to clear it when Skank grabbed him from behind. He brought his booted foot down on the goblin's bare one as hard as he could, causing the creature to howl with pain. Gorp struck him with a club on the side of his battered head and Solomon crumpled to the ground.

He was unconscious when the rain began, a cold downpour, accompanied by lightning that blinded his captors with its brilliance. He missed the spectacle of two huge, hairy forms that leapt from the dark forest while the

Goblins screeched in fear. Buck and Rolf latched onto the Goblins and shook them like rag dolls.

The sound of their screeching, barely audible amid the crashes of thunder, raised the hair on the back of Joseph's neck as he desperately sought a clearing large enough for the Dragons to land. The wind had risen quickly with the arrival of the storm. They were no longer safe in the air. Flashes of lightning once silhouetting the mountains to their left now struck close enough to illuminate the dense canopy below. They found a small clearing he prayed was not far from the origin of the terrible screams that still echoed in the night.

Holly was listening for Solomon's voice, but no Elf could make the noises she heard. It was a goblin's shrieking mixed with the snarling of the dogs. A sharp crack of thunder and a bolt of lightning simultaneously rent the night, followed by the sound of a tree falling nearby. The Goblins were on the run now, their shrieks accompanied by the baying of the pursuing dogs.

By the time their feet were on solid ground, the only sound they could hear was the pounding rain. All other sounds had faded into the distance. They looked at one another in despair. They had lost the dogs and there was no way to find them in the dark and the rain. Very little evidence would remain of anyone's passing now. Their only hope was to wait for dawn and hope the rain had ended by then. Each of them feared by then it would be too late to save Solomon if he were still alive even now.

Holly was fighting tears of desperation when Buck appeared out of the rain and darkness, tail wagging madly, anxious to lead them into the woods. They hesitated only long enough for the Dragons to light makeshift torches that hissed and sputtered in the rain, before Kate sent Buck into the woods ahead of them.

He led them impatiently through the dense pines, stopping to let them catch up occasionally, whining until he was on the move once more. At last, as if unable to wait any longer for them, he disappeared from sight. Kate, Holly, and Joseph stood huddled together as the rain became drizzle, uncertain of the dog's whereabouts until they heard him barking furiously nearby. They pushed their way into a small clearing and looked about.

The recent camp seemed deserted at first glance until Holly caught sight of a patch of white beneath a fallen tree. Closer inspection revealed Solomon lying on his side beneath its branches. Holly could not help the sob that escaped her as she reached through the branches to touch him. This was not the way the life of a Dragon Rider should end, beaten to death and left lying in the mud.

He appeared dead, his hands bound behind him, the rough cords cutting into his wrists. Blood, thinned by the rain, now ended as quickly as it had begun, trickled from a wound on his temple. He was sodden and filthy, but to everyone's immense relief, he moaned softly when Buck pushed his way into the branches beside Holly and began to lick his exposed ear.

Joseph soon cut through the branches that pinned Solomon and knelt beside his friend probing gently, seeking to determine the extent of his injuries.

Solomon lay curled on his side, wondering why someone was washing his ear with a warm, wet cloth. It seemed strange someone should have resorted to tying his hands simply to wash his ears. The washing ceased and someone cut his hands loose. He lay still, dreaming of Joseph's deep voice, calling his name. He did not wish to wake and lose his hold on the dream. He was still trying desperately to hang on to it when a woman's voice spoke his name.

"Bess?" he murmured weakly.

He rolled onto his back and opened his eyes, searching for something on which to focus.

Holly was bending over him. He thought how beautiful she looked in his dream, even dripping wet. "Holly," he sighed.

If it was Holly bending over him, perhaps he was not dreaming. The thought struck him he might still be alive. His head throbbed too painfully. He could not be dreaming. He struggled to sit up and found Joseph's arms supporting him from behind. He could see the rain glittering in the torchlight on Holly's face as she knelt beside him and he wrapped his arms around her as much to be certain she was solid and truly there as to comfort her.

"Holly," he murmured into her hair. "I cannot believe it is you. You and Joseph have found me. How is that possible?"

Holly let him go reluctantly and gestured to Solomon's right. When he turned his head to look, Buck rewarded him with a wet tongue that, with one swipe, washed the mud from the right side of his face.

That explained the washing of his ear. Holly scolded Buck and he sat back, unoffended, his muddy tongue hanging from his mouth as if it were ready if needed.

Solomon had to laugh at the big friendly dog he had thought might be a Nasua. He recognized him as Kate's and greeted her warmly when she approached. He was delighted when she spoke to him in his own language. He had never had the chance to learn hers.

She seemed nearly overwhelmed with emotion when he thanked her for her help with the water skin she brought to him.

Supported by Holly and Joseph, Solomon was soon on his feet. Buck led them back to the safety of the meadow and the company of the Dragons where Antares greeted Solomon with profound relief. Solomon soon sat with his eyes closed, resting his aching head against the Dragon's warm side, while Holly and Joseph went off with Buck to find Rolf and determine the fate of the Goblins he had pursued into the darkness. Kate remained with Solomon.

By the light of a small fire, she cleaned and bound the wounds on his wrists and head with bandages from Holly's pack while Polaris and Procyon kept watch for any danger that might threaten.

When she had finished, Solomon opened his eyes and took her hand in his. "I was afraid something might have happened to you, Kate. I am sorry I have not been watching over you as I promised."

Solomon could not quite understand what Kate found so funny. He did not think she would even understand him, but he thought she must have forgiven him when her arms went around him and she hugged him close.

Holly and Joseph soon returned with the two dogs and a cringing goblin.

"Here is something interesting," Joseph said as he shoved the goblin to the ground before the small fire. "It speaks our language."

Skank stared wide-eyed at the three Dragons that glared down at him. Polaris and Procyon rose as one and brought their heads close to the goblin.

He began to squeal in terror. "No, no, don't kill Skank! Skank take good care of your little friend. Skank take him to Great Lord only to talk. Great Lord wants peace with Dragons and Elves."

Antares snorted, a spurt of flame shooting in the goblin's direction, sending him groveling and wailing in the mud.

Kate straightened from where she had knelt to wrap Solomon in a blanket. "We can see plainly the care you took to beat him senseless and deprive him of food and water. If you lie to us again, you miserable piece of carrion, we will set the Dragons on you and feed what scraps are left to the dogs,"

Skank sat up and stared at her as if she were even more frightening than the Dragons. "You! You!" he shrieked, pointing and scuttling as far away from Kate as the point of Joseph's sword would allow. "I know you! The Great Lord sees you! You are the great Wizard from another place. You not belong. He will kill you now. He only watched before. Now he will kill you!"

Joseph realized the truth in the goblin's words. They had persuaded Kate to become involved in their troubles. Now the Dark Lord would no longer tolerate her presence. She was no longer a curiosity, but an enemy he would hunt down and destroy. Their only hope was that the Dark Lord might not know what happened to his kidnappers or at least of Kate's involvement. Perhaps the Dark Lord would attribute the death of Gorp to the Nasua that roamed this region.

Kate laughed at Skank, shaking her head. "He is mistaken if he thinks I am a Wizard. I am not. Your lord is not all knowing if he believes I possess magic of any sort. As for killing me, he has to find me first and even if he does, I will not be as easy to kill as you might think."

Skank fell to muttering under his breath as he eyed her warily. Joseph was not through with him, however.

"Speak, Skank, or I will end your miserable life now," he threatened. "Who helped you capture Solomon? You could not have taken him from the Hall without help from someone. Even unarmed he could kill you easily."

Skank thought of resisting for a moment, but the dogs, sensing Joseph's anger, rose to their feet growling, their bared teeth inches from the Goblin's face. He remembered watching one of them kill Gorp, shaking him until his neck snapped. He could still hear Gorp's screams as he Rolf pulled him down and the final muffled gurgle as he died. Skank did not particularly care that Gorp was dead. He just did not want the same to happen to him.

He tried again, as he had when first cornered, to strike a bargain with the Elves, abruptly turning away from Kate as if she were beyond the reach of his scheming. "Great Lord will give you power. Much power if you join his cause," he whined. "I take you to him. We are close to his kingdom. He will reward you if you join with him."

Joseph shifted his blade in his hand as if even his unlimited store of patience was wearing thin. "Perhaps you are of no use to us after all. Perhaps keeping you alive is not worth the trouble." Joseph said, filled with loathing for the creature cowering before him.

He fully intended to end the creature's worthless life until Solomon stepped up beside him and laid a hand on his shoulder. He looked battered and weary, but his eyes shone in the firelight as he regarded the goblin scrabbling about in the mud. Joseph wrapped his free arm about Solomon to hold him upright.

"I know who he struck a bargain with, Joseph," Solomon said. "I think Augustine was the original prize offered to the Dark Lord. I just happened along when things went awry. Augustine was still alive when I found him. He wanted me to warn the Riders. Marcus is the traitor among them. Even Skank admitted. Marcus was in service to the Dark Lord."

"Marcus! I knew it!" Holly cried. "This wretched creature can testify on your behalf, Sollie. Perhaps we could let him live a bit longer if he cooperates."

Skank groveled at Holly's feet while she backed hastily away from him, trying to avoid his touch.

"Pretty Elf lady. Thank you. Thank you. You are most kind to lowly Skank. I will serve *you* now. Yes? Skank will help you, serve you, as he served the Great Lord if you let Skank live."

Holly thought she had never seen such a pathetic creature. For what he had done to Solomon she would have gladly bashed his ugly skull in with his own club and left his body to the crows, but if he would bear witness to Solomon's innocence she was willing to let him live for a while.

Solomon was anxious to return to the Hall to deliver Augustine's warning to the Riders. The storm had passed as quickly as it had come, and the moon once more shone brightly through the shredded clouds remaining, but Joseph, Holly and Kate overruled him.

"You are in no condition to travel tonight, Sollie. We will be safe enough here with the Dragons and the dogs to watch over us. As for Marcus, none of the Riders are as trusting of him as he thinks. He said he saw you kill Augustine. Obviously, he has mastered the art of lying. Ephraim is watching him closely," said Holly.

Buck barked once at Solomon as if to lend his support.

Solomon found it difficult to persuade them otherwise when he could not hide the fact he could barely stand. Joseph had no trouble pushing him back down against Antares' side, threatening to sit on him if he could not keep still. He consented to rest for a short time, but by the time Kate had wrapped him once more in a woolen blanket, he was asleep.

Holly sat watching over Solomon as he rested, one hand on his curly head and the other lying on Buck's head where he lay curled against her leg. Joseph and Kate sat watching Skank where he lay bound with Rolf on guard.

"Do you think he knows how much Holly loves him?" Kate asked quietly after watching the pair in silence for a long time.

Joseph shook his head. "I think he is afraid to love anyone right now. Holly and I discussed her feelings for him before she left to find him. I was willing to speak to him on her behalf if he returned. She said it was too soon. I think she was right. He has been through so much in the last year and even more in the last few days. I wish he could rest for a while and regain his strength. No, maybe I do not mean strength. He has strength enough for ten. Perhaps I should say instead that he needs to regain his balance. He will not rest easily until Augustine is avenged and Anduin is safe. Then, I fear there will be another task facing him of some sort or another. The Dragon Riders need his leadership. We are a long way from peace as long as the Dark Lord and this evil stone Solomon speaks of exist."

"Well," Kate chuckled, "he seems peaceful enough for the moment." She sighed, happy with the outcome of their search. "I think Holly has chosen wisely. He will see her as more than just a friend some day. Your world is a dangerous place now. Solomon is wise to be wary. I hope that some day you and the other Riders will make it a safe place to raise your children. Maybe even in my lifetime." She sighed again, looking off into the dark sky.

"Perhaps I could take more of a hand in the affairs of this land, but as I have said before, I am not the powerful ally you might think I am. I am just a teacher in my land. I had once thought to be resting by now, retired and puttering about the home I left behind when I came to your world. Perhaps I would become bored with it. I know the dogs would become bored with me."

Joseph and Kate spent the night keeping watch and talking over the fire. Joseph learned a little about the amazing machines that populated the land of

Kate's birth and Kate was fascinated by the life of the Dragon Riders. Joseph told her the rest of Solomon's tale, of Euwyn, the Wizard, and his adopted son who was actually the Prince of Anduin. He told her what he could of Bree and Chess and Thorny and little Mica and Solomon's encounter with the Dwarves and Giants on his way back to the Hall. Kate's eyes shone with delight as she listened.

When dawn approached and he had run out of stories to tell, she thanked him sincerely, and offered him a token of their friendship. She slipped a small, round sphere of glass into his hand. Within the sphere, a rainbow of colors swirled. She called the tiny sphere a marble and assured him it was merely a toy for children and that it was very old and not of much value in her homeland.

Joseph admired the weight and smoothness of it and the brilliant colors it held captive within its depths. She laughed when he thanked her as if it were a rare jewel and dropped it carefully into his pocket.

"I have brought something for Holly," she said, pulling a small box from her pack. "This is a box of writing tools called pens in our world. There are a dozen of them in this box. They will write without dipping them into ink. Look, Joseph, they contain their own ink," she said, producing a scrap of paper and writing her name on it before Joseph's astonished eyes. "They will run out some day. They do not contain an infinite supply, but Holly can do a lot of writing with these. Perhaps some day we will meet again and I will see she gets more of them. I have something for Solomon as well," she continued, pulling something more from her pack. In her hand, she held the small photograph she had taken of Joseph and Holly the night before. She had given Holly and Joseph each a picture of the two of them together and now she offered another of the same picture for Solomon. Joseph took it and held it gingerly in his hand.

"Solomon will treasure this," he said, "and Holly will put these pens to good use."

"Please wait until I have left to give Holly and Solomon these things," said Kate. "You must understand, Joseph. I do not want any thanks from them. They are very small gifts in my world as is the glass marble I gave you. I suppose I am hoping you will remember me when I am long dead and gone from your world. You will still seem as young as you do now when I am dust in some graveyard."

"For what you have done for us Kate, we will remember you all our lives. Never doubt that," Joseph assured her. "Holly will write of you in her journal."

Joseph agreed to do as she asked, but as they watched the sky lighten, he tried to persuade Kate to return to the Hall and the protection it offered. She adamantly refused. He could not even persuade her to accept a ride back to her home.

"The dogs and I have had enough of flying about for now. The rain has ceased and with the dogs to guard me, I will reach the outpost safely," she assured him. "Once I am there, very little can harm me. I can easily cross the barrier into my world."

Joseph was not sure what she was trying to tell him. He wondered exactly what she meant when she referred to her world as if it were not a part of his, but he let it rest for now. He would return to learn more from Kate if he could some day, but for now, he would concentrate on getting Solomon back to the safety of the Hall. Kate only asked to photograph the three of them and their Dragons together before she left them.

"A remembrance," she said, "of the night we rescued Solomon and our lives became entwined."

Joseph puzzled over Kate when he thought of her later. He wondered if Kate had children and a husband who loved her in her own land. It was something that had not occurred to him until now. The more he learned of Kate the more mysterious she seemed.

## Chapter Thirty-eight

## RETURN

A gray dawn found Solomon anxious to travel. Joseph was concerned when he found him standing atop Antares, staring southeastward, the poisonous mists that shrouded the wastelands just visible from his vantage. Solomon seemed much steadier on his feet after a night of rest.

When Joseph joined him atop the Dragon and turned a questioning look in his direction, Solomon continued to gaze into the distance. His eyes glittered dangerously. "Evil dwells somewhere near this place. I can feel it in the earth and the air. Some day, Joseph," he said, "I will return to find the Dark Lord's lair. I know the direction the Goblins were taking. Skank told me we were close to our destination. 'Guest of the Great Lord by nightfall,' he said. Some day he will pay for the pain and horror he has brought to the people of our land and the lands around us."

Solomon turned abruptly and slid to the ground. Joseph cast another look in the direction Solomon had indicated and nodded to himself. He could sense the evil as readily as Solomon could, and he did not doubt Solomon's resolve. Other matters needed their attention now.

They took to the skies as soon as Kate and Holly had changed the bandages on Solomon's wrists and inspected the wounds to his head.

Kate's farewell was brief. Joseph knew it was difficult for her to leave them. He could feel it plainly when he took her hand in his as they parted. He felt concern for Solomon and concern for his safety and Holly's as well, but her loneliness was most plain to him and a sharp feeling of loss that did not seem connected to their parting. The feeling that disturbed him most of all was the absence of fear for her own safety.

She strode off through the pines, Buck and Rolf at her side, turning only once to wave at them a short time later as they flew overhead. True to his word, Joseph gave Holly the box of pens and Solomon the photograph after Kate had left. Holly was much taken with her box of pens, but not as pleased as Solomon was with the photograph. He studied it for a long time before he tucked it carefully away.

Skank was strapped to Procyon's back where he shrieked in terror during the first few minutes of their flight. When Joseph drew his blade and offered to cut him loose to find his way back to the ground by whatever route he wished, the goblin's shrieks subsided to a pitiful moan. Joseph soon wished he had cut the wretched creature loose as he had threatened.

Antares carried Solomon through the air with a contented rumbling, leading the way back to the Hall.

They arrived in the great meadow before the Hall of the Dragon Riders soon after midday. Matthew and Noah, on guard at the gates, had seen their approach. By the time they landed, Riders were running from the Hall to meet them. Holly and Joseph stood beside Antares, waiting for Solomon to dismount when Marcus appeared, flanked by Elijah and Peter.

Joseph noticed that Marcus looked a bit pale and more than a little uneasy when he found Solomon had returned with them. Still, he advanced on Solomon brazenly with his sword drawn, shouting for Elijah and Peter to seize him and put him in shackles even before Solomon had set his feet upon the ground.

Joseph's sword rang menacingly as he drew it, stepping between Solomon and Marcus. Marcus had the presence of mind to step back, putting Elijah and Peter between himself and Joseph. One look at Solomon, weary, battered, and still unsteady on his feet, and Elijah took his hand from the hilt of his sword and motioned for Peter to stand down as well.

Elijah was the most analytical of all the Riders. He could see at once that Solomon had spent his last days bound hand and foot. The fact Joseph and Holly had brought him back unbound made it seem to Elijah as if Solomon had spent the days he was absent as a prisoner and not as a fugitive from the Dragon Riders, as Marcus would have them believe. Nothing he saw seemed to fit the tale Marcus was telling. Elijah respected Joseph too much to think he would draw his sword against another Rider to protect an Elf who had killed his friend and leader, Augustine. He stood looking from Marcus to Joseph, waiting for one of them to speak.

"Marcus," Joseph said, his voice ringing loud enough to reach the ears of all present, "we have returned to accuse you of murder and treason for the death of First Rider Augustine and the abduction of Second Rider Solomon."

"What?" roared Marcus. "If you have been listening to the ranting of this madman again, then you are as mad as he is! Solomon murdered Augustine. I saw it with my own eyes! By what fanciful evidence do you accuse me of his crime?"

Joseph was pleased to hear Ephraim's voice cut through the general uproar that followed his pronouncement. He strode toward the newly arrived Riders, calling for silence as he took charge of the situation. He looked at Solomon closely, taking in the bandaged wrists and the bruises and cuts that decorated his face. With an angry glance in Marcus' direction, as if daring him to interfere, he asked Peter and Holly to help Solomon to his rooms where he would meet with him shortly. Another withering glance silenced Marcus' objections.

Joseph motioned for Ephraim to follow him around to Procyon's side. There, he unceremoniously cut the straps binding the goblin to the Dragon's back. Skank landed in a gibbering, scrabbling heap at Ephraim's feet.

"Where did you find this sorry creature?" Ephraim asked, stepping back in distaste as Skank groveled too close to his polished boots for comfort.

"We found this creature and another like him, headed for the realm of the Dark Lord, according to the tale this one tells. It is interesting that he speaks our language fairly well. He would have us believe the Dark Lord wished to discuss peace terms with the Riders and when Augustine died, Solomon was elected to be our representative. Solomon was beaten senseless, of course, to make him more willing."

Ephraim hauled Skank to his feet, his face dark and angry. Even Joseph almost cringed before the look his friend directed at the goblin.

"You dare to abduct a Rider from our very grounds," he growled. "Not just any Rider, but one who is a particular favorite of mine. I suspect you have played a part in the murder of a very dear friend as well. You will come to rue the day the Dark Lord spawned you, goblin. You will howl in fear at the mere sight of me if you do not tell me the truth. Get your facts in order, Skank. We will question you before all the riders this very night. If I suspect you are lying, you will wish you were dead."

Skank appeared to have been struck dumb. His mouth worked feverishly, but he could not utter a word or even tear his eyes from Ephraim's face until Ephraim himself turned him about and shoved him forward.

When Ephraim and Joseph propelled the cringing goblin into plain sight before the gates, they did not miss the way Marcus' face turned deathly pale. Marcus suddenly seemed to feel he had something very important to do elsewhere, fleeing ahead of Joseph and Ephraim as they propelled their captive toward the fortress. A word whispered in Noah's ear as he stood guarding the gates, sent him running after Marcus, a fierce grin on his boyish countenance.

"There has been a gathering of the Elders, Joseph," Ephraim said as they pushed their cowering prisoner through the halls toward the prison area. He stopped to face Joseph with an uncertain look on his lean face. "They have chosen me to serve as First Rider." He stood before Joseph, uneasy, waiting for his reaction.

For the first time in the past two days, Joseph found he was able to smile. "They have chosen the Rider most fit for the job, then. That is the best news I have heard in a long time."

Ephraim returned his smile. "I hope you are right, Joseph. We are living and fighting in dangerous times. When they named me, I would have refused if my conscience had let me. If all goes as I wish tonight, Solomon will once more be our Second Rider and Marcus will face punishment for his crimes."

"You believe Marcus is guilty, then," said Joseph.

"It is his word against Solomon's. Who would you believe? I cannot think Solomon capable of such an act. Nor do I think he would lie to me. I will speak to him personally as soon as we deliver our prisoner safely to a cell. I only hope the Brotherhood feels as I do."

Solomon sank wearily into a chair while Holly sent Peter for some water to bathe in. She helped Solomon out of his ruined shirt, wincing when she caught sight of his blackened ribs. Still, she had seen him survive injuries much more severe. She knew he would heal in time.

He sat staring silently at his hands, hands that still held traces of Augustine's blood. "He was still alive when I found him," he said softly. "He spent the last of his strength trying to warn me I was in danger."

He fought for control of his emotions. He did not want to weep in front of Holly. He covered his face with his bloodied hands, but he could not stop the tears that trickled between them. She put her arms around him and her tears mingled with his.

Ephraim followed Peter through the open door, both bearing pails of hot water. He set his down to lay a hand on Solomon's shoulder.

"He was very proud of you, Solomon. Your return made him as happy as I have seen him in the past year. Do not feel responsible for what happened to Augustine."

Solomon took a deep breath and nodded. He knew the Elf responsible. He would not falter now. There was much for him to do.

Bathed and clad in his dress uniform, all traces of blood washed from his hands, he felt ready to face whatever lay ahead. Ephraim and Holly were deep in conversation when he rejoined them. Holly informed him the council of elders asked Ephraim to serve as First Rider and he had accepted.

Solomon was relieved to hear they had chosen another First so quickly, amazed and pleased that Ephraim had consented to fill the post left vacant by Augustine's death. Ephraim was the best choice to lead the Dragon Riders. Solomon told him so as he took his hand to congratulate him. He felt more confident now that Ephraim was in command.

Elijah soon joined them. Ephraim had requested his presence while Solomon told of Augustine's death and his own capture. Solomon did not question his presence or that of Elijah's brother, Peter, who made their number four. They shared a meal over the small table in Solomon's room, while Solomon talked. Elijah took charge of ferreting out the details. He had a keen, inquisitive mind. By the time Solomon's story had been heard beginning to end and Elijah had probed for more bits of information, Solomon was surprised at how much more at ease he felt at the prospect of repeating the same story before the rest of the Riders.

Elijah and Peter left soon after their meal was finished. Solomon noticed a mysterious look that passed between Ephraim and Elijah as they left. Something was afoot. Solomon was sure of it. The last of his uneasiness retreated, replaced by a curiosity to know what Ephraim and Elijah were up to.

## Chapter Thirty-nine

## TRIAL

There was a chamber in the Hall of the Dragon Riders large enough to seat comfortably all the active Riders and the elders of their Brotherhood. Solomon sat wishing he had been present when Ephraim had accepted the position of First Rider. This is where the Elders placed the silver medallion of the office about Ephraim's neck with all of the Riders and their families present, all but Holly and Joseph and himself. Solomon had never witnessed such a ceremony since Augustine was First Rider before Solomon's birth.

The elders were already seated when Solomon entered the hall and took his place. Marcus occupied the seat reserved for the Second Rider. He still held that post. Solomon hoped that would change by the end of the evening. He did not care who held the post as long as it was not Marcus. It would be for the entire Brotherhood to decide, just as they would decide who was guilty of Augustine's death. He would not let himself hope for more than that the Brotherhood would accept his story. If they did not, if the evidence they had gathered against him was irrefutable in the eyes of the Riders, he would accept his punishment.

No Rider had ever been accused of murder. Would he be executed if they found him guilty? Somehow, the idea his comrades would think him capable of such an act seemed more disturbing than the thought he might die because of it. It would come down to the word of Solomon and a goblin against that of the Second Rider of the Brotherhood when all was said and done. Skank spoke of Marcus as one who served the Dark Lord. The only other evidence of Solomon's innocence was the word of a dying man to the one accused of his murder.

The rest of the Riders were nearly all seated when Elijah came to sit by Solomon's side. He laid his hand on Solomon's shoulder as he spoke to him. "Rest easy, Sollie," he said. "All you need to do is tell the truth. Marcus is the one whose task will be difficult tonight. He will have to lie convincingly enough for the Brotherhood to believe him."

Solomon gave him a grateful smile, but his mouth went dry at the thought of addressing Elves that thought he might be insane enough to murder his closest friend.

When all were seated, Ephraim stood and called for silence, wearing the medallion of First Rider hanging outside his coat for all to see, reminding everyone present of his station. He and Elijah would need every advantage to clear Solomon of the charges against him. A little reminder of his importance to the Brotherhood could not hurt their cause.

Solomon noticed the goblin was not present yet. His attention returned to

Marcus, there in the Second Rider's chair. Uneasiness again turned to anger as Solomon watched Marcus sitting there. He pushed it down as best he could. He needed his wits about him now.

Ephraim read the charges against Solomon and then those against Marcus. Marcus stood to state his case before the gathering. He smiled confidently as he told of seeing Solomon stab Augustine on the shore of the lake, reminding the Riders that Solomon's blood stained-coat and the sleeve of his shirt lay nearby.

"It should be obvious to all present. Solomon is insane. He went after Augustine with a knife and stabbed him to death as he walked on the beach. Noah saw him follow Augustine from the Hall. During the struggle, his sleeve was torn. He then fled. That fact alone proves he is guilty. Did you not see the blood that remained on his shirt and hands when Joseph and Holly brought him back to the hall? Ask him whose blood it was!" Marcus' voice had risen to a shout. He looked at Solomon as if daring him to lie.

"The blood was Augustine's," Solomon answered quietly. He could not suppress a shudder at the memory of his friend's blood escaping through his fingers despite his efforts to stop it. A murmuring of dismayed voices began to echo about the hall.

"You see!" Marcus was nearly foaming at the mouth now. "See the guilt on his face? He admits the blood was Augustine's"

"Are you finished, Marcus?" Ephraim asked.

"I reserve the right to say more if I can refute the lies this madman Solomon is about to tell the Brothers," he said, strutting now as if he had already won.

"Very well, Marcus," Ephraim sighed. "You will have a second chance to speak, but I will extend that courtesy to all present, including Solomon."

It was then Solomon's turn to speak. He told the story as completely and clearly as he could. He could not fill in the details of the times when he lay unconscious. He only had Augustine's final words to him and Skank's mention of Marcus to offer. They would have to believe him without much evidence to prove he told the truth. Holly and Joseph had not heard Skank speak Marcus' name. Only Solomon heard it pass from the monster's lips. He was a madman. Why should they believe him? Still, he found his story easy to relate. He would tell them the truth. If no one believed him, at least they would have the truth in their possession. It was all he could offer.

Elijah asked to speak next. He held a knife in his hand and offered it before the assembled riders. "Does anyone recognize this knife?" he asked.

Half of the riders recognized it as Solomon's knife.

"Have you ever known him to carry any other knife than this one, carried by his father before him?"

There was a general shaking of heads.

Elijah turned to the elder Anthony. "Is this knife the one you took from Augustine's body?"

"No, it is not," he answered. "The knife I took from his body was unremarkable. One that could have belonged to anyone."

Solomon thought he saw Anthony's gaze shift briefly toward Marcus.

Marcus obviously wanted to say something, but at Ephraim's stern look, he held his peace.

Ephraim turned to Joseph. "Did you find Solomon captive at the hands of Goblins?"

"Yes, Holly and I enlisted the help of Hound Mistress Kate to track them."

"Was he injured?"

"He was bound and unconscious when we found him. He had been beaten."

"He was not injured by Holly or yourself?"

"No, of course not. He was grateful when we rescued him and anxious to return to the Hall."

Marcus stood abruptly, shouting, "Lies, all lies! He was captured by Goblins after he fled the Hall if he was indeed an unwilling captive. Perhaps Solomon was the Elf they were dealing with. As I have said before, who knows what alliances he has made in the past year?"

"That is ridiculous, Marcus!" It was now Joseph's turn to shout. "He was nearly dead when we found him. Why would the Dark Lord's creatures treat him so if he were an ally?"

"We have only your word and the word of Holly to attest to that. You are his brother. Who knows to what lengths you would go to save him?"

Ephraim was calling for silence. The Riders subsided once more. He motioned for Elijah to continue.

Elijah turned to Marcus. "Your list of Riders who have become capable of lying grows long, Marcus.

"You have never seen this goblin, then? You and he have never met to bargain for a hostage on behalf of the Dark Lord?"

"No, of course not," Marcus sneered. "That is a lie and an insult. I am not personally acquainted with any of the Dark Lord's creatures."

"So, then," Elijah continued, "If I were to bring the creature into this room, he would not know you. Say we take your medallion off," he said, slipping the chain bearing the medallion marking him as Second Rider over Marcus' head before he could object, "just in case that makes you stand out from the others, and you stood with all the other Riders in this chamber. He could not pick you out as the one he had dealings with among all the other Riders. Is that what you are telling us? If we all stand together, and no one points you out to him, he could not recognize you because he has never met you. Noah has been guarding you since the prisoner's arrival and he assures me you have not gone to introduce yourself to the Goblin or come anywhere near him."

Marcus turned to glare at Noah. Noah grinned back.

There was a surprised and curious murmur among the riders. Solomon caught some of them smiling in anticipation.

Marcus licked his lips nervously. "I do not deal with Goblins!" he shouted. "What is this lunacy? My word should be enough! I am Second Rider!"

Elijah sent him a disgusted look and turned to Ephraim.

Ephraim sent Noah and Matthew to bring the prisoner. They left grinning at each other. Solomon could only watch with wonder as the remaining Riders let Anthony herd them into two lines, facing each other across the room. He was amazed at the cleverness of Elijah and Ephraim and the lengths to which they had gone to prove him innocent. He half-expected Marcus to try to escape before the goblin could point him out.

Skank slunk into the chamber between Noah and Matthew, his teeth bared, his yellow eyes darting about the room at the Riders assembled there. He hissed and shrank from the sight of Ephraim, standing in the middle of the chamber between the lines of Riders. The points of Noah and Matthew's swords kept him from backing away as far as he would have liked.

Ephraim now held the Riders' attention as he stared at the creature cowering before him. "Tell me the truth, goblin. Do you know any of the Elves in this room?" he asked. Skank nodded, hissing and baring his teeth, his eyes darting uneasily at the Riders surrounding him. "Point out to me the ones you know and their names."

"Solomon!" he squealed. Throwing an arm out and pointing a scrawny finger at Solomon who nodded in agreement. "Mistress Holly, Joseph," he hissed, giving Joseph a second look as if expecting him to attack at any moment. Indeed, Joseph looked angry enough to throttle him to death then and there.

Skank seemed to be enjoying his part in the proceedings entirely too much for Joseph's taste. He wondered if the creature would actually point Marcus out as the one who dealt with the Dark Lord. Skank was squinting at the Riders gathered about him now as if he were done pointing out those he knew.

Marcus began to smirk triumphantly.

"Oh! Oh!" Skank squeaked, suddenly capering grotesquely on his long legs, sidling away from his guards to fling a bony arm about Marcus' shoulders. "Must not forget friend Marcus!" he giggled. "He is favorite Rider of Great Lord."

Marcus shrieked in dismay, trying to disentangle himself from the goblin's long arm draped affectionately about his shoulders.

"He is lying! I do not know him! For the Creator's sake, kill this wretched thing!"

Skank danced away from Marcus, a look of sorrow upon his face. "You are no longer Skank's friend," he moaned. All promises you make to Skank and Great Lord. Lies.... Lies," Skank said, shaking his head. "Great Lord will be very angry with you. You said Riders would make you leader and serve our Great Lord within a year. Great Lord counted on you. He will be angry." Skank started to giggle and then to laugh, shrieking madly, dancing about until Noah and Matthew hustled him from the room.

Marcus stood alone now in the center of the room, his eyes darting about like those of a caged animal. The rest of the riders stood silent, staring at him with a mixture of disbelief and anger.

"You cannot take the word of a goblin over mine," he whined. "Ask him how he knows Solomon! He pointed him out!"

"Solomon was the hostage you delivered to him bound and unconscious, Marcus," Elijah said in his even voice. "Skank met Joseph and Holly when they took him captive. I hope you are not accusing Ephraim of treason since the creature only met Ephraim when he arrived here. The only mystery is, how did he pick you out of the crowd? Where did you meet this wretched creature?"

"Well, yes," Marcus said, a sickly sort of smile on his lips, "I must have fought him once. Yes, that is where he learned who I was."

"Do you often introduce yourself to the Goblins you do battle with, Marcus?" said Ephraim. "I find that hard to swallow."

"Especially since he does not get very close to many of them. We do most of the fighting while he shouts orders from a safe distance," muttered Peter.

A brief ripple of laughter followed Peter's statement.

It died abruptly when Solomon and Marcus stood face to face, the Riders watched silently as Solomon's golden eyes sought those of Marcus and held them fast.

"*Why*, Marcus? What could the Dark Lord possibly offer you that was worth Augustine's life? You were a Dragon Rider, Marcus. Second Rider. What could you desire more than that? What brought you so low you could kill Augustine and then lie to cover your crime?" There was more sorrow than anger in Solomon's voice.

Marcus gave a bitter laugh. "He was after *you*, Solomon. He wanted me to bring *you* to him. He offered me the post of Second Rider. I already *am* Second Rider! I have gained that post on my own. I would never have let you take that from me. First Rider, on the other hand, that was what I wished for above all else. I offered the Dark Lord Augustine in your place. You were too far gone, I told him. You were as good as dead. He accepted my offer easily enough.

Things went a bit wrong that night. Augustine was not easily taken and I was forced to kill him, but then, you were there. Augustine's plight and my approach kept you distracted just long enough for the Goblins to club you senseless. It was *you* the Dark Lord desired all along. So, you see, Solomon, it worked out for the best. Augustine was dead. You were out of my way.

"Who would have thought Ephraim would accept the position of First Rider? I had not counted on that. Still, if your friends had not rescued you, I would have remained as Second Rider and you would have been the Dark Lord's honored guest."

Marcus smiled as Joseph's hand went to the hilt of his sword. "Will you kill me, then, Joseph? Will you shed the blood of a fellow Rider? How will that make you feel?"

Joseph stood silently, considering, but he did not unsheathe his sword. Solomon knew he would not.

"Do not look at me in that way, Solomon!" Marcus shrieked, his cool manner suddenly evaporating as Solomon stood looking at him. "It is your fault, not mine! Augustine died by my hand, but the Dark Lord wanted you! You, the most beloved Rider, Augustine's favorite! *Everyone's* favorite! You should have died a year ago! I told them where to find you! I told them you could be easily taken on that day, and yet you come back now to haunt me!"

"Enough!" Ephraim shouted. "Take him to a cell. We will decide his fate at a later time. We have a vote to take and more matters to discuss."

Peter, Elijah, Timothy and Samuel hustled Marcus in the same direction as the goblin. They returned in time to participate in the vote to declare Solomon guilty or innocent. It was a mere formality. None voted against him.

The Riders gathered about Solomon, congratulating him and vowing they never doubted his innocence. Solomon tried to respond as he should. He felt numb. An entire village had died because the Dark Lord was after him. Marcus had sent the creatures of the Dark Lord to kill an entire village so they could capture him. Solomon struggled just to remain standing.

Holly smiled at him from outside the crowd. He was grateful Joseph kept close by his side, one strong arm about his shoulders. Holly and Joseph had never doubted him. He had the feeling he could say the same of Ephraim. Still, he knew Marcus' words would haunt him. Why was he so important to the Dark Lord? He could not imagine how the evil lord even knew his name. He would ask Antares when the opportunity presented itself. Antares knew all the answers.

He was grateful to find Holly and Joseph seated on either side of him when Ephraim called the meeting to order once again.

"I would now like to ask the Riders present who they would have as Second Rider. As your First Rider, I was chosen by the elders. This is your chance to select a Second Rider. Choose wisely. He or she will lead you into the coming battles against the Dark Lord, an evil that grows ever stronger and reaches ever farther beyond his present domain. I think you know my choice. Search your own hearts for yours," said Ephraim, taking his seat and picking up a quill to mark his vote.

Solomon did not hope to reclaim his post as Second Rider. His recent past was too uncertain. Who would trust him with such a responsibility now? He penned Joseph's name on his scrap of parchment and handed it to Elijah when he came to collect the ballots.

The Riders shifted impatiently in their seats while Ephraim looked the ballots over carefully. He was chuckling as he stood to pronounce the results. "I have one vote for Joseph. The rest have chosen Solomon. Solomon, do you not want the job? I know your hand. You voted for Joseph."

Solomon was stunned. *All* voted for him? He sat staring at Ephraim, afraid it was some cruel joke. Ephraim gazed back at Solomon.

"Well, Solomon, will you return to your post? Obviously the other Riders wish you to lead them into battle as you did before."

"Yes... Yes, I would like to lead the Riders as your second, Ephraim, but I cannot stay here. I have given my word to return to Anduin," Solomon managed finally. He rose to look about at the men who would put their lives in his hands, wishing his answer could be different.

"If you have given your word, Solomon, you must honor your vow, but perhaps your return to Anduin does not mean you cannot return to the post of Second Rider. We have all discussed this matter at length and all the Brotherhood has been given some time to think upon it. Let us retire to the great meadow before the gates. The Dragons await us there. We will decide the matter of Anduin with their help," said Ephraim.

Φ             Φ             Φ

Torches lit the great meadow where the eighteen Dragons pledged to the Dragon Riders lay waiting. They formed a semicircle about the gates of the fortress, their jewel colored hides glittering in the flickering light. Their deep voices echoed off the stones as they spoke among themselves, awaiting their chance to speak to the Riders. Each Rider took his place before the Dragon pledged to him, facing inward toward Ephraim who stood before the gates. His red Dragon, Vega, and Marcus' red Dragon, Mira, were the only two whose riders did not join them. Solomon was glad to be close to Antares again. He sat on the Dragon's taloned paw, leaning gratefully against the side of his huge head. Antares sighed a deep gusty sigh of contentment.

"It went well, then, Sollie," he rumbled. "I see you walk free and Marcus is absent from your number."

"Yes, Antares," Solomon answered. "If you can consider discovering one of our number has had dealings with the Dark Lord going well. I cannot believe an Elf would do such a thing."

"Ah, Sollie, that is what the desire for power can do to one who does not deserve it. All Elves are powerful in themselves. If they are not satisfied with the innate power they already possess, the quest for another power will destroy them. It is said the Orcs were Elves once, Elves who allied themselves with the Dark Lord. Now they are his servants with no power of their own. Not even that power they were born with so many thousands of years ago."

Solomon nodded. The motion set his head pounding. He closed his eyes for a moment.

"Marcus said the Dark Lord wanted me as much as he did Augustine. What would cause him to single me out above all the other Riders?" Solomon asked. Antares did not miss the weariness in his voice.

Antares' voice was hushed as he spoke, taking Solomon back thousands of years. "It is time, little friend. Time I told you of something only the elders and the Dragons know. It is time you heard the song of the Dragons and so, I will tell it to you exactly as I saw it unfold.

Φ                Φ                Φ

The peaks of the Hoary Mountains sat bathed in starlight, throwing plumes of snow into the wind from their topmost spires. Daystar and the rest of us added our own glittering plumes, trailing behind us like the tails of earthbound comets.

We were the Dragons. We were eternal. We feared nothing in these mountains. We were as stars, fallen from the heavens to wrap our sinuous forms about the highest peaks.

Below in a small valley, a fire contended with the pure light of the stars. Daystar circled lower. Had there not been a village here once upon a time not so long ago? Now, only one lonely flame lit the darkness.

Curious.

Where had the village gone so suddenly? What trickery did the Elves perform to hide a thing once so solid from his Dragon's eyes? He slid from the sky like a silken scarf dropped from a careless hand, wrapping himself about the fire in the valley.

He was amused to find a Mountain Elf attending it. A small, insignificant, creature that scrambled to his feet in fear. He held something close, wrapped carefully against prying eyes. Daystar laughed at him, drawing closer to see the precious thing the man clutched to his breast so desperately. The man had the temerity to hide it from him.

He would take it.

He looked about for more of the creatures, but there were none to be seen. The village lay in ruins about the single Elf, trailers of snow and mist shrouding the scattered stones and the Elf's fallen brothers. Daystar could sense their lifeless bodies beneath the freshly fallen snow.

He turned back to the little man. "What have you there, Elf?" he demanded. "What treasure lay hidden from my sight in this village? What did you and your brethren defend from the evil creatures of the dark until all but you lay dead? You must know all of value in these mountains is mine. Show it to me!"

"This treasure is of no value to you. Your claws are too clumsy to hold it, your heart too cold to appreciate its worth," the Elf said softly. "You cannot possess this treasure. Even I will not hold it as close as I do now for long."

"All in these mountains belongs to me and my brethren!" Daystar roared. "All things of great value are mine!"

"You will kill me, then, to possess my treasure," the Elf cried. "If you do this, the treasure will surely cease to exist. It is treasure to me, but of no use to you."

"Treasure is treasure," the Dragon snorted.

"This treasure will wear you down. It would cause even you sadness and pain to hold it along with the great joy it will give you, for it will not be held for long and even you would find guarding this treasure more than you bargained for. This treasure is not for you."

"I will take it from you."

"If you do, it will not last."

Daystar inspected the small creature closely. The Elf shivered. His blood stained the snow at his feet. Daystar could hasten his death and take the thing he so treasured, but the creature's golden eyes were too much like his own, the bravery it showed before him too much a curiosity. It was said these creatures could not lie.

Amusing.

"A wager, then, little Elf. If you show me your treasure and I agree I cannot keep it, my brothers and I will serve you until you are gone from this earth."

The little Elf regarded the Dragon silently, holding his treasure even more closely than before.

"You have my word, little man. I will not harm you. If you win this wager, my first service to you will be to find someone to heal you of your wounds."

"I will accept your offer, Dragon. If, win or lose, you agree to keep my treasure safe."

"Agreed!" the Dragon roared, his patience growing thin. "Show me what you value above your own life. Show me!"

The Elf sighed, sinking down by the fire within Daystar's coils to display his treasure before the great golden Dragon.

Daystar drew closer yet, eager to glimpse the riches he would soon possess. He drew back in surprise at the contents of the small bundle.

"A child?" he roared, a small gout of flame escaping him. "A child? This is no treasure, but a lowly creature like yourself!"

The Elf held the child close once again, shielding it against the Dragon's anger. "He is my greatest treasure, Dragon. He is my son."

"I cannot care for an Elf child! I am a Dragon!"

"You admit it, then, Dragon. You were wrong. Treasure is not treasure. I have won the wager."

"You have deceived me, Elf, and for that, I will simply watch you die and therefore be released from my oath."

"I will not be gone from this earth even then, Dragon. I have a son and your word you will keep him safe until all trace of me is gone. Part of me will still live on in him."

"I cannot care for such a tiny creature."

"I can," the Elf said softly, hope dawning in his golden eyes.

Thus began the alliance between Dragons and Elves for there has always been a descendant of the man with golden eyes to serve. Let it be said Daystar came to accept his service to them as did his brethren.

Eons passed before Daystar would admit he had found his greatest treasure that day in the Elf who first became his friend and then, in that man's infant son and his golden-eyed descendants.

Φ            Φ            Φ

Antares' story ended. Solomon looked at the dragon in astonished silence. "I have told you this much, little one," Antares said, "because you hold the key to our service to the Elves of the mountains. You are a direct descendant of that man who made a wager against Daystar and won. You are your father's son, the only true remnant of the Goshawk line left upon this earth. The Dark Lord will take you if he can, Sollie. If you become his, the Dragons will come to serve him as well. If we serve this evil lord, your people, the people of this world will perish."

"I am sorry, Antares," Solomon said. "I did not realize you were bound to us in this manner."

Antares chuckled softly. "Do not think we were not offered our freedom. The Elf who made that wager was your namesake, Solomon. He offered us our freedom, but we did not take it. At the time, it seemed unimportant. We had found a purpose to our existence and we were content. Looking back, we should have taken his offer. Nothing would have changed. We would still serve you. Now, that debt could be our downfall."

"That night in the village…the night I would have taken my own life…" Sollie said. "You did not try to stop me. Were you wishing for your freedom, Antares? If I was no longer alive, you and your brothers would be free and you would be safe from the Dark Lord."

"Sollie! You cannot think I wanted you to die that night!" Antares said. "It was what you wanted. Our agreement prevented me from going against your wishes if you must know the truth. It pains me to tell you that you have such power over me, but there you have it. I cannot refuse you anything. I can argue with you. I can attempt to persuade you otherwise, but if you cannot be persuaded, I must do as you ask.

"As for the Dark Lord, I cannot believe you would betray us. You would die first. It is your safety that truly concerns me."

"Who knows of this, Antares? Why did my father keep this from me?"

"Only the elders know. Your father was not told of it. We found it safer for your ancestors if few knew of this. We have decided to make an exception in your case, Sollie. The Dark Lord knows. He has found out our secret. He will stop at nothing to take you. You must be careful, Sollie."

Suddenly, Solomon's thoughts held the memory of his father. He often thought of him in the moments before battle or in the quiet hours of the night. He could see his face as plainly, as if he stood before him. Thoughts of his father's death brought tears to his eyes even now. He would never forget the day Augustine came to tell him of it. Somehow, he had accepted the death of his father. Jonah had died in battle as Riders often did, and yet, the death of Bess and the people of her village had nearly destroyed him. What power did the Dark Lord have over him? Could he be forced to betray his people?"

He was still considering these things when Ephraim stood to address the Brotherhood and the Dragons.

"The Brotherhood has discussed the plight of Anduin during the last two days. We have spent much time on this matter. You all know I feel it is in our best interests to face the enemy in Anduin while the other races are still free to fight at our side. We cannot spare all of our number, but perhaps some will volunteer to go if our allies, the Dragons, agree it is wise to do so. Have the Dragons reached a decision regarding Anduin?"

Vega spoke for the Dragons now. Traditionally, the First Rider's Dragon spoke for them all. His eyes glowed eerily in the flickering light as he turned his head to look at each of the Riders and their Dragons before he spoke. "We have discussed this matter at great length," he growled. "We Dragons feel the lives of a few Humans, a race whose lives are so fleeting in any case, are of very little value to the Elves who dwell here in the mountains. Indeed, one must wonder what value their puny race is to any of the Elven races."

Solomon's hopes fell as he listened to Vega's words. He recalled Antares had voiced the very same feelings on their way back to the Hall. Evidently, the rest of the Dragons felt the same.

"Still," Vega continued, "it does seem the Dark Lord would dearly like us to remain here in the mountains. Antares and I have flown a scouting mission. He has left a few Goblins to harass us here while the remainder of his forces, those who have not already done so, move by the cover of darkness ever northward. Even the Myoti mass in that general direction and they also fly by night as if wishing to hide their movements from us.

"We are agreed half of our number could be spared from our duties here. Some do not wish to leave these mountains. They are our home as well as yours and we would not leave our lands vulnerable. However, some of us are prepared to join with the Humans of Anduin if it is the wish of our Riders. The war against the forces of the Dark Lord has begun. He has sent his forces against those he feels are weakest and therefore most easily taken. We shall see how willing the Humans are to risk their lives to remain free of the Dark Lord's rule. We do not want to be the last to join in. We want to be one of the first. No part of our world, even that inhabited by Humans, should fall under the control of the evil that must, even now, be at Anduin's very gates. If the Riders are determined to go, then there will be Dragons to carry them."

Ephraim pulled Solomon into the center of the gathering. "What do you say now, Solomon?" he said, the medallion of the Second Rider dangling from his hand. "Will you return to us as Second Rider? That seems to be the wish of all present. Can you refuse us now?"

"No, Ephraim, I cannot refuse," he said simply.

There was a deafening roar of approval from everyone as Ephraim placed the medallion about Solomon's neck and embraced him. "You are the best Second Rider the Brotherhood has ever known, Solomon. You always have been," he said, speaking close to Solomon's ear. "Perhaps we need to become part of the rest of our world now or be swallowed up. You have set it in motion, Sollie. I am very proud of you."

Solomon did not have a chance to answer. He did not know what to say in any case. He had set events in motion that might cost the Brotherhood dearly. He felt the weight of the medallion about his neck, much more heavily than before.

Matthew and Peter lifted Solomon to their shoulders. "Sollie!" Matthew shouted. "You have not been formally bonded to a Dragon!"

"Let me see...," he mused, pointedly ignoring Antares' eyes. "Who will bond to Solomon? He is Second Rider again. Any Dragon would be honored to have him."

"Most of the women, too!" shouted Peter. Causing all sorts of ribald comments and much laughter from the crowd.

"Dragon first, Peter. They are much less dangerous," said Matthew.

When all was said and done, Solomon bonded to Antares that night, as was expected by all present. Solomon was relieved when his fellow Riders did not bring up the question of a woman again.

They cremated Augustine's body with Dragon's fire at dawn, his ashes spread over the lake by Solomon as he led the Riders who volunteered for the task, northward toward Anduin. As he expected, there was no lack of volunteers to accompany him. Ephraim wished desperately to go, but his broken shoulder still troubled him. It would not do for the First and Second Riders both to be absent from the Hall on such a dangerous mission in any case.

After a bit of wrangling, the Riders chose nine who would accompany Solomon to Anduin. Joseph would go, of course, refusing to part from his brother. Solomon would have rather seen Holly stay in the relative safety of the mountain hall, but he chose her to go as well, failing to find a good reason to keep her from it. He did not have the right to refuse her, simply because he did not wish to see her risk her life in battle. He himself had trained her to do that very thing.

Elder Anthony, asked to be included, expressing a desire to take to the skies again and to serve as healer during the coming battle, and was gratefully accepted. Marcus' Dragon, Mira, consented to carry him, grateful to atone for her rider's treachery. Elder Sarah and her Dragon Altair asked to accompany them. Young Noah and golden Aldebaran were eager to go as well as the brothers Elijah and Peter on their Dragons Achernar and Mizar. Dragonmaster Matthew and his Dragon Sirius made nine Riders and their Dragons that would fly to Anduin under Solomon's leadership. Half would stay behind to guard their home. Solomon prayed there would be enough of them for both tasks.

## Chapter Forty

## SIEGE

Despite a summons delivered by a messenger of the king and queen, Althus spent the night on the walls of Anduin looking out at the forces massing there. Bree, Thorny and Chess roamed the walls as well, helping prepare the men of Anduin for what would be required of them when the forces surrounding Anduin finally moved against them. Althus knew the Elves were seasoned warriors. He, on the other hand, was not. Euwyn and Gilden were at his side, discussing the tactics their enemies might possibly take and the ways in which they might counter them. Althus tried to remain hopeful. He was looking at a force of over three thousand fell creatures that would soon move against the thousand or so men within the walls of Anduin capable of holding a weapon. The odds did not seem favorable.

Along with the ever-faithful Mica, Rowan was at his side at all times. He pointed out the aspects of the enemy Althus missed. He knew the weaknesses of each creature they faced and suggested ways in which they could turn them to their advantage. He looked out at the enemy as if he did not fear any of them and gave Althus the courage to do the same, at least outwardly. Inside, Althus feared the battle to come.

Dawn brought Kestrel winging to Rowan's shoulder with a message. Rowan held the tiny scrap of paper before Althus so they could read it together.

"It seems Captain Cedar has our forces in place, hidden in the foothills to the southwest of here. They will wait for the Dark Lord's forces to make their move and then attack them from behind," said Rowan, gazing off to the southwest as if he could see his Elves there, waiting.

"I do not like to think of your people risking their lives. It seems a hopeless cause, Rowan. If Anduin falls, you will need every Elf to defend your homeland," said Althus.

"Ah, but Anduin may not fall, Althus. We have a powerful Wizard on our side and perhaps the Dragon Riders as well if all goes as we hope with your friend, Solomon. I have learned never to give up, even when all seems lost. We are the hope of the future of our two lands, Althus, you and me. Some day we will rule side by side. I mean for us to be close allies. No one will have the power to conquer us if we are bound to each other in such a manner."

Althus told Rowan of the night when they pledged themselves as allies to the Dwarves and Giants and the Wizards as well as the three Elven nations.

Rowan nodded in approval. "We will see what the future holds, Althus. Such an alliance will make our world a safer place for the people of all races."

A messenger delivered a second summons from the king and queen.

Euwyn brought it to Althus and stood looking out over the wall while Althus read it.

"You must go to them sooner or later, son," he said when Althus had read the summons, angrily crumpling it into a ball before flinging it over the wall.

"I do not want to dance attendance to them, father. They hide in the castle while you and the Elves risk your lives to save their kingdom and its people."

"Althus, do not be foolish. We risk our lives to save *your* kingdom and *your* people."

"I will never be king of Anduin!" Althus shouted. "I do not wish to be king!"

"I understand you, son," Euwyn answered quietly, "but you cannot tell me you do not care for your people. I have taught you better. Some day they will need you to become their king. You are King Allen's only heir and the only one who can help these people. No one will ask you to take the kingdom from your father's hands until the proper time, Althus, but you are Prince of Anduin. The lives of your people will some day again lie in your hands as it does now. Will you leave the fate of the kingdom of Anduin to chance? Who is to say who will rule after your father if you will not? Even now, once this battle is over, will you abandon them, leaving your people's fate wholly to the king who betrayed them? Now is your chance, Althus. You can make a difference now. You have returned as Prince of Anduin. Gilden and I will see the king names you as his son. He owes you his life. He cannot deny you what is rightfully yours."

"He is not my father! *You* are my father!" Althus shouted.

"Regardless of how you feel about him, King Allen is your father!" Euwyn replied angrily. "I would give anything if you were my true son, but you are not!"

Althus clutched his head in his hands, as if Euwyn's words hurt him. "I do not wish to be like him! I cannot be like him. I could not kill my own flesh and blood." Althus was weeping now, ashamed of his weakness and terrified he was becoming as mad as King Allen.

Euwyn put his arms about Althus and held him tightly. "I never said you were anything like the man your father has become. If you were, I could not hope for you to take his place. I see myself in you always, for better or worse. Even without a Wizard's power, you have the courage and principles of my race and it is more difficult to have courage without power. You *are* my son. You will always be my son because of what I have taught you."

"I still hear the words of the prophecy in my head. Your prophecy. It was the same as that of Borgas. It says I will kill King Allen," Althus whispered against Euwyn's shoulder.

Euwyn pushed Althus back, his hands on his shoulders so he could look directly into his eyes. "You are still fretting over that idiotic prophecy? Did I not tell you prophecy is a dangerous game?  You have fulfilled the prophecy, Althus.  Think about it!   Who was the true ruler of Anduin?  Certainly not King Allen!  Borgas controlled him.  Why do you think Borgas was so eager to see you dead?  He saw his own death at the hands of the true Prince of Anduin."

"What of the dead who would rule by my side?" Althus shuddered, chilled at the thought.

Euwyn spun him about. "There," he said, pointing, "there is the frightful dead thing that will rule by your side!"  Rowan waved back and smiled at the Wizard as he pointed at him. "You cannot deny we thought he was dead and it was only Chess' quick thinking that brought him back to life."

Althus felt foolish that he had not seen it himself, since Rowan had brought up the subject of them ruling side by side some day.  He smiled back at Rowan.

"Althus, do not fear the power of kingship," Euwyn said turning him back to face him. "I will stay by your side and advise you as long as you wish it. Perhaps together we can improve the lives of your people.  Even now, as Prince of Anduin, you will be able to help them."

"But first," he continued, drawing Althus to the wall to look out over the occupied Anduin valley, "we must defeat the Dark Lord's army and then find a way to stop him from raising another.  You must also face your father and make your intentions clear to him.  He is still king of Anduin and I suspect will be for many more years."

Althus nodded, sighing in resignation, "Will you come with me?"

"I will, gladly," Euwyn answered.

## Chapter Forty-one

## THADDEUS

The palace seemed empty and cold as Euwyn and Althus trod the empty halls in the messenger's wake. Althus could see the uneasiness in the young boy's eyes as he glanced at the Wizard and the young man dressed in the uniform of the Elven patrol walking on either side of him. Their boots echoed hollowly on the bare stone floors as they passed down the corridors in silence. The youth would take a deep breath at times as if wanting to say something he could not find the courage to say. Euwyn broke the silence first. "What is your name, son?" he asked.

"Thad, sir, I mean, Thaddeus. Thaddeus Miller," he answered.

Althus smiled at the youth when he glanced uneasily in his direction.

Thad turned to look up at the Wizard. "Sir, Euwyn, I mean," he stammered.

"Just call me Euwyn, Thad. I doubt I will ever carry the title of sir unless the king has greatly changed his opinion of me," Euwyn chuckled.

"Euwyn, then. I want to thank you for saving my life. When I was younger, I mean. My mother says if it were not for you, I would have died of the fever when I was ten. She thanked you, but you were gone while I still slept and I never got the chance to thank you myself. I remember you well, and Althus, too except he was much younger at the time.

"All of Anduin is glad you have returned safely. It gives us hope, somehow." Thad's voice trailed off and he took another deep breath. "But what I would like to ask is .... Well, what gives us more to hope for is ...." He took a deeper breath and plunged on, "I heard Althus is the prince who we thought lost to us years ago! Is it true? People are saying it is so. Please tell me it is true."

Althus stopped, taken aback by the look on Thad's face. The boy's eyes searched his as if he might find the truth written there.

"What makes you think having me as your prince would be such a great thing?" Althus asked him.

"We mostly all know you. You were always with Euwyn when he came to help us. We feel like you are one of us. That cannot be a bad thing, you knowing us and all, like having a friend in the castle who can speak for us."

"Yes, Thad," Althus answered, flattered and somewhat alarmed by the young boy's faith in him, "I am your prince. Back from the dead, you might say."

Thad performed a brief capering dance of joy before leading them onward, grinning from ear to ear. Althus could not help but smile at Thad's enthusiasm until he thought of the danger facing even this innocent child from the enemy laying siege to Anduin. Thad announced them to the guards at the doors of the king's chambers and stood at attention as they entered, as if he intended to be there when they were finished. Euwyn allowed Althus to precede him into the King Allan's chambers, choosing to walk a step behind. He would stand close to his foster son, but Althus would have to learn to speak for himself before the king if he would help the people of Anduin.

The king turned from gazing out the window as Althus entered and stepped closer, studying him. "I am told you are my son and Prince of Anduin," he said. "I see no reason for Queen Maris to lie to me in this matter. How she has kept you a secret from me for nearly twenty years is a mystery, although I would suspect Euwyn's hand in this."

Euwyn bowed his head in acknowledgment, but did not speak.

"I see a strong resemblance I did not see before. Tell me, young Althus, what would you ask of me, if I were truly your father? Would you take my kingdom from me? If what my queen says is true, then I have certainly wronged you. You must hate me. What would you have me do to atone for my sins?"

Althus looked at the king coldly. "I do not want your kingdom, sire. My fondest wish would be to live as I always have in the stone tower with Euwyn."

"He has turned you against me, then?" the king said. He sighed as if he were weary, turning back to gaze out the window.

"If not for Euwyn I would still be on the city walls planning the defense of your kingdom! I have no time to play games with you, your majesty. Your kingdom, your people are in peril! Because of your refusal to see what Lord Gilden left his own people to warn you of, they face this army unprepared. Say what you will to me and then I ask that you let me be!" Althus shouted, losing patience. "Are my feelings toward you your only concern? Are you truly so shallow? If so, then you have little to worry about. I have no feelings for you! None at all!"

Althus turned away as if to go, but the king grasped his arm to detain him. The look in Althus eyes as he turned back to him caused the king to remove his hand hastily. Euwyn noted that Althus looked more like a king than the true king did at that moment.

King Allen collapsed into a chair, his head in his hands. "I have been a fool, Althus. I could have had a son who loved me, a son I could have loved in return. I chose instead a foul sham of a Wizard who promised me power I never held. The power was his from the moment I agreed to wear his stone about my neck. Forgive me, I cannot undo what I have done!"

Althus' face softened, but he did not move from where he stood. "You will have a chance to regain the love and respect of your people. It will not be an easy task, but Anduin is a rich kingdom. You and your Wizard regularly levied and collected heavy taxes in the past few years. Where have they gone? At least I do not see the palace bathed in luxury. I cannot accuse you of squandering it on gold and riches to adorn this place, but children should not go hungry in such a land, rich in resources. *You* must find a way to remedy the problems in your kingdom.

"I have other matters to which I must attend. I cannot rest until the Dark Lord is defeated and I will not stop here if by some chance your kingdom survives this siege. If you can find a way to make this kingdom what it should be, then I may forgive you if only for Euwyn's sake, as he seems to wish it. As for thinking of you as my father, it is too late. Euwyn is the only father I have ever known and the only one I will ever need."

"I hear you, Althus," the king said. "The queen has spoken the same words in my ear. She said I could win you by helping your people. I see she is right, as usual. There is one thing I can do for you. I will proclaim your name to the people as Prince of Anduin so none will doubt your claim, and I will not interfere with your wishes in the matter of Anduin's defense. You have my blessing to do what you must to defend Anduin. If you wish for me to ride into battle either at your side or as the least of your men, you need only ask."

"I do not wish to see your face until I have settled matters with the Dark Lord's army. If we win this battle, I will seek your counsel on what will be done next. If we lose, I will not live to trouble you further, but I fear life without me will not be pleasant, even so."

"I shall stay out of your sight if that is your wish." King Allen said.

Althus nodded in agreement and abruptly left the chamber. Euwyn followed after one last glance at King Allen. He sat staring at nothing as if he were digesting the words Althus spoke to him. "Well," thought Euwyn, "it is a start."

Thad fell in behind them as soon as they left the king's quarters, trotting to keep up with them as Althus swept through the halls, his Elven cloak billowing behind, Euwyn at his side easily pacing him.

"You are still angry," Euwyn said.

"Yes."

"You have every right to be."

"Thank you, father."

"Will you see your mother before you go?" Euwyn asked cautiously.

Althus rounded on him, a look of frustration on his face. It disappeared at Euwyn's look as suddenly as it appeared. He sighed in resignation. "I suppose I should."

Thad was dancing before them like a puppy. "I know where she is! She is in the garden waiting for you. I was supposed to bring you to her, but you looked so angry I was afraid to say so."

Althus laughed at him and ruffled his shaggy head. "I am sorry, Thad. I did not mean to frighten you. Lead on, messenger."

They found the queen waiting in the gardens as Thad had promised. He left them with the queen and went to play in a nearby fountain, pretending he was not listening.

Queen Maris embraced Althus, who tried to respond as he should. He had spent too many years thinking of himself as the queen's subject to think of himself as her beloved son so quickly. He supposed it would come more easily to him as time went on. He was truly glad to see her. He noticed she smiled readily even though her eyes were troubled. She would be worrying over the fate of Anduin. Her heart was ever with her people. She remarked with some asperity that Althus still wore his Elven uniform and offered to find him more appropriate garb. Althus refused politely. Somehow, the uniform he had now worn for so long seemed a comfort to him. He could not give it up yet. He would soon wear Anduin black and silver as Crown Prince, but not yet. He would wear Gilden's green and gold for luck until Anduin was safe. The queen asked to know what had passed between Althus and the king and Althus gave a brief account of their meeting. The queen seemed satisfied and they were soon on their way back to the walls of the city.

Thad seemed intent on following them until Althus turned him back toward the palace.

"I would like to stay with you," the boy said softly as Euwyn bent to speak to him.

"You are Ryder's son, are you not?" Euwyn asked gently.

Thad nodded.

Althus realized that this boy had just lost his father to the Myoti that had attacked Tristan the previous morning.

"Then your mother needs you now. We will see you later, Thad," said Euwyn, pushing him back toward the palace.

"Thad?" said Althus.

Thad turned with a hopeful look.

"Will you keep an eye on the horses for me? We left them in the stables and I would like to know they are cared for properly. I remember your father telling me how good you are with horses. I need to know they are safe."

Thad nodded, a grin spreading across his face.

"And look after the queen as well," he called after him.

"I will!" Thad shouted as he headed back to the palace at a run. Althus could not help but wonder how many sons would lose their fathers before the fate of Anduin was decided.

Φ          Φ          Φ

Drums sounded beyond the walls when Althus and Euwyn rejoined Mica and the Elves. Euwyn and Gilden conferred for a moment before Gilden took Mica, Chess and Thorny off to patrol the walls. Euwyn, Rowan and Bree stood watching their father and brothers depart.

"I do not like the sound of those drums," Rowan said. "Perhaps they are just an attempt to instill fear in the men on the walls. I hope that is all. Still, I do not like the sound of them."

The look on the Elf's face made Althus shiver as Rowan continued to stare out over the valley below. It seethed with a mass of dark forms, changing shape like fouled oil on water, stirred from beneath.

"I wonder where the wraith that inhabited Borgas' body has fled." Bree said as if to herself as much as to Althus or her brother.

"I wish I knew, Bree. We will find out in time. He has not left this place. Of that, I am certain. He is out there, somewhere, in command of this army." Rowan's voice was as cool as his expression. Althus wished he felt as brave as the Elves appeared. The drums and Rowan's concern put a knot in his stomach.

"There!" Rowan was pointing at something beyond Althus' vision. Suddenly, he was running along the wall, shouting for the men to arm themselves with torches and pikes. Althus still could not see what threatened, but he did not doubt Rowan's warning. He helped light torches even though the sun had barely passed its zenith and passed pikes to those armed otherwise. When Rowan stopped to look out over the wall, Althus did the same and then wished he had not. There were creatures headed toward the walls. They appeared to be gigantic spiders, large enough for Althus to stand upright beneath them

"Will they breach the walls, Rowan?" he asked, trying to keep the panic from his voice.

"There will be no need for them to breach the walls, Althus. They will climb them as easily as any spider of normal size climbs a wall. Their bite is deadly," Rowan answered grimly.

Althus' hands were suddenly slick with sweat as he gripped his pike. Bree stood at his side, a torch in each hand. He wanted to shout at her to run, but he could not make his voice obey him. He gritted his teeth to keep them from chattering as he watched the first of the huge black creatures scuttle up the wall.

Rowan's voice cut through the din. "Aim for their undersides! Do not let them cross the wall top and enter the city!" Rowan was quick as lightning with his pike, sending three of the creatures backward off the wall, their entrails spilling from them before Althus had dealt with one. Bree held them off with her torches, shoving them at the creatures' eyes until Althus could dispatch them. His arms soon ached from the weight of them as he heaved them back. He could hear the shouts of the men at his side and saw flashes of blue to his right where Euwyn was dashing along the wall, accounting for many more than his share of the beasts.

Thanks to Euwyn, it was over in less than an hour, the beasts mindlessly scuttling over the walls where the defenders of Anduin slew them and threw them back. There seemed no strategy to their attack. They moved as one mass until every one of them had died at the end of a pike or by Euwyn's hand. Men who were stung by the creatures fell dead where they stood. There was no saving them. Death took them the moment the venom touched them. Althus tried not to think how many children the twelve dead left behind. Tristan appeared at his shoulder to tell him that, thanks to Rowan's warning they had fared very well against the creatures. Althus did not feel fortunate.

None had reached the city within the walls except one and Chess accounted for that creature. Althus soon found what price the Elves paid for that good fortune for Mica came running along the wall to fetch Euwyn with word the beast Chess killed within the walls of Anduin had stung Gilden as he pulled others from its path.

They found Chess cradling his father in his arms with Thorny trying to keep Gilden from injuring himself on the rough cobbles of the street as seizures racked his body. Euwyn's hands sought the wound in Gilden's thigh. He murmured an incantation while the Elf lord's children watched anxiously. Althus watched Gilden's eyes at first clouded with pain, gradually close as his seizures ceased and his body relaxed. The anxious look that remained on Euwyn's face did not allow him to take any comfort in the peace that followed. Edmund, the castle physician arrived with a litter at once. He was obviously nearby, tending to the wounded. He and Captain Manton carried Gilden to the rooms he occupied in the palace, Euwyn pacing anxiously at his side. Althus was surprised to find Bree, Rowan, Thorny and Chess still with him when he regained the top of the wall.

He drew Bree aside. "You and your brothers should be with your father, Bree," he said.

She shook her head, her eyes bright with tears. "Father would want us here at your side. To leave you would be to betray him. Euwyn will care for him. If Euwyn cannot save him, then he is beyond hope. I have left Kestrel with him so Euwyn can send word to us if need be."

Althus could think of nothing more to say. There was no comfort for her or her brothers. He could not protect her from worry. He held her in his arms as he studied the Dark Lord's army.

The drums continued through the night. He could see a harried look forming on the faces of the men about him. The sound was relentless, assaulting their hearing and giving them no peace.

A ray of hope arrived with the dawn. Eagle arrived with a message from Bull, spiraling down from a great height while Bree watched. She shared the message with Althus and her brothers while Eagle stood preening himself on the wall with the morning sun warming his back. Eagle's cleverness greatly impressed the common soldiers of Anduin. He had obviously flown at a great height to avoid the notice of the army encamped below. When Bree penned an answer, he spiraled upward until Althus could no longer see him before heading off southward toward the mountains. Bull informed them Granite's army lay hidden in the foothills to the southeast of Anduin, ready to attack the Dark Lord's flank from that direction when his army finally turned its attention totally toward Anduin.

Althus clearly remembered refusing help from the Dwarves whose numbers were already depleted by the battle for Stonehaven. He also remembered the stubborn light in Granite's eyes when Althus refused him.

Mica did not seem at all surprised to hear his father's army lay hidden in the hills to their southeast, spoiling for a fight. He looked off over the wall to where his father would lay in hiding and said, "We'll give 'em what fer until they don't know which way is up!" This was followed by a cheer for the Dwarves from the men of Anduin that put a grim smile on Mica's face for the rest of the day.

Althus' thoughts wandered to the night spent with Bull's wife and children. He risked all of that to fight for Anduin. Althus could not help wondering if he and his people were worthy. Would Bree and her brothers sacrifice their father to Anduin's cause as well? A message from Euwyn was not encouraging, but said Gilden still fought for his life.

Althus prayed for all of them as he gazed over the walls of the city of Anduin.

## Chapter Forty-two

## BATTLE

On the morning of the third day after he had left the wall, Euwyn rejoined them. His haggard look told Althus at once all was not well. The Wizard slumped against the wall and stared at his hands as Althus took a seat beside him on the cold stone.

"I cannot seem to hold him, Althus," he said softly. "His life trickles away like water through my fingers. He will not live more than another day, perhaps two." He rubbed his palm against his forehead and shut his eyes.

"There is no way to save him and I cannot watch him die any longer. I have left him in Elinor's care."

Euwyn lapsed into silence as Althus looked up to discover Bree, Rowan, Chess and Thorny gathered before him, hoping for news of their father. He looked up at them helplessly while they looked at Euwyn in stunned silence. Rowan took a seat on the other side of Euwyn as his sister and brothers moved off to comfort each other.

"Euwyn," he said softly, laying his hand on the Wizard's where it rested on his knee.

Euwyn started as if he had dozed off and opened his eyes to look at Rowan sadly.

"You have done all you can, Euwyn. Rest here for a while. We will need your strength soon," said Rowan.

He drew Althus away to where Captain Manton stood waiting for them, his face grave.

"They wait for us to weaken, Althus," Rowan said. "Food and water grow scarce. Your men grow weary and they will soon go hungry. The drums grow louder and more incessant, if that is possible, making tempers short."

"What we are trying to say is, whatever strength the men have left should be spent fighting the enemy, not one another," Captain Manton said. "Our situation will soon become even more desperate as we try to keep order when food and water are scarce."

Althus could not suppress the fierce smile that crossed his face as he grasped what they were suggesting. "We attack, then," he said simply. He was beyond fear now. Gilden's impending death made him angry beyond reason. This evil had hurt the Elves beyond healing. Suddenly his desire for revenge outweighed any other consideration.

With Althus' permission granted, Rowan and Manton went their separate ways to prepare for an attack that would commence at dawn the next day. Bree sent Kestrel out with word to the Elven army and then to Bull who lay in wait with the Dwarves.

Althus stood atop the wall, his hand about the Dragon scale that hung glistening about his neck and wondered where Solomon was. He wondered if the pendant would give him any clues to his friend's whereabouts, but if it held such powers, he could not discern them.

He could no longer hope Solomon would return in time. Something had delayed him. He sent a prayer to the Creator that he and Antares were safe whatever skies they flew. The knowledge that Solomon would have been in Anduin already if he were able made Althus fear for him.

He turned away from the wall to find something with which to occupy himself until dawn. He spent some time sharpening his sword and testing his bow, adding to his supply of arrows. Bree gave him Elven arrows, saying they would fly truer than any others. Althus looked for Rowan among the milling soldiers, but he could not find him anywhere. Chess and Thorny joined him for a meager meal. Chess ate in uncharacteristic silence while Thorny attempted to make conversation, but his gaze kept wandering to the castle where their father lay dying. Althus was grateful when Mica appeared at his side to keep him company. He spent a good amount of time showing him how to sharpen the broadsword he carried, finally remembering that Dwarves made some of the finest weapons in the world at their forges and although few carried the swords they made, they certainly knew how to sharpen them. Mica hung on his words as if he had never held a weapon in his life until Althus looked at him and laughed. Mica laughed as well.

"I guess I jest needed ta hear a friendly voice, Althus," he said. "You coulda told me anythin and I'd listen to ya."

Althus realized he needed the same.

He and Mica slept for a while atop the wall, but for most of the night, they talked to each other on a myriad of subjects until the approaching dawn lightened the eastern sky.

Rowan met Althus and his sister and brothers at the main gates of the city at first light. The horses were with him, arrayed in fine Elven mail that glowed even in the faint light of the coming dawn. The Elves seemed to take it as a matter of course. Althus was not so sure he wanted to ride his friend Gust into battle.

"They are war horses, Althus," Rowan informed him. "That is what they are born and bred for. Did you not wonder why they were bred for agility and endurance and not for speed?"

"Please, Althus," Bree begged, "Gust can keep you safe. Trust him to carry you."

"I trust him, Bree," Althus replied. "I only hope I do not endanger him. I have never fought from the back of a horse."

"Trust him," Bree repeated.

"I do and I will," Althus answered, settling himself on Gust's back. Gust danced before the gates as if eager to face the enemy.  He snorted and tossed his head, keeping Althus busy as he held him in check.  Althus knew Gust felt his uneasiness.  The horse played with him to keep his mind occupied and his fear from overpowering him.  He looked to where Euwyn sat astride Mars wishing he could look as coolly confident as the Wizard and the Elves.

Φ          Φ          Φ

Rowan glanced down at the young Dwarf standing at Argent's side.  He doubted young Mica had ever found himself facing a battle such as this.  He was certainly no coward.  Rowan doubted a coward existed in the entire Dwarven kingdom.  He had outfitted Mica with a helm and a coat of mail, but the Dwarf refused to exchange the heavy broadsword Althus had given him for a lighter Elven blade.  Rowan bent down to speak to him.

"Mica, would you do me the honor of riding into battle behind me?  I would have you guard my back."

Mica gave him a fierce smile as he accepted Rowan's hand, climbing up behind him.  "I kin see better from here.  All's I can see down there is men's chests and horses' bellies.  I can't say I'll stay behind ye fer long, but I'll ride with ye until we reach the thick of it."

Rowan laughed.  Such fierceness in so small a package.  Still, he wondered if the end of the battle would find Mica still alive.  He would look out for him if he could manage it.

Φ          Φ          Φ

Althus' heart lurched in his chest as the gates opened and they thundered out into the open followed by Captain Manton and his foot soldiers and a horde of undisciplined volunteers.  A howl went up from the enemy forces as the Anduin army massed before the gates, fanning out between the walls of the city and the enemy that surrounded them.  There was stillness as the armies faced each other across the intervening ground.

A chill ran up Althus' spine as he surveyed the creatures of the Dark Lord's army from a closer vantage.  The majority were Orcs and Goblins.  Most were afoot with some mounted on Nasua, both riders and mounts drooling in anticipation.  Many rode unfamiliar creatures he did not care to examine too closely.  Too many limbs or heads, a multitude of eyes or mouths marked them as the Dark Lord's most evil and twisted creations.

No light escaped the dark horde.  No weapon reflected the rising sun.  No ornament glinted or shone.  All was black as night save the yellowed fangs and red or yellow eyes of the creatures they faced.

Althus wondered if his fear showed on his face.  Did his men look as frightened as he felt? He did not dare look at their faces. His deep desire to avenge Gilden's death still burned in his breast, but it was no longer alone. The knot had returned to his stomach.

He was their leader, Prince of Anduin. As he considered the army facing him he felt it was a very small thing indeed. Manton and Tristan reined their horses in on either side of him.

"I do not like it," the Captain growled. Why do they wait? I would rather they made the first move, but there they sit. What are they waiting for?"

"They want to draw us as far from our own walls as possible," Althus said. "Without the walls at our backs we are more easily surrounded."

"You have a point there, Althus," Manton agreed. "Still, it is unusual for such creatures to show such restraint. It is possible they wish to draw us away from our walls, but I suspect their motives are more complex. Still, either we charge them or we turn tail and run. I do not like the thought of turning my back on them. What do you say, Althus?"

"I say we attack."

"At your signal then, my prince."

Althus stood fast until he was sure all had taken their places. Gust stood as still as stone now, his eyes upon the enemy. Althus drew the sword of Anduin, its blade flashing crimson as he raised it to the rising sun. With a roar of defiance, he swung the blade downward and Gust pounded toward the waiting horde.

The forces clashed with a mighty sound like thunder, more than a thousand weapons met, steel against steel. The first swing of his sword sent the head of a huge Orc rolling in the trampled grass. Althus lost all sense of time from that point on as the Dark Lord's creatures closed about him.

He was grateful for Gust who protected him from those he could not face as he turned this way and that, hacking at the creatures that flung themselves at him mindlessly. Protected by the Elven mail he wore, Gust wheeled and reared, placing himself between Althus and danger time after time accepting blow after blow without hesitation.

Althus wondered how his friends fared. Were the Elves still standing amongst their foes? Had the Dwarves and Giants and the Elves of the Dark Forest joined the fight? He could not spare the time to look for allies or even to look for his friends.

The skies darkened above him, but he dared not look away from the fighting. Were clouds rolling in? "The Dragons," he thought suddenly. His heart leapt until he heard the awful shrieks of the creatures darkening the sky above him. Myoti, he realized, the cold knot in his stomach clenching even tighter. Now he knew why their enemies wished to draw them from the safety of the walls. They were in the open now and surrounded. The Myoti would have all the space they needed to maneuver above them as well as behind them. He heard the cries of his men as the horde of foul creatures attacked. The screams of his men and the shrieking of the Myoti filled his ears until he thought he would go mad. He managed to kill the first bird that tore at him, but the skies were dark with them. He knew there were many more to come.

He tried to shut out the cries of terror and pain echoing about him as razor sharp beaks and talons slashed at his men. He could not help but listen for the voices of his friends above the din. The body of an Elf fell from the sky, nearly on top of him. He fought to keep his eyes focused on the enemies who surrounded him, but he could not help glancing at the fallen Elf. It was Maple, his body torn almost beyond recognition. Althus sat paralyzed by the horror of it. Gust shook his head, jerking at the reins in Althus' hands until he came to his senses. It seemed they would all die here on this bloody field, left as carrion for the Myoti.

He pressed on. He saw no other options. The Myoti continued to prey on them from above as they faced the foul creatures on the ground. His forces seemed doomed. A roaring filled his ears until he wanted to drop his sword and cover them to shut it out.

Suddenly, it seemed as if a blast furnace opened at his back. Enemies fell about him. Those who could, scrambled to their feet and ran from him. He stared after them in astonishment until he heard his name called from above in a voice loud and deep enough to vibrate him to the very soles of his feet. Glittering green scales passed above him as Antares swept back into the battle. Solomon had given him a moment to breathe and look about. Masses of Myoti still filled the skies, but within their seething mass, there were Dragons of all colors. He caught sight of a sleek white Dragon doubling back on itself to catch a Myoti in midair whose intended target was Bree. "Thank you, Holly," he breathed. He heard cheers from his men as they fought with renewed hope.

Φ　　　　　　　Φ　　　　　　　Φ

Rowan was pleased to find Mica at his back for much of the battle. He slew almost as many of the enemy from there as Rowan, his reach limited by his size, but giving a good accounting of himself, even so.

They parted company only when Mica caught sight of an enemy he could not bear to lose. An enemy he wished to punish more than all the others.

"Magool!" he shouted as he leapt from Argent's back to face the huge half Orc. The ugly creature turned with a look of astonishment and then, a look of fiendish pleasure.

"You!" he shouted. "Thought you dead long ago. I'll take care of that now." He paused as if a thought had suddenly occurred to him. "How did you get here? Thought you little vermin were locked up tight in your warren?"

"Stonehaven's free now, Magool. Me father's brought the Dwarves ta fight fer Anduin. Euwyn's free and here as well. Yer days as our tormenter is over. Look about ya, Magool. I come ta tell ya Althus, the Prince of Anduin is returned. I speak fer him now. I fight fer him. The Dragon Riders fight fer him. The Wood Elves fight fer him. The Giants fight fer him. The days of you and yer kind are numbered. If I wasn't about ta kill ya I'd tell ya to take that message to yer boss!"

Magool did look about him. He could see for himself that Mica spoke the truth. His only hope was to kill the Dwarf quickly and escape. He swung his sword, unexpectedly, aiming to take the Dwarf's head from his shoulders and be done with him, but Mica was deceptively quick. He met the blade with his own and ducked away.

Rowan could not free his attention entirely from the foes about him. He spared a glance in Mica's direction, wondering if he should interfere. He was not so sure he *could* interfere while so totally engaged in battle himself. He nearly lost his own head to an Orc sword as he watched Mica parry the blow meant to remove his.

Mica stood his ground, parrying and ducking the wild swings Magool aimed in his direction. The longer Mica stood before him, the angrier the Orc became. One so much smaller than he should not be able to thwart him. Mica swung at him, connecting a solid blow to his side, his powerful swing opening a gash even through the Orc's protective mail.

"Ya don't think we'd use our best iron ta make protection fer an Orc, do ya?" Mica laughed as Magool regarded the blood flowing from the wound with dismay.

Magool's anger reached the boiling point. His swings became wilder. Mica was grinning fiercely as he parried blow after blow, managing to open a few more holes through the mail Magool so depended on to keep him safe. Mica would have finished him if he had not fallen over the legs of a dead goblin as he danced backward from one of the Orc's wild swings. Rowan watched in horror as the Orc, grinning evilly, raised his sword overhead to finish him.

Antares, whether by chance or design, was now making a pass close enough to the ground to ruffle the horses' manes with the wind of it. Magool, glancing upward, distracted by the massive Dragon passing overhead, was rewarded with a blast of fire that served to back him up a step.

Mica, coming back to his feet with roar, took advantage of the opportunity presented him and stuck his broadsword through a hole conveniently made through Magool's mail on a previous strike, extending that hole to include the Orc's lungs and his black heart.

He found Rowan at his side, smiling down at him as he withdrew his blade. He rejoined the Elf on Argent's back.

"Hope ya didn't miss me at yer back, Rowan. I had some business ta attend to," he said.

"You were sorely missed," Rowan said, "but I managed for a time without you."

"I might hafta have a word with that interferin' Dragon later."

Rowan's laughter brought an answering grin from the Dwarf.

Φ        Φ        Φ

The voices of the Dwarves and the Elven Patrol were ahead of Althus now. When the allies met on the field, the battle would be nearly over. Althus was amazed as he turned back into the main battle to see the sun had passed its zenith and was beginning to sink toward the western horizon. The numbers of Myoti were thinning and the Dragons turning some of their attention to the battle on the ground.

There could be no wholesale slaughter there as there was in the skies. They had to be more careful as friends mixed among the foes on the battlefield. Althus caught glimpses of the red coats of the Dragon Riders joining the fighting afoot, reminded of Antares' words of warning regarding the deadly ferocity of Solomon. Evidently, all of the Riders shared that trait. He was relieved to see Holly atop a small hill, still astride her white Dragon with Bree astride Moon, standing in the safety of their shadow. Both had sheathed their swords in favor of their bows, none of the enemy horde anxious to approach the white Dragon close enough for swordplay.

Chess and Thorny were still mounted and fighting as well. An Orc nearly beheaded Althus as he looked about desperately for Rowan. When Gust wheeled to deflect the Orc's swing, he caught sight of Rowan atop Argent in the act of lifting Mica onto Argent's back. The Elven patrol surrounded them, shielding them while Mica and Rowan paused to catch their breath.

More often now, Althus fought beside Dwarves or Elves. Bull towered close for a moment and then was lost in the melee. Althus deflected a blow meant for Sailor from the Elven patrol and was swept away before he could hear the words Sailor shouted to him. He did see the direction the Elf was pointing, however.

Throughout the day, he caught flashes of blue out of the corner of his eye or from a distance. It was not until mid afternoon when Sailor pointed him out that he caught sight of Euwyn standing atop a small rise some distance away. The enemy had pulled back from that small patch of ground, giving Euwyn a wide berth, the ground about him littered with the smoking carcasses of the enemy. Gust pushed his way doggedly to Euwyn's side. Althus could see the toll the battle had taken on the Wizard. He looked exhausted and bewildered. Looking in every direction as if searching desperately for something.

"Althus!" he shouted above the noise of the battle around them, some of the weariness fading from his face. "You are a welcome sight. I feared you might have fallen."

"I had him, Althus," he panted. Shifting his grip on his ebony staff, his eyes searching the battlefield. "I had the wraith that inhabited the Wizard Borgas. He has taken another form, one of the Dark Lord's foul creations. Its body was like a Goblin's, but taller than all the rest. His head was a bit wolf-like, I think. I hoped to put an end to him. Evidently, he feared I would. He cannot have gotten far. We must find him and destroy him! We cannot let him escape!"

Euwyn paused to look up at a blue Dragon, passing overhead only to touch down a moment later in an area where the fighting was fiercest. "We seem to be winning this battle thanks to your friend Solomon and his people. Without them, we would have been in dire straits."

Althus had to agree. The appearance of the masses of Myoti had meant certain defeat for Anduin's army. Solomon and his Riders turned the tide of battle in their favor. Althus was anxious for it to end so he could find Solomon and thank him and the other members of the Dragon Riders who had come as well to risk their lives in the battle for Anduin.

"There!" Euwyn shouted, wheeling Mars about and sending him plunging away over the littered battleground. Gust needed no urging to send him thundering after. Rowan appeared as if by magic at Euwyn's side, mirroring Althus as he overtook the Wizard. Euwyn was intent on his quarry, barely giving them a second glance as they did their best to clear a path for him through the battle still raging about them.

A sudden deafening boom stopped Euwyn in his tracks so abruptly, Rowan and Althus nearly lost track of him. All eyes, friend and foe alike, looked to the source of the sound. Althus took advantage of the sudden pause in the fighting to follow Euwyn's gaze upward. A creature appeared overhead as if the sky were a piece of cloth, torn by some unseen hand to allow its passage. At first Althus thought it might be a Dragon, but although it flew like a Dragon and there were many kinds of Dragons, Althus could not believe this hideous creature was in any way related to the glittering jewel-like Dragons of the Brotherhood of Dragon Riders. The creature was as black as night, as black as the army they fought against so desperately. It was as if something cut a hole in the sky in a shape vaguely like that of a Dragon. Althus could see the great length of its talons and the even greater length of its limbs. Unlike their Dragon allies, it flew with its limbs hanging, ready to grasp and rip apart whatever came within its reach. A horn sounded ahead of them and the creature shrieked as if in answer.

"A demon," Euwyn shouted. "Summoned from the bowels of the earth. It is sometimes called a cold Dragon, although its relation to a Dragon is distant. It breathes no fire, nor does it need to. The power for its summoning will have weakened the wraith we seek. If we can reach him before he recovers we may be able to defeat him."

"What of this demon, Euwyn?" Rowan asked. "How will it be defeated?"

As if in answer, a green Dragon lifted into the sky followed by a white and a blue. A golden Dragon followed soon after.

"The Creator help you and protect you and your brothers, Solomon," Althus prayed as he watched the huge green Dragon he knew to be Antares overtaking the monstrosity that fouled the skies above them. They pressed onward toward their quarry.

## Chapter Forty-three

## WRAITH

Solomon watched the cold Dragon slip from the bowels of the earth, summoned to hunt the skies above. He looked to Joseph and Holly to see if they were aware of its presence. They stared at the monstrosity cleaving the skies above as he did, a look of mingled horror and disgust on their faces. They lifted from the ground as one with Noah and Aldebaran close behind.

Antares was the first to reach their quarry, racing to intercept it as it dove to attack the forces of Anduin. He blasted it with fire, drawing a deafening shriek of pain and rage from the creature. Polaris was close behind, slipping beyond the creature and turning agilely about to drive it back toward the others. Holly put an arrow in its eye as Polaris turned again, narrowly avoiding its slashing claws. Procyon and Aldebaran worked in concert, slashing at the creature's wings as it dove to avoid them.

It was Aldebaran and Noah who lingered too close. The black Dragon twisted as Aldebaran slashed at its wings one last time, slashing back, tearing the golden Dragon's wing with one set of talons and opening a gash in his neck with the other. Solomon watched in horror, faltering for a moment as Aldebaran rolled over and plummeted toward the ground, bearing Noah with him. Antares' roar of rage brought him back to his senses and to the battle abruptly.

Antares made another pass, his powerful wings interrupting his dive long enough to send another fiery blast, singeing the creature as it twisted in mid air to avoid him. His second pass took him past the creature's blind side where Holly's arrow still protruded from the creature's eye.

Polaris dove beneath the creature, disappearing from sight as Holly sought a vulnerable place to stick another arrow. The creature's shrieking told Solomon she had found her mark. He held his breath until Polaris turned swiftly, sliding away from the creature's talons once again.

On the opposite side, Procyon managed to grasp the creature's wing in his powerful jaws and held on doggedly, wings beating rapidly in an effort to keep the wing stretched to its full length and avoid the creature's flailing talons. He ripped a respectable hole as the creature struggled to escape him. Antares flew in to grasp the opposite wing, effectively trapping the creature between them while Holly put another arrow in the demon's remaining eye.

Antares and Procyon played tug-of-war with the creature until the wing Procyon held tore completely through, spinning the demon out of control. Joseph watched in dismay as it spun toward Antares. The last thing Solomon saw before he was struck from Antares' back was a flailing black tail headed straight for him.

Φ                    Φ                    Φ

Althus, fascinated by the battle in the skies above him, could barely keep his eyes from it as the Dragons worked in concert to defeat the demon. He glanced skyward often, and again just as Solomon fell. Antares roared in frustration, still entangled in the grasp of the dying demon. Holly and Joseph sped toward him, but Althus could see they would not reach him in time. He cried out as Solomon plummeted earthward. Euwyn turned quickly, but too late as well. Solomon fell from sight and Althus forced his mind back to the battle, choking back tears. Euwyn turned back to his search for the wraith, looking more determined than ever.

The creature stood as tall as a giant, its limbs as skeletal and sinewy as those of a Goblin, its skull-like head bearing the features of a hideously deformed wolf. Its deeply set eyes shining red from beneath a greasy mane of matted hair. It smiled a twisted, ugly smile as, with a grasping gesture in his direction, it drew the falling Rider through the air and into its claws.

Solomon opened his eyes. There were cries and shrieks all about him as he faced the creature and, amid the sounds of struggle, familiar voices and blue fire.

"Let him go, wraith!" he heard Euwyn say. "The battle is lost for you and your foul creatures!"

It was true. Most of the Dark Lord's remaining forces had gathered about the wraith, that creature calling them to his side when he found Euwyn hunted him and the battle was all but lost. Only a few small skirmishes were occurring elsewhere on the battlefield, widely scattered, Dwarves and Elves sending those they did not kill running for their lives.

The wraith would escape the battleground by whatever means possible. The rest of the Dark Lord's creatures were expendable, their lives now spent in order that he might escape as soon as his powers, drained by the summoning of the demon, returned.

The Wizard and those that rode at his side made short work of the creatures gathered about him. This small Elf was his protection now. He would hold the Rider hostage until he could flee this place, taking the Elf with him as something to appease the Dark Lord's anger at the crushing blow the Humans of Anduin had dealt him.

The demon turned Solomon about and shook him roughly until he shut his eyes to keep them from leaving his head. When Solomon dared open them again, many of his friends and allies were standing about them, surrounding the creature that held him captive.

Euwyn pointed his staff menacingly, Althus looked on, a look of near panic on his face. An Elf he did not recognize stood with Althus, an angry, calculating look in his eyes that seemed out of place on such a fair face. Antares was there as well with Joseph and Procyon.

"Let him go!" Antares roared, echoing the Wizard's demand.

"Is he yours, then, Dragon? I would think you would be more grateful. I saved his life, you know. You were very clumsy to lose him," the creature said, shaking him in Antares' face. Solomon was surprised to hear a Human voice emanating from such a hideous creature. Those who were familiar with the Wizard, Borgas' voice recognized it as his.

"Come and get him, then, Dragon. Or do you think I might twist his head off before you reach him?" The creature set his free hand atop Solomon's head.

Solomon could feel trickles of blood running down his cheeks from where the creature's claws dug into him. Joseph made a move to rush the creature and with an idle gesture, the wraith sent him flying backward to land in a heap at Euwyn's feet. Procyon roared in anger, but did not dare attack while the wraith held Solomon. Joseph did not move again. Euwyn stepped between Joseph and the wraith, again raising his staff threateningly.

"We cannot let you escape, wraith," he said. "We will sacrifice the Rider if we must."

"Do it, then, Wizard if you truly have the courage to do such a thing. Why do you hesitate? A true Wizard would have killed this form by now. What are you waiting for?"

Euwyn's face darkened with anger. "Put Solomon down!" he roared. "Are you too cowardly to face me without him?"

"Solomon?" the creature turned Solomon about to regard him curiously, "Ah, yes. I remember Solomon. He has always been a thorn in my lord's side. He was not what I pictured when I first beheld him a year ago, the fiercest warrior among those who ride the Dragons. The last I saw of him, he was crawling on his belly and whimpering like a small child. He left quite a lot of blood behind for such a puny creature. Perhaps I can recreate the scene for your friends, Solomon."

The creature laughed, looking closely into Solomon's face as if he found Solomon amusing. "You should have become one of the Dark Lord's creatures a year ago, Elf. You would not be facing death now. You can thank Augustine and his Dragon for keeping you from the power you could have possessed."

"I do not wish for power," Solomon said, facing the creature fearlessly.

"Perhaps you are right. We found another among the Riders who greatly desired it. He was most anxious you should not return to take the medallion of Second Rider from him. I see you have done what he most feared, however, as you wear the medallion he was so proud of.

"Enough idle chatter," the wraith said abruptly. "I know your story and I know what I must do. You are missing some memories, are you not, little Elf? I will have mercy on you. I will not kill you. The Dark Lord is most anxious to have you at his side. In addition, I will give something back to you that you seem to have lost.

"I am brother to one who took great pleasure in killing your friends. Wraiths are bound closely and all know the knowledge and memories of one. How would you like to know how it feels to take the lives of those you loved? It was done very slowly and with great care, although you do not seem to recall witnessing the artistry of it now. I can share the memories with you since yours seem to be missing. You may not feel the pleasure of it, not as my brothers and I did, but I can make you hear their cries and you can know what it is to tear their limbs from their still struggling bodies. You can know the feel of their blood as it bathes you in its warmth."

Solomon's face was a mask of fear now, his eyes drawn to those of the wraith as if he could not look away. The creature's clawed hand caressed his head gently as if searching for the place that was most vulnerable. The creature laughed as Solomon struggled desperately to free himself.

Antares heard Solomon cry out to him. He knew what Solomon begged him to do. He looked at his friend for a last time and drew a deep breath, prepared to end his suffering and destroy the creature that would cause it.

Solomon's single scream of horror as the creature's claws fastened about his head pierced Althus to his heart. He watched as streams of blood began to flow down Solomon's face. He could not sit astride Gust and let this happen. Against all odds, Solomon was still alive. He could not waste this second chance to save him. Althus felt no fear, only a white-hot rage. Antares would soon turn Solomon and the creature to ash. He had to move now.

Gust sprang into action, fearlessly bearing Althus in a direct collision course with the wraith before Althus could finish the thought, as if mere thought was permission enough. His powerful strides sent great clods of turf into the air. The creature struggled to fling Althus aside as it had Joseph, but Althus wore the Dragon scale atop his mail now. It absorbed the dark powers flung his way. Althus could feel it heating, even through the Elven metal.

Gust turned aside at the last moment, hitting the creature with his shoulder and rolling past, ears pinned and teeth bared, wheeling about for another pass. Althus was encouraged to hear a shriek of pain from the wraith as it came in contact with the Elven mail Gust wore. It left a large smoking wound on the creature's hip. Unlike the Wizard's form the wraith had previously inhabited, this creature could not bear the touch of Elf-forged silver. The wraith swatted at Althus in rage as Gust danced aside, lessening the force of the creature's blow. The creature pawed at the mail Althus wore, turning his hand into a smoking ruin.

Rowan was on the move as well, circling and charging from the opposite side, harrying the distracted wraith. Althus prayed the creature was too distracted to realize the charging Elf was nearly as vulnerable as Joseph without a Dragon scale about his neck. Althus and Gust made another pass and the sword of Anduin sang through the air, severing the hand that held Solomon. The creature shrieked with anger, grasping the Second Rider medallion that hung about Solomon's neck with his remaining, ruined hand as Solomon fell, leaving the Elf struggling at the end of the chain that held it. Euwyn stepped in to finish the creature, but a curious thing was happening to the wraith. He seemed paralyzed, rooted to the ground where he stood, the medallion still grasped tightly in his hand, his eyes rolling wildly as he vibrated with power from some unseen source.

Rowan charged in once again, severing the chain with amazing accuracy, pulling Solomon safely onto Argent's back with his free arm as he fell.

Euwyn stood puzzled for a moment longer and then added his power to the mix. Moments later, the creature exploded, showering them with ash and pieces of the soil upon which it once stood.

There were a few minutes when they all stood gaping at the spot where the creature stood only moments before. There was nothing left to see, save a smoking hole in the sod. Euwyn retrieved Solomon's medallion and something else Althus recognized from the blasted ground.

Rowan still held Solomon tightly, shielding him from the flying debris, his arm pressing the smaller Elf against his chest, as the beat of Solomon's heart steadied. He could feel his ebbing fear and confusion plainly, as if the feeling of fear was one with which Solomon was unfamiliar.

"That is some medallion you wear, little friend," he said, looking down at the Elf sitting before him with deep respect.

"The medallion has no such power, at least, not that I know of," Solomon said. "I believe it must have been Augustine's Dragon scale, given to me before we left the Hall of the Dragon Riders that killed the creature. It hung beneath the medallion. Perhaps the next time I ride into battle, the Dragon scale should not lie hidden. Antares said it would protect the one who wore it, but I had no idea its touch could do that to one of the Dark Lord's creatures."

Solomon slid to the ground to kneel at Joseph's side. Euwyn was there before him and, to Solomon's great relief, Joseph was soon sitting up, holding his aching head, but not seriously injured.

Solomon looked across the field to where the golden Dragon Aldebaran and his friend Noah had fallen and was astonished to find Noah limping slowly toward them. He looked at Euwyn, who grinned back at him and winked. They would mourn Aldebaran, but with his last dying breath, and some help from Euwyn, he had managed to bring Noah safely to earth.

Althus reached for Solomon, wrapping him in a fierce embrace before his attention returned to Rowan who had swung Argent about and was looking toward Castle Anduin.

"I must go to father's side, Althus," he said softly. "He still lives. I still feel his presence. I would tell him the battle is over and Anduin is free. It will ease his passing."

Althus nodded sadly and Rowan was off. Althus saw Bree, Chess and Thorny overtake him in his gallop toward Castle Anduin.

The gates swung open as they approached. They passed a group headed by the physician, Edmund, and Elinor filing out of the gates as they swept in.

Althus turned to Euwyn, who stared after the Elves as well, a look of sadness and frustration on his weary face. "I can do no more for Gilden, my son, but there are those here who will die as well if I do not heal them."

"I know, father,"

Solomon looked up at Althus who still stood with one arm wrapped about his shoulders. "What is it, Althus? What has happened to the Elf lord? I felt a great sadness in the Elf that held me. Who is he?"

"You were rescued by Rowan, crown prince of the Dark Forest. He is Gilden's eldest, Sollie, and Gilden is dying. He was bitten by one of the Dark Lord's spiders," Althus answered sadly.

"Come, little friend, you are bleeding from a dozen places. Let Euwyn care for you."

"No!" Solomon cried, pulling away to face Althus, "if Gilden has been poisoned, Antares can help him, but we must go to him now before it is too late!"

Althus looked at Euwyn who now helped Joseph to his feet. Euwyn raised his eyebrows and shrugged.

"It is true, your majesty," Joseph said.

For a moment, Althus nearly looked about to see who Joseph was addressing.

Solomon had already leapt aboard Antares, who grumbled as he lay down for Althus to climb aboard. Althus looked into Solomon's face for reassurance as he took his hand to climb the Dragon's slick side. If only Solomon was right, he thought. If only they were not too late.

Antares took off with the same heart-stopping leap Althus remembered and they were soon winging their way toward the castle.

"Where?" Solomon asked.

"He lies high in the southwest tower."

"Is there a way down from the ramparts?"

"Yes, I have stood watch atop the tower. I can get us to Gilden's rooms from there."

"Sollie, what are you going to do for him that Euwyn could not?"

"It is what a Dragon can do for him, if he is willing, Althus. You are willing, Antares, are you not?"

The Dragon landed with a heart-stopping drop atop the tower before answering. There was barely room for him there. In order to keep his head over solid stone, his tail hung over the castle wall. Althus could hear shouting in the streets below as the population of Anduin caught sight of the Dragon atop the castle.

"I have come through a great battle nearly unscathed, Sollie. We have fought a cold Dragon, perhaps the same demon that killed your father, and we have won. Now you wish to let my blood for an Elf I do not know in any way. Still," Antares sighed as if embarked on a long oration, "he is the father of Chess and I find Chess amusing in a foolish sort of way. Have at it Elf, but do not take more than you must, and... OUCH!" the Dragon roared as Sollie stuck him near the base of his neck with his sword and caught a few drops of blood in a vial from his pack.

They did not stop to apologize to the Dragon, who continued to grumble as they ran for the door that opened onto the winding tower stairs. Althus was amazed to see that Dragon's blood was not red, but a shining, viscous substance in which colors swirled and changed, glittering in the light of the windows like liquid opal as they passed.

Althus could barely keep up with Solomon, who was more sure-footed than he on the narrow, winding stairs. Solomon nearly passed the doors to Gilden's rooms, skidding to a halt as Althus called to him. He burst into the room and found himself standing between Bree and Rowan, looking upon the Lord of the Dark Forest as he lay near death. The Elves had been singing softly, hand in hand until Solomon burst into the room. Althus entered, hard on his heels. All eyes turned toward them as Solomon held the glittering vial toward Bree.

"Please, Bree, I think this will help your father," Solomon said. "Will you give it to him?"

Bree looked from Solomon's earnest face to her brothers. Chess and Thorny looked doubtful. Rowan shrugged with a sad smile for the small Elf.

"He certainly has earned our trust," he said. "Father is dying. We have nothing to lose."

Althus noted Gilden did not give off the faint light his children did in the darkened room. Even Solomon glowed faintly through the trickles of blood that continued to run down his face. The vial of Dragon's blood added its own light to Solomon's face as well as he offered it to Bree.

Without hesitation, Bree took the vial and went to her father's side. There was no resistance from him as she gently tipped the contents of the vial down his throat a drop at a time. Solomon took Gilden's hand in his and joined in as the Elves began to sing softly once again. Solomon's gaze never left Gilden's face, his golden eyes shone as if his faith in his cure still held as the minutes passed and Gilden's breathing grew shallower. It was not until

Gilden gave one last shuddering gasp that Solomon's face began to show doubt. The elvensong ended.

Bree laid her hands on his shoulders. "You tried, Solomon. We are grateful to you. It was simply too late."

Althus was turning away, scrubbing at his tears with the tattered sleeve of his uniform when he heard Gilden take another shallow breath and then a much deeper one.

Gilden's eyes opened and he stared at Solomon, still hoping, still holding his hand tightly. His eyes shifted then to rest on Bree who stood behind Solomon, her hands still resting on the smaller Elf's shoulders.

"Who is this handsome little fellow, Bree?" he said, his voice weary, but still clear to all present. "Have you brought me a Dragon Rider? It has always been my wish to meet one."

"Indeed, I have, father. He is the greatest Rider of all," Bree said, tears of relief coursing down her face.

Gilden looked Sollie over carefully. "You should take better care of him, then, Bree. He is wounded and bleeding."

"I am sorry, my Lord Gilden. I would not have come to you in such a state if it were not imperative I reach you quickly," Solomon said.

Gilden waved a hand at him weakly. "I only think you should have better care. That is all."

Gilden closed his eyes and fell silent for a moment. Althus thought he slept.

"Althus," he whispered.

Althus was at his side in an instant. "Yes, Gilden?" he asked.

"Did you win the battle?"

"With the help of Solomon's Dragon Riders and the Dwarves and Giants and, of course, the Elves, we did," Althus answered proudly.

"I am so weary I cannot keep my eyes open, but I would like to meet them all and to hear their accounts of the battle. We still have much planning to do as well if we are to prevent such a force from gathering again. The Dark Lord must be defeated."

"I will ask them to stay until you are stronger, sir," Althus reassured him.

"You are a good man, Althus. I will put my trust in you," Gilden sighed. He was soon asleep, a glow beginning to show faintly about him.

Bree and her brothers followed them to the door of the room where Bree kissed Solomon and thanked him for his help. Chess, Thorny and Rowan thanked him as well, each taking his small hand in theirs. Rowan and Bree then hustled him off, protesting, to find supplies to dress his wounds. Chess and Thorny watched them walk out of sight before turning back to Althus.

"Thank you, Althus," Thorny said.

"I did not save your father, Thorny. Solomon did," he replied.

"True enough, but if you had not befriended him, our father would have died. You see how valuable Solomon is, as well as the Dwarves and the Giants. You are the glue that holds them all to us, Althus. I cannot say exactly how, but I feel certain that is true."

"I owe my life to Solomon and Antares as well, Thorny, but it was only chance that brought us together."

"Chance?" Thorny mused, smiling at Althus, "Perhaps, but I prefer to think it is fate that drew you and Solomon together. He has great strength for one so small. Rowan is quite taken with him and no Elf can read another's worth better than Rowan."

"He has survived events in the past year that should have killed him, and still, he found the strength to ride to the defense of Anduin. I do not doubt his strength," Althus said. "It seems all of Anduin owes Solomon and the Dragon Riders a debt of gratitude. I only hope I can repay him some day."

Thorny shook his head. "There is more to the story of you and Solomon than you are telling, Althus. Rowan tells me Solomon feels indebted to you in some way."

Althus laughed, then. "He owes me no debt, Thorny, not after what he and his Riders have done today, but I will leave the story of our meeting to Solomon, if he chooses to tell it. In the meantime, I must return to the battlefield, see how my people fared, and make sure the wounded are cared for. I cannot leave all to Euwyn. He is exhausted and only one Wizard after all. When the wounded are cared for, there are the dead on both sides to be taken care of."

"You are the Prince of Anduin, Althus," said Chess. "No one expects you to do more than what you have already done. You have led your people to a great victory."

Althus shook his head. "Euwyn is still out there and I still feel more his son and aide than a prince. Many lives have been lost today. As the son of a healing Wizard, it pains me to think of it. The men who died are sons and fathers, not mere numbers to be tallied as the cost of war. The cloak of general will never sit easily on my shoulders. I do not think I am meant for that role even though tradition dictates I must fill it. It is my fondest wish never to see battle again. Too much is lost, even in the winning."

"You have struck the truth of the matter, Althus," Chess agreed. "We have lost Maple and Cedar in this battle. I do not look forward to telling father that two of his dearest friends and a captain and lieutenant of the Elven Patrol are among the dead."

The death of Cedar and Maple saddened Althus as well. He remembered Cedar's kind words to him at their last meeting and the night they enjoyed their company. They had a hand in his rescue from the Orcs as well, although he did not remember it.

Solomon and Bree reappeared, Bree speaking earnestly to the smaller Elf as they approached. Solomon was shaking his head adamantly and hurrying as if he were trying to escape.

"Althus, he should not be going back to the battlefield in this condition. He should be resting," Bree said. "He has been beaten unconscious twice in the past few days, even before he led the Dragon Riders here. I could see it plainly when I touched his head."

Althus regarded Solomon sternly. "Is this true, Solomon?" he asked.

Solomon looked up the winding stairs, a stubborn set to his jaw. "I believe I left a Dragon on your roof. I must be going."

Althus caught his arm as he turned to go.

Solomon turned back to look up at his friends. "Bree would never have known if she could not read my thoughts," he said. "Please, Althus," Solomon pleaded, "I have been accused of madness so many times in the past few days.... I cannot let my men down again. I cannot stay here. I left the field so abruptly. If I do not return, you know what they will think. I will come back when all of the Riders can come with me."

Althus looked at Bree over Solomon's head, questioning. "You read his thoughts?"

"Yes, when I touched his head I could read his thoughts. It happens sometimes between Elves whose thoughts are unguarded. Believe me, Solomon. I found no madness in you, but you really should be in bed."

"What happened to you at the Hall, Sollie? Is there some strange ritual that requires Riders returning to their posts to be beaten?" Althus asked.

"No, no, there was some difficulty, though. That is what delayed us."

The wraith's words came back to Althus then. He had spoken of a traitor among the Riders.

"I will tell you about it at a later time. Holly and Joseph should be present as it is their tale as well," Solomon said.

"They were the ones who beat you, then," said Chess.

"No! Do not be ridiculous, Chess."

Althus sensed Solomon's growing impatience. "I will watch over him, Bree and I will see that he stays close to Euwyn. If I think he should return to the castle, I will drag him back here," Althus assured her.

Chess looked skeptical. "I have my doubts you could do that unless he was unconscious, Althus."

"Antares will look after him, then," said Althus. "He has been nursemaid to Solomon for over a year now."

"You and your brothers should be at Gilden's side when he wakes again, Bree. We will take care of things beyond the walls of Anduin. I will return as soon as I can," Solomon assured her.

"Father will be asking for you when he awakens, Sollie," said Bree looking at him sternly. "I would not like to have to disappoint him. He told me to take better care of you."

Solomon and Althus made their escape from Bree when Rowan returned. They soon rejoined Antares who by then, was, entertaining the people staring up at him fearfully by breathing fire about the wall. Althus looked sternly at him when he set one of the few remaining pennants decorating the castle walls afire. In addition, some of the stones were beginning to melt.

Antares was unabashed. He chuckled as he left his perch with Althus and Solomon aboard, swooping low over the few brave enough to gather close and scattering them in all directions.

"You are a shameless showoff, Antares," Althus laughed. "As if the people of Anduin had not suffered enough."

"They should know us for friends by now," Antares said. "If they do not, they deserve to be frightened."

No one could argue with that.

**Chapter Forty-four**

**AFTERMATH**

Althus and Solomon joined Euwyn, the Dragon Riders, and the surviving Humans, Dwarves, Giants and Wood Elves on the battlefield. Those that were able searched the battlefield for those who still lived among the fallen. They spread out in a long line, the various races mingling as they paced the trampled meadow, trying to save those who still lived and performing the sad task of numbering the dead. The eight remaining Dragons followed behind, burning the bodies of the enemy where they lay. The air filled with smoke and ash that spiraled lazily upward in the evening air. Euwyn paused to replace Solomon's medallion and Dragon scale about his neck, the bits of chain mended together by magic. Some of the weariness left Euwyn's face as he stood back to admire his handiwork.

"I was a bit fearful of using even such simple magic around that marvelous Dragon scale of yours, Solomon, but evidently white magic does not arouse its power," he said.

Edmund and Euwyn soon tended to the immediate needs of the injured with the help of the Riders and all were brought safely within the walls of Castle Anduin before nightfall.

Althus was overjoyed to find Captain Manton and Tristan among those only slightly wounded. The Captain reported more than three hundred dead. Among the dead lay the Giant, Gideon, and twenty-three of the Elven patrol, including Captain Cedar and his lieutenant, Maple.

Fifty-two Dwarves died. Althus winced at that number, knowing how many had already given their lives in the liberation of Stonehaven. Still, Granite greeted him like an old friend with a smile and a rough embrace. Mica came safely through the battle, delivered to his father's side by Rowan even before the battle ended. Bull was just as happy to see Althus and Solomon even though he wept for his brother Gideon as he embraced them. Sailor and Willow came to greet them as well, followed by the members of the Elven patrol.

Althus invited all to rest within the walls of Castle Anduin, but the members of the Elven patrol elected to spend the night outside the city walls. From there, they would begin their journey back to the Dark Forest at dawn, reluctant to leave their borders undefended for long. Euwyn healed those few among the Elves who were injured, even their horses, allowing all who had survived the battle to return at once to the Dark Forest.

Althus said a reluctant goodbye to Sailor and Willow and their fellow patrolmen on the battlefield.

The Dwarves consented to return to the castle for the length of time it took their wounded to recover enough to travel.

Bull and his brothers, Apollo and Gabriel agreed to grace Castle Anduin as well and would return to their valley in the company of the Dwarves.

The nine Dragon Riders all consented to return to Castle Anduin, relatively unscathed save the loss of Aldebaran.

His body was cremated by his fellow Dragons and his ashes taken aloft and spread to the four winds as the sun was setting in the west. Althus thought he could see a golden Dragon dancing above the sun as it touched the horizon. Perhaps it was a trick of the light and the spiraling smoke and ash. He wanted to think it was not.

It seemed ages before they all stood within the castle walls. The castle staff had risen to the occasion, providing the heroes of the battle to save Anduin with all the comforts they could imagine. Althus and his companions sat at a table laden with food, but had little strength left to eat or even to speak more than a few words.

Mica introduced his father and the Giants.

Holly, who stood between Solomon and Joseph with a hand on each Rider's shoulder to keep them seated, briefly introduced the Riders and named their Dragons.

Althus thanked them all on behalf of the king and queen and the people of Anduin before they all retired to their beds. Althus found himself installed in quarters befitting the Prince of Anduin. He had a bed for Solomon set in one of the rooms he occupied, reluctant to let him far from sight after Bree's warning regarding the state of his health. Solomon refused to go to the infirmary and would have liked to sleep with his men, but was too weary to protest, especially when all the riders seemed to be well cared for and each occupied their own rooms. Joseph looked a bit gray as well, but Holly was keeping a watchful eye on him. Castle Anduin was soon silent except for the few servants who still scurried about and those in the infirmary who cared for the wounded.

Φ        Φ        Φ

Solomon's hand on his shoulder prodded Althus from sleep the next morning. Solomon, already washed and dressed, wore his red coat with the golden Dragons winding their way up the sleeves and buff colored breeches, his well-worn boots polished to a shine. Solomon was looking rather shiny himself, his hair combed as neatly as his wild curls would allow and bearing only a trace of the weary look he wore the night before. Althus wondered how he could look so cheerful when every muscle in Althus' body warned him not to attempt to rise from his bed.

Althus undertook and accomplished the task eventually with a little help from Solomon. When he finally stood before the small Elf, Althus was startled to find him openly gaping at him, his eyes wide with shock.

"What?" Althus asked uneasily, looking himself over carefully. "Is there a limb missing that I did not notice? Something worse missing? No, everything is still here," He grinned at Solomon, waiting for him to laugh.

Solomon continued to stare, reaching out to touch the golden Dragon burned into the skin of Althus' chest. "What is this? I do not remember that you bore this mark when we were in the mountains."

"Oh," Althus laughed softly, running his hand over the small but perfect Dragon, "I had forgotten this. I learned you should never wear a Dragon's scale next to your skin when a Wizard is trying to kill you. Chess said you had put your mark on me."

Solomon was still staring. He did not look as shocked, but he still did not seem able to tear his eyes from the mark.

"It does not hurt," Althus reassured him.

Solomon smiled slowly as if some inner thought pleased him, but he did not share that thought with Althus.

Althus felt a sudden urge to cover the mark that seemed to fascinate Solomon. He turned to look for something to wear and groaned anew at the clothes laid out for him. He supposed they were fitting for a prince, but he refused to wear clothing decorated liberally with pearls and bows.

The appearance of Tristan at his door, moving as gingerly as Althus did, was fortuitous. He offered to find clothing more to Althus' taste and managed to return with his black and silver dress uniform. He examined the clothing Althus had rejected, laughing at Althus' horrified look as he held it up before him and turned him about to face the mirror. Solomon laughed at them both as Tristan danced about with the velvet breeches, liberally decorated with bows, swaying about his knees. Althus wondered what had become of his green and gold Elven patrol uniform, hoping the servants did not discard it.

Solomon retrieved something Althus and Tristan missed that rolled from atop the pile of finery. He took the plain silver circlet set with a small, flawless blue stone and set it upon Althus' head. He had to stand on tiptoe to do so, standing back when he was satisfied with the set of it to admire the effect, his head tipped to one side.

"It suits you, Prince Althus," he said, gently forestalling Althus' hand when he reached up to remove it. "Besides, I think Gilden may have forged it for you to wear. It is definitely Elven craft, although I have never seen one exactly like it."

When Euwyn entered the room, Althus let the circlet remain where it was.

Euwyn looked as fit as ever, his dark eyes shining as he studied Althus in his uniform. "I wondered if you would really don that outfit the servants chose for you. I am most glad you did not. I am glad also to see you in

Anduin uniform instead of that of the Elven Patrol. It is time you addressed your people. As much as we owe our freedom to the Elven nations of Solomon and Gilden, you should be dressed for the occasion as a man of Anduin. Do not fear. I have rescued your Elven uniform from the servants."

Euwyn stepped to the window and pushed it open. "Can you hear them?" he said, turning back to look at Althus and gesturing out the window.

Until that moment, Althus had dismissed the noise outside as the usual noises of a crowded city. He realized now his people were cheering, singing, chanting his name. At the open window, the noise was deafening.

"King Allen and Queen Maris await you on their private balcony. Unless you want the people to declare you king of Anduin today, you must appear with them and show your support of the present king," Euwyn said.

Althus found the prospect a bit distasteful. Could he trust King Allen? He had no choice unless he was ready to take the king's place. Trust. He trusted so many with the lives of his people. Many he had known only a very short time. He wished he could trust King Allen as well. He would need to stay in Anduin. That was plain to him. He would see what the next months would bring. As for the king and queen and the crowds gathered about the castle walls, they could wait.

Euwyn, Althus, and Solomon spared a moment to see how Gilden fared this morning while Tristan went to explain the delay to those who waited. Althus asked him to inform the king and queen he would meet them on the front steps of the castle and not the small balcony from which the king usually addressed the people of Anduin. Tristan seemed to enjoy the prospect of making Althus' wishes known to the king.

Gilden was sitting up, toying with his breakfast when Chess escorted them in. The Elf lord's smile was warm and welcoming, his hands steady and strong as he took theirs in greeting.

"So you have brought Solomon back to see me," Gilden said, keeping the smaller Elf's hand in his possession while he looked him over carefully. "You look as if you have been better cared for than when I last saw you. I was not sure if I had dreamed you until Chess told me you saved my life last night. I am grateful to you, Solomon. If they would let me get out of this cursed bed, I would repay you better for your kindness."

"There is no need to repay me, Lord Gilden, it is enough to see you well again. I have become very fond of your children in the last few days and I would hate to see them lose you. Rowan saved me from the Dark Lord's wraith only moments before I came to you, so, you see, it was only right."

"Well, I was only a small part of a rescue that was for the most part performed by Althus," said Rowan, entering the room.

Gilden laughed. "You are all so humble, but Chess fills me in on the details. He is not so humble, you see, and he loves a good tale."

Bree entered the room dressed in a white gown that floated about her as she walked. Althus found his mouth had dropped open and hastily shut it, hoping Gilden did not notice him openly gaping at his daughter. He had seen her only in uniform and had thought no clothing could suit her better, but he could only stare at her as she moved toward them, his tongue stuck to the roof of his mouth as she paused to kiss him softly on the cheek.

She bent to look closely at Solomon, touching his head gently as she bent to look into his eyes. He looked as if Bree had nailed him to the floor. Evidently, with her hand on his head she could still read his thoughts. She looked at him curiously and then laughed.

"Father likes to see me dressed so. It is in honor of his recovery that I wear this. I am still the same maiden that rode into battle yesterday."

Solomon was blushing.

Althus freed his tongue enough to say that the king and queen awaited them and to ask Rowan if he would stand by his side in Gilden's place. Rowan agreed with a chuckle, but mercifully, no comment and left the room in their company, promising Gilden they would return before long.

Althus sought out Granite and Mica and then Bull. Bull created quite a stir wherever he went, his dark face and his size sending servants scurrying away at his approach. Althus was amused to think that the smallest of his companions, Solomon and Granite, were the fiercest and deadliest warriors. Bull was as reluctant a soldier as Althus, and possessed a tender heart. His eyes were still red from weeping over Gideon. Althus' heart went out to him.

Solomon left his side briefly to gather his Riders. They appeared wearing the same red and gold uniform as Solomon. The only difference marking Solomon as the one who led them, the golden medallion about his neck. They entered the king and queen's presence together, gathering in the main hall, whose massive doors opened on the steps of Castle Anduin. It pleased Althus to have them all there at his side, representatives of the five races who had come to the aid of Anduin.

He feared the Dragon Riders would not understand his speech on the steps of the castle. They had so little contact with the world beyond their mountains, he wondered if any of them understood the language of Humans. Althus had spent so little time speaking his own language in the past few weeks that it felt strange, even to him, to speak it once again. Gilden's people were fluent in his language as well as their own since their lands bordered upon each other and trade between them was constant. Mica and Granite, true to their heritage, were traders as well and spoke many languages including the language of Humans, as did most of their people.

The crowd gathered before Castle Anduin, still chanting Althus' name, fell silent as the huge doors swung open and the king and queen stepped out onto the sunlit stone at the head of the broad stairs. Althus noticed King Allen's uneasiness. He was no longer the beloved king he was years ago. Few of his subjects had set eyes on him in the past twenty years. The king and his subjects regarded each other warily with the guards standing watch between. Althus wondered if it were the crowd's respect for the king or their respect for the guards who had left their king's side to fight for the freedom of Anduin that caused them to keep an orderly silence. It did not occur to him that the people of Anduin were waiting to see how Althus wished them to regard the king.

"I have come forth today to celebrate the return of our son, Althus, Crown Prince of Anduin," King Allen began," and to celebrate his victory over the evil that threatened our fair city and the whole of our kingdom."

The crowd roared its approval while the king took Althus by the arm and led him forward to stand by his side. The noise increased in volume until Althus raised his hand to silence them. The cheering subsided with much shushing and hand waving in the crowd. All present seemed to hang on his words. His mouth suddenly felt very dry. The crowd's rapt attention, their faith he was about to speak of matters that were deeply profound, frightened him nearly as much as the battle had. What should he say to his people? What did they want to hear? Bull stepped up behind him, laying both hands on his shoulders. The crowd gave a collective gasp at the sight of him looming over their new hero, but neither Althus nor the king's guards showed any sign of apprehension, so they continued to wait for him to speak.

Bull leaned down and whispered in his ear, "You have a good heart, Althus, the heart of a Wizard's son. Tell them what is in your heart. It will be enough."

Althus took a deep breath.

"Most of you know me as Euwyn's adopted son and Euwyn as friend to those in need," he began. "I would like you to remember I am still the same man I was then, with the same desire to help the people of Anduin. Now I have the power to do so. In the next week, we will mourn our dead and the dead of our allies and we will care for the wounded. At the end of that week, there will be a festival for all of Anduin before the gates of the city. It will be a festival to honor those who came to our aid when all seemed lost. I will introduce them to you so that should you see them before that time you will know them."

He proceeded to introduce Bull and his marriage brothers, Gabriel and Apollo and told them of the sacrifice of their brother Gideon. He introduced Mica and Granite and told them of their losses in both the battle for Stonehaven and in Anduin and of their long journey through the mountains to reach Anduin in time. Althus introduced Rowan. Most already knew of him and his sister and brothers and their father, Gilden, who had helped lead the people of Anduin to safety within the city walls. Althus felt deeply the loss of

Cedar and Maple and other members of the Elven forces who were immortal and yet willing to die in defense of Anduin. He watched the eyes of his people turn toward Rowan as he spoke, and thought he saw gratitude in them

He introduced Euwyn as well, even though all knew him on sight, but he took the greatest pleasure in introducing Solomon and his Dragon Riders. He introduced each of them in turn, beginning with Solomon, their leader, and ending with Holly, the newest member among them. He named their Dragons, who rested beyond the gates of the city and invited the people to visit the Dragons and speak with them as well as their riders. He wondered again if any of the Riders understood a word of his people's language, but he suspected the ancient race of Dragons would.

He hoped his words would help his people understand the sacrifice all of those standing with him before Castle Anduin had made for them.

There was thunderous applause when he had finished. He waved to the crowd and stepped back through the massive doors, leaving the king and queen and their personal guards to follow in his wake.

Althus found Holly was translating the speech he gave before the castle gates for some of the Riders even before the doors had closed behind them. He stood entranced by her skill as she translated his speech word for word with complete accuracy. Joseph stood at Althus' side.

"She is amazing," he said watching her fondly.

"How does she know our language?" Althus asked curiously.

"We learn what languages we can from the Dragons. If we are to help those who travel in our mountains, it is necessary to speak more than one language as many races stray into our realm. Some learn other languages so that, although we all speak more than one language, we do not all learn the same ones. It increases the chances one of us can communicate with the many races we encounter. Holly seems to learn languages so easily. She knows many while I struggled to learn what little Procyon taught me. I know only some of your language and some of the language of the Dwarves. Holly's skill is part of being a chronicler, I suppose. Still, I find it amazing. I would give anything to possess her skills. You should ask to read her journals. She would be pleased to show them to you and you might find them interesting. At the very least you should know what has transpired in the last few days."

"Solomon did not tell me how he came to be injured," Althus said. "He said you and Holly should be present for the telling."

"Yes," said Joseph, "it is a tale worth hearing. Euwyn will need to hear it as well. Mica and Granite and the Giants and the Wood Elves also, of course. It will concern all who will join us in our search for the lair of the Dark Lord."

"Us?" said Althus raising his eyebrows at the Rider. "Will you join us in our search? I was hoping for Solomon's help, but any of the Riders and their

Dragons would be more than welcome."

"Holly and I have been there, Althus, so near the Dark Lord's underground lair that we could feel evil on the wind," Joseph said.

Althus wondered again at the courage and loyalty of the Dragon Riders, shuddering at the thought of entering the Dark Lord's domain. There would be no Dragons to help them in that foul place. Still, that was their intention, he and the allies he had gathered.

Φ        Φ        Φ

They retired to Gilden's rooms where Holly entertained them all that day and into the night with her tales of the Dragon Riders. The king and queen joined them. Euwyn sat close to Gilden, enjoying his company as he had many years ago. They admired the courage of Solomon and his people who lived precariously close to the evil that threatened their lands.

Holly's account of Solomon's journey over the past year moved everyone. Bull sobbed loudly while Mica and Granite tried to quiet him. Gilden and Euwyn now understood the bond between Althus and the little Elf and why the wraith's threat to replace his memory had terrified Solomon and sent Althus riding against such a deadly foe. They came to understand the strength of the bond between Joseph and Solomon and Holly and what it meant to be part of the Brotherhood.

Surely, with such an alliance, Gilden thought, there was more than a slim chance the Dark Lord could be destroyed. He could not help but worry for the safety of his children and their allies. They had drawn the eye of the Dark Lord now. Euwyn would protect them, as he had since the day two centuries ago when he had saved them from the Goblins at the edge of the Dark Forest, but Euwyn was only one Wizard. Were there others willing to join their cause? He was certain there were if they could only find them. What of this Kate Riders spoke of so fondly? Was she as Human as she claimed? Was she another land's version of sorcerer? Solomon had shown them the image of Joseph and Holly he carried. It truly seemed the work of a Wizard, or at least someone with powers that might be useful.

Gilden and Euwyn continued to consider their course over the next week as the people of Anduin mourned and buried the dead and cared for those who would live on.

The festival on the lea before the city gates was a huge success with all the Riders and their Dragons in attendance. The tiny children who followed them about, gaping up at them, amused Bull, Gabriel and Apollo. Most of them ended up riding on the Giants' shoulders for the better part of the evening, much to their parents' dismay.

Granite drank enough ale for ten men, showing no ill effects while Mica was only able to drink half as much before he began to refuse more. Althus was amused to find some of the Dwarves that had stayed behind to recover from their wounds were women. He saw Mica and Granite holding them too close to think otherwise as they danced in the moonlight.

The Elves danced and sang, shining like suns amid the rough farmers and craftsmen. Chess danced with every girl he could find who was willing and a few who were not so willing. Rowan produced a flute and Thorny a drum and joined the rest of the musicians on the grass. Bree sought Althus and held her close, kissing him behind Antares' wing while the Dragon rumbled with laughter.

Holly and Solomon spent the evening together. Althus smiled to himself when he saw Solomon's arm stealing about Holly's waist as they stood in the moonlight listening to the music. Holly leaned her head on his shoulder and Solomon was smiling.

"He will find the courage to love her," Bree whispered, following the direction of his gaze as she danced in his arms. "It may take some time, but he will."

The celebration lasted far into the night. Althus dreaded its end. The Dragon Riders were set to depart at dawn and the Dwarves would depart the next day. Bull and his marriage brothers would go with them. He feared Gilden and his children would depart very soon as well. They had been away from Borias and the Dark Wood for far too long. He felt cold at the thought of their leaving and sought out Antares for a last word with him.

Antares was stretched full length on the grass amid his fellow Dragons, gnawing on the remnants of an offering left by the grateful people of Anduin brave enough to approach the huge Dragons.

"Your people are most generous, Althus" he replied when asked if he were getting enough to eat. "Perhaps I was wrong when I doubted it was worth the trouble of saving them. They fought bravely as well. It seems Humans are not such a bad sort after all."

Althus laughed at Antares, settling himself in the grass and leaning against the warmth of the Dragon's side. How many days ago had he done this for the first time? Not so many when he thought about it. It seemed so long ago now.

Antares occupied himself with the last of his dinner and Althus found he did not have much to say after all. He leaned his head back and closed his eyes.

"We will return, Althus," Antares rumbled softly after they had enjoyed each other's company in silence for a while. "Gilden would have us come to Borias at the equinox if Ephraim agrees. Perhaps Ephraim will come as well and you will meet him. He is our First Rider now that Augustine is gone and he is a warrior equaled only by Solomon."

"I will miss you and Solomon terribly until then, Antares," Althus sighed. "Gilden will be leaving and his children will go with him. Granite and Mica and Bull and his brothers as well. Still, I will miss Solomon most of all save Bree."

"Parting with friends is always difficult," Antares agreed. "I will miss you also and Solomon will not find parting easy. He is very much attached to you now and to the Elves of the Dark Wood, but he must return to the Hall to serve as Second Rider for a time. The Riders restored him to his post only hours before we left for Anduin. There is much for him to do there as you have much to do here. Time will pass quickly. You will see. You have Euwyn back and you will need to come to know the king and queen better and they you if you are to leave the kingdom in their hands when you leave once more."

"It all seems so strange, Antares. How did all this happen? I am a prince now, although I am not sure at all that I wish to be one. I am to think of this kingdom as mine, although the king is still a stranger to me and he still rules Anduin."

"You rule Anduin now in the hearts of your people, Althus," Antares replied. "King Allen rules still only by your consent. Your people are not foolish. They know to whom they owe their lives. You have named your allies as those who freed Anduin, but your people know who brought us here. You have only to say the word and you could be king in your father's place."

Althus cringed at the thought and at the thought of King Allen as his father.

"You will have to accept him as your father, Althus, whether you like it or not," Antares said simply.

"I do not know if I can forgive him. He is not the man Euwyn is."

Althus opened his eyes to stare across the fields to the stone tower just visible in the distance, shining in the moonlight.

"I agree with you there, Althus. Who is the man Euwyn is? Very few are. Your feelings for Euwyn need not change, but you have a big heart, Althus. You have taken so many into it in the last few weeks. Do you not have some room left in it for your king? He needs your help to become the king he once was. The man he was before he took in the evil that nearly destroyed him, the man who fathered such a fine son. You are the very image of him, you know."

Althus nodded. "I have been told as much. I will try to follow your advice, Antares. Who am I to argue with a Dragon?"

"Before we leave Anduin I must thank you for what you did for Solomon that night in the ruined village," Antares said. "I must admit I had given him up for lost that night. You knew him for only a few hours and yet you could not accept his death. I was willing to let him go. You were not." Antares tipped his head to pin Althus with one golden eye. "How did you know he would not turn on you? How did you know he would not kill himself there in the moonlight?"

Althus laughed. "I knew no such thing, Antares. I just *hoped* there was something I could do to help him. Do Dragons never hope?"

Antares looked at Althus thoughtfully, "I suppose we are not very good at it. We are practical creatures. We are best at seeing what is and do not easily see what could be."

"I guess it was the lost look in his eyes that I knew would haunt me forever if I did not do what I could," Althus continued. "Even had I done what I could and he still died that night, I think those amazing eyes of his would haunt me."

Antares snorted. "He would have chosen his own path if that were the case. You are too soft hearted by far, Althus. I would have soon forgotten him entirely."

Althus laughed, patting the Dragon's scaly head. "You lie, old Dragon."

Antares did not deny it. He merely sighed and went back to his dinner.

## Chapter Forty-five

## PARTINGS

Dawn came too soon and Althus found himself the last of the company to say farewell to each of the Riders and their Dragons as they mounted. Holly wept as she hugged him fiercely. Joseph embraced him just as fiercely before he took his place on Procyon's back. Solomon was the last to face him. They stood looking at each other for a long time, reluctant to part. Despite the sadness in Solomon's eyes, they glowed with an intensity Althus had not seen before.

"I hope to return soon, Althus, but I am Second Rider once more and subject to the decisions of the Brotherhood concerning such matters now," Solomon said.

Althus nodded. "I know and I understand. I think I understand it better now that I have met the men you lead and their Dragons. Your responsibility is to them first. You will keep them safe, Solomon, as you did before. Lead them well and I will hope our paths cross again soon."

Solomon mounted Antares, who gave Althus a nudge with his broad head before he leapt into the sky. The seven Dragons remaining followed quickly, circling once above Anduin as the people waved and cheered and shouted their farewells below.

Φ                        Φ                        Φ

Althus wandered to the stables again to be sure Gust and the other horses were well cared for. He found them turned out in the lush pastures just north of the castle walls, their coats gleaming in the sun. Their injuries were minor. A few nicks here and there and a bruise or two, all well tended now. The mail they wore and their cleverness had kept them relatively unscathed during the battle. He found Thad watching over them as they ate, taking his pledge to care for them very seriously. He informed Althus that Gilden and his children had been there earlier. The horses had been one of Gilden's first concerns when he was up and about. Althus felt he had been a bit neglectful of Gust, but the sturdy horse greeted him only briefly before returning to the green grass, evidently too busy to need his master very much. Althus was glad to see him resting after their grueling journey and the ensuing battle. He left him to his grass.

Althus wandered from there to the western battlements where he last stood watch over Castle Anduin on a day that seemed long ago. He could see the farmers in their fields once more. The siege had taken its toll on their lands, but now they were free to live as they wished. Althus would see their needs met in the days to come. He was determined to make their lives better. Euwyn would help, as would the queen. He would speak to King Allen when he had said his farewells to the Dwarves and the Giants tomorrow. He tried not to think of Gilden's departure.

He was lost in thought, his gaze wandering over his kingdom, his mind working over what should be done when he felt a tug at his sleeve. He looked down to find Mica at his side. He smiled at the sturdy Dwarf as he climbed the battlements and sat with his feet dangling over the edge.

"Lookin' over yer kingdom, Althus?" he said, his wide green eyes following the direction of Althus' gaze as he returned to looking over the battlements.

"Yes, Mica," Althus answered. "Hoping and planning for the days to come."

"Dwarves are good at plannin' and such. 'Specially when it comes ta diggin' dikes and fixin' roads. There's lotsa things to be done out there. Seems you could use some help," Mica said.

Althus turned to stare at the young Dwarf.

"Me dad says you might be needin' help with things. He's leavin' tomorra fer Stonehaven. Lotsa fixin' to be doin' there, too. He says I kin stay with you if you says it's all right and I could kinda help you with the plannin' and such. If you would like me ta stay, I could. Maybe ...." His voice trailed off uncertainly as Althus continued to stare.

"You would rather stay here than return to your home, Mica? Truly?" Althus asked when he found his voice.

"Yeah," Mica answered, shoving his hands deep into his pockets and staring hard at nothing.

Althus wrapped him in a bear hug and dragged him off the parapet, setting him down and putting his hands on his shoulders. "You and I will make Anduin the best place in all the land, Mica!" he shouted.

Mica's grin nearly split his face in two.

Althus spent the rest of the morning pacing the battlements with Mica, pointing out things that needed attention. Mica had ideas of his own. When Althus left the battlements, with Mica in tow, he cast only one last look toward the mountains to the south beyond which the Dragon Riders had disappeared.

They spent the afternoon with the Dwarves and Giants, Euwyn and the Wood Elves, further refining their plans and putting their ideas to paper.

Althus knew the value of a Dwarf's advice when it came to the moving of earth and the building of mechanical devices. Granite assured him no Dwarf had more skill in such matters than his young son.

"I hafta admit there was a few things that didn't work as they was supposta, but the explosions was minor and each time the rubble was cleared in less than a week.

Althus felt a bit of doubt creeping in, but Granite assured him there had been no explosions lately. Althus wondered if that were because Stonehaven was occupied by its enemies for the past few years. Still, Mica's enthusiasm was hard to deny. Althus was so pleased to have him stay that he was willing to face the risks it might entail.

When Althus looked back on that afternoon, he remembered that Euwyn was uncharacteristically quiet. He later recalled the Wizard sitting silently as they discussed plans for the future of Anduin. Caught up in Mica's enthusiasm, he did not notice something seemed amiss with Euwyn. His failure to take notice was to haunt him for days to come.

Bree found him in his rooms that evening to tell him Euwyn had left for the tower. Althus was slightly annoyed the Wizard had not seen fit to ask him to accompany him or at least to tell him in person of his plans. Still, with Bree at his side, he soon dismissed the Wizard's absence as his attempt to find some peace after the chaos of the past few days.

Bree pushed Euwyn further from his thoughts when she announced they intended to leave for the Dark Forest the next morning when they had said their farewells to Granite and Bull. He wanted to beg her to stay. His first instinct was to throw himself at her feet and declare his love for her, but his regard for Gilden kept him silent. He could not leave Anduin to accompany her to her home and he could not find the courage to ask her to forsake her family and her homeland for him. He felt trapped by his duty to the people of Anduin and concerned for Gilden's still fragile health. Bree would return to Borias in the heart of the Dark Forest and he would remain here to serve the people of Anduin until Gilden gathered the allied races to the Dark Forest on the night of the autumnal equinox. From there they would set out in search of the Dark Lord and attempt to destroy him. Perhaps they would succeed. Until that time, he would seek to strengthen Anduin for the darkness that would follow if they did not.

This night he did not want to think of the uncertain future. He took Bree to the battlements and held her in his arms. She was wearing a gown that floated about her in the soft breeze, so delicate he could see her shining skin through the material from which it was made. She felt at once solid and insubstantial in his arms as if she might disappear, as evanescent as the moonlight. Would he awake to find he had dozed off at his post and the past few days had been only a dream?

They said very little of consequence to each other. Bree watched the moonlight glittering on the broad river. A few boats lay moored on the riverbank, their lights moving with the gentle current beneath them. Music drifted up from the city below, but nothing more intruded on their evening together.

Althus studied the moonlight reflected in Bree's eyes. He longed to put into words the feelings he had for her, but of course, he did not need to. She would know his feelings and understand them better than he did himself.

"I will await your arrival in Borias at the turn of the seasons," she said when they parted. "I will look forward to the day we are reunited, Althus. You must remain safe until then."

"When that time comes, Bree, nothing will keep me from your side," he answered softly.

Φ        Φ        Φ

Bull and his brothers and the remaining Dwarves left the next morning at first light. Althus was troubled to find Euwyn had not returned from the tower to bid farewell to their friends.

Granite dismissed it as the way of Wizards. "They're always appearin' and disappearin' at odd times. He wuz there when it mattered. Leave him be, Althus. He's probably hatchin' a new plan fer when we go off ta get that Dark Lord that's causin' us all so much trouble. We'll see him in Borias in a few months."

Bull did not seem reassured. He kept gazing toward the tower as he bid farewell to Althus, tears trickling from his dark eyes as he almost broke Althus' ribs with his farewell embrace.

"Will you come to Borias as well, Bull?" Althus asked when he could draw breath again.

Bull gave him his beautiful smile. "I am embroiled in this until the end, Althus. I will travel to Borias with the Dwarves when the time comes. I will be their guide. After all, it is where I grew up and I long to see that beautiful city again."

King Allen was present to bid farewell to Anduin's allies. He was very gracious, presenting Granite and Bull with gifts for them and their people and offering to meet with them to discuss possible trading agreements.

The king's presence only emphasized Euwyn's absence. Althus was not accustomed to feeling angry or disappointed with Euwyn. It was not a pleasant feeling.

Gilden and his children were there as well to wish Granite and Bull and their people a safe journey before they departed for the Dark Forest.

Mica bid a brief farewell to his father and the Dwarves and Giants departed from Anduin. Althus could hear them singing as he watched them disappear southward, their gruff voices heard far into the distance. Bull's deep laughter was the last sound to reach him as the Dwarves and Giants marched off toward the Hoary Mountains.

Gilden turned Slate toward Euwyn's tower when their departing friends had faded from view. He shaded his eyes with his hand as if expecting Euwyn to appear. Althus could not read his face. Did the Wizard's absence trouble him?

"We will say farewell to Euwyn before we go. Will you come with us, Althus?" he said finally.

Althus agreed readily. He had planned to journey to the tower when the Elves had departed and had brought Gust along for that purpose. He turned Gust toward the tower as well, taking up a position between Rowan and Bree, happy to delay their parting for a while.

Rowan soon drew Argent to a halt, motioning Althus to do the same. He let the others draw ahead beyond the sound of their voices and then continued on before he spoke.

"Althus," he said, pausing as if to choose his words carefully. "Are you not in love with my sister?"

Althus, surprised by the directness of the question and afraid of the words that might follow, was compelled by Rowan's look to be equally direct.

"Yes, Rowan," he said, "I love her with all my heart. I am sorry."

"You are sorry? How so, Althus? Why are you sorry?"

It was now Althus' turn to search for the right words. "Because I believe she loves me in return and I am afraid I cannot live forever." Althus looked at Rowan with a look of anguish. "Rowan, if I die, will she die also? Have I condemned her to become as mortal as I am? I tried to think of her only as a friend, but I failed."

Rowan was regarding him quietly as the words he had feared to say until now tumbled out of his mouth in a rush.

"Althus," he said finally, holding a hand up to stop him from continuing. "You place too much importance on immortality. We have fought the darkest foes you could imagine all our lives. Few of us enjoy our immortality. Our lives are taken as easily as yours. If not for you, Bree would have died the day she nearly drowned in the Anduin River. Chess and I would have died as well. Who is to say when death will take us? In addition, you are of Elven blood. Your mother is half Elven, descended from the Sea Elves. Their blood is very potent. Who is to say you will not survive the normal lifetime of a Human by many times?"

"You speak of possibilities, but I need to know, Rowan. If something happens to me, will Bree die?" Althus asked, his anxiety mounting.

"Oh, Althus," Rowan said, his frustration beginning to show. "Think about it, man! If you love one another and cannot be together, *that* would break her heart more surely than anything! If you do love each other and you marry, then you will give her something to live for if you die an untimely death."

Althus was puzzled now more than ever. What could he possibly give an Elven princess that she did not already have?

Rowan ran his hand through his hair, looking expectantly at Althus, waiting for him to come up with the answer.

"Children, man!" Rowan shouted at him, unable to contain himself any longer. "You will give her children! Little ones that are the image of their father! By the Creator, Althus, you are such an ass at times! Bree wants to stay here in Anduin with you. You only need to ask her!"

"But, Rowan, what will Gilden think of all this when he finds out I have fallen in love with his only daughter?"

"Who do you think asked me to speak to you? Father is not blind nor is he stupid. In addition, he is extremely fond of you. Nothing will please him more than to see you and Bree together."

Althus looked at Rowan and then at Bree who rode ahead. A slow smile spread across his face. "Thank you, Rowan. I will ask her."

Rowan sighed, a look of relief crossing his face. "You know, Althus," he said more quietly, "we are twins and when she is sad I cannot help but feel it too. I am only thinking of myself."

Althus looked at Rowan, who began to laugh at his look of deep concern. They were still laughing at each other as they caught up with the rest. All Althus needed was the right moment to ask Bree to stay. Thanks to Rowan, he knew she would if he asked.

He would remember their ride to the tower as his last moments of real happiness that summer. They passed between the fertile fields of Anduin where the weathered farmers dropped their work to wave at their new prince and the Elves as they rode by. They passed a few stone cottages where children stopped to stare at them, their mothers running to the door to smile and wave and call down blessings from the Creator on them. It was all somewhat embarrassing to Althus, but he considered it a measure of his people's regard for him and their growing hope for the future of Anduin.

They soon stood before the weathered wooden gates that would admit them to the courtyard surrounding the tower. They were standing open as they often did. Althus could hear Euwyn's footsteps and Mars' hooves on the cobblestones, approaching the gate from within. They barely had time to dismount before Euwyn appeared. Althus took in the gear packed behind Mars' saddle and the dismayed look on Euwyn's face and he knew without a doubt the Wizard was about to depart from Anduin without him once again.

"You are leaving," he said, making it a statement and not a question. The simple words carried enough anger and accusation in them to make Euwyn recoil a step.

He seemed to struggle for a moment before he answered. "Yes, I am." His voice was quiet, carefully controlled.

"You would leave without a word of farewell to Gilden after all he has done for Anduin?" Althus said. "You would leave without a word to me?"

"I have to go, Althus," Euwyn answered. "I cannot explain."

"When will you return?"

"I will not return."

Althus stared at his father, dumbfounded. Euwyn looked back at him with eyes that tried to look unmoved, but failed.

"You cannot go now, Euwyn," Gilden said. "Althus needs you here by his side. Where are you going? Who needs you more than he does at this moment?"

Euwyn wore a look of desperation as he faced them. "I have to go. I cannot explain," he repeated.

No one moved out of his way. Althus could not think of what to say. How could Euwyn leave now? What could he say to make him stay?

He was still looking into Euwyn's dark eyes when they seemed to lose their focus. He watched in horror as the Wizard's hands went to his head and he fell to his knees, crying out in pain. Althus was on his knees beside him in a heartbeat, his arms about Euwyn as he howled in agony, his hands clawing at his head.

Gilden was kneeling beside him as well.

"What is wrong with him?" Althus cried. "What is happening?"

Bree knelt to lay both hands on Euwyn's head, speaking softly in the Wizard's ear. Euwyn's cries subsided to ragged gasps as he struggled for control.

"What is it, Gilden? What is wrong with him?" Althus repeated more quietly.

"It seems Euwyn paid a high price when he destroyed the Dark Lord's stone. There are shards of it lodged in his head, I fear," Gilden replied. "You knew this would be the outcome. Euwyn! Answer me, Wizard! You planned to leave Anduin all along when everyone else was safe. You were crawling off to die somewhere, alone."

Euwyn nodded, still looking at the ground, his head, still clutched between his hands, now resting against Althus' chest as Althus held him tightly.

"You have always let your heart rule your head, Euwyn. At times I have loved you for that, but it is at times like this I would like to beat some sense into you," Gilden growled.

Euwyn dropped his hands and sat back on his heels to look into Gilden's face. His dark eyes met Gilden's brilliant blue ones fearlessly.

"Antares warned me what the destruction of the stone might cost. It had to be done. There was no other choice."

"You will stay here, father," Althus said. "I will care for you. We can find a way to make you well again."

Gilden was shaking his head even as Euwyn answered him. "I am sorry, Althus, but It is very possible I will go mad before I die. You cannot have a mad Wizard in the midst of the people of Anduin. The shards will make me even more powerful before that happens. No, Althus. I have to leave here. I cannot stay with you no matter how much I wish it."

Althus and Bree both looked to Gilden for some shred of hope.

"He is right, Althus. Euwyn cannot stay here. He would be a danger to your people. He must leave Anduin."

Euwyn struggled to his feet. "Thank you, Gilden. I knew you would see what I must do."

Gilden shook his head at Euwyn. "I do not see it as you do. Not at all. You will leave Anduin with us. We will take you to the healers in Borias. The Elven healer, Taxus, is without equal. He may be the only one who can help you."

"No, Gilden, I cannot endanger your people any more than I can the people here." Euwyn stood, leaning heavily against Althus.

"I can help you, Euwyn, as I did just now," Bree said. "I can take some of the pain from you and keep watch on the state of your mind. I can give you a potion to make you sleep if I must. We will get you to Borias safely and once there, Taxus can surely help you."

"Rowan will stay here with Althus and Kestrel will keep him informed of your progress," Gilden said, the command in his voice leaving no room for argument. "Bree will help us tend you on the way there. She is an excellent healer. All is settled. You are ready to travel. You will come with us."

Euwyn looked troubled still, uncertain of the wisdom of entering a city full of Elves in his precarious condition.

Gilden gave him little choice. Chess and Thorny gently set him on his horse and, like it or not, Euwyn was on his way to Borias. Althus rode at his side until they crossed the Anduin and reached the Forest Road, wishing he could go to Borias with them and knowing he could not.

"I am sorry I was angry with you. I should have trusted you," Althus said to Euwyn as they crossed the bridge over the Anduin.

Euwyn shook his head, wincing in pain as he did so. "I was wrong to think of leaving without a word to you, Althus. I am the one to be sorry. I could not bring myself to tell you I was dying. It was stupid of me. I thought I would have more time. When I realized how quickly the shards were taking control, I was unprepared, afraid to come near you and the people whose lives you worked so hard to save. I feared I might lose control where I could harm you or others. I had hoped to finish this business before that happened. Is it selfish of me to hope Taxus might give me more time to seek out the Dragon's Egg and the Dark Lord that possesses it and the strength to destroy them both?"

Althus did not trust himself to answer. He hated seeing Euwyn so vulnerable. He felt turned about as if he were the father and Euwyn his son, but he had no fatherly advice to give.

"I hope Gilden does not regret his decision to take me to Borias, but I must admit I would like to see it again before I die."

Euwyn looked out over the river, for a time before he continued. "I am sorry things have turned out this way. I was hoping to be at your side when you became king of Anduin. At the very least I wanted to see with my own eyes the difference you are going to make in the lives of your people as their prince." He turned to look intently at Althus' face, his dark eyes studying him as if seeing him for the first time, or perhaps the last. "No matter what happens to me, Althus, know that you are more precious to me than anything else in this world and I am more proud of you than I can say. You are a grown man now and crown prince of a mighty kingdom. Let no one tell you that you were not born to lead these people."

Althus tried to smile, but failed. "Nothing will happen to you. Gilden will get you to Borias safely and once you are there, his healer will find a cure."

Euwyn nodded in response, looking between Mars' ears. He looked tired and worn, not fully recovered from his captivity in Stonehaven and now facing another battle for which he did not seem to have the strength. Althus wondered if he would ever see Euwyn again.

They dismounted in the middle of the dusty Forest Road to say their farewells. Euwyn gave his ebony staff into Althus' hands, asking him to keep it safe until he could be trusted to carry it again. Chess and Thorny assured him they would see Euwyn safely to Borias. Gilden told him not to worry and briefly held him close. Althus and Bree wrapped their arms about each other. There was no need for words between them. Althus knew he must stay and, for Euwyn's sake, Bree had to return to Borias. Before the eyes of her father and her brothers, he found the courage to kiss her one last time before they parted.

On their way back to the castle, Rowan expressed a wish that he had left well enough alone instead of giving Althus false hopes, but the knowledge that Bree would have stayed if she could have was some comfort to Althus.

Euwyn's words to him ran through his head often that summer. He wondered just as often if they would be the last to pass between them.

He, Mica, and Rowan tried to keep their minds otherwise occupied as they set about the tasks that would bring security and prosperity to Anduin. They presented their ideas to the king and found him a willing participant.

King Allen truly seemed on his way to becoming the king he once was. Queen Maris grew even more beautiful as her husband grew more like the man she had loved years ago. Althus seldom saw her now without a smile on her face and he spent time with her often as she regularly rode by his side when he went to inspect the various projects under way.

There were new dikes and ditches to see, and Mica's windmills that pumped water from the river to water the farmers' fields to admire. The construction of granaries to store surplus grain was well under way and the roads over which the farmers and craftsmen moved their goods were improved.

As Althus' popularity grew by leaps and bounds, the king's popularity also rose. Lords and Ladies once more began to visit castle Anduin for extended periods. Some were welcome additions. Some were there to curry favor with the new prince in their own interest. Althus studied them all carefully, struggling to separate those who were to be trusted from those who were not. Rowan was more perceptive in these matters and they spent much time discussing the motives and morals of the local royalty.

Althus was careful not to let a word of criticism of King Allen pass his lips. He had to admit that he had little to complain about regarding the king. Allen gave him his way in all things with only a few suggestions that proved of great value from the true ruler of Anduin and he found a small measure of fondness for the king. He still thought of Euwyn as his father, but King Allen became someone he turned to more and more for advice in Euwyn's absence. It became his habit to take his meals with the king and queen if he was within the castle walls. Rowan and Mica, ever at his side, were as welcome at the king's table as he.

Rowan entrenched himself even more deeply in Althus' heart as a brother and confidant, as did the irrepressible and amazingly resourceful Mica. Kestrel flew between Anduin and Borias almost constantly, but did not seem to mind. He became as attached to Althus and Mica as he was to Bree and Rowan.

News of Euwyn sent with regards from Bree was always welcome. The Wizard reached Borias safely and was in the care of the highly regarded healer, Taxus. Althus gathered that although he was not completely free of the stone's influence, Taxus was able to help him resist the effects of it. The healer still searched for a permanent cure, but it seemed that, although still in danger, Euwyn was holding his own for now. Althus was encouraged by the news, but worried constantly about Euwyn all the same.

He thought of how his world had changed. He had expected always to be Euwyn's son and had wished for no more than that. The life span of a Wizard was many times that of a Human. Now he was Prince Althus of Anduin and seemed in danger of losing Euwyn while they were both still young. He had often joked that he would call Euwyn father when he himself was old and gray and the Wizard still looked as he did now. Althus had no choice but to put his trust in Gilden and Bree and Taxus, an Elf he did not know, to keep Euwyn alive. He could not help but hope for the best.

The summer was passing quickly. Rowan and Mica would help keep his spirits up until they could leave for Borias. It was enough for now.

## ABOUT THE AUTHOR

The author was born and raised in western New York State and lives on a small horse farm with her husband and daughter. Her profession is photography and her passion is writing. This is her first attempt at writing a full length novel.

## INDEX OF CHARACTERS

### -A-

Aaron - Dragon Rider, son of Noah, bonded to Deneb

Achernar - Dragon, bonded to Elijah

Adam – an elder of the Dragon Riders, bonded to Pollux

Adolphus – Dark Lord to his enemies, Great Lord to his followers, a fallen Wizard

Aldebaran – golden Dragon, bonded to Noah

Alphard – Dragon, bonded to Samuel

Altair – Dragon, bonded to Sarah

Althea – Black Giant, Liddy's sister

Althus – adopted son of Euwyn, mostly Human

Antares – green Dragon, bonded to Solomon

Anthony – an elder of the Dragon Riders, Sarah's mate, healer

Apollo – Black Giant, Liddy's brother

Arcturus – Dragon, bonded to Esther

Argent – Rowan's horse, steel gray

Augustine – First Dragon Rider, an elder and healer

### -B-

Bartholomew – an elder of the Dragon Riders, a smith

Bellweather – a member of the Queen's guard of Anduin

Beryl – Dwarf, Granite's mate, Mica's mother

Best – a member of the Queen's guard of Anduin

Black Giants – a race of dark-skinned giants, 10 to 12 feet tall, a peace-loving agricultural society living between the northern and southern arms of the Hoary Mountains

Borgas – court Wizard of Anduin, in league with the Dark Lord, controlled by one of his wraiths

Bree – Wood Elf, daughter of Gilden, Rowan's twin, Chess and Thorny's sister

Buck – Kate's youngest dog

Bull (Bullroar) – Black Giant, Liddy's mate, raised by Wood Elves

**-C-**

Canopus – Dragon, bonded to Timothy

Cedar – Wood Elf, a captain of the Elven Patrol

Chess (Chestnut) – Wood Elf, son of Gilden, Thorny's twin, Rowan and Bree's brother

Corny – a member of the Queen's guard of Anduin

Crucis – Dragon, bonded to Isaiah

Cully – Human, one of Borgas' men

**-D-**

Dark Lord – a fallen Wizard, Adolphus

Dell – a member of the Queen's guard of Anduin

Deneb – Dragon, bonded to Aaron

Dogs – If you look up the breed called Bernese Mountain Dogs, you will see what Kate's dogs look like.

Dragons – There are two races of Dragons. Those from the southern mountains have the power of speech and in fact can speak all languages. They vary in hue, but are all richly colored, their faces broad and almost dog like. Sea Dragons are smaller, always white and do not speak, their heads more similar in shape to horses.

Dwarves – a short, stocky race, ranging from three to five feet tall, preferring to live underground, excavating huge halls and passageways into the mountains; great miners and lovers of precious stones and makers of weapons, armor and all sorts of machinery.

### -E-

Eagle – an eagle from the mountains, Bull's messenger to Bree

Edmund – Human, castle Anduin's physician

Elijah – Dragon Rider, Peter's brother, bonded to Achernar

Elinor – Captain Manton's wife, Tristan's mother, a nurse

Ephraim – an elder of the Dragon Rider, bonded to Vega

Esther – an elder of the Dragon Riders, bonded to Arcturus

Euwyn – Wizard, foster father of Althus

### -G-

Gabriel – Black Giant, Liddy's brother

Garth – Human, one of Borgas' men

Gideon – Black Giant, Liddy's brother

Gil – Bull and Liddy's youngest child

Gilden – Lord of the Wood Elves, ruler of the Dark Forest

Goblins – A race of gangly creatures who serve the Dark Lord. Scavengers preferring to eat any type of fresh or rotten meat, including the corpses of other races. Flat footed and stupid, their skin is a dusky brown from filth or their coloration (no one seems certain which). Their eyes are large and round, yellow in color, their teeth pointed and yellow-brown.

Gorp – a Goblin

Granite – leader of the Dwarves, father of Mica

Gust – Althus' horse, black with white points

**-H-**

Holly – Dragon Rider, bonded to the Sea Dragon Polaris

Horses – The Wood Elves' horses are stocky, short bodied and agile, bred for war. Anduin's horses are generally lean and swift. Both come in varying colors.

**-I-**

Isaiah – Dragon Rider, bonded to Crucis

**-J-**

Jonah – Dragon Rider, Solomon's father

Jonathan – Dragon Rider, bonded to Rigel

Joseph – Dragon Rider, Solomon's adopted brother, bonded to Procyon

Joshua – Dragon Rider, bonded to Regulus

**-K-**

Kate – Human, often called Mistress of Hounds, a photographer studying the land of the Mountain Elves

Kestrel – Sparrow hawk, Bree's companion and messenger

King Allen – King of Anduin

## -L-

Liddy – Black Giant, Bull's mate

Lin – Bull and Liddy's oldest child

Linden – Wood Elf, Gilden's mate

## -M-

Magool – Orc, commander of the force occupying Stonehaven

Manton – Captain of the Queen's guard of Anduin

Maple – Wood Elf, a lieutenant in the Elven Patrol

Marcus – Dragon Rider, bonded to Mira

Maris – half-Elven, Queen of Anduin

Mars – Euwyn's horse, bay

Matthew – Dragon Rider, keeper of the Dragons, bonded to Sirius

Max – a member of the Queen's guard of Anduin

Mica – Dwarf, son of Granite

Mira – red Dragon, bonded to Marcus

Mizar – Dragon, bonded to Peter

Moon – Bree's horse, grey

Mountain Elves – The smallest and oldest race of Elves, the origin of all Elven races, from three to almost five feet tall, sentient beings, able to sense emotions or injury through touch,

protected in their mountain villages by the Dragon Riders
who are themselves Mountain Elves

Myoti – huge leathery-winged creatures, a perversion created by the Dark
Lord partly from the genetic material of dragons

## -N-

Nasua – huge, rangy wolf-like creatures, a perversion created by the Dark
Lord partly from the genetic material of wolves

Noah – the smallest of the Dragon Riders, bonded to Aldebaran

## -O-

Ochre – Thorny's horse, chestnut

Opal – Dwarf, one of the imprisoned children

Orcs – Servants of the Dark Lord, huge, red-eyed beasts with tusks curving up
from their lower jaws and flattened faces, fond of the flesh of their
Human and Elven enemies

## -P-

Peter – Dragon Rider, Elijah's brother, bonded to Mira

Polaris – White Sea Dragon, bonded to Holly

Pollux – Dragon, bonded to Adam

Procyon – blue Dragon, bonded to Joseph

## -R-

Raven – Queen Maris' horse, black

Regulus – Dragon, bonded to Joshua

Rigel – Dragon, bonded to Jonathan

Rolf – Kate's older dog

Rowan – Gilden's son and heir, Bree's twin, brother to Chess and Thorny

Ryder – a member of the Queen's guard of Anduin

## -S-

Sailor – Sea Elf living with the Wood Elves, Willow's mate, a member of the Elven Patrol

Samuel – Dragon Rider, bonded to Alphard

Sand – Chess' horse, dun with white legs and face, one blue eye, one brown

Sarah – Dragon Rider, and elder, Anthony's mate, bonded to Anthony

Sea Elves – a race of elves that sail the Western Sea, always raven-haired with blue or sea green eyes, a very proud and fierce race having little contact with the other Elven races who they consider inferior to theirs.

Shale – Dwarf

Sirius – black Dragon, bonded to Matthew

Skank – Goblin

Slate – Gilden's horse, blue roan

Solomon (Sollie) – Dragon Rider, once second in command, bonded to Antares

## -T-

Tarsus – Tristan's horse, fleabitten grey

Taxus – Wood Elf, healer

Thad (Thaddeus) – Human, messenger for the king and queen of Anduin

Thorny (Hawthorne) – Wood Elf, son of Gilden, Chess' twin, brother of Bree and Rowan

Timothy – Dragon Rider, bonded to Canopus

Tristan – member of the Queen's guard, son of Captain Manton and Elinor

**-V-**

Vega – red Dragon, bonded to Ephraim

**-W-**

Willow – Wood Elf, a member of the Elven Patrol, Sailor's mate

Wizards – most powerful of the magical races, sent by the Creator to help those in greatest need, usually solitary and nomadic

Wood Elves – the tallest and fairest race of Elves, calling the great Dark Forest their home, diligently guarding it from those creatures who serve the Dark Lord. A sentient race that can read the emotions of others and find hidden injuries through touch.